THE
ROYAL
ARTISAN

Praise for Tessa Afshar

No one brings the Bible to life like Tessa Afshar.

Debbie Macomber, #1 *New York Times* bestselling author

Tessa Afshar combines adventure and romance in a fast-paced novel that kept me turning the pages. I loved the way she brought so many historical figures to life. I highly recommend *The Hidden Prince*!

Francine Rivers, internationally bestselling author
of *Redeeming Love*

What an extraordinary story of Esther! This tender and touching tale of what might have happened in Esther's later years is simply—well, delicious.

Angela Hunt, *New York Times* bestselling author
on *The Queen's Cook*

I loved this book! Tessa's brilliance shines on these pages. . . . What a great read!

Susie Larson, talk radio host, national speaker, and bestselling
author on *The Queen's Cook*

Afshar's writing shines in this brilliant perspective shift on Queen Esther's story. . . . Searching biblical fiction relatable for today's reader.

Mesu Andrews, bestselling and award–winning
author on *The Queen's Cook*

Afshar gets better with every book. . . . Readers will not want this book to end.

Library Journal starred review of *The Queen's Cook*

[R]ich and resonant . . . A twisty plot full of intrigue and divided allegiances, set against an intricately rendered ancient Persia.

Publishers Weekly on *The Queen's Cook*

The Queen's Cook is a sensory accomplishment that blends gripping palace drama with immersive culinary artistry.

Booklist

QUEEN ESTHER'S COURT

THE ROYAL ARTISAN

TESSA AFSHAR

BETHANYHOUSE

a division of Baker Publishing Group
Minneapolis, Minnesota

Published by Bethany House Publishers
Minneapolis, Minnesota
BethanyHouse.com

Bethany House Publishers is a division of
Baker Publishing Group, Grand Rapids, Michigan

Printed in the United States of America

Library of Congress Cataloging-in-Publication Data
Names: Afshar, Tessa, author.
Title: The Royal Artisan / Tessa Afshar.
Description: Minneapolis, Minnesota: Bethany House, a division of Baker
 Publishing Group, 2025. | Series: Queen Esther's court
Identifiers: LCCN 2025013965 | ISBN 9780764243707 (paperback) | ISBN
 9780764245572 (casebound) | ISBN 9781493451166 (ebook)
Subjects: LCGFT: Christian fiction. | Novels.
Classification: LCC PS3601.F47 R69 2025 | DDC 813.6—dc23/eng/20250424
LC record available at https://lccn.loc.gov/2025013965

Cover design by Jennifer Parker

Published in association with Books & Such Literary Management, BooksAnd
Such.com.

Baker Publishing Group publications use paper produced from sustainable forestry
practices and postconsumer waste whenever possible.

25 26 27 28 29 30 31   7 6 5 4 3 2 1

To my readers.
You make writing a joy.

Black Sea
THRACE
Byzantium
CAPPADOCIA
LYDIA
Athens
IONIA
Sardis
Zagros Mountains
Tarsus
Haran
Mediterranean Sea
BEYOND THE RIVER
Sidon
Damascus
Babylon
Jerusalem
LIBYA
BABYLON
Memphis
EGYPT
Red Sea

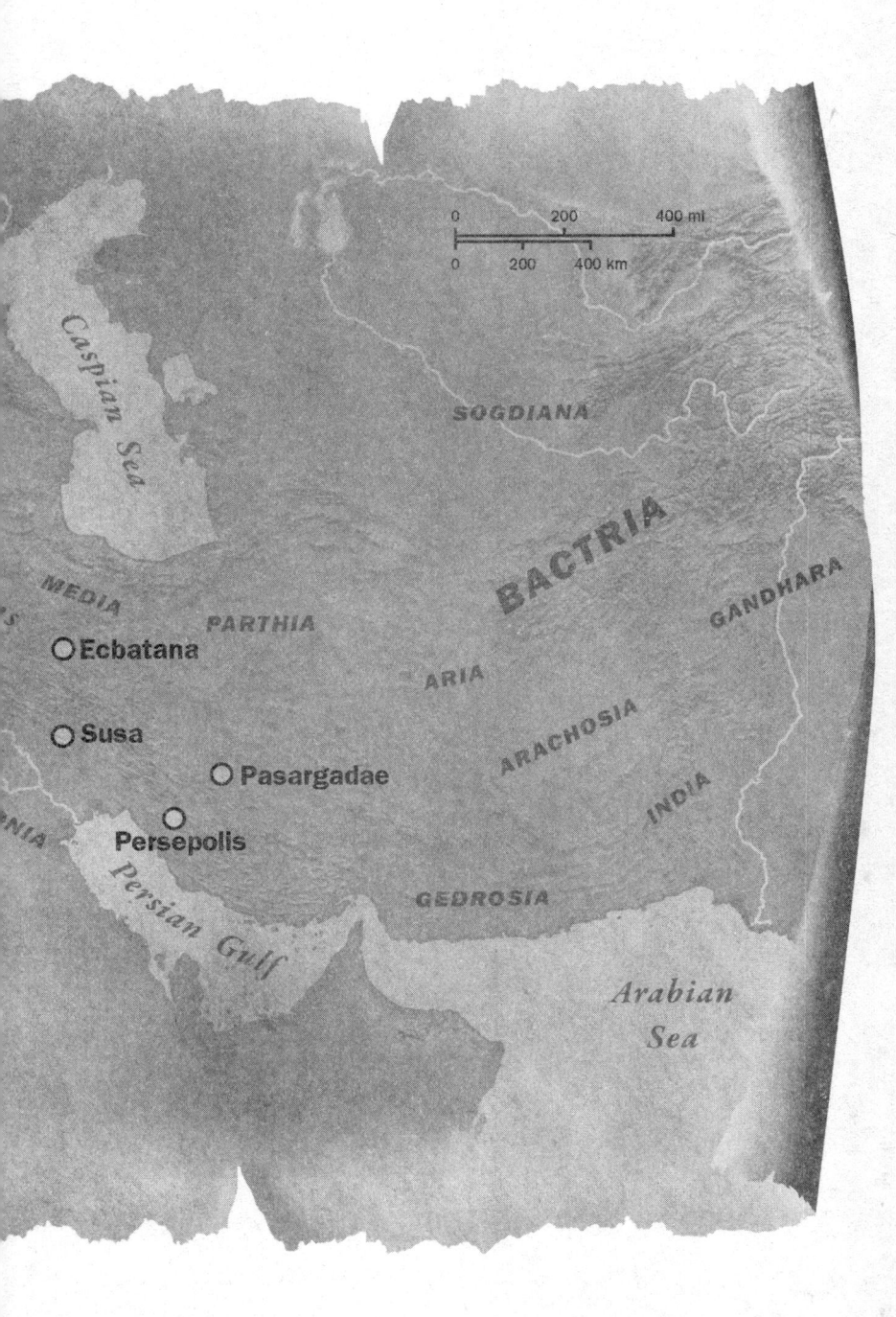

From the Secret Scrolls of Esther

And the young woman pleased him and won his favor.

Esther 2:9

The Twenty-Fifth Year of King Artaxerxes's Rule

Let me tell you a secret: Being queen will not fill the empty places in your heart.

I arrived at the Persian court on trembling legs, a stranger to its rigid protocols and sharp-edged rules. All the priceless jewels and alluring garments in the world could not chase away the chill of loneliness that plagued me those early days.

At eighteen, I was one of the oldest girls brought into the palace for that absurd competition—for though no one called it that to our faces, we all knew we were contending against one another for the crown.

My age and my faith had garnered me enough wisdom to recognize a few things by the end of my first month at the court. My companions in the women's quarters were ruled by their longings. The longing to be the loveliest, the wittiest, the best liked, the most admired. The longing to be chosen, wanted, desired.

The longing to be queen of an empire.

Longing flowed over the polished marble of the women's chambers like an invisible river, its currents pounding against every wall, demanding fulfillment. But I knew that the way of my companions would lead to discontentment. To disappointment so deep it would swallow them whole.

All their yearning, palpable in its reaching, snap-jawed hunger, rose out of empty places in hearts that had been starved of better things. My companions thought the crown would fill those old aches.

I knew better.

But looking at them, I felt the first quaking of real fear. I had my own empty places. The child of dead parents, I had learned loss at an early age. No heart is whole in this fractured world. I could easily fall into the same pit as the young women whose craving eyes looked upon me and thought, *rival*.

Which is why I determined I would never be queen, not even when Hegai, who had charge over the virgins, set me up in the best chamber. I had no desire to win the king's love, nor had I any interest in surrendering my heart to him.

I kept my own counsel and hid my Jewish heritage as my cousin Mordecai bade me. Like Abraham, I laid the Isaac of my hopes and dreams at God's feet.

I was almost twenty when I completed my year of beauty treatments. The night before my first visit to the king, I slept like a sated babe. I asked Hegai to choose my garments and went to the king not with the fluttering of desperate hopes, but with the ease of a woman who did not care.

Imagine my surprise to find Xerxes staring at me as though enchanted when I told him his beard needed a good trim.

I found love when I had thought to protect myself from the pain of it. The pain came, sure enough. But love also brought something unexpected. It opened the door for the salvation of my people.

In that vast palace, I discovered that I was not alone after all. God brought me the companionship of a few dear friends. And together we were able to stand up to dark forces that were greater than us as individuals.

I am older now and live a quiet life. The life of Hadassah. The queen is forgotten, as I meant her to be. My hidden life keeps me safe from those who still wish me harm in a palace full of sharpened knives.

But even here, my friends surround me. Together, we sometimes remember the wonder of days when a fragile queen was able, against all odds, to save her people.

Prologue

Turn to me and be gracious to me,
for I am lonely and afflicted.
The troubles of my heart are enlarged . . .
Psalm 25:16–17

FORTY-FIVE YEARS EARLIER
THE YEAR BEFORE XERXES BECAME KING

Three solitary stars pierced the sullen clouds, their bright glow like a whispered promise in the otherwise uninterrupted gloom. Shoshanah set her gaze on that cheery corner of the sky as she tucked her body against her mother's side, seeking comfort in the familiar curves.

Her mother kissed the top of her head. "We'll arrive at the inn soon, my love."

Shoshanah wriggled closer. "I like the cart. Can we sleep here again tonight?"

Her mother gave a mock shudder. "My back still aches from last night's adventure. I need a proper bed." Her father and Arta nodded in unison, their heads bobbing in vigorous assent.

As if in apology for not granting Shoshanah's request, her mother gave her another kiss, followed by a cuddling embrace that had more than a touch of a mother babying a child. At eleven, Shoshanah made it a general rule to remind adults that she had outgrown childhood and stood on the verge of becoming a proper woman. But reading the worry on her mother's normally serene face, she let the cuddle pass without comment.

These were extraordinary times, after all.

The end of her family's world as they knew it had arrived four days earlier when they had walked into their pottery workshop and discovered the place in utter disarray. Pots broken, wheels upturned, baskets toppled. The culprit, whoever he might have been, had even rummaged through the cold kiln in the yard, spreading ashes in his wake. For a thief, he had certainly searched in odd places. What had he hoped to find?

Shoshanah, who spent two hours every afternoon training at the pottery wheel under Arta's expert tutelage, had stared slack-jawed at the disaster. The sight of the vandalized workshop made her ache, like a sharp-nosed trimming tool jabbing her innards.

She had expected her parents to mourn the senseless destruction. The workshop had once belonged to her mother's father. Years of memories lay hidden in every nook and cranny of the place. Her mother had learned her trade there, had become the only female potter well known for her craft by laboring in those dusty rooms. The shop was more than a trade. It had become a heritage. A place of belonging and becoming. Seeing it so abused clawed at a deep place for all of them.

Shoshanah understood her parents' grief. She expected tears. Anger, even.

Instead, after a few hours of secret discussions, her parents proclaimed that Babylon was no longer safe. With a haste that made her head spin, they sold her mother's precious inheritance to her competitor and found a buyer for their family home as well. In three days, they severed every ancient root they had set in Babylon's soil and left behind the life they loved, departing for Susa.

Nothing Shoshanah said persuaded them to change course. "You will regret it," she said, her voice pleading. "You love this place too much."

Her gentle father treated her to a stern gaze. "We would not leave if we did not have to, child. You must trust your mother and me. This place is no longer secure. Not for us."

Child. In moments like this—moments when life's hardest decisions stared them in the face—she found herself relegated to the schoolroom once again, her burgeoning womanhood shoved aside unacknowledged.

She loved them more than life, the man and woman who had been the center of her world since birth. But nothing they had done in the last four days made any sense.

In the swaying cart, the heaviness of sleep pulled on her eyelids. The cart had belonged to her father's father and was one of the few familiar things they had with them. Years ago, when her grandfather had felt homesick and lonely while on a long journey, he had carved his name into one of its wooden panels. That name, written neatly in Hebrew rather than one of the languages of Babylon, seemed to ask for a little company now. Or perhaps it was Shoshanah who needed the companionship.

She scrambled to her knees, remembering the task she had set for herself. "Father, may I carve my name next to Grandfather's?" She pointed at the curling letters that spelled *Libni ben Mispar.*

In an upside-down world where a strange new landscape met her gaze from one hour to the next, she needed a reminder that she was still Shoshanah bat Bani. Without home, without the workshop, without her favorite wheel and the feel of the clay between her fingers, she could still remain herself.

Her father took a quick look before returning his attention to driving the donkeys. "Yes, daughter. You may. Perhaps Arta can help you. Wielding a knife can be tricky in this teetering cart." His voice was soft, tinged with what Shoshanah recognized as regret. He understood why she needed this tiny claim upon the wood that cradled all they had left.

The handle of a short knife appeared before her. Arta, her parents' dearest friend and the man who had been like a beloved uncle to her all her life, held it aloft with a winsome grin. "What language shall it be, then?"

"Hebrew, like my grandfather's," she said.

Her name was one of the few words she knew how to write in the tongue of her ancestors. Born and raised in Babylon, she had never set foot on Israel's soil. And unlike her scribe father, and his before him, she had not inherited an aptitude for languages. Instead, she had come into the world with clay in her blood.

"Bani, can you slow the cart for a moment?" Arta called to her father. "We are trying to create a work of art back here."

Her father nodded. Shoshanah gave him an appreciative smile when the cart's bouncing steadied. She whittled the curves of a Hebrew *shin* into the wooden slat just next to her grandfather's name. The letter always reminded her of a short lampstand with three branches. Arta helped hold her hand steady when the cart dipped into a long rut. She drew a straight line, followed by another *shin*, a *nun*, and a *heh*, each letter carved right to left, and as straight as she could make it, until her name was complete. שׁוֹשַׁנָּה

She blew away the last of the wood chips and sat back to examine her work.

Arta gave a nod of approval. "That's fine work. Of course, I can't tell if you spelled it correctly since I don't speak Hebrew," he teased.

Her mother gave an arched look. "You can be certain it contains no mistakes. Bani taught her himself, so you know it will be perfect."

Her father glanced over his shoulder. "Couldn't have done better myself. Well done, daughter."

She had finished just in time, for in a short while her father pulled the cart onto the edge of the road alongside the inn where they would spend the night. A popular stopping point on the road that stretched from Babylon to Susa, the inn seemed full to bursting on this cloudy night, for its yard was crammed with carts of every size, donkeys, mules, oxen, and horses taking up every spare spot, leaving no room for them to turn inside.

"You and Shoshanah go and see if you can arrange for a room, please." Her father passed a purse to Arta. "And you will be among the blessed if you can procure some bread and cheese for our supper." He handed the reins of the donkeys to a servant boy. "Elihana and I will have our baggage brought in."

The aroma of Babylonian stew greeted Shoshanah as she entered the main dining hall of the inn, making her stomach grumble. The smell of butter, milk, and herbs mingled with lamb, a recipe that her Jewish lips would never taste, for the law forbade the mixing of dairy with meat. Bread and cheese would suffice until they found a new home where they could cook their own meals.

She sighed. Even insignificant events like an ordinary supper became a barbed reminder that they had lost all that felt good and familiar.

Arta spoke to the innkeeper about procuring a room for the night while Shoshanah scanned the busy dining room. Spotting a narrow table whose occupants were about to leave, she headed in that direction, Arta in tow.

The innkeeper's wife brought over a wooden platter piled with flat, steaming bread alongside two round plates she balanced with one hand, one full of soft white cheese and another bearing a little hill of dates. She bent to set down the bread when the sound of a scream, followed by loud shouting, brought the cheerful hubbub in the dining hall to a standstill.

One of the outdoor servants who had helped them upon arrival ran inside, his gaze searching until it fell upon Arta. With an abrupt motion, he signaled for Arta to follow him. "Stay here." Arta's voice emerged a croak. "I'll see what's happened."

A knot twisted in Shoshanah's belly. Without a word, she rose to follow him. Seeing the expression on her face, he jerked his chin into a nod and led the way.

Outside, a nightmare awaited them. A few steps from their cart, her parents lay in the rutted road, limbs bent at odd angles, moaning.

A scream clawed up Shoshanah's throat but emerged only as a strangled whimper. She threw herself next to her mother, reaching out a hand to her father's shoulder.

"I didn't dare move them," the servant boy said to Arta. "Feared I'd do them more harm."

Arta fell to his knees. "Lord's mercy! What happened here?"

"They were standing on the edge of the road, taking some baggage out of the cart." The boy's voice shook as he recounted what he had witnessed. "Out of nowhere, I saw a wagon hurtling toward them. The driver did not even try to stop. I cried out to warn them. But they stood no chance."

The innkeeper had now arrived upon the scene, shaking his head. "The driver must have been drunk. Where did he go? Where is the dog who mowed them down?"

"He drove off, master. Never even gave a backward glance."

Shoshanah did not care. All that mattered now was that her parents should recover.

"Ima! Ima, can you hear me?"

With some heroic effort, her mother opened her eyes. "My daughter. My sweet child." She swallowed, a stray tear disappearing into her tangled hair. "I love you," she rasped. "Never forget. I'm proud of you."

"Ima!"

She coughed, and a thin thread of blood stained the side of her lip. "Arta."

Arta sobbed. "Yes, Elihana?"

"You are my own brother. Dear . . . dear to me. I trust you with our treasures. Raise my daughter well. Cherish her."

Arta took off his felt hat, his head dropping over his chest. "Yes, Elihana. As long as I have breath."

She reached a trembling hand to her husband. For a moment, bloody fingers grasped bloody fingers. "Love you . . ."

"Always," Bani said, his chest shaking.

She went still as a dew drop on a blade of grass. Still and peaceful.

"Oh, Abba! Is she . . . ?"

"Gone from us, child. As I will be soon. How I love you, dear heart."

"No," she moaned. "No, no. Don't say it. Don't say goodbye."

"Forgive me. I know you wished to stay in our home. But it wasn't safe."

"Don't worry about that now."

"I place you in Arta's charge. Be good to him. He has never raised a child." He managed a pained smile. "Arta?"

Arta choked on his breath. "Yes, Bani?"

"My girl is your girl now."

Arta's tears rolled down his cheeks. Mutely, he nodded.

"With the money from the sale of the workshop, buy a house where you can be safe in Susa," her father said. "Look after them, Arta. Keep them secure with your life."

Arta squeezed his friend's bloody hand. "I promise, Bani. I will give my life for them."

Her father took a deep, gurgling breath. She could see each inhalation had become an effort. Still, he held on to her and gave a small smile. "My beautiful girl. You have been a joy to me."

He lingered for another half hour, though he spoke no more words. Shoshanah abided with him in anguished silence, her heart in her eyes. Love, she found, did not always need words.

1

Sazana

As one whom his mother comforts,
so I will comfort you;
you shall be comforted . . .

Isaiah 66:13

The full moon looked pockmarked, its pale light creating shadows on the pottery wheel, giving its flat surface a sinister cast. Drawing her lamp closer to dispel the gloom, Sazana tried to ignore the spasm of pain that shot up her back. She might only be twenty-three, but in the wake of an endless day, she felt like an old woman.

She exhaled. Two more pieces and she could stop.

Across from her, the boy whose head had started nodding into his chest straightened hastily at her gesture and set the wheel into motion with several powerful turns. To his delight, Arash had been promoted to the post of her wheel boy three months ago after serving for a year in the grueling clay yard. She grinned. A fifteen-hour day like today might cause him to regret the privilege.

At least she had sent Cambyz and Rashda home at a reasonable hour. The two youths who reported to her in the fine ware section of the workshop had completed enough pieces to meet their quota for the day. They had not reached her level of mastery at the wheel, which left her with the lion's share of the more complex pieces for which the workshop had become famous.

Wetting her hands in a bowl of water, Sazana cradled the ball of clay she had placed at the center of the wheel. Under the knowing pressure of her hands, the clay rose quickly into a cone. Her fingers curved over the point she had just created and pressed until the clay became round and flat. Twice more she built up the mound, only to demolish it. The clay, fine as it was, needed this brutal rising and falling before it could be shaped, else it would not be centered, producing an uneven vessel.

The jar she had to make, though no larger than the length of her forearm, presented several challenges. For one thing, its fluted design required a thicker wall. At the same time, the clay could not be so thick as to make the vessel ungainly. She wet her hands again, and hooking her left foot in the lowest rung of her stool, tucked an elbow against her thigh to keep her arm steady, and began the part of her labor that was more art than craft. Again and again, her fingers traveled up and down the clay, until the shapeless mass transformed into the hollowed body of a delicate jug with a long, slender neck.

With a sigh, she sat back and signaled Arash to let the wheel slow to a stop. Using a wire cutter, she separated the base of the jug from the stone wheel. Tomorrow, when the clay turned leather-hard, she would carve out the flutes and attach the handles at the same time. Those handles needed to be shaped tonight, though, or the difference of moisture in the clay would cause them to break in the kiln.

She moved to her table to roll out the clay, shaping thin tubes into two matching arcs, decorated on top with a tiny swirl. Wiping her hands on a damp rag, she told the boy to carry the fragile wet jug and newly fashioned handles to the drying shelf reserved for Sazana's pieces.

Her arms had started to tremble with exhaustion. She stretched, trying to restore her strained muscles. As usual, Sazana's hair, straight and slippery, had fallen loose from its tie. She bundled the thick mass into a knot at the base of her neck and secured it with a leather strip.

A large hand settled on her shoulder. "Enough," Arta said in his gravelly voice. "You're done for the day."

She flashed him what she hoped was a reassuring smile. "Just one more. I can do it."

"No." His thick brows knotted over his prominent nose. "You're too exhausted. He can wait an extra day."

It took her a moment to form her answer. Even now, irritated as he was, Arta did not interrupt her, but waited patiently for her words to come.

She shot him a grateful smile, then swung her head backward, the Persian signal for no. "Lord Haman, wait?"

It would only land Arta in trouble if she did not complete the order. As the foreman of the workshop, he carried the responsibility for every failure and received none of the praise from its owner. Since Lord Haman had requisitioned the order for his own private use, he would consider it a personal affront if they fell short by even one vessel.

Arta hissed a frustrated breath. "It's an unreasonable request. That many complicated vessels in so short a time. I may just give that man a piece of my mind."

"The only piece we'll give him is made of pottery. I told you. I can do it."

"I don't suppose Lord Haman would put up with even a hint of complaint from me. But once this order is finished, you will have a whole day to yourself."

She gave him an appreciative nod. To her, Arta was a father first, then a foreman, protecting her where he could.

Before she settled at the wheel to begin the final piece, she reached for the instinctual comfort of the clay oval that lay snug under the fabric of her tunic.

Her mother's seal.

Those dear hands must have wrapped around the smooth-edged oval a thousand times as she put her stamp into every pot she had made. As always, the touch soothed Sazana like balm. The seal's Hebrew words flashed through her mind.

Elihana, daughter of Shaphan.

The name and lineage were followed by a discrete second line that featured a single word: *Potter*. As a workshop owner and expert potter, her mother had had the right to her own seal.

She would have been no stranger to days like this. Days that lasted too long at the never-ending turn of the wheel. She, too, had ached, back and shoulders sore from bending. But she had persisted until her vessels were formed before pressing that oval seal into the wet clay.

It had been twelve years since the seal had made its mark on clay. Now it had become a hidden object, a secret consolation rather than a public declaration.

Sazana signaled the boy to start the wheel and began to shape the last piece. Like her mother before her, she would fulfill her duty.

By the time she completed the final vessel in Lord Haman's order, Sazana longed to crawl into bed and not rise for ten hours. Not that she would have that luxury. Sunrise would arrive too soon, and with it, more labor. Tomorrow, she planned to carve delicate flutes into the vessels she had prepared today.

A longer delay in Susa's hot, dry climate, and the clay would become too hard to carve.

Dismissing Arash to his home and waiting mother, she placed the final piece on the drying rack. In passing, she drew a soft finger down the side of a jug, her touch as tender as a mother's hand on a toddler's sleeping head. Tired as she was, she could not suppress a smile of satisfaction. The row of jugs she had thrown that day stood next to one another, perfect in height and thickness, their walls smooth and unmarred.

Hearing a loud noise behind her, she spun around. Her toe caught on the edge of the reed mat, causing her to lose her balance, pitching her forward. She stretched out her arms to keep from tumbling to the floor. Coming to a teetering stop, she took a deep breath.

That could have been a disaster! She could have shattered a whole row of pottery with that kind of careless floundering.

She winced at the sight of the muscular man who seemed to have appeared out of thin air, watching her with an unfriendly expression, arms crossed over a massive chest. "Nabonassar?" Why was he sniffing around the fine ware section so late at night?

"You sound surprised to see me," he said in his thick Babylonian accent. "Who did you think it would be? The satrap of Bactria come to carry you away to his golden palace?"

It took her too long to form an answer for Nabonassar's liking, and he decided whatever she had to say wasn't worth the wait. "You are making such a commotion in here, I could not sleep."

She scowled. The man slept in an alcove all the way on the opposite end of the workshop, and her wheel was not noisy enough to keep him awake. More likely, he had come to spy on her. As Haman's not-so-secret informer, he reported every detail of the workshop to his master. For his pain, he had been elevated to head potter in the common ware section, where he and eighteen other men made rough vessels for food and wine storage. Next to Arta, that gave him the highest rank in the place, though his skill hardly merited such a position.

"As you see, I am finished now." She moved to walk past him.

A thick hand snaked out to wrap around her arm. "What's that?"

Before Sazana could step away, greedy fingers grabbed the chain at her neck. Her seal! It must have slipped out of her tunic when she stumbled.

"Let go!" A sheen of sweat dampened the top of her lips. She tried to pull away, but Nabonassar held fast.

"What have we here? Is this a love token? Do you have a sweetheart, girl?" He pulled the seal toward him, studying it with inquisitive eyes.

The Hebrew letters were written backward, since it would be their mirror image that would be stamped into the clay. She prayed the reverse alphabet would baffle Nabonassar. She knew her prayers had not been answered when a slow smile dawned on the man's handsome face. "Well, well. What are you doing with a Hebrew seal hanging from your scrawny neck, eh?"

Sazana had grown up at the potter's wheel and had the toned physique to prove it. She knocked the seal out of the man's hand, and stepping away, tucked it back inside her tunic.

"What goes on here?" Arta growled.

Nabonassar faced the foreman. "She is a Jew, this one. You must have known."

A dull flush spread from Arta's neck to his pate. "What nonsense is this?"

"She wears a Hebrew seal around her neck. Saw it with my own eyes, just now. Lord Haman will be very interested in that news."

"Don't be ridiculous, man," Arta said, trying to sound casual and failing miserably. "You will only make yourself look like a fool if you carry such empty tales to the master."

Nabonassar laughed as he walked away. "We'll see."

Sazana swallowed hard. "I can't believe I let him see it."

Arta put a comforting arm around her shoulder. "I can't believe he has the wit to figure out what it is."

Her watery laugh dried up quickly. "Arta, I've gone and ruined us."

"Your mother used to laugh just like that, all white teeth and sweetness." He tapped her on the cheek. "And we are not ruined. At worst, we may find ourselves without employment. But there will be other workshops that will jump at the chance to hire you."

"There are no other pottery workshops in Susa that produce fine ware. I would be reduced to making rough amphora for grain storage."

"We can seek work in Ecbatana or Persepolis."

"They don't know me, Arta. My name is only known here, in Susa."

"Which is why Haman would never let you go. Your fine pottery earns him a small fortune. He won't dismiss you merely because he disapproves of your heritage. He'll growl and sneer for a season and then forget about it."

She shook a finger at him. "If those words were a pot, they would crack at the first sight of the furnace."

Arta rubbed the back of his neck. "I suppose." He exhaled. "What's done is done, in any case. Let's go home and sleep for a few hours. Tomorrow will come soon enough."

"I'm sorry Arta."

"For what?"

"For insisting on wearing my mother's seal. If I had left it at home, this would never have happened."

"You did nothing wrong. You have every right to cling to a precious keepsake. The Lord knows you've lost too much already. I would never expect you to give up so small a comfort as well, Shoshanah."

She felt her shoulders ease at the sound of that name. The one she had been born with, Hebrew like her blood.

She poked a finger in his arm. "You'll find yourself without a job because of me."

He waved a dismissive hand. "After twelve years, I was tired of working for the man, anyway."

"Are you tired of eating too?" The position of foreman was an honored and highly competitive one. Vacancies did not come around every day.

Arta drew her close. "It won't come to that, my dear. I have a little bit set aside for just such a day. Besides, I haven't forgotten how to throw a pot."

Sazana rewarded him with a wan smile. She loved the way Arta always saw the hope in every situation. Which was why she did not remind him that making common ware was young men's work. Arta might have the technique, but he no longer had the strength.

But she did. She would find work in one of the other workshops. Coarse or fine, it made no difference. She would look after Arta the way he had always looked after her.

2

Jadon

But to you also the cup will be passed . . .
Lamentations 4:21 NIV

Jadon surveyed the stale bread and shriveled cheese sitting on his shelf and covered them again with a piece of cloth. He was not that hungry.

He had just returned from a village north of Susa where the queen owned a prosperous farm. She had sent him to verify the overseer's claim that poor soil and disease meant they expected a much smaller crop of barley this year.

Jadon had arrived at the overseer's door disguised as the servant of a Lydian merchant, seeking to purchase barley at a generous rate.

"Lydia has been struck by a terrible famine," he told the overseer. "You are fortunate to have charge of such good land. The price of grain will likely double and triple soon."

The overseer's eyes took on a gleam Jadon did not like. "Will it?"

Jadon nodded. "My master is willing to be generous if your barley is good quality."

"You will not find better." The overseer emptied a bag on the table between them. "Here is a sample from last harvest."

Jadon waved a hand. "This could be from anywhere. Show me your fields, and I will decide for myself."

The overseer obliged. For an hour, they rode their donkeys from one end of the expansive field to another, tasting from the ripening crop.

"Nothing wrong with this grain," Jadon said, examining the green head of barley that sat in the palm of his hand. Clearly the man's claim that the barley would not yield a rich harvest that spring had been false. A ploy to pocket the difference in income between what he declared and what he actually sold the grain for.

The overseer missed the irony in Jadon's voice. "As I said, this is the finest grain you'll find anywhere."

"Someone from my master's household will contact you soon." They certainly would, though not in the way the overseer expected.

Now Jadon settled behind his desk, preparing to write a report to the queen's chief steward, Hathach. Before he had a chance to dip his stylus into ink, a polite knock sounded at the main entrance. He peeked through the slats of the window and, recognizing the man outside, pulled the bar free from the door.

"Benyamin!" It had been a few months since he had seen the carpenter who had built his writing desk for him.

Benyamin drew a sheepish hand down his beard. "Forgive the intrusion. I know the hour is late. I came earlier but found no one at home."

"Not at all. Come in."

Benyamin thanked him, taking the cushion Jadon offered.

For a few moments, he spoke of mundane concerns: the oppressive heat, unusual so early in spring; the rising price of wine; his daughter's approaching wedding. But Jadon could tell that the man had something particular on his mind and decided to put the carpenter out of his misery.

"How can I help you, Benyamin?"

His guest colored. "You remember Jacob? My youngest?"

"The boy who could climb trees faster than a squirrel?"

Benyamin grinned. "That's the one." He leaned close. "Well, Jacob has his heart set on going to the palace school."

"Ah." It was a point of Persian pride that any boy could enter the exclusive school that taught its pupils reading, writing, ethics, basic medicine, and the art of war. Commoners as well as aristocrats could reap the rewards of this privileged education. "Have you applied?"

Benyamin's smile held a world of satisfaction. "Applied and accepted."

"That is a great accomplishment. My congratulations."

Jadon leaned back. Young Jacob now faced another hurdle, in some ways more challenging than the first. The palace school, though open to all, cost a fortune. Students had to have their own horse and pay for its keep and fodder as well as pay for their clothes, their weapons, and their armor. Few commoners could afford all the expenses.

"I have saved enough to buy him a horse," Benyamin said. "Nothing like the beasts the gentry can afford. But it has four legs and knows how to trot. His grandfather will pay the stable fees. But the weapons . . ." Leaving the sentence unfinished, the proud father dropped his head.

"Say no more. I would be happy to help. My kit, though old, is still usable. Your son is welcome to it."

"Bless you, Jadon!" Benyamin cried. "I will repay you, somehow."

Jadon waved a hand, embarrassed. "It's not as if I use it. Wait here. I will go and fetch what he will need."

In his chamber, Jadon lifted the lid of the ancient chest he kept in a curtained alcove. The hinges creaked in protest, reminding him that it had been a long while since they had been used.

He sifted through a lifetime of keepsakes. His father's cloak. His own formal garments that he used to wear in the days he had served as an Immortal. A gold-embroidered bedcover. Underneath, he found the cache of his boyhood weapons and armor.

His father, a minor Persian lord who had fallen in love with a Jewess and become a follower of the Lord before marrying her, had insisted on this one Persian tradition: that his son attend the palace school. Which was why Jadon could now help Benyamin's son.

As he drew out the fat bundle from the bottom of the chest, a silver object clattered against the side and rolled to a stop. He went still, staring at the goblet.

So many threads of memory clung to each intricate line and serpentine carving of that cup. His grandmother's laughter turning into a knot of anger. His mother's pale face, silent and combative.

And Shoshanah. Shoshanah smiling that ravishing smile. Shoshanah teasing him, her silky black hair slipping free from its knot to frame a face he had never managed to forget. Shoshanah staring at him with a love that melted his bones.

Shoshanah, white with hurt.

He slammed the chest shut and shoved his bundle under one arm, bolting to the front room.

3

Sazana

> . . . because he is at my right hand, I shall not
> be shaken.
>
> Psalm 16:8

The Twelfth Year of King Xerxes's Rule
The Thirteenth Day of Spring

In the workshop's expansive yard, two large mounds of clay
looked like the humps on a giant camel's back. The sun's
first rays brushed the pointed tips just as Sazana plodded
by, lighting her path as she navigated the various heaps of debris
that were a permanent fixture in the landscape of the pottery
yard.

Inside, the workshop greeted her with a somber hush. Usually, this was her favorite time of day. The quiet hour before
everyone arrived and turned the large rectangular building into
a hive of sweat and activity. Today, the stillness failed to work
its soothing magic. She settled on her stool and grabbed a lump

of clay, fisting her fingers over the cool, malleable surface like a child finding comfort in the folds of a well-worn blanket.

Her head drooped as she considered the steep price she would have to pay for wearing her mother's pottery seal around her neck.

Lord Haman made a dangerous enemy. His influence had spread its tentacles faster than a pottery wheel could turn. She marveled at the way his wealth had grown to legendary proportions over the past decade. Susa's largest pottery workshop was now one of many business concerns he owned, though, according to Arta, it remained his most profitable venture.

She squeezed the clay until her knuckles turned white. It wasn't merely his wealth. Haman came from an aristocratic family on his mother's side. His bloodlines, bolstered by his mounting wealth and oily charm, had catapulted him into the king's inner circle. The previous year the king had promoted him above his other officials, a position that endowed him with incomprehensible power.

She wanted to bleat like a wounded sheep. To have *this* man turn the arrow tip of his hatred upon her boded ill. And Arta, though Persian through and through, had committed the sin of protecting her. He would be no less a victim of Lord Haman's hostility than she.

Haman had never been fond of the Jews. Which was why Arta had insisted that Sazana take on a Persian name when she had started helping in the workshop at the age of eleven. She had hidden behind her secret identity over the years. But in recent weeks, she had noticed that Lord Haman's hatred for her people had ascended to new heights.

The source of this increased hostility seemed ridiculous to her. A Jewish official by the name of Mordecai refused to bow before him in public. That was all. One man's scorn. Yet since then, Lord Haman had demanded that all his workshops cease doing business with Jews, no matter where in the kingdom they resided or how good their merchandise was. The thought that his star potter worshipped Adonai, right under his very nose, would likely drive him into an incandescent rage.

She swallowed the bile that rose up her throat. After years of living incognito, the disguise of adopting a Persian name had started to make her feel safe. But that security had proven an illusion, shattered beneath the weight of one simple blunder.

With a sigh, Sazana rose. Her worry may yet be for nothing. She had not been dismissed yet. And the vessels she had made yesterday still needed her attention.

Picking up the first jug from the drying rack, she measured the base and top and calculated the number of flutes that would fit evenly into its body. With sure, experienced fingers, she carved steady lines into the leather-hard clay using a wooden tool. She painted each end of the handle with slurry—a special liquid clay she used as glue for joining parts—and positioned the curved pieces on the vessel.

One by one, the eighteen potters in the coarse ware section slipped into the workshop, greeting her with smiles and waves. She had known most of them since she started here. Over the past twelve years, they had grown accustomed to having a woman in their midst and had come to think of her as a younger sister. They were simple men, hardworking and forthright. Their very presence settled her heart and made the workshop feel almost safe.

Cambyz and Rashda hurried in with the rising sun. "Pardon, mistress." Cambyz threw himself on his stool. "I overslept."

She crossed her arms. "And Rashda?"

"I overslept even more." The youth with the drowsy eyes yawned and offered a sheepish grin. "My parents gave a feast for my seventeenth birthday last night. Cambyz joined us. We stayed up late."

"Well, now that you are seventeen, I will expect even better work from you." Sazana winked at the boys before assigning their day's tasks. They had been under her tutelage for a full year, and she could now trust them with some of the less complex pieces in the fine ware section.

By early afternoon, she had completed the final piece in Haman's order. As she studied the line of jugs drying on the rack, Sazana felt lulled by the rhythms of a typical day. Perhaps Arta was right. Perhaps Haman's greed would prove more powerful than his hatred. Maybe he would refuse to act upon Nabonassar's intelligence, seeing the logic of holding on to his highest-earning potter regardless of his personal feelings.

She came to her feet. The jugs would need several days to dry before she could glaze them. But she could prepare the glaze beforehand so long as she kept it well sealed and set Arash to stirring it regularly.

A loud gasp drew her attention. Turning, she found the workers in the coarse ware section gathered around one of the potters. Parnaka had gone with Arta early that morning to make a delivery. Through the buzz of voices that were speaking over one another, she picked up fragments of questions: *Why . . . ? How . . . ? Surely not . . . When . . . ?*

She drew closer, curious. Arta stood silently at the edge of the crowd, his face ashen. Sazana frowned, about to make her way to him when Parnaka's words rose above the crowd.

"I am telling you. That is what the royal messenger said. Every single Jew is to be killed, by order of the king!"

Sazana froze. *What?* She must have misheard him. She swiveled toward Parnaka, listening with care.

"I heard it in the market. The king has issued an edict to annihilate all Jews who live in Persia."

Sazana shook her head. It could not be true. But she knew Parnaka to be an honest man. He would never lie about such a thing. Somehow, he must have made a mistake. Persia had 127 provinces. From the borders of India all the way to Egypt, the Persian territories spread over half the known world. If every

Jew in every province was to be killed, there would hardly be any of her people left.

This must be an empty rumor. No such edict had ever been issued in the empire. Not against the Jews or any other people group unless in war or as a response to outright rebellion. But the tight knot in Arta's brows told its own story.

She gave him a wide-eyed look. Arta sent everyone to their stations, and snagging her wrist, drew her into an alcove in the fine ware section. He pulled the thick curtains closed behind them, offering them a measure of privacy.

"Shoshanah, I fear what you heard is true." His gravelly voice, always deep and certain, sounded oddly constrained. "In eleven months, the Jews are to be killed on a single day and their property seized by whoever chooses to attack them."

Sazana sank onto a stool. Her mind whirled with sharp-edged alarm. Questions and objections screamed in her head. But the words took their time to emerge. Arta waited patiently for her to form them. "Why would the king command such a thing?" she finally managed.

Arta knelt before her. "No one knows. The messenger offered no reason."

"There must be a mistake. His head will cool, and he will change his mind."

Arta's lips pinched. "He cannot. He set his royal seal on the cursed thing and turned the pronouncement into permanent law. The messenger showed it to us."

Sazana exhaled. That morning her greatest worry had been the possibility that Lord Haman might dismiss them both. To her, that had seemed a monumental catastrophe. Now such an outcome hardly seemed to hold any significance. What was a mere job when compared to the annihilation of her whole people?

Arta reached for her hand. "What did your mother used to say about the potter's wheel?"

Sazana closed her eyes. "'When you sit at the wheel, tuck your elbow against your thigh. That's the anchor that will keep your arm from quivering.'"

Arta joined his voice to hers, and together they finished her mother's oft-repeated advice. "'But anchor your heart to God, and he will keep you from being shaken.'"

Arta squared his shoulders. "That's what we will do. We'll anchor our hearts to God. He will find a way for us."

He enveloped her in his bearlike embrace, the way he had done all those years ago when she had been a girl of eleven, half shattered from watching her parents die. Back then, the world had felt like it was ending. But she had survived it. Survived that cruel loss to make a life for herself.

This time, the loss was magnified, for it threatened not only her personal future, but the future of her whole people. She sank to the floor, tucked her elbow against her thigh the way she did when she sat at the wheel and tried to herd her heart until it became anchored to God. She found her heart more defiant than her elbow. It refused to find a steady place. It refused to cling to God.

Arta knelt to wipe the tears that squeezed unbidden beneath her lashes. "I am sorry, my dear."

She looked up. She might be helpless to come to the aid of her people. But there was one person she could help. "Dear Arta." She laid a hand against his cheek. "You are a Persian. This edict has no bearing on you even though you follow the Lord. We must keep you safe."

His head snapped back as though she had slapped him. "If you are about to say what I think you are, don't. Don't you dare."

"My presence exposes you to needless danger. I must leave you. Surely you see that. It's the only way."

"It's the only way to break my heart." Arta drew a trembling hand over his graying beard. "You are my family. My own daughter, though I did not have the privilege of fathering you. What you suggest is not safety. It would be the end of me."

Sazana's eyes softened. How she treasured this man. For his sake, she made her tone stern. "Be reasonable."

"This is reasonable. You might as well try to separate the clay from its glaze after it's been fired. No. We stay together, no matter what."

She felt ashamed to admit it. But at Arta's declaration, the tight fist squeezing her heart loosened its clutching hold a little.

From the Secret Scrolls of Esther

Esther had not made known her people or kindred, for Mordecai had commanded her not to make it known.

Esther 2:10

Thirty-Three Years Later
The Twenty-Fifth Year of King Artaxerxes's Rule

From the day I arrived at the palace as a virgin, I had one defense against any who might object to my lineage. My name.

I became Esther the day I came to the court. That name, bearing no allusion to Israel or Judea, guarded me from wagging tongues and evil intentions. My true name, Hadassah, would have been a weapon in the hand of those who meant me ill. No Persian king would rise to the defense of a queen whose bloodlines belonged to a conquered nation. Or so I believed.

For six years, my life, my position, and my marriage all found shelter beneath my false name.

A human ploy, for Mordecai himself had commanded

me not to make my true heritage known. But I had leaned into that name for so long that it became a part of my very soul's security.

Mordecai, dressed in sackcloth and ashes, demanded that I smash this trusted armor with my own hands. You cannot imagine the resistance that rose up in me at his suggestion. Tell the king that I was not Esther, but Hadassah? A soldier in the midst of bloody battle would be as likely to shed his breastplate as I was to cast off the bulwark of my name.

I am older now and have learned many things. I have learned, for instance, that God allows us to hold on to our human defenses for only so long. At times, he himself calls them forth, permitting them to function for a season in order to guard us from harm. But a day will come when, in his eyes, they have served their purpose and must be removed.

The hour your soul grows attached to that defense—the moment your heart clings to it too much for safety—is the moment God rises in his mercy to destroy it.

And so he did for me.

I had to lay down what I had thought was my true protection in order to pick up the Lord's armor. I had to fold Esther like a silken robe and set her aside before the king, my husband. How my heart shivered at the very thought.

But not until I did so could the power of God's true protection cover me. Only then did I discover that every other shield to which I clung would prove temporary in the end.

4

Jadon

Letters were sent by couriers to all the king's provinces with instruction to destroy, to kill, and to annihilate all Jews, young and old, women and children.

Esther 3:13

Like a man thrown by a horse he had believed biddable, Jadon stood slack-jawed with amazement. Amazement at discovering that the queen he had served for two years was not Esther at all, but Hadassah. He blinked at Hathach. "She is a Jew?"

The queen's eunuch exhaled an annoyed breath. "As I said."

Jadon tried to wrap his mind around this revelation. Like his own mother, the Persian queen belonged to the lineage of Abraham. She had guarded the secret of that heritage tightly

44

for the past five years. Six, if he counted her year of preparation in the palace.

In light of the king's freshly minted edict, this revelation put an even darker spin on matters. The queen herself lived in peril. Unlike Jadon, whose aristocratic Persian father would act as a shield against the new law, the queen's Jewish bloodlines left her exposed. Her enemies could easily use the new decree as a means of destroying her.

He pressed the bridge of his nose between two fingers. "Has she heard the news of the king's proclamation?"

"I have not informed Her Majesty yet. I need to understand matters before I approach her."

Jadon bowed his head. "How may I serve?"

Hathach leaned close. "The rumor is that someone is behind the edict. Someone other than the king. We need to discover if that is true. And if so, find the identity of the one who engineered this decree. To keep the queen safe, we must know her enemy."

Dipping his chin in acquiescence, Jadon rose. "If he exists, I will root him out."

"There is a man who might be able to help you."

"Yes?" Jadon expected a royal name, someone highly connected, or failing that, one of the shadowy royal spies.

"His name is Mordecai."

For the second time that morning, Jadon was thrown. "Mordecai? Isn't he a minor official?" Neither a spy nor a highly connected courtier, Mordecai rated as an ordinary man in the hierarchy of the palace.

"That's the one." Hathach's thin lips tipped up in one corner. "He also happens to be the queen's cousin. You shouldn't underestimate these minor officials. Sometimes they have more useful connections than a dozen senior men." He leaned close. "More importantly, this one will do anything for her. He is faithful to the bone."

Jadon sped down a wide path that ran alongside the massive palace wall. The famed blue-glazed bricks protected the sprawling royal complex from the outside world, furnishing its inhabitants with both security and privacy. But that barrier had proven impotent before the power of words.

Now Jadon had to do all in his power to keep the queen safe. Even her crown could not shield her from the malevolent edict that had wormed its way into law.

Two years ago, Jadon had been serving as an Immortal, a member of the king's elite guard, when Hathach sought him out with a flattering offer. Becoming the commander in charge of the queen's security meant a substantial promotion. It represented royal trust, for the king himself had to agree to release him into the new position.

Although he had left the formal ranks of the Immortals in order to fulfill his new duties, his ties to his fellow soldiers went deep. While they would never betray a royal trust, they would bend a few rules to help one another. A fact that could prove useful in moments like this.

Jadon had known many of these men since their boyhood days at the palace school. They had served together in the Persian military, saved one another from dangerous scrapes, shared sleepless nights, and been chosen from amongst the ranks to join the world's most skillful soldiers. As Immortals, they protected their king—sometimes at the cost of their own dreams. Those were not bonds that could be easily forgotten.

He turned right on a lane that led straight to the Immortals' barracks. His friend Mazares would be off duty now, which meant he would be found either snoring in his bed or eating. At the sight of a neatly rolled-up pallet, Jadon headed for the courtyard attached to the barracks. Here, soldiers sat in clumps, conversing as they ate their midday meal. Spying Mazares in the midst of a particularly boisterous group, he waved.

Mazares grinned. "Trust you to show up just when they

serve the best meal of the week. Still starving yourself with your own cooking?" He pointed his knife at a sizable piece of meat. "Roasted ox. Come join us."

"Not today. My thanks. I need to have a word."

"Ah." Mazares threw a regretful look at his plate and rose without complaint.

Hidden behind the private curves of a whitewashed arbor, Jadon came straight to the point. "I must discover who is behind the king's new edict."

Mazares arched a brow. "The one about the Jews?" The brow dipped down at Jadon's nod. "Of course. I had forgotten your mother was a Hebrew." He reached a hand to Jadon's shoulder. "I am sorry, my friend."

"Can you help me? I need to find one of the couriers who announced the decree in Susa. He might still have a copy of the original edict in his possession."

Mazares tapped a finger against his neatly bearded jaw. His expression brightened. "Come! I know just the one. He lost at dice to me not a fortnight ago. Had to give up a week's pay. I am quite fond of the boy."

He had already taken off before the words finished coming out of his mouth, Jadon bounding behind him. In another courtyard, one often used by various attachments of palace guards and messengers, Mazares homed in on a lanky youth. Before the messenger had a chance to finish his first bite of savory bread buried under a mound of meat, Mazares had him cornered.

The young man groaned. "I already paid you what I owed."

"You did. But I am looking for something else." He pointed at the brown leather satchel that lay next to him on the grass. "Still have a copy of the king's latest edict?"

"As a matter of fact, I do."

Before the young man had a chance to argue, they had his satchel open, the king's edict lying before them. Jadon studied the clay tablet with its small blob of red wax at the bottom, which depicted a man battling a roaring lion. He recognized the seal from his days serving the king. He had seen it carved upon a ring Xerxes favored. Not a general royal seal, then, but a personal one, which suggested Xerxes himself was involved in the issuing of the edict.

Like all palace documents, this one had been fashioned by a royal scribe. Most scribes produced their work anonymously. But upon occasion, they left clues to their identities. A small name carved on the backside of a tablet, a particular word exchanged for another in the body of the text, even a fingerprint in the wet clay.

Jadon's brow furrowed. This particular scribe had not been thoughtful enough to name himself. Not being familiar with the singularities in the handwriting of royal scribes, Jadon failed to recognize any other clue. Thanks to Hathach, however, he knew just the man to ask.

First, he would have to convince the young messenger to part with his official document. He directed a stern glance at him. "Why are you still in possession of this tablet? You have already made the announcement in Susa. Why have you not returned it?"

Jadon knew that although tablets were supposed to be returned to the scribes immediately after a public proclamation, messengers often held on to them for several hours. They returned from their duties hungry and thirsty, covered in the dust of unpaved roads. No one begrudged the delay in the return of their documents while they refreshed themselves.

Still, the letter of the law, though lax in practice, demanded immediate return of all official documents. A fact Jadon intended to use to his advantage.

The messenger's mouth flapped open. "You are the one who insisted on seeing it."

"Good thing I did. Another man would report you for dereliction of duty. Mazares shall return it to the scribes for filing. As an Immortal, it is his duty."

The messenger's shoulders drooped. "Please, sir. I know I am a little late. Perhaps you can overlook my error this once." His tone turned pleading. "I need this job."

Mazares tucked the tablet under an arm. "Calm yourself, boy. After winning half your wages the other day, I am in a good mood. I won't get you into trouble."

They strode away with the young messenger's thanks ringing in their ears. Mazares laughed. "You are too sly for everyone else's good, Jadon. What do you want with this tablet, anyway?"

"I have to discover who wrote it."

Jadon had seen soldiers in the field of battle who had received a grievous wound dealt by a lightning-fast strike that had amputated a limb. Mordecai had that kind of look about him. Disbelief. Shock. His bruised eyes hinted at an odd mix of outrage and terror. The king's edict had obviously hit him hard.

Jadon lowered himself on one knee to face the magistrate where he sat before the King's Gate, one of the main entrances to the palace. "Mordecai ben Jair." He spoke in the firm, authoritative tones he had learned to use in the confusion of a bloody fight.

The magistrate looked up, his gaze unfocused.

"My name is Jadon, son of Arsaces. I work for the queen."

That snapped him back to attention. "I've heard of you."

"Then you know the one who has sent me. I have need of your assistance."

"I will serve Her Majesty however I can."

Jadon withdrew the clay tablet. "This is an original document bearing the king's edict from this morning. I need to know the name of the scribe who penned it. There are a few Jewish men in the king's employ who serve as scribes. I assume one of them might be able to help us discover the identity of the man who prepared this edict. Can you assist me?"

Mordecai's slumped torso straightened. "Why do you need him?"

"Because he will be able to tell us whether the king himself dictated the words of the edict, or if another was behind it."

In an instant, the despair that had glazed Mordecai's eyes disappeared. Jadon smiled. The man had a sharp mind. Sharp enough to have grasped the implications of Jadon's words. If another was behind the edict, then there might be a whisper of hope. A sliver of a prayer to help the Jewish people.

Mordecai took the tablet with trembling hands. "Leave it to me."

A whole day passed. Then another, leaving Jadon squirming with impatience, before Mordecai finally brought his news to his door in the cover of night.

"Lord Haman? Are you certain?" Jadon's fingers curled into a fist where it lay on his desk.

Mordecai sank against his chair. "There is no doubt. Ezra heard it from the scribe who took down the words. Haman himself dictated them in the presence of the king. Xerxes handed him his own ring. But Haman's hand pressed the seal into the wax."

"And Xerxes made no objection?"

"None. Haman had already won him over by then." His voice turned bitter. "Haman promised the king ten thousand talents of silver to cover the expense of the messengers he would have to send to the four corners of the kingdom. He paid a fortune for the destruction of our people."

"You are certain of this?"

"I spoke to a man in the treasury who confirmed every word."

Not good news, this. Haman had lately become the most powerful lord in the empire after the king himself. He had risen so high, and waved his stupendous wealth about with such impact, that little chance remained of opposing him. The fact that the king had freely handed his royal seal into his keeping, even for a short while, indicated the depth of his influence.

Jadon nodded at Mordecai. "My thanks. I will let Hathach know."

Mordecai held up a hand. "Allow me to be the one to tell Esther."

Jadon raised a brow in question.

Mordecai pulled a hand over his long beard. "You know who she is? To me?"

"Hathach told me."

"Of all the women the king could have chosen as his queen five years ago, his heart was drawn to a Jewish maiden. Do you think that came about by accident? Do you not see the hand of God in this?"

Jadon hesitated. "Perhaps you place too much on her shoulders, Mordecai. Under her crown, under the magnificent jewels and clothing, you will only find a young woman. Haman is a treacherous snake to have for an enemy. If she missteps, her life will be forfeit."

"I know that better than any. Yet God is a greater friend than Haman can ever be an enemy. Trust me in this, young man. If you or Hathach tell her the news, all you can do is shake her heart. But I can strengthen her—even as I tell her the worst tidings of her life."

5

Sazana

My times are in your hand;
rescue me from the hand of my enemies
and from my persecutors!

Psalm 31:15

The Twelfth Year of King Xerxes's Rule
The Fifteenth Day of Spring

Sazana studied the gray lump that lay on her palm. The clay had been quarried from the banks of the Karkheh River with permission from the king. By the time Sazana received the fine clay, it had passed through several extensive processes. Arta, who had charge over both the fine and the coarse clays, added a special temper made of limestone and sparkling quartz to Sazana's batch. The addition modified the clay, increasing its strength while also making it more pliable for Sazana's complex designs.

She wished she could find a temper to add to her own soul.

Something to increase strength in her shaking spine as she contemplated the king's insane edict.

At her signal, Arash started the rotation of the wheel. Her mind wandered as she went about the familiar task of building up the clay and flattening it. Where could she and Arta go? Where would thousands of her people, now in danger of their lives, find shelter? They would have to abandon their homes and leave behind land they had tilled for decades. Lose their farms and orchards. Everything they had worked so hard for generations to build would be stripped from them.

"I think you have beaten that poor clay to death," Arta said at her elbow, making her jump. He pressed his hand over her restless fingers and, with a nod, dismissed the wheel boy. "What were you trying to make, anyway?"

"A fortress where you can be safe."

He laughed, patting his expanding belly. "You might need a little more clay for that." Looking up, he froze.

She turned, her breath catching at the sight of Lord Haman, resplendent in an embroidered silk tunic with wide, pleated sleeves and enough jewels sewn into his golden belt to feed a family for a lifetime. Arta nodded toward Rashda and Cambyz, dismissing them as the master approached. Pale-faced, they scrambled out of the fine ware section to find refuge amongst the other potters.

The unpleasant edge in Haman's smile put Sazana in mind of a ranging wolf. Not until Arta's fingers pressed against her arm did she remember to offer a hasty bow.

Haman made an expansive movement with his arm, giving them permission to rise. His mouth turned down at the corners. "I am disappointed. I see by your sour expressions that you have already heard my news. And I so looked forward to telling you myself."

Arta choked. "News, my lord?"

Haman laughed. "Oh, you are going to let me tell it, after all. How thoughtful." He wiped away an invisible speck on his tunic and pressed a scented kerchief under his nose. "So much dust. This place is not fit for civilized people. Then again, we are talking about a Jew, aren't we, dear Sazana?" He shook a finger at her. "How wicked of you to keep that piece of information to yourself."

Haman's teasing banter covered a grinding threat, like a thin layer of glaze enveloping hard clay.

Though her body quaked, Sazana lifted her chin. She might bow to him for the sake of protocol, but she refused to bow before him in spirit. "As you say, my lord. I *am* a Jew."

The smile vanished. "You admit it freely? I daresay you will not be quite so proud in eleven months when the king's edict comes into effect. On that day, when you and your people stare death in the face, I suspect you will find a hole to hide in and keep your lips sealed about your cursed heritage."

Sazana had been born with a slow speech. Her tongue took time to express the thoughts in her mind, cautious not to say the wrong thing. Careful to express what was appropriate to the situation. The more tense she felt, the slower her speech became. But for once, she felt reckless enough to refute Haman to his face. Enough even to think of the right words.

Sensing the brash heat of her anger, Arta rushed to speak. "My lord, she is a Jew. That cannot be helped. But she is also the best potter in Susa. And she has the privilege of working for *you*. Ask your steward. He receives my accounts each month. He knows how much she makes for your workshop. Think of the financial loss if she were to be killed."

The sharp-edged smile returned to Haman's lips. "That is a sensible argument. I cannot fault it. Indeed, the same thought occurred to me."

Arta exhaled, the tight knot of his brow loosening. Sazana would have warned him not to breathe too easily just yet. Haman's satisfied expression boded more ill than good—he looked like a wolf that had cornered its prey.

"As always, my lord displays fine judgment." Arta's deep voice boomed with its usual good cheer. "Shall we leave her to ply her fingers to the wheel? The sooner she gets to work, the more vessels she will complete for you."

"Oh, she will complete more vessels for me. But there is a price to be paid."

"Price, lord?"

"Well, I would have to keep her safe from a violent attack. That can't be done for free. And I would have to put up with her in my own workshop, when I refuse to bear with her kind anywhere in the entire kingdom. Someone has to pay the price for my inconvenience." His head bent close over Sazana. This close, she could smell his hot breath. Like the rest of him, it was cloyed with expensive things. Cinnamon and clove. She wondered how so vile a man could smell so pleasant.

"That edict was my own work, you know."

Sazana snapped up her bent head, almost catching Haman in the nose. "The king's edict? The one against the Jews?"

Haman smirked. "I was the one who put the idea into the king's head. Cost me an eye-watering sum. It is no cheap undertaking to send messengers to 127 provinces. And after all that, I am now supposed to keep a Jew safe? The very thought leaves a bad taste in my mouth."

Sazana pressed her hand against her chest, trying to keep herself from splintering. She worked for the man who had engineered the coming murder of thousands of Jews. And he knew that she was one of them.

Arta hesitated. "May I know what you have in mind?"

Haman shrugged. "Simply this. You will work for me. Both of you. Since you obviously chose to betray me by protecting her, Arta, you too shall pay."

Sazana tasted something acrid. "We already work for you."

"Yes, and I pay you handsomely for the privilege."

Handsomely, he called it? Their rations kept their home in

tolerable repair and food in their belly. Little remained for anything else. "You wish to cut our pay?"

Haman laughed. The sound echoed with malice. "As of today, you shall have *no* pay. You will work for me. You will make everything I demand. You will come when I want and go when I say. And you will do it without remuneration. You own your own home, I hear. No doubt you have a nice pile of silver set aside thanks to my liberality. What more do you want? You can sell your house if you grow hungry."

Sazana's hand crept against her throat. "You mean to make slaves of us."

"Better than being dead, isn't it? Consider yourselves fortunate."

A hot shaft of anger loosened her normally recalcitrant tongue. "Arta is Persian. You cannot enslave him. And the king's edict has no bearing on him."

"Sazana!" Arta gave her a warning look.

Haman pressed his lips together until they turned white. "Arta may be a Persian. But he is a Persian who cares for you, else he would not work so hard to protect you. Of course he can leave. Find employment in another workshop. But then he will watch you get slaughtered with the rest of your kind. Sooner, if I choose. You can see that I have the ear of the king. It won't be hard to obtain a special order for your early demise." He turned toward Arta. "You understand?"

Arta bowed. "Perfectly, lord. You need not worry. No one is leaving. We will continue to work at your pleasure."

Haman smirked. "I thought you might say that. Nabonassar will keep an eye on you, to ensure you do not trespass the new terms of your employment." He withdrew a scroll of papyrus. "Here is your next order. See to it that I suffer no delay." He waved a hand before his straight nose. "And now, I really must quit this place." His gaze settled on Sazana. "The stench is unbearable."

By the time Haman had departed, leaving the sharp tang of too much perfume in his wake, Sazana had reached a conclusion. They had eleven months to figure out a way to escape Haman. Until then, she would obey the man no matter the cost. She would do whatever it took to keep Arta safe.

6

Sazana

Fire tests the purity of silver and gold,
but the LORD tests the heart.

Proverbs 17:3 NLT

Midnight had come and gone by the time she and Arta plodded home. This was their first taste of the days to come. Of endless hours of labor, trying to accomplish the work of four men between the two of them. Every muscle screamed its objection as she sank into bed.

Too much had happened over the course of one day. Too many hard things to process and accept. Tired as she was, she needed time to digest the sudden upheaval of her whole life.

On a shelf built into the wall sat the three-branched ceramic lamp her mother had made years ago. She lit the wicks and repeated the process with the matching lamp on the shelf in the opposite wall. From the depths of her trunk, she fetched the delicate ebony box where she kept her treasures.

Cradling the smooth black wood on her lap, she settled on the bed. In the warmth of the amber light, she searched for a faded woolen bag and, finding it, spread its contents on the sheet before her.

Her father's scribal tools. He had come from a long line of scribes and, like his father and grandfather before him, had served at the royal palace in Babylon. She kissed a wooden stylus that he had sharpened with his own hands and carefully lined it up next to the rest on the blanket.

"Shoshanah?" Arta's whisper came through the curtain that separated her room from the living area. "Are you still awake?"

"I'm awake. Come in."

His face softened at the sight of the implements before her. "Bani's tools." He picked up a stylus made of bone, yellowed with age. The corners of his eyes flared with lines. "Do you remember the time he walked by a guard at the palace in Babylon, and when he noticed the man oiling his sword, Bani whipped out a stylus and held it before him like a weapon, telling him his pen could beat any blade?"

"And the guard held up his arms in mock surrender." Sazana laughed. "Or when he asked my mother to prepare his clay scrolls and tablets for him? When the senior scribe at the palace told him that he ought to make his own like every other scribe, Father said, 'My wife makes the finest clay tablets in Babylon. If their content proves boring or unreliable, the future generations can always use them as ornaments.'"

Arta fingered the tools, his touch almost reverent. "He was my best friend."

"He always said you were like a brother to him."

"I came to Babylon a lost man. I thought to learn your grandfather's technique and return to Susa a better potter. Instead, I found something better. I found a family." His smile flashed, unsteady. "I never knew what a real father was. Watching Bani with you, I learned. The way he held your little hand as he helped you jump over potholes, never letting go. The way he whispered every night that he loved you more than the whole world and its stars above. The way he prayed over you before putting you to bed. A thousand things I saw him do for you, and finally it dawned on me that this was what it meant to be fathered.

"I've tried to be that to you, Shoshanah. I am no Bani, the Lord knows. But I do love you."

Her eyes welled. "You have been the best of fathers, Arta. I was blessed to have two such good men in my life." Her gaze turned fierce. "Haman better not touch a hair on your head."

Arta lowered himself on the edge of her bedroll, the sound of his creaking knees betraying his age. "We will see each other through this trouble, Shoshanah. We have eleven months to find an escape. Meanwhile, we own this house and won't lose it. We'll have a roof over our heads and enough savings to put simple food in our bellies. Just don't talk of leaving me again."

Sazana's heart convulsed like a beached fish. "Not if you don't want me to."

They sank into silence. The worries of the day squeezed an old regret out of her. One she rarely spoke aloud. "I wish we had never sold Grandfather's workshop in Babylon."

"It would not have changed anything. The king's edict is as valid in Babylon as it is in Susa."

"Yes, but at least we would not have Haman to contend with. We would be managing our own workshop in Babylon. Why on earth did my parents decide to sell the place? Now my grandfather's legacy is lost forever, and we are under Haman's power."

As always, when she mentioned the sale of the workshop, Arta's face shuttered. She assumed the odd reaction to be born out of regret for the loss of his dearest friends. It was one of the reasons she rarely brought up the subject. But, tonight, for the first time, she noticed something shifty buried beneath the grief. Something secretive.

"Those were hard days." Reaching for her mother's pottery

tools, which lay snug in a linen pouch, he pulled out a scraper, cradling it in his large hand. "I had forgotten how dainty these were!"

She emptied the contents of the pouch onto her lap, studying the ivory-handled tools. "Grandfather once told me he knew she would be a great potter the very first time she threw a pot. She was only nine at the time."

Arta eased the scraper back into its pouch. "Before she turned twenty, she was producing better pots than your grandfather. By the time he passed on, she could run the place with her eyes closed."

Sazana treated Arta to an unwavering gaze. "All the more reason for them to keep the workshop. It was my mother's heritage as well as her trade."

Arta dropped his head, his expression tinged with regret and exhaustion. "We can't change the past."

No. But explaining it might help. She did not express the thought aloud. Like so many words over the years, they went unspoken, buried alongside all her unanswered questions. After her parents' deaths, she and Arta had fallen into a pattern of shielding each other. He did his best to protect her from the hurt of loneliness. The ache of being an orphan. She returned the favor by not pestering him with questions that clearly discomfited him.

"Shoshanah?" Arta picked up a loop tool and twirled it between his fingers. "If something should happen to me—"

"Nothing is going to happen to you."

He tapped the tool gently on the back of her hand. "But if it should . . . I left you some things in your chest, in case."

She gave him an odd look. She went through that chest every day and had never seen anything from him in it. Shaking her head, she promptly put the words out of her mind. She had no desire to think of the possibility of losing Arta.

After he left, she rummaged under her small pile of treasures to find an old square of folded linen. The dried pink petals tucked within had long since lost their sweet perfume. But the memories attached to them still evoked the enchanting scent of a perfect damask rose.

It had been the first flower Jadon had given her. After that day, he had brought her other blooms: irises, jasmine, roses. Armfuls of flowers. But none ever charmed her as that first single rose, which he presented to her shyly, his young face flushed and earnest.

When she had pressed her nose into the whorls of petals, drinking in their sweetness, he had drawn close and whispered the words she had longed to hear. "I love you, Shoshanah."

His voice had been solemn and tender, as though his whole life were wrapped around the simple declaration. As though he would never, *could* never, take those words back. That had been its own kind of false promise.

She had returned all his gifts to him when he had broken their betrothal. The gold-and-turquoise ring with its matching necklace. The silver belt beaded with crystals. The lengths of embroidered fabric. She had packed every single item with infinite care and sent them back to him, with the thin stack of notes and letters he had written to her over the months of their courtship sitting neatly on top.

But the rose petals she kept. When she had tried to tuck them into her goodbye package, her hands had refused to cooperate. They could not let that perfect moment go. The memory of it, of his tender voice, still had a hold over her that she could not shake. Though all that solemnity had proven a lie, she still clung to it, like a woman falling off the edge of a mountain who reaches for a fragile weed to secure herself.

She blew out the lamps and lay down in her bed, the yellowed bundle of rose petals pressed to her chest. Arta was right. She couldn't change the past. But she couldn't seem to let it go either.

The next morning, sitting at the wheel, Sazana recalled how her mother used to say that making pottery was like raising children. The potter never truly knew what awaited at the end of all her efforts. She gave each vessel her best effort, guided by experience and knowledge and that indefinable thing called intuition. But in the end, it was impossible to know what would emerge from the fires of the kiln. Impossible to predict how the clay would react with the heat. Would it come out of the fire strong and resilient or, in spite of the potter's best efforts, would it emerge a broken thing?

Sometimes the clay would bake so light a gray, it looked almost white, while another clump from the very same batch would emerge a completely different color. The same design and an almost identical clay would produce a distinctly unique vessel every time.

New potters often struggled with this reality, with the fact that all the talent and experience in the world still gave them no way of knowing how a pot would look when it emerged from the kiln. The fire ultimately determined the clay's personality. The potter's creation could only become its true self when exposed to the harsh lick of the flames.

Sazana wondered what the flames of her life would reveal about her.

She had lived through harsh flames already. Once, when she had lost her parents at the age of eleven. And again, when at eighteen, she had lost her heart to Jadon and watched it shatter when he walked away.

What had those fires revealed about her? That she had never lost her smile? Never lost her hope? That she had cocooned herself in a lonely shell and made the world shrink down to just her and Arta and her pots?

And now she faced another furnace, hotter than any she had known before. What would the fire of slavery to Haman reveal? Or the flames of her people's approaching doom?

"What are you doing staring at the wall like a half-wit sheep?" Nabonassar sauntered in front of her, an ugly sneer marring his handsome face. "Get to work."

Sazana exhaled. She anchored her elbow against her thigh, did her best to anchor her heart to God, and centered the clay on the wheel.

From the Secret Scrolls of Esther

Until the day breathes
and the shadows flee . . .

Song of Solomon 2:17

Thirty-Three Years Later
The Twenty-Fifth Year of King Artaxerxes's Rule

When I was a young woman in love, one of my favorite pastimes was reading Solomon's poetry, written for his bride. Now that I am older, a humble couplet of the king's lines speaks more deeply to me than all the rest. You might be surprised when I share them with you, for they are words many may easily pass over.

Until the day breathes
and the shadows flee . . .

You might wonder why, of all the famous lines Solomon spun together, these are the ones I choose to tell you about. The answer is in the word *until*. In the hope that single word breathes into the aching heart.

In every life, a time may come when love is hidden, happiness is lost, and the heart is weighed down. A

65

season when the shadows rule, and all the light of day is absent.

You have to remember, in times like this, that there is an *until* around the bend. Bear the weight of darkness, because the day will breathe again and the shadows will flee. Somehow, your soul has to lean into the *until* of life. Learn to navigate the shadows until the day breathes and light dawns again.

All those years ago, when my senior handmaiden told me that Mordecai had camped at the entrance of the king's gate, covered in sackcloth and ashes, I knew some terrible calamity had come upon us. I sensed the deep shadows approaching, for my cousin is not a man easily shaken. He knows how to carry unbearable burdens without being crushed.

I sent two of my women to him with fresh linen garments, hoping to revive him. But he refused my offering. I realized that I needed someone with more spine. Someone who could reason with my cousin. I sent Hathach, the head of my household and my dear friend.

Hathach returned with a copy of the decree the king had issued, declaring the destruction of my people.

The words of that decree rendered me mute. What can you say when faced with so great an outrage? How can you respond to such senseless annihilation?

I will own, though I love him, that my husband had a predilection for having the wrong people as relatives and choosing even worse ones as friends. In his battle to escape the terrible loneliness of kings, he allowed those friends too much influence upon him.

Until then, I knew little of Haman. Like others, I had been aware of his fast rise and seen him from afar at public dinners and state affairs. He had charm, I grant you. Always dressed in the latest fashion and wafting the most expensive perfume. But his ingratiating smile struck me as so thin a veneer that I often wondered what lay beneath.

Now I knew.

Mordecai's request arrived when I was already suffocating in the shadows. For a whole month, my husband had not sent for me. I had become what I feared most: an abandoned wife. And now Mordecai wanted me to go to the king on behalf of our people and beg his favor. How could I make my cousin understand that I had no influence, though I still wore a crown? Xerxes had removed the shield of his love from me when he had cut himself off from my presence.

But Mordecai was not as convinced as I that the strength of my husband's abandonment could outmatch the power of God's intention.

"Who knows but that you have come to your royal position for such a time as this?" my dear cousin asked me. As far as he was concerned, with or without the king's affections, God could open the doors of favor to me.

I had a choice before me then. In the darkness of despair, in the gloom of rejection, would I turn to my beloved? Not to the king, my husband, whose love seemed to have dimmed. But would I turn to God until the shadows fled and a new day breathed?

I faced a great impediment in this battle. The fading light of my husband's love consumed me. Thirty days of rejection had shaped my every thought, my every expectation. I faced death for approaching him without being summoned. According to the law, I would have but one recourse. That the king should choose to extend his golden scepter as I came into his presence, uninvited.

My abandoned heart held no hope for such an eventuality. If he had rejected me for a whole month, why would he receive me now?

I walked into his presence thinking myself doomed to death. In an astonished court, none was more shocked than I when he held out his scepter of authority and offered me up to half his kingdom.

I would have been satisfied with a kiss.

My friends sometimes ask why I chose to invite the king and Haman to so intimate a dinner. Why not simply make a request of the king when he offered me his kingdom?

I was still the woman he had ignored for thirty days. I wanted to buy time with him. To sit in the same chamber with him. I wanted to look both my enemy and my beloved in the eyes. To remind one of the love he once bore me, and the other of the queen he had for a foe. And, in the meantime, to wait for my *until* to come. Until the day breathed and the shadows fled.

One day stretched to two.

And in between, God moved in ways I could not have imagined.

7

Jadon

This is what Cyrus king of Persia says: "The LORD,
the God of heaven, has given me all the kingdoms
of the earth and he has appointed me to build a
temple for him at Jerusalem in Judah. Any of his
people among you may go up, and may the LORD
their God be with them."

2 Chronicles 36:23 NIV

THIRTY-THREE YEARS EARLIER
THE TWELFTH YEAR OF KING XERXES'S RULE
THE THIRD DAY OF SUMMER

J adon resisted scratching the itch that had started at the
back of his neck. It was not often that he was summoned
into Esther's personal quarters for a private meeting. As
a man, even one in charge of her security, such intimate visits
would have been considered inappropriate. More often than
not, they met in Hathach's office, or if they had to conduct their

business in her rooms, she came surrounded by a clutch of her women. Hathach, being a eunuch, had more free access to her, passing on her messages to Jadon.

Now he stood alone in her hexagonal audience hall, the criss-cross collar of his formal robes biting into his chest. He cast a surreptitious glance at his shoes, hoping they hadn't dragged any dirt upon the priceless carpets.

It was an odd time for Esther to summon him. In a few hours, she would be dining with Haman and the king. If she intended to beseech the king for his help this night, then she had greater concerns on her mind than any routine matter relating to her estate. Which must mean she had some special errand for Jadon. An important commission that required his presence on such a night, when the fate of the Jewish people hung in the balance.

A silver table had been set for two in the center of the room, and to the side, an arched arbor framed a throne-like chair. Folds of purple and white silk hung from the silver framework, deco-rated with fresh flowers. The chair was specially set up for the king, who never shared anyone's table for a meal. Eating apart from others protected him from an unpleasant encounter with a variety of deadly poisons. A diaphanous net hanging in front of the arbor would provide him with both privacy and visibility.

It must be a lonely way to live, often separated from others.

Jadon shifted his weight from one foot to another. He could not imagine what commission Esther had for him. The not knowing made him restless, and for the twentieth time, he shifted, fidgeting as he was not supposed to do in royal presence.

Finally, Hathach strode through the door. Slim and short, the eunuch had the aura of a much larger man, as though the atmosphere had to resettle itself to make room for him.

Without a word, he led Jadon to a plain reception chamber, in the center of which the queen occupied a leather chair, before bowing himself out. Tall and regal, she adorned the place like a jewel, her flawless posture unmarred, though her foot rested on an upholstered stool. Beneath the layers of embroidered hemline, his sharp gaze glimpsed white bandages around her ankle. His heart picked up its pace. Had she been attacked?

She smiled. The dewy soft skin, barely touched by the paint pots so popular at the palace, made her appear younger than her twenty-five years. But the eyes seemed older today, and weary.

"Do not look so anxious," she said, as though reading his mind. "It was an accident." She waved at her raised foot. "I tripped on a carpet. The physician has taken care of it. I will be able to entertain my lord the king as I planned this evening."

Jadon bowed. "I am delighted to hear it."

"In other words, you wish to know why I have sent for you on such a night."

He could not suppress his grin. Her humor often caught him by surprise. "The thought had occurred to me, Your Majesty."

"I have a special mission for you."

He pressed his hand to his heart. "My life for your service."

She leaned forward. "I want you to find me the original Cyrus cylinder."

Jadon's brow puckered as he tried to parse her meaning. Cyrus, the king's grandfather, was the legendary Achaemenid king who had carved out an empire from humble beginnings. He must have dictated a thousand tablets and cylinders in his lifetime.

"The Cyrus cylinder, lady?"

"The famous one. The one he made in Babylon."

The pieces fell into place. The queen was speaking of the edict where Cyrus declared that the people of enslaved nations were free from the yoke of Babylon and released to return to their homeland.

"The declaration that set our people free from their seventy-year bondage to Babylon," he said.

Esther nodded. "With one stroke, Cyrus granted them permission to return to their homeland, to worship their own God, and to rebuild his Temple."

Certainly, for any descendant of Abraham, Cyrus's edict was the most crucial pronouncement ever issued from the lips of a Gentile king. For one thing, it fulfilled God's prophecy. It proved the Lord faithful. The Jewish people loved the old king for this unique act of grace in a world that showed little care for the plight of conquered people.

They were not the only ones who held Cyrus in high esteem. The Persians loved him above all their rulers and considered him the very model of kingship. One that the rest of his lineage wished to emulate.

Esther's request was beginning to make sense. "You wish to remind Xerxes of Cyrus's uncommon decision."

"I wish to remind *everyone* of that decision. The court. The men who are planning to destroy us. Cyrus became great in large part due to this very attitude. His empire spread wider than any other because he welcomed people of other nations as friends. Jew, Gentile, Median, Babylonian, Lydian. He called them friends and gave them freedom to worship as they chose. You would never find Cyrus committing the kind of genocide Haman's words have crafted. Let the Persians remember that."

"You think reading the words of the cylinder afresh will help our people in their present plight?"

She waved a golden fan before her face. "I cannot change the king's edict, nor can I directly say anything that would undermine my husband. We have no magic solution that can undo Haman's damage. But the content of Cyrus's cylinder can diminish that harm substantially. For many, it will take away the desire to strike at, and destroy, a whole people. Used rightly, it can reduce the number of attacks visited upon the Hebrews."

Jadon realized how in *her* hands, Cyrus's edict could play a crucial role. "Our own people also need to remember that the greatest king of this nation once shielded them from slavery and injustice."

"You begin to understand." She moved her foot with a restless motion and winced. "As they face that day of reckoning, the Jews must call to mind that God has used unlikely forces to protect them before, and he can do so again. We need that cylinder to give courage to the ordinary men and women who will face an extraordinary attack in eight months."

Jadon bowed his head, a little awed by the queen's foresight. "It's an excellent strategy, my lady. I wonder that no one else has thought of it before now. Cyrus's words will shame those who wish to harm the Jews. That cylinder can serve to stem the tide of the current hostility rising out of Xerxes's edict. And it will calm the hearts of our people."

Still, he failed to see why he in particular had been called upon. He had little to do with tablets and records. "How may I help, Your Majesty? Would you like me to fetch one of the royal scribes? They must have copies of that famous cylinder somewhere in the archives of Susa."

Esther's lips flattened. "You would think so. And yet we cannot find a single one. Not even in Akkadian. All the transcripts in Susa have vanished."

Jadon's brow knotted. Persians were notorious for their love of records. They kept triplicate copies of the most prosaic documents. A historical relic of such significance should have multiple records in each of the five capitals in the kingdom. "That seems odd."

"I have dispatched messengers to the royal palaces in Persepolis, Anshan, Babylon, and Ecbatana. It will be two or three weeks before I hear back from all of them. I only hope to have better news there than we have found in Susa."

"Do you suspect the copies have been lost due to incompetence, or that they have been intentionally removed?"

Hathach returned to the chamber in time to hear his question. "How often do you hear of an important document vanishing entirely?" he answered. "One copy may be misplaced. But all? I have no proof, of course. Yet if you ask me, the matter indicates forethought. Someone intentionally planned the disappearance of the Cyrus cylinders. Someone who understood their significance as well as my lady did."

Jadon finally understood why he had been sent for. "You believe Haman was behind the disappearance, my lord?"

"It makes the most sense. He must have had the same thought as the queen before he set his plan into motion. It would explain why he went to the trouble of removing the very documents that could help our cause."

Esther adjusted her foot on the stool. "We have heard an interesting rumor. There is a hidden copy here in Susa, some say in the possession of a scribe. I want you to discover if that is true, Jadon. And if the rumor proves legitimate, I want you to find that copy and bring it to me. You are my man of many talents, after all."

Jadon cleared his throat. Sometimes he wished the queen did not place so much weight upon his supposed capabilities. He could not voice that objection out loud. Not to the woman who had only one day earlier risked her life by appearing before the king without being summoned. She had broken the law in a desperate attempt to help her people.

He could do no less, though he cringed at the assignment. Pursuing rumors was a little like trying to corral smoke.

"Tell me where you heard this rumor, lady."

8

Sazana

You have captivated my heart with one glance
of your eyes...

Song of Solomon 4:9

Arta had the responsibility of delivering their orders to
market stalls and shops four or five days a week. Usually, he made the trip alone. But for the first time in
weeks, Sazana was allowed to go with him.

Pottery glazes came in shades of brown, buff, red, black, or
ecru. The blue bricks of the palace walls had given her an idea
for something different, however.

Since this would be a trial run, she did not want to place a
large order from their suppliers, lest the whole enterprise prove
a failure. Egyptian blue, a dye that mimicked the deep color
of lapis lazuli, cost a fortune, and she only intended to buy a
small quantity.

After all, this was one of the reasons her pottery had gained recognition in Susa. Her work stood out due to her ability to create fresh concepts.

She had managed to convince Nabonassar to allow her a visit to the market to buy the precious dye. Arta loaded the cart with the day's wares and drove it to the familiar stables just outside the Artisans' Market. Isaac, one of the established Jews of Susa, owned and managed the place, a popular spot where many merchants dropped off carts or mules early in the morning before entering the congested market.

The man himself came to greet them, pointing at the rear wheel shaft. "Looks a bit unsteady, Arta. Want me to fix it?"

Arta gave him a friendly thump on the shoulder. "Sure, if you don't intend to charge me half the king's treasury."

Isaac bent to study the damaged wood. "You have to pay for what you get. Want a proper repair or a shoddy job that will loosen your wheel at the first sight of a pothole and break all your pots?"

Arta sighed. "How long?"

"Three days."

"Make it one, and you have a deal."

"I see what you want." Isaac pulled on his gray beard. "Slow prices for fast service."

Sazana hid her smile. Arta had fierce instincts when it came to saving silver.

"You are a wise man," he said without a blink. "The Lord bless you for it."

Isaac rolled his eyes and took charge of the mules as Arta unloaded the pots, stacking them on a handcart. "Meet me at the market pool in an hour," he told Sazana. "Go enjoy yourself."

She did not need another nudge and began to wend her way toward the market proper. The aroma of a hundred spices perfumed the air as she wove between the stalls. The freedom, though temporary, buoyed her spirits. She smiled at the sight of the wild colors and clever designs that splashed across endless textiles, some of which had been produced right here in the city's famous workshops, while others had traveled oceans to grace Susa's markets.

For weeks, her days and nights had been consumed by fulfilling Haman's greedy orders, which never seemed to end. Every morning, she rolled out of bed when the world still lay in darkness, pressing her body to begin afresh. She pushed through the ache of her muscles to meet Haman's ever-growing demands. As a slave, she had no choice.

But for this moment, she could pretend to be free again. Pretend Haman had not chained her to her wheel.

She had just completed her purchase after a bit of haggling when, from the corner of her eye, she saw a man lean in to speak to a merchant a few tables over. Something about the line of his back drew her attention, and without thinking, she turned to study him.

Her breath stuttered. She felt as if she had been hit on the head by one of the fat posts holding up the stall's awning. Her vision clouded.

Jadon!

For five years, Jadon and she had danced around each other, doing their best to avoid the sight of the other, though they occupied the same city. They had done such a fine job that she had not had a single glimpse of him in all that time. Until now.

She swung in the opposite direction, walking away blindly. The slap of her leather soles rang loud in her ears. Her steps picked up speed, as though bolting from memories that chased her. But the old images proved faster than her feet.

They caught up with her, every scene playing in her mind's eye with clarity, as though five excruciating years had not passed since the day they had met . . .

The workshop's location, far from Susa's walls and inconvenient for most shoppers, meant that individual buyers rarely stopped in for a casual purchase. Which was partly why she stared dumbstruck when a man appeared unannounced at her elbow. The other reason had to do with . . . well, she might be surrounded by men every day. But none of her simple potter companions looked like *him*.

He cleared his throat. "I wonder if I may trouble you for some help?" He sounded like a prince, though his clothing, crisp and new-looking, marked him as an Immortal.

"Yes?"

"I need a present for my mother's birthday. I only have a moment." He pointed his chin outside. "I must return to duty."

She came to her feet. "What would you like?"

"What would you recommend?"

She smiled at his deer-caught-in-torchlight look. "A vase? A platter?"

"Vase, please."

Sazana fetched three different vases to show him.

"You made these?" He ran a finger down the length of a pedestaled vessel. "They're beautiful." Her belly tightened at his admiring glance. He tapped the side of the iron-red pedestal. "I'll take this one."

"I will fetch a bit of rag so you can wrap it. It's a delicate piece." When she handed him the faded square of linen, for a brief moment, their fingers touched. He fumbled, dropping the rag. Both of them bent at the same time; his long arms reached it first. When he straightened, his face was as pink as a Damascus rose.

The workshop felt hollow after he left, though he had only been there a handful of moments. All day long, Sazana found herself thinking of him, the young Persian whose name she did not know and whose face she would never see again.

The following day, Arta had a late delivery to make, and she left the workshop to walk home alone. There he stood, her Immortal, waiting outside the pottery yard. She came to an abrupt stop. "Was your mother displeased with the vase?"

His eyes widened. "Not at all. She admired it. You saved the day."

"Oh." For an awkward beat, neither spoke. "Well." She indicated the road. "I am walking home."

"Perhaps I could accompany you?" The Damascus-rose flush colored his cheeks again. "I noticed some wild dogs on the road yesterday. They can be dangerous."

She blinked. He wanted to walk with her? As usual, her words dried up when she most needed them. She gave him a quick nod. His eyes, she noticed, were pure blue when he smiled. It took some effort to look away from the full effect of that smile.

"I am Jadon, son of Arsaces." He fell into easy step at her side, matching his gait to hers. "And you are Sazana."

"Jadon?" She stumbled. Placing a hand at her back, he steadied her before withdrawing his touch. She cleared her throat. "That's a Hebrew name."

He raised a brow. "It is, though not a common one. I am surprised you recognized it."

Her heart picked up speed. She had given away too much.

He lifted a hand as though to calm her. "Do not be alarmed. My mother is a daughter of Abraham. Rachel, she's called. And my father, though Persian, is a follower of the Lord." The blue eyes warmed. "Would I be right in assuming that Sazana is not the name with which you were born?" He lifted his hand toward her. "You are one of us, I think."

One of us. It sounded so inviting, the way he put it. As though he had decided that she belonged already. The unforeseen connection between them made him seem safer, somehow. More accessible. More real.

"Yes. I am one of you."

"May I ask why you work under a Persian name?"

She bit her lip.

He shrugged. "I have my own theory." His voice sounded serious.

"And what is that?"

"That your real name is so horribly difficult to pronounce, you had to make up an easier one to sell your pots. Your true name, I believe is . . ." He tapped his forefinger against the tip of his nose. "Hazzelelponi. No? Jechoaddan? Not beastly enough. I know! Meshullemeth!" He wagged his finger at her. "I'm right, aren't I?"

"Not even a little." She shook with laughter. "They must not train the Immortals as well as I have been told." A smile lingered on her lips even when the laughter died.

He stared as though mesmerized. Gulping, he said, "What then?"

"Shoshanah. My true name is Shoshanah."

"That's a lovely name," he said. Next to being told that she was one of them, it sounded like the sweetest compliment anyone had ever given her.

A gentle hand wrapped around her arm, shaking her out of her reverie.

"Gone off to gather wool, have you?" Arta said. "Didn't you hear me call your name?"

She glanced over her shoulder, furtively sweeping the landscape of the market, searching for Jadon. No sign of him. Thankfully, he had not spotted her, and she had managed to lose him.

She had quite a talent for that, it seemed. "Let's go back, Arta. I've had enough of the market."

From the Secret Scrolls of Esther

Many waters cannot quench love,
neither can floods drown it.

Song of Solomon 8:7

Thirty-Three Years Later
The Twenty-Fifth Year of King Artaxerxes's Rule

As I sat across from the man who intended to murder a whole generation of my people, I had to admire his table manners, which were better than mine—and better even than the king's, if I am allowed that small indiscretion. It made me distrust him all the more. He seemed so intent upon impressing others that nothing of his insides matched the outer shell.

He was certainly determined to impress his queen that first night. A losing battle—if only he knew who it was that sat across from him.

In spite of the elegance of his deportment, a piece of chive had found its way between his two front teeth, stuck there like mud on a pig's snout. The sight of that clinging bit of greasy herb gave his self-important visage a silly air. I found a childish pleasure in it and made him laugh at every opportunity so that I could see it again.

What a challenge to smile at him and nod encouragingly over our golden plates as he spoke some piffle about art. I had to make him believe I found him as charming as he thought himself. If only he knew how hard I had to fight the desire to kick him in the rear in spite of my purple, swollen ankle.

Instead, I smiled and flattered him until his defenses came down. Not for a moment did he suspect that he faced a deadly foe across that lavish table. I held that advantage over him. I knew him to be *my* enemy, while he thought me a dim-witted girl who had fallen under his spell. I would use that and every other advantage allowed me in order to destroy him before he could annihilate us.

When Xerxes joined us at our table after dinner, I could sense his curiosity. We had not spoken for over a month, not until that strained moment when I approached his royal throne uninvited. I had taken my life into my own hands to come to him. He knew I would not do such a thing for the pleasure of his company over a mere dinner. Certainly not with Haman in tow.

I had confounded the king.

Now his every glance asked me a question. He was waiting for the favor I would want from his royal hand. Finally, as he sipped his wine, he gave in to the sharp edge of his curiosity. "What is it you wish, Esther?"

After surviving my initial request, I had considered this moment with care. How would I tell Xerxes what I needed? The answer had come to me only when I let go of my sorrow as a wife. I could not entertain him as a rejected woman. He would never find the stench of my self-pity attractive.

No. I had to stop thinking as an abandoned wife and

start planning as a queen tasked with the saving of her people.

I needed wile.

That's when it came to me. Xerxes loved suspense. So that's what I would give him.

Now I let the moment stretch, dangled before him like a treasure he had to hunt. It had become an itch, the need to discover what I was up to with this feasting, laying at his feet all my charms as a hostess.

I refused to scratch that itch.

His fascination grew with every passing moment.

"Come to the feast I will prepare tomorrow," I said. "Tomorrow, I will do as you ask."

I am told Xerxes could not sleep well that night. As the occasion led to my cousin Mordecai receiving great honor from the hand of the king, I cannot, in any case regret it. Only once did I ask my husband what had kept him awake the night of the first feast.

"I could not sleep, you wretch, because I was trying to tease out the riddle you had set me. I had grown too interested for rest." He pulled me against him. "And because I missed you."

The king and I never spoke more about that night. The subject brought us too close to the events of the second night, when I finally gave him the answer he sought. I satisfied his curiosity, but that satisfaction came at a high price for us both.

I knew I would wound him by revealing how unworthy a man he had trusted. Wound him by proving that his dearest friend was a schemer who had exploited him. Wound him by revealing that I was not who he believed me to be.

To save my people, I made my husband feel weak and stupid and betrayed.

My husband, once more tender than Solomon had been to his bride, offered me no comfort after I revealed my secret that second night. He did not reassure me. He wrapped no hand about my shoulders, placed no kiss upon my lips. The heat of his rage burned away any desire he once would have had to offer me consolation.

He gave me the help I sought to save my people, then walked away from my chambers, his back rigid, his face a frozen mask. He hated me a little that night, I think. I had held up a mirror to his face and exposed his folly in order to achieve my ends.

To save my people, I had wounded the man I loved. To protect them, I had ruined my marriage.

That was not the end of our story. Love survives many a wreckage. What was it Solomon said to his beloved? *Many waters cannot quench love.*

But that night, when I watched his retreating back, I felt drowned by the flood of bitterness and betrayal that swept over our marriage.

9

Jadon

A king's wrath is like the growling of a lion,
but his favor is like dew on the grass.
Proverbs 19:12

THIRTY-THREE YEARS EARLIER
THE TWELFTH YEAR OF KING XERXES'S RULE
THE FOURTH DAY OF SUMMER

The following night, when the queen entertained the king and Haman once more, events took such a shocking turn that Jadon all but forgot the Cyrus cylinder. He was standing guard at the edge of the chamber, almost hidden by long linen curtains. Across from him, two Immortals stood at attention.

After a two-hour meal, the king, wearing a genial half smile, sauntered over to Esther's side, and setting his goblet upon the silver table, said, "What is it you wish, Queen Esther?"

Jadon's frame went taut. He knew in his bones that she would reveal her secret now. But what would Xerxes do? How would he respond to her plea? Would he take Haman's side or hers?

Jadon's blood thrummed in his ears as the silence stretched. In the short history of the Achaemenid line, no king had chosen a foreign queen. It was not done. How would Xerxes respond to the dawning realization that the woman to whom he had bestowed a crown was not even a Persian?

How could he take her word over Haman's, a man whose bloodlines and astounding wealth gave him boundless influence in the court? Even if he wished to help her, the politics of the situation tied the king's hands.

Esther straightened her shoulders and took a gulp of air before she began, her words humble but unflinching. By the time she finished, she had made sure the king knew Haman was her enemy.

The king's face, alight with warm curiosity only moments before, darkened. For the length of a breath, he said nothing. Jadon could almost see the wheels of his mind turning, trying to calculate if Haman had known the queen's background before instigating his plot. Had he meant the whole scheme as a way of getting rid of the woman he loved? Or had he merely lied about her people, falsely accusing them of breaking the king's laws for some unknown personal gain?

Wordlessly, Xerxes turned on his heel and stormed through double doors into the garden, his Immortals flanking him.

Esther sank into the couch, looking ashen. As soon as her trembling back leaned against the cushions, Haman threw himself upon her. Jadon was at her side in a blink, but it became obvious that Haman intended her no harm.

The intensity of the king's silent wrath had clearly shaken the man. Setting aside his famous pride, Haman fell before Esther, hands reaching out in supplication, clinging to the purple silk of her hems. Any fool could see he meant no violence. Haman wanted mercy, clearly concluding that the king would take Esther's side over his.

Before Jadon could pull the man away, the king returned from the garden. "Will he even assault the queen in my presence," he said through tight lips, "in my own house?"

Jadon frowned. Could the king have misinterpreted Haman's actions? Even Esther stared at him in confusion. The king's chin dipped in a subtle motion, and the Immortals sprang forward to cover Haman's face, stifling the man's cry with a fold of linen. The action revealed a wordless indictment. Xerxes had already decided the man's fate.

He threw the queen a short glance. There was no confusion in that look. It held the sharp edge of calculation. Of intention.

Then it dawned on Jadon. Xerxes must have grasped Haman's real motive for clinging to the queen. But his twisted interpretation, the one he had pronounced loud enough for everyone to hear, had given him the legal excuse he needed for dealing with the man. With one stroke, he had removed Esther's enemy, while also repaying Haman for abusing their friendship.

Not a single courtier in the court would object to the swift justice due to a man who assaulted a queen. No man could be allowed to go around laying hands upon royal wives, whether in violence or passion, no matter how high his position. The king's punishment of Haman would face no protestations in the court now, for it had nothing to do with the queen's foreign background or her people's actions. It was his supposed attempt at touching the king's own wife that ended Haman's schemes.

Jadon raised an astounded brow. Xerxes wasn't confused. He was a crafty fox.

10

Sazana

And the city of Susa shouted and rejoiced.

Esther 8:15

THE TWELFTH YEAR OF KING XERXES'S RULE
THE FIFTH DAY OF SUMMER

Arta drew Sazana into the alcove and pulled the curtain shut. "You'll never believe what I heard in the market."

Sazana's heart slammed against her chest. "What now? What else has Haman cooked up for us?"

Arta shook his hand, negating her words. "A new command from the king that gives the Jews permission to defend themselves against anyone who attacks them on the designated day. They can fight back, Sazana! They can kill in self-defense without being punished. And just as the king permitted those who would attack the Jews to take their property, he has now allowed the same right to the Jews."

"What?" That sounded like an unbelievable reversal. If true, the king had made the ground of the fight even.

"By royal edict, he has turned the Jewish people from victims into combatants. It puts a different face on the coming battle." Arta pulled a restless hand through his disheveled hair. "You should have heard the people in the market, Shoshanah. Everyone burst into wild cheers. Jew and Gentile. How Haman would have hated those celebrations!"

"He would despise the new edict even more. Lord Haman is not going to be happy that in eight months, when the attacks come, we shall stand a chance. A good chance at survival! I wonder what caused the king to write the new edict? Why go against his own earlier words? Why weaken his support of Lord Haman's plan?"

Arta lowered his voice even more. "A rumor is going around that Haman has been arrested. Nabonassar has gone to check on the veracity of it. Given that the king has reversed his support of Haman's plot, perhaps there's some truth to it."

Sazana went still. "Haman arrested? I don't believe it. He is the king's pet."

"Kings have been known to change pets. We must wait and see. Nabonassar will unearth the truth and let us know."

But Nabonassar never returned to the workshop that day, or the next. For the first time in almost three months, Sazana and Arta were able to resume their normal work routines. In Nabonassar's absence, even the common ware section grew more lighthearted than it had been for weeks. Sazana's muscles, which had twisted into constant painful knots, began to loosen.

Standing back, she examined the final brushstroke of raw glaze she had applied to a bowl with a flanged rim.

"You've found your smile again," Arta said. "What has you so happy? Aside from the absence of Nabonassar, of course."

She indicated the bowl. "Blue glaze. I have high hopes for it."

He studied her handiwork. "Perhaps so. But Egyptian blue is too expensive."

"I think I have dealt with that problem." One of the reasons no one made blue pottery was the exorbitant cost. If people wanted to spend that much, they preferred to invest in metal vessels. But she had used less of the dye, creating what she hoped would turn out to be a lighter but pleasant hue. That small economy might make the resulting pottery affordable for someone of the merchant class. "I won't know for certain if it will work until I fire it."

"We are potters. In the end, it always comes to the fire."

The same could be said of people, Sazana thought. Life always came down to the fire. Though she had enjoyed two days of relative freedom, something in her bones told her that the blaze of the furnace in her life had not burned itself out yet.

On the third day after the pronouncement of the edict, they received astounding news. It was no rumor. Haman had been arrested. More shockingly still, the king's dear friend had been executed.

Sazana stared loose-jawed at Arta when he told her. "Is he truly dead?"

"Hanged on the gallows he had built in his own house."

Sazana shook her head, trying to dispel a wave of dizziness. "It seems God has granted us a miracle," she whispered. Like a dry well filling with water from an underground spring, her chest swelled with wonder. "Do you know what this means?"

Arta rubbed his hands together. "That we can go home early and make a big dinner with chickpea and lamb cutlets and fresh herbs instead of supping on stale bread." His grin spread wider than the potter's wheel. He snapped his fingers to a catchy rhythm and shook his shoulders to its beat. Coming to a slow stop, he held up a questioning hand. "I only have one question. What kind of person builds a fifty-cubit gallows in their own backyard? Most folks are content with a shrub or two."

Sazana laughed. Too quickly, the sound dried up in her throat. "But Arta, who owns the workshop now?"

He shrugged. "Not Haman is all I know."

"But he has ten sons. What if one of them inherits? He might prove worse than the father."

A week passed without a whisper from the workshop's new owner. Nabonassar failed to return to work, a detail that Sazana could not help celebrating on an hourly basis. After the way Lord Haman had met his death, the man was probably afraid to show his face. Given the swiftness with which his master had fallen, he had probably sensed the shadow of a severe punishment hanging over his own head and beat a hasty retreat. All the way to Babylon, Sazana suspected.

In the absence of a master, Arta took over the running of the workshop once more, and without Nabonassar's interference, the sound of easy conversation and laughter rang out during working hours again.

Sazana spent more time training Rashda and Cambyz. "A sharply upturned lip on a large platter offers a challenge even to an experienced potter." Her hands moved quickly on the clay as her apprentices followed her every move like a couple of eaglets. "The trick," she explained, "is to angle the floor of the plate thus." She forced the clay upward, squeezing just enough between thumb and index finger to create the short lip. "You have to be fast with this design. If you press it for too long, you will weaken the clay and it will break, either in the shaping or in the fire." She sat back, revealing the finished rim of the platter.

"That's perfect!" Cambyz rushed to his wheel. "I will try it." But his attempt at creating a rim crumbled under his fingers. "Agh! I am a clod."

Sazana frowned. "No such thing. Every failure is a victory in the making if you learn from it. What can you do better next time?"

The young man pulled on a thick clump of hair, leaving a streak of wet clay in the tangles. "Move faster?"

"That will help."

"And he did not pinch enough clay between his fingers. The rim became too thin." Rashda pointed a skinny finger at a collapsed lump.

She gave him an approving nod. "Very good."

He gave her a wistful look. "How long did it take you to become so skilled, Mistress Sazana?"

She gentled her voice. "There is no set timetable for these things. They take as long as they must. For everyone, it will prove different. You are trying to become as good as you can be. Not as good as anyone else. Your gift will emerge with its own particularities, and in its own time. And it will be good, I can already tell."

The young man's eyes moistened. She gave him a pat on the shoulder and returned to her own wheel. Being a teacher could be overwhelming at times, for there were days like this when she felt that she held the boys' hearts in her hands.

Sazana knew that their respite would prove temporary. Any hour now a steward would stride through their doors and announce the workshop belonged to a new master.

But she was wrong.

The workshop did not belong to a new master. It belonged to a new mistress.

And that mistress decided to make a personal visit to her property rather than send a steward in her stead. She came without prior announcement or preparation. The gate simply opened and in she strode on dainty, gold-stitched leather boots.

The sight of her brought the whole place to a standstill.

Pottery wheels turned, spinning untended as tongues lolled out in shock. Though none of them had ever met her, they recognized the two Immortals who flanked her, their fancy uniforms and their apple-tipped spears familiar to any resident of Susa. Their presence, alongside the simple circlet of gold in her hair, revealed her identity before anyone announced it.

Sazana stood frozen, the wheel forgotten as she studied Queen Esther.

Three weeks earlier, the Jewish community had been rocked by an extraordinary fact. Queen Esther, the woman who wore the royal crown of Persia, was in fact Hadassah, a Jewess like Sazana.

And like Sazana, she had taken a Persian name and lived under an assumed identity for years, until Haman's edict had forced her out from the shadows of hiding.

For three days, Sazana and Arta, along with the rest of the Jewish population of Susa, had fasted, praying that Queen Esther would win the king's favor and find them help against the edict that sought to annihilate them. Days later, the king had provided his codicil to the edict. Had it been the queen's doing, this chance for their salvation?

Sazana felt a sudden conviction that Esther was behind it all. And behind her, the wall of fasting and prayers of a whole people.

She was a rare beauty. She had to be to snag the attention of a king. But beneath the enchanting face, Sazana sensed an avid intelligence.

For some moments, Esther took in her surroundings, her eyes alight with keen interest. At first, Sazana assumed she had come to place a sizable order and wondered why so lofty a royal would dirty her feet by coming to their hot, smelly workshop. She could have sent her steward, likely the slim, elegantly dressed eunuch who stood one step behind her. Then it came to Sazana in a swoop, like a pot emerging out of the kiln, fully formed and glazed.

The king had given Haman's workshop to Esther.

The queen was their new mistress!

The eunuch stepped forward, gazing at everything with an assessing eye, and introduced himself as Hathach, the queen's chief steward. With little fanfare, he announced that, as Sazana had suspected, Esther had indeed been granted ownership of the workshop.

The queen's gaze searched through the coarse ware section, eyes bright with curiosity. At the sight of Sazana, she seemed arrested. "It is unusual to see a woman in a pottery workshop," she said with a smile.

Since the queen appeared to expect an answer, Sazana offered a bow. The queen strode forward until nothing but an arm's length separated them. "Are you the potter they call Sazana?"

Astonished that Esther had heard of her, again she could manage no words and responded with an awkward jerk of her chin.

Esther's expression softened into something almost motherly. "I own one of your pots. A long-necked ewer with flawless proportions. One of my handmaidens gave it to me as a gift. I have always admired its perfection. It is a pleasure to meet you."

Sazana gulped, and still lost for words, offered another awkward bow. Esther did not seem offended by her dumb response. "Tell me, how did you learn the craft? How did you find your way to pottery when it is considered a man's work?"

Sazana finally gave voice to one of the many thoughts that swirled around in her head as fast as her wheel. "My mother was a potter, Your Majesty. She learned from my grandfather." And then inspiration came, and she pulled the oval seal over her head to offer to Esther.

The Immortal at her side took a step closer. The queen waved him back and reached for the seal, studying the short, inverted Hebrew text.

Elihana, daughter of Shaphan.

Potter.

The kohl-lined eyes widened. "Your mother was a Jew."

"My father, also." Thankfully, her words were flowing more readily now.

"Yet *Sazana* is a Persian name."

"My guardian, Arta, thought it would be safer if I took such, seeing as we worked for Lord Haman. My true name is Shoshanah, lady."

Esther's gaze tangled with hers. In that infinitesimal moment, the two women connected on a fundamental level, without words, without explanations. They lived worlds apart, one a queen who occupied splendid palaces, the other an artisan whose haunt was a dusty workshop. But they both comprehended the fears and sacrifices that came with a life of secrets.

11

Sazana

> When the righteous triumph, there is great
> elation . . .
>
> Proverbs 28:12 NIV

Esther returned the oval seal to Sazana. "You have a guard-ian?"

The eunuch indicated Arta with a hand. "His name is Arta. He serves as the overseer of this place."

Sazana's eyes widened. The man must have done his home-work before accompanying his mistress here.

Arta bowed. "My queen."

"Did you also take on a Persian name when you began work-ing here, Arta?"

"No, lady. This is the name I inherited from my parents."

"How is it that you came to be guardian to a Jewish maiden?"

"Shoshanah's parents were like brother and sister to me. I worked in her grandfather's workshop in Babylon. What was meant to be a one-year apprenticeship stretched to fourteen. When they sold their workshop and headed to Susa, I came along."

"Where are they now?"

"We lost them to a terrible accident. Shoshanah was only eleven at the time. It was my honor to raise her."

Esther's smile held an unusual warmth. "I, too, was raised by a loving guardian after my parents died within days of each other." She turned that clever glance Sazana's way, and once again, a deep understanding passed between them. They had both weathered an impossible loss as children, their lives upturned overnight. And they had both found the nurture of a good father after that loss.

Esther waved toward the wheel. "Would you demonstrate for me how it works?"

Sazana bowed her head. "With pleasure, lady. What would you like me to make?"

"Choose what you wish. I have never seen a potter at work. I am curious to see how you go about it."

Sazana seated herself at the stool, trying to ignore the bite of self-consciousness at being the center of so many eyes. Arta began to turn the wheel. It reminded her of their early days here, when she had been a young girl and he the teacher, turning the wheel and teaching her the speeds she would need for each task.

The memory soothed her. Taking a lump of clay, she raised and flattened her cone.

"Why do you do that?" Esther asked, her tone curious.

Sazana threw a quick glance at Arta. While she could easily explain such basic techniques to Rashda and Cambyz as she worked, the idea of coming up with the right words before the queen and her entourage felt overwhelming.

Arta gave her an imperceptible nod. "Allow me to explain, my lady," he said. "We cone the clay before making a vessel for two reasons. First, the process helps to center the clay, which will result in an evenly formed vessel. Second, by raising and knocking down the new clay, we expel any air caught inside. This protects it both from cracking as it dries and later, when it is exposed to the flames of the furnace."

Within moments, Sazana had a goblet to show the queen. Esther clapped. "Marvelous. You make it look easy."

She waved at the wheel. "Would Your Majesty like to try?"

"Really!" the eunuch interjected with a dark frown, and Sazana's heart caved.

She was about to apologize when Esther said, "It's all right, Hathach. In truth, it is an enticing offer. I believe I shall attempt it."

The whole workshop had gathered a respectful distance from the queen. Although they had been too far to hear her conversation with Sazana and Arta, they cheered when the queen sat gingerly at the wheel. It was not every day when a royal came for a visit. And no one had ever heard of a queen getting her hands dirty with the stuff of their trade.

By sitting at the wheel, she had endowed a new dignity to their work.

Esther gestured for Sazana to sit across from her. In moments, Sazana prepared the clay for the queen. Under her tutelage, the queen's vessel emerged, a bit lopsided perhaps, but the small bowl had sturdy walls, and it did not collapse.

Using the wire cutter, Arta released the bottom of the vessel from the wheel with one clean slice, and to loud cheers, held it up for all to admire. "That is fine work for your first try, Your Majesty," he said. "You have the knack."

Esther wiped her hands on a pristine handkerchief that Hathach produced from somewhere. "You are too kind. I am certain anyone brave enough to attempt to drink from this bowl is sure to dribble upon his tunic."

She returned the soiled kerchief to Hathach. "The experience only makes me appreciate your fine work more." Coming to her feet in a smooth, elegant motion, she faced the back of the room where the rest of the workers had gathered. Raising her voice to ensure they could hear, she added, "I am indebted to you. I now appreciate that all your vessels, fine ware or coarse, require much talent and hard work."

The cheers were deafening. Sazana realized that with a few words, Esther had won the workers' loyalty for life. Heart and soul, they were her men after this, because they knew she valued them.

The queen returned her attention to Sazana. "Perhaps you can show me some of your finished pieces."

Sazana fetched two vessels to show the queen. One, a narrow-lipped jug, had been dipped in a light buff glaze and decorated with black embellishments. The other, her most recent piece, the pale blue bowl with a flanged rim that she had recently fired.

She had added a pinch of red into the Egyptian blue to produce a slightly purplish hue. Leaving the design plain, she had allowed the unusual color to take center stage.

Esther gave a small gasp. "Exquisite. You have a rare talent."

Beneath the faint trace of cosmetics and the complicated hairdo, she looked no older than Sazana. Yet something in her voice conveyed a maternal nature suited to an older woman. Before Sazana could thank her, the queen turned away, holding up the blue bowl. "What do you think, Hathach?"

The eunuch shrugged. "Everyone and his neighbor is going to want one."

Esther gave Sazana a considering look. "Can you make more?"

"Yes, lady. Though Egyptian blue is not cheap."

"Give me a breakdown of the cost," the eunuch said. "We'll see if it holds any potential for profit."

Esther returned the pale blue bowl to the table, her fingers lingering on the metal-smooth glaze. "And even if not, I shall want a few pieces for my own private collection."

"Should I offer the bowl to the lady?" Sazana whispered to Hathach. "Her Majesty seems taken by it. Only, I do need it as a template if you wish more like it."

Hathach's smile held a world of amusement. "If waiting means that she can have a shelf full of pottery instead of only a single specimen, I think the queen can manage to exercise a little patience. She means to make a success of this workshop. We do not wish to let the king down after he has displayed such generosity, do we?"

"No, my lord."

Hathach, seeming satisfied, turned his back, and with as little fanfare as they had displayed upon their entrance, the queen and her entourage left the workshop to take a quick tour of the yard before leaving.

"I can hardly believe it! Queen Esther came here! She sat on my stool, Arta!" Sazana plopped down on said stool, her legs too unsteady to hold her up.

It seemed utterly inconceivable that the queen not only owned their workshop but had gone to the trouble of personally inspecting it.

Cambyz, who had doffed his hat at Esther's appearance, smashed it back on his head and stared at the queen's lopsided bowl. "She made that with her own hands!"

Rashda elbowed him. "Did a better job than your first time."

Cambyz made a face. "Did a better job than your *last* time."

Arta broke into his dance, feet skipping in sprightly steps as his fingers snapped their jolly rhythm. "Our troubles are truly over, my girl. Haman's sons won't get their hands on us now. And the queen clearly admires you." He squeezed and jiggled her chin the way he used to when she had been a child. "As any person of good sense should."

Before Sazana could respond, the door opened again, admitting Hathach. This time, the eunuch came alone. He walked straight to Arta and Sazana. After surveying the area, he pointed at the frayed curtain bunched at the side of the alcove. "Does that work or is it just for show?"

In answer, Arta dismissed Cambyz and Rashda to the coarse ware section, and following the eunuch and Sazana into the alcove, pulled the curtain closed behind them.

Hathach gave a nod of approval. "Now then, Master Arta. The queen's scribes have been studying Haman's accounts. I assume you have figures of your own for this place?"

"Yes, Lord Hathach." Arta, whose knack for organization matched his ability for shaping clay, fetched several scrolls of papyrus and handed them to the eunuch. "You will find everything in order."

Hathach tapped a scroll against his palm. "If all the accounts show a satisfactory management of this place, you will continue in the role of overseer."

Arta beamed. "Thank you, my lord."

Hathach frowned. "The scribe tells me he finds no record of payment to you or Mistress Sazana for many weeks. Is that an error?"

Arta scratched the tip of his ear. "No, Lord Hathach. It's no error. Lord Haman decided he no longer needed to give us our agreed-upon rations when he discovered that Sazana is a Jew. He said if we wanted to keep her alive, we would have to work for free."

Hathach's eyes narrowed into slits. "The toad turned you into slaves, did he? We'll set that outrage straight immediately. You needn't be concerned that such treatment will continue. The queen will treat you right. Her Majesty has commanded that you receive whatever back payment you are owed."

Arta threw Sazana a startled look. She grinned, as astonished as he. The queen owed them nothing. She did not have to make up for the misdeeds of the former master of the workshop. This unusual generosity, in addition to the queen's warm manner and grace, convinced Sazana that no better woman could have worn the crown. "Please offer Her Majesty our sincere gratitude."

Hathach inclined his head. "I am told Haman had a man here who reported to him directly." His brow lowered. "You grasp my meaning?"

"I do, master," Arta said. "He is called Nabonassar. I may have been the overseer in name, but in recent months, I did the work while Nabonassar wielded all the authority."

"Where is he now?"

"He vanished the day we heard Lord Haman had been arrested. Never returned to work after that."

"Not a fool, then. Do inform me if he shows his face. Are there others besides this Nabonassar? Men who were in the pocket of Haman?"

Arta fidgeted. "Not that I know, Lord Hathach."

"But you are not certain?"

"Lord Haman was a thorough man. It would not surprise me if he had more than one source. I just cannot imagine who. Our men are truehearted. None would play the informant."

"And you, Mistress Sazana? Do you suspect anyone?"

"I have never seen anything but respect from these men. As Arta says, I find it hard to believe any of them would serve Lord Haman in a manner beyond their work as potters."

Hathach tapped his lips with an index finger. "Haman was well-connected. And he is survived by ten strapping sons who feel this workshop should rightfully belong to them. They are none too pleased by the current state of affairs. I would not be surprised if they try to hatch some mischief, especially if they still have one of their people planted here."

Arta bowed. "Though I trust my men, it is wise to be careful under the circumstances."

"I will assign someone to watch over the place for a while. My man will arrive tomorrow. I will instruct him to come incognito. Give him a job here. Any job. He will stay until we know everything is safe and settled."

"Is he a potter, my lord?"

Hathach rolled his eyes. "Queen Esther is more of a potter than he, I should imagine. He can read and write. Hire him as a scribe. Or make him the wheel boy. Or whatever you have to do to get him in here without giving him away as the queen's man. He'll do the rest."

It seemed they were exchanging one spy for another. Yet Esther's man wanted to keep them safe from mischief rather than create it. He was not spying on them. He was spying *for* them.

When Hathach left, Arta collected Esther's lopsided bowl and with exquisite care set it upon a drying rack. "We will give the queen's bowl a place of honor after it is fired in the kiln. It may be the only pot made by royal hands in all of Persia's history."

12

Jadon

"Go, return." And he returned.

2 Samuel 3:16

THE TWELFTH YEAR OF KING XERXES'S RULE
THE SEVENTEENTH DAY OF SUMMER

Jadon's work, being fluid in nature, held many complexities. At times, he had the responsibility of managing the queen's guard, especially when she ventured out of the palace. He did not like the added risk to her person on such occasions. No one asked his opinion, however, and he made the best of it when the queen embarked outside the walls that kept her safe. Sometimes, he served as a glorified messenger. Often, he acted as her agent—part steward, part inquiry man—chasing after suspicious trails, detecting anything that smelled rotten.

In short, he had charge of keeping both her and her business interests, which had grown large and prosperous, safe from bad intentions.

The variety of his work occasionally caused some inconvenience. It required a lot of foresight and planning. But until today, none of his assignments had ever turned his life upside down. They had never caused his heart to lodge in his throat, refusing to budge.

"Haman's pottery workshop?" He gaped at Hathach when the eunuch informed him of his new commission. "But I am busy trying to find Cyrus's cylinder."

Hathach glared. "Do both. What's the matter with you? This workshop is part of the property the king gave Esther as a gift after Haman's execution. I am concerned that he may still have a man there. One who now reports to his sons. Haman was a sly rat."

Jadon fidgeted in his chair. Of all the places the eunuch might send him, he had to go and pick *her* workshop. "Perhaps we should consider sending one of the king's trained spies instead."

"And perhaps we shouldn't. The queen does not wish to ask the king for another favor. What ails you, man? It's a simple enough job. Go in, sniff around, and make your report."

"It's only that . . . well, they know me. I couldn't sneak in unnoticed."

"Who?"

"The overseer, for one."

"Arta?" Hathach leaned forward. "Do you suspect him?"

"Of course not. He is honest to the bone."

"That's what I thought. What is the problem, then? I have already informed him that I am sending my man. He will help you blend in."

"There is also . . ." Jadon tried to loosen the crisscross collar of his tunic that seemed to be cutting off his breath. "Well, you see . . ."

"By Nebuchadnezzar's bald head! Spit it out before I lose my teeth to old age."

"I know Shoshanah as well."

"Shoshanah? Who might that be? Wait. You mean Sazana, the main potter?"

Jadon nodded miserably.

Hathach's stare grew sharp as a tiger's tooth. "How well do you know her?"

Heat traveled up Jadon's face. "I knew her very well, once."

"I see. In that case, I should think you would want to keep her safe."

Jadon's back went rigid. "She is in danger?"

"Might be. Haman discovered her Jewish heritage several months before his death. He forced her to serve him as a slave."

"What?" Something scarlet-hot and blazing exploded inside him.

"The problem is that the king left Haman's sons alive after he condemned their father to death. Ten of them, all seething with resentment, looking for someone to blame. They cannot reach Esther. We have made certain of that. But they might want to expend their wrath on someone closer at hand. It's bad enough that the king gave their house in Susa to the queen. The workshop was one of Haman's most profitable ventures. His sons consider it rightfully theirs. Part of the inheritance stolen from them by the Jewish queen. They will not want the place to succeed."

"Where are they now? I will set a man to guard their house and report any suspicious movements."

"That's part of our problem. They have gone to ground. Vanished from sight. I have heard from their village in Agazi. They have not returned home." Hathach tapped the top of his desk with a restless finger. "Your Shoshanah is the most profitable potter in that workshop. If they move, it may be against her."

Jadon's throat turned dry. "I will report to Arta right away."

"Good man. And try to get some color back in your cheeks before you show up at their door. With that pale face and sweat glowing on your brow, you look like you are suffering from a fatal contagion. I doubt the other potters will want to cozy up to you."

Jadon would almost prefer a deadly contagion to the coming encounter.

After all these years, he would have to face Shoshanah again. Walk through those doors as he had done when he had been a green twenty-three-year-old, too sure of himself and the world around him. As a newly minted Immortal, he'd had no time to go to the market and pick up a birthday gift for his mother. Riding past the workshop, he had decided to step inside and find something his mother would enjoy. He had found the perfect gift . . . and lost his heart.

Alongside the clenching twist of nausea in his gut, an entirely different sensation spiraled through him. Something he could not name. Something altogether too sweet for comfort.

13

Sazana

Refrain from anger, and forsake wrath!
Fret not yourself; it tends only to evil.

Psalm 37:8

The glaze seemed perfect. Sazana felt the thrill of creation as she considered how the final design might emerge from the kiln. She had used the blue glaze on a dozen completed pieces that sat on the shelf, dried and ready to receive their new skin.

Joy sprang from the bottom of her belly and spread all the way up, seeming to reach into every limb in her body until it broke out on her face, like the sun bursting over a mountain range.

She sensed Arta's sudden shift rather than saw it. Raising her head, she caught her guardian in an arrested pose, his mouth half open as he stared toward the coarse ware section. Had the queen returned? Her smile warmed at the thought as she swiveled toward the door.

Under the stone threshold, a tall man stood, broad shoulders rigid, lips pressed tight and flat. The shock of recognition nearly sent her tumbling onto her behind. Their eyes caught and locked across the expanse of the workshop.

Slowly, her smile died. His glance slid away, looking at everything but her.

Without her permission, her mind tabulated the many changes in him: the corded muscles that had thickened, the ridged hollow of his cheeks, the broad column of his neck. Everything about him seemed to have shifted from the pliability of youth to something hard-edged and more unyielding, as though the passing of time had robbed him of the last vestiges of boyish softness.

In spite of the many changes, every part of her leapt in instant recognition, and with it, a painful longing she would have given anything to conquer, for there at the door stood the man who had haunted Sazana's dreams and nightmares for five years.

Every beat of Sazana's heart turned into an explosion, booming in her ears until she felt deaf to all else but the sound of her own body turning traitor. What was he *doing* here?

Finally, one of the potters approached him and asked his business. A few words passed between them that Sazana could not hear. The potter lifted a hand to catch Arta's attention.

"For you, master," the potter called.

Arta shook himself out of his stupor and moved to the threshold. "May I help you?" he asked as though addressing a stranger.

Sazana gave him a confused look. Had he not recognized Jadon? Had she misread the shock on his face—the shock that must have mirrored her own expression?

Why had Jadon strolled into her workshop, standing there as if a thorny history did not divide them? What had possessed him to do such a thing?

After a long, frozen moment, it finally dawned on her.

Jadon was the queen's agent. The man they were supposed to welcome into their midst. The man who would become a regular worker here while he tried to unearth whether Lord Haman had left a mole behind.

She squeezed her eyes shut. She would have to spend days with him milling around, days of seeing him in the periphery of her vision, days when she might even have to speak to him. Of all the people Esther might have sent to their aid, why had she chosen this man?

And why had he agreed to come?

Sazana turned back to her glaze, hunching her back, desperate to disappear. The glaze that seemed so perfect only moments ago had lost its magic. It had turned into something ordinary—a watery solution that contained various dyes. Her hand wrapped around her mother's seal, no longer hidden, but hanging over her tunic for the whole world to see. It felt cold and hard, lacking the usual comfort it always offered.

"Sazana," Arta said as he drew flush against her table. "We have a new employee."

Sazana tried to school her features into something bland before lifting her chin.

"This is Jadon. I am hiring him to run errands."

Jadon bowed—not the courtly bow he had learned from his father, the one she had always secretly admired. The one that turned her knees a little wobbly when directed at her. Instead, he gave an awkward sketch like a country bumpkin unused to Susa's sophisticated ways. "Mistress. You want anything done, just say."

Her eyes widened. His cultured accent, another legacy from his gentrified Persian father, had disappeared. In its place, he spoke like a peasant, every note capturing the musical tones of a village farther north. Up close, she noticed his clothes, which were frayed and old, washed so often that the color had faded into a nondescript hue that might once have been brown. Now it brought to mind the dung of a sick cow.

No wonder Esther had chosen him for this job. Jadon had

transformed himself into a poor, unskilled man with the ease of a chameleon.

She realized the two men were still standing in front of her as though waiting for an answer. But she could not think of a single word to say in reply to Arta's introduction. Nodding an acknowledgment, she dropped her gaze to her lap.

"Sazana is busy." Arta pushed his bulk between them, his tone protective. "We must not interrupt her."

"Yes, master." Jadon followed after Arta. He turned to look over his shoulder, throwing her a final glance. The blue eyes, which she remembered as shockingly bright, were cloudy today.

Something stirred inside her, an ache too old to be so raw.

She watched him return to the coarse ware section. Arta set him to moving the heavy, swollen-bellied vessels made for the transportation of grain and oil, lining them neatly in a rack against the wall. Apparently Arta intended to put him to real work while he snooped.

The thought sparked a sudden idea. She had a long list of chores that had gone untended while they had tried to meet Haman's ever-increasing demands.

She fetched a scroll of papyrus. A tiny smile played at the edge of her lips as she thought of task after task. Not that she was holding a grudge against the man or anything. But if he was going to be around, he might as well make himself useful. She looked at the broken wheel that had been collecting dust in one corner for as long as she had worked in the workshop, and her smile widened.

"It isn't his fault that the queen assigned him to us," Arta said with a shrug, dipping bread into his bowl of bean soup. Over the course of the day, he had adjusted more readily to Jadon's presence in the workshop than Sazana had. Now, in the privacy of their home, he appeared as calm and cheerful as ever. "He is her man, after all. He must go where she sends him."

"Why is he in the queen's service at all? The last time I saw him, he was an Immortal. What's he doing working for Esther?"

Arta scratched his head. "Hathach recruited him a couple of years ago when her head of security retired."

"Of all the Immortals, they had to go and pick him." Sazana twisted a piece of bread with restless fingers. "He could have refused to take on this assignment."

Arta stopped chewing. "Refuse the queen? Be reasonable."

"Fine. He could have at least warned us. Sent a note to let us know he was about to intrude upon us."

Arta shrugged. "Perhaps he did not have a chance."

Sazana threw the mauled bread into her bowl. "Why do you defend him?"

Arta held up his hands. "I don't. I am happy to accuse him of all manner of wrongdoing. But pick something fair."

She narrowed her eyes. "Fine. He is an oath-breaking, life-ruining, love-spurning destroyer of hearts. Is that more to your liking?" The anger, intense and hot, shocked her more than Jadon's appearance. She had thought she had burned through her rage long since. Believed herself free of the offense. Yet it had risen up like the noxious fumes that inhabited the dank tunnels of a silver mine.

Arta scratched his head some more. "No argument from me."

Sazana's skin heated. Arta deserved to have his meal in peace. She reeled back the flow of resentment as best she could and stuffed it beneath years of practiced silence.

After dinner, she fetched the papyrus she had been working on earlier. She might as well put this unexpected lava of emotions to good use. Adding a few more unpleasant chores to her growing list, she amused herself by making each task more ridiculous than the next.

When she had finished, she went over the spelling of each word. She had stopped her studies when her parents died. She could still read and write Aramaic, the common language used by merchants and other working classes in the far-flung provinces of the Persian empire. Thanks to its uncomplicated alphabet, she found the language manageable. It was certainly easier to learn than Persian or Akkadian.

Unlike Jadon, who had studied several languages as well as texts of poetry alongside ethics and mathematics at the palace school, her reading and writing skills were simplistic. Adequate enough for a potter, and better than many women of her class who could not read at all. But a long way from the proper education Jadon had received. She found herself jabbed by the sharp prick of pride. She did not want to appear incompetent in front of him.

Carefully, she weeded out every mistake she could detect from her words. When she finished her revision, she set the scroll aside. Tomorrow, she would ask Arta to give it to Jadon. She bit her lip. If she were honest, she did not want to miss the expression on his face when he began reading the tasks she had assigned him.

Better hand him the list herself. After all, he would need her guidance with some of these chores. She practiced the words she would say to him, not wanting to stand like a lump of clay, all silent before him again. When she had her short speech memorized, she lay her head on her pillow and fell asleep as soon as her eyes closed.

14

Sazana

They repay me evil for good;
my soul is bereft.

Psalm 35:12

These chores are for you." Sazana held out the scroll to Jadon, proud that her hand remained steady. "I have listed them in order."

Jadon's eyes widened. "Thank you, mistress. I am happy to serve you." He offered her his awkward bow.

Her chest tightened at the spark of genuine pleasure that warmed the blue eyes, turning them into the Susa sky on a summer day, as though he truly looked forward to helping her. He bent his head over the list to study every item.

Nothing in his expression changed. But when he lifted his head, the warmth had leaked out of his eyes. He held out the parchment to her. "Would you mind reading this to me? I can't read."

She should have known better than to try to play games with him. He was fast on his feet, his mind sharper than a lion's claw. She should have remembered that a peasant would likely be illiterate and realized that Jadon intended to remain in character.

She schooled her features into an impassivity that she hoped matched his. "To start, I need you to move that broken wheel out of here and into the yard."

He turned to study the wheel. It must have weighed more than one of the stones in a pharaoh's pyramid. "Today?"

"Yes. It's urgent." As his silence stretched, she felt the need to explain. "I want that spot cleared."

Spider webs stretched from one end of the stone to the next, a layer of dust thicker than her thumb covering its surface. Anyone could see it had sat there for years without being shifted.

"I see."

She offered him a sweet smile, starting to enjoy herself. "Next, I want you to move all the vessels from this drying rack to the one over there. Mind you be careful. If you break any, it will come out of your rations."

He dipped his chin.

"Tomorrow, you can move them back."

"Move them back?"

"As I said. I want them in precisely the same location you find them in today."

"You do that often?" His voice had grown cold. "Take your vessels for a walk around the workshop? Do you have a leash, or should I just take them free hand?"

"I want to dust the racks. Even a country fellow like you must see that we cannot clean a shelf while it's full."

"I didn't understand. Beg your pardon, mistress."

Her eyes narrowed. "Do you?"

He seemed lost at her meaning. "Do I what?"

A vein pulsed against her temple. She had set aside the script she had prepared for this meeting when he had forced her into reading the list. Now the conversation was about to veer a long way away from what her original intent had been. Yet the flame in her chest demanded a quenching. A reckoning of sorts. She lifted her chin. "Beg my pardon?"

His expression shifted. The impassive mask crumbled, softening the hard, expressionless features into something else entirely. Something warm and full of regret. "With all my heart."

She almost believed him, except that the mask slipped back on so quickly, she must have imagined the whole thing.

"I will start on your chores, mistress." He bowed his head. "You can read me the rest when I finish with these ones."

She retreated to her stool and stared at the wall. It took her a long time to corral her thoughts into some semblance of order. Enough, at least, to nod at the wheel boy and start shaping a pot. The jug she intended to make refused to behave, and halfway, she had to smash the clay down. It had been a long time since she had missed a throwing. Even if something refused to go her way, she usually managed to turn it into something else on the spot.

Not today. She shifted on her seat, looking at the misshapen clay like it might be a viper about to strike.

When time stretched and she still had not moved, Arash pulled on his ear and allowed the wheel to come to a stop. Judging by the state of his hair, which lay flat on one side and stuck out like porcupine needles on the other, he must have rolled right out of bed and run all the way to the workshop. At twelve, he appeared still more boy than youth.

She rooted around the cloth bag she had brought from home and drew out a piece of bread and a hunk of white cheese. She pointed at the clean kerchief hanging from his belt that his mother laundered for him every day, and when he handed it to her, placed the food on it. "Didn't break your fast again this morning, did you? Go eat something. Take an hour off." She wasn't going to accomplish anything useful at this rate. Might as well allow the boy a break.

With a whoop, he jumped from his stool, and sinking his teeth into the bread before even taking a step, thanked her with a full mouth.

She watched him skip out into the yard, relieved to be left alone for a short while. Perhaps speaking to Jadon had been a mistake. The sound of his voice, the way his eyes lingered before shifting, the familiar scent of him . . . Everything about him, in fact, was stirring too many memories.

Bad memories.

Memories of the night that had broken the back of their love.

They had signed the betrothal agreement just one month earlier. The bloom of devotion, of happiness, and the expectation of the life to come had colored everything in her world in those days. In her naïveté, she expected the best to be waiting around every corner. Her life had been consumed by dreams of weddings and the home she would share with Jadon.

She had been too innocent to know that sometimes dreams turned to ashes.

That night, they had supped with Jadon's parents. His mother, Rachel, had sat, nervous fingers playing with her treasured silver cup, following the whorls and designs on the chalice. She was a quiet woman, given to staring at nothing and barking out anxious comments at odd moments. Sazana had done her best to put her at ease, trying to draw her out from the well of silence that she often sank into.

"Such a beautiful cup, Mistress Rachel," Sazana said, knowing how Rachel treasured the ornate chalice.

"My grandmother worked in the household of a silver mine owner for years," Jadon said. "In gratitude for her faithful service, her mistress presented her with this chalice. It held a place of honor in Grandmother's house. She drank from it every day for the rest of her life, until it passed to my mother. Now my mother upholds the tradition."

"The workmanship is rare." Sazana indicated the complicated silver whorls. "I can see why you treasure it."

Certain that her praise of the cup would bring a smile to Jadon's mother, Sazana was astounded when instead Rachel's eyes rounded, spots of color staining her cheeks.

"You want it for yourself, don't you?" she snapped.

"What? No, I—"

Rachel's voice rose. "I know you. You are just waiting for me to die so you can take it from me." A trembling finger pointed in accusation. "First, you take my son from me. Now, as if that's not bad enough, you want to rob my inheritance."

Jadon went pale. "Mother!"

Rachel began to weep, fat tears dripping down her chin. She was still a beautiful woman, her cheeks unmarred by sags and wrinkles. But between the sobs and the twisted expression, all the loveliness seemed to seep out of her.

Sazana's lips trembled. "Mistress Rachel, I beg your pardon. I didn't mean to cause you distress. I—"

Jadon's mother did not give her time to finish. "You are not good enough for my son! Who is your father? Who is your mother? Dead, the both of them. No one in Susa even knows them. No, I say. You cannot have my Jadon. He deserves better."

Rachel lunged, one hand raised in wordless threat. If Jadon's father had not held her back, she would have raked her nails across Sazana's flesh. She was still screaming when her husband dragged her from the room.

Jadon had turned bone-white, staring after his mother. His fingers shook violently as he pulled them through his hair. Sazana had never seen him so discomposed.

She knew how he felt.

She waited for him to come to her, to take her into his comforting embrace. But he seemed frozen. "Jadon." Her voice emerged pleading and soft. Finally, he turned to face her.

"I . . . I didn't know she felt that way," she said.

"Nor I." His voice was as unsteady as his fingers. He took a gulp from his cup, as though his throat was closing.

An awkward silence settled between them. Sazana's whole body trembled in the aftermath of Rachel's screaming accusations. She dropped her head into her hands. She and Jadon had a hard road ahead of them. Winning Rachel's good opinion would not come easy. But Sazana could do it. With Jadon's help, she could manage anything.

"I think I had better take you home." Jadon moved toward her, his eyes shaded.

She came to her feet. "I can make my own way. Stay with your mother. She needs you."

"I will take you."

It had been a strained walk. She tried a few times to speak of what had taken place. But Jadon's short answers had made it clear that he needed time to sort through his tangled thoughts. Time she had given him.

But in the absence of his reassurance, her own mind grew as unsteady as a lopsided urn, unable to stop wobbling. She promised herself that tomorrow they would find a way to win Rachel's approval. They would think of a way to reassure her.

Tomorrow came, and no reconciliation with it. The day passed without even a single note from Jadon. For three whole days he avoided her. Hard as it was to wade through those hours, waiting for word, for reassurance, never once had she suspected the conclusion he would reach. Not once.

On the fourth day, he came to her house, looking like all the life had been drained out of him. "Shoshana, I beg your pardon." He stood rigid as a marble sarcophagus. "I . . . I have come to break off our betrothal."

"What?" She collapsed onto a cushion, her mind refusing to comprehend the words he had spoken. "*What?*"

His throat bobbed as if he could not swallow. Wiping a

trembling hand across his lips, he dropped down on one knee. "Listen. I am to blame. I . . . You deserve better."

"Jadon!" She reached for his hand, but he pulled away. She blinked. "It's because of your mother, isn't it?"

He lowered his gaze. "It's not what you think."

"Tell me you are not breaking our betrothal because of her."

He remained silent, the unspoken words making their own statement. "Jadon, we can change her mind. We can try to win her over."

"No."

His eyes filled with tears as he gazed at her. He pressed them closed, shuddering. "You are the best thing that ever happened to me. But we are wrong for each other."

Without another word, he turned his back and walked away.

In the months that followed, she decided it was the sight of his tears that made it impossible to let go. The anguish with which he had looked upon her made it impossible to truly hate him, even when the scribe arrived bearing papers and money.

Unbelievably, unbearably, Jadon had officially broken their betrothal. His letter bore three short words. *I am sorry.*

His hard-earned money, which he had thrown at her with offending generosity, supposedly paid for the damage to her reputation and her heart.

She had sat for a week and stared at the scribe's fat package in disbelief. This was the measure of Jadon's love. This sparse letter sitting atop a broken legal document, accompanied by a bag bulging with guilt-ridden silver.

One objection from his mother, and Jadon's love had caved like a cracked vessel in the heat of the kiln.

Sazana tucked her cold hands under her arms, trying to escape the weight of bitter memories. Jadon was busy moving a jug from one rack to the next, his movements full of the unconscious grace she remembered. She knew with sudden conviction that queen's agent or not, having Jadon here was a profound mistake. Being in his company every day, watching him hour after hour, would destroy her hard-won peace.

She had to be rid of him.

15

Jadon

And I have filled him with the Spirit of God, with
ability and intelligence, with knowledge and all
craftsmanship, to devise artistic designs . . .

Exodus 31:3–4

J adon grunted as he threw his weight behind the tall,
wooden rack and slid it a forearm's length to the right.
Standing back, he studied his handiwork, rubbing his
aching back.

He had better check with Her Highness before loading the
pottery back on the shelf. The last time he had moved a rack
to her exact specifications before replacing the vessels, she had
made him take everything off again and scooch the shelves a
finger's length to the left.

She was wasting his time, throwing him an endless list of
useless jobs. In spite of himself, a smile twitched at one corner
of his mouth, refusing to be squelched. A part of him could

appreciate the humor in that scroll filled with ridiculous, back-breaking tasks.

He would have enjoyed doing something that might actually help her in some way. But this waste of his time rankled more than he liked to admit. Given everything that had passed between them, she was not going to trust him with any important tasks. He accepted that. But the admission hurt like the biting tip of a leather whip.

Guilt burned its way through both humor and annoyance.

He deserved it. He deserved her small attempts at torture. Deserved the thunderclouds building in her doe eyes every time she looked at him. In truth, he deserved a lot worse.

He wiped dusty hands on his tunic, forcing himself into character. Shoshanah's long list armed him with one useful weapon: a perfect means with which he could fulfill his mission for Esther and also keep Shoshanah safe.

He scuttled next to one of the potters called Parnaka. "Has she always been such a pain to work for?" He made his voice whiny as he rubbed his shoulder.

Parnaka slapped a large lump of clay on the wheel. "Who?"

"The mistress." Complaining against Arta or Shoshanah was the best way to unearth a spy if any still remained in the workshop. Haman's man would not be a fan of either of them.

"Sazana?" The potter centered the clay. "She isn't difficult to work with."

"You must be thinking of another Sazana, then. This one never stops nagging me."

The potter frowned. "Then you are doing something wrong. Now, clear off. I'm working."

The potter missed Jadon's satisfied smile as he walked back to the rack and began to dust the shelves. He had been the fifth worker who had proven loyal to Shoshanah and Arta.

He slapped his rag against a knee. Though he had rid the shelf of its last speck of dust, he could not go on to the next task until he had Shoshanah's approval. Which meant he had to seek her out again.

He doubted that she had foreseen this inevitable outcome of her ploy. Her list of silly tasks forced them into stilted conversations with throbbing undercurrents that he found more painful than the physical labor she had dreamed up for him. Yet he sensed that she found proximity to him every bit as agonizing as he did.

He lingered in the periphery of her vision, studying her as she shaped a tall vessel. Her fingers had an enchantment to them as they formed the clay into curvaceous lines. Like Bezalel, the craftsman endowed by the Spirit of God with skill to furnish the Temple in Israel, she seemed blessed by something beyond human talent, something from God. An innate gift to create beauty from the very dust of the earth.

Her hair slipped out of its leather thong, coming loose down her back in a slow unfurling of its braid. His throat turned dry. How well he remembered that silky waterfall. Once, he had been free to run his fingers through it.

He ground his teeth. God help him. He had to conquer these memories.

It didn't help that she had grown lovelier over the years. The girl's beauty had turned into a woman's maturity, like a hand-knotted Persian carpet, attaining an irresistible glow that had been absent in her younger years.

He turned, determined to walk away. To find Arta and ask for some other work. But she spotted him just as he took the first step.

"Did you want me?"

An unfortunate turn of phrase. He squeezed his eyes shut and swallowed the ready answer that leapt to his tongue. Schooling his features into a bland mask, he turned back, facing her. "The rack, mistress. You want to look it over before I move the pots back on the shelves?"

She waved a careless hand. "Go ahead. It's fine."

He raised a brow. It wasn't like her to give up an opportunity to exact more work out of him. He wondered if she had decided that vexing him might not be worth the bother.

Relief fought with disappointment. He might feel tormented by her presence. Yet at the same time, with her, he had discovered the first thrill of real joy he had experienced in five years. It was maddening.

"Jadon?"

He whipped around. "Yes?"

"After you replace the pots, ask Master Arta for your errands. I am finished."

His stomach twisted. "Finished, mistress?"

She bit her lip. Jadon held his breath as she struggled with some internal dilemma. "For today, I mean. I'm finished for today."

He exhaled. "Very good, mistress."

16

Sazana

Above all else, guard your heart,
for everything you do flows from it.
Proverbs 4:23 NIV

I n its own childish way, her little charade had felt satisfying at first. To saddle Jadon with ridiculous tasks and then watch him grunt and sweat with strain had made her grin with satisfaction.

But now it had become a torment as it brought Jadon to her side again and again.

The anger that had ruled her heart since he walked through the door had abated, settling into a beating pulse rather than a roaring explosion. In its place, the old memories rose up—not of the hard, incomprehensible ending between them, but of the days when life had seemed perfect.

Now, when Jadon drew close, she had to fight sudden images of them laughing together at a silly jest only they understood or holding hands as they crossed over a slippery bridge. Memories of his fingers spanning her waist as he lowered her from his horse; of his voice, warm and serious, as he explained the history of some battle. The memories she had buried were now rising, prodded by his closeness, pelting her like hail in a gathering storm.

She had done it to herself. She had shaped her own torture. And she was not even ready to let it go.

In the late afternoon, when all the potters had left the workshop and Arta had barred the doors, Jadon set aside his broom and joined them for their nightly conversations. Over the past four evenings since his arrival, he had shared his day's discoveries before heading to the palace to make a more formal report to Hathach.

"What did you find out today, Jadon?" Arta sat on a stool, heaving a sigh. He still had not regained his full stamina after the weeks of Haman's brutal treatment. She would have to cook him some ox broth to add strength to his bones.

"I have ruled out three more potters as potential spies. They seem loyal to you."

Arta rubbed his hands together and smiled. If Jadon had found loyalty among the men, it was because of Arta's wise leadership. They knew they could expect fair treatment at his hands.

"Who did you speak to today?" he asked.

Jadon named the men. "When I pressed them to betray some dissatisfaction, they grew angry. That is a good sign."

Sazana placed a hand on Arta's shoulder. "The men love Arta."

Jadon shifted his gaze to her. "Perhaps. But today I complained about you. It was you these men defended. They are faithful to you also. Body and soul, I'd say." His expression soured. "I'm surprised one of them hasn't snatched you up, the way they jump to your defense."

A shocked silence met this comment. Jadon had turned pale,

clearly as astonished by the words that had slipped out of his mouth as Arta and Sazana.

"Beg your pardon," he said, his lips barely moving. "None of my concern."

"No, my boy, it isn't." Arta's cheerful voice seemed at odds with the tense moment. "But you are right. There is a long line of men leading to Shoshanah's door."

Sazana snapped her head toward Arta, her mouth open. No line led to her door, long or otherwise.

Arta, ignoring her wide-eyed look, had more to say. "If they haven't snatched her up yet, it is because she has learned to be choosy."

"I am glad to hear it." Jadon sounded like a man suffering from a plague. "If you will pardon me, I must make my report to Hathach."

As soon as he slipped out the door, Sazana rounded on Arta. "*A long line?* What were you thinking, Arta?"

He pulled on his beard. "A little too much?"

Words failed her. Finally, she croaked, "Don't do that again. Please!"

"If you insist. But I will tell you something. I enjoyed watching the boy squirm."

"You think he squirmed?"

"Like a fish at the end of a barbed hook. Didn't you notice how downright vexed he looked when he mentioned one of the men snatching you up? I know a jealous man when I see one."

She could not swallow back the puff of air that escaped her lips. "You've never even been married. I doubt you are an expert in these matters."

He shrugged. "I don't have to ride a horse to know what it looks like."

"Please leave this particular horse alone."

"As you wish, my dear." He rubbed his hands together like a man who had been handed a free bag of silver.

Sazana cringed. She recognized in him the signs of hope. Ridiculous, senseless hope. She recognized the signs because there had been a time she had seen them in herself. In the early days, after Jadon broke off their betrothal, she thought he would return to her. Give some manner of excuse. Temporary loss of sanity, perhaps. A fat hole in his head, possibly.

He never came.

Six months later, when his mother died, she thought, *Now! Now he will return to me.*

Now that he no longer had to worry about his mother's violent disapproval, he would come for her. She assured herself that she would never take him back. Not if he begged on his knees. Not after seeing how shallow his love ran. But under the layers of wounded pride and genuine hurt, her heart sat patiently, longing to say yes. Yearning to take him back.

He did not come.

Even his mother's death did not reverse his decision to part from Sazana. She had learned, then, what she had not wanted to believe. Jadon had never loved her. Arta would learn the same lesson soon enough.

She straightened her sagging shoulders. Tomorrow, she would put an end to her silly game. She would stay as far from him as the span of the workshop allowed. In a few days, he would find his answers and be out of her world once again, this time for good.

She blinked fast until the world cleared and she could see again.

"Sazana!" Arta stopped next to her wheel a little before noon the next day, shaking a wad of papyrus in her face. "Guess what I have here."

"I believe it is called papyrus, Arta. The Egyptians invented it a long time ago."

"Ha! But what is written on there, Mistress Clever? You

won't guess, so I will tell you. They are orders for the dozen blue vessels you fired. I wanted to know how they would fare in the market."

She turned to face him, her interest sparked. "You sold them?"

"Sold them? There was nearly a riot over them, my girl! I have never seen so much interest in pottery. The merchants were fighting over the samples."

She felt her chest fill with warmth. "They're all gone?"

"Every single one." He shook the papyrus in her face. "Plus, orders for more."

"Master Hathach will be pleased." She grinned. "That means the queen's workshop will do well. I am so happy, Arta."

He took a few dancing steps. "So am I, my girl. Our new mistress will be well-pleased with you. And she can hold her head up before the king." He patted her cheek. "I thought this idea of yours would never fly. Too costly, I said. I am so glad you didn't let my doubts hold you back."

"You may not have believed it would work, but you have never stopped me from trying, Arta. You have always encouraged me to attempt new designs. If not for that, I would probably not have made half the things I have created over the years."

Arta grinned, his face aglow with the compliment she had paid him. Sometimes she thought he valued nothing so much as her praise of him as a father.

Watching his retreating back, Sazana decided to go for a short stroll to celebrate their success. On the way to the door, she noticed Parnaka slip his hand on the mound of clay that occupied the fast-turning wheel before him. An intentional slip that sent a fleck of clay flying.

The clump whirled through the air, and with perfect precision, landed on Jadon's cheek with a splat, sliding like honey into his short beard.

Jadon flinched. He wiped the clay from his cheek and studied it for a moment before sauntering over to Parnaka. "Lost something?"

"Is that where it landed?" Parnaka gave Jadon a wide-eyed look. "How unfortunate. My hand must have slipped."

The potters who sat close enough to see the exchange snickered. Sazana covered her own smile with a hand. Jadon's ploy to get the potters to open up to him had not made him popular.

He marched away, his expression stony. But she caught the twitch of a dying smile when he walked by her. She had to admire his good humor. Another man would have fumed.

In the afternoon, he sought her out at her table where she was shaping a row of jug handles.

"I have come for my chores, Mistress Sazana. What do you have for me today?" If she had not known better, Sazana would have thought he was hiding another smile. He probably expected another chunk of flying clay, this time at her hand.

She came to her feet. "You need not consult me about your work anymore. I am finished assigning your chores. Master Arta will give you his own tasks."

She exhaled after delivering the words she had practiced that morning. At least she had not tripped over her tongue.

Jadon took a step toward her. "I have time to do what you need. Whatever you want. Tell me."

She had expected him to look relieved. But instead of making a hasty retreat, he drew closer. Without meaning to, she retreated one step. He stopped in his tracks. Neither spoke as they faced each other. It dawned on her that he would not budge unless she answered.

She cringed inwardly. It took her some time to think of the right response. As if sensing her struggle, he remained silent, giving her time to form her thoughts.

It had been one of the first things she had noticed about him. His willingness to wait without running over her unformed words. He had always made her feel as though what she had to say was worth his patience. At the time, she had thought it a gift, one few outside her family had offered.

She had lived through years of teasing as a child because of her slow speech, first in Babylon, and later in Susa, being told she was a dolt, or worse, a bore, too dull to befriend. By the time she thought of the answer to one thing, the conversation had often moved in a different direction. People her own age had found her tedious, not having the patience to wait until she said her piece. To them, she was hardly present. Not worth the effort of friendship. She had learned to protect herself by not risking new friendships, a habit that had stuck into adulthood.

Jadon had been different from the start. He had waited on every word, his easy smile reassuring her anxious heart. Never once had he made her feel unwanted. At times she wondered if he had been born to understand her.

Now his patience seemed annoying. Why couldn't he simply walk away?

She ground her teeth and came to a painful conclusion. It was time to put aside childish games and speak the truth.

She swallowed past a dry throat. "My list is nonsense, as you must know. I wanted to rile you." She waved a hand in the air. "I am finished. Tend to your proper business."

It was his turn to fall silent. "You never used to be this forth-right."

She shrugged. "That was a long time ago."

He looked away. "I deserved your nasty chores."

"You deserved worse. I simply couldn't think of any."

His lips twitched. "I will be here a few days yet. Perhaps something will come to you."

The wall of anger that had risen against him crumbled a little more, as though it could not bear the weight of the honesty that had sprung between them. Or the laughter.

He took another step toward her, this one more hesitant. His voice emerged a whisper. "If there is a man here, a spy from the time of Haman, you might be in danger. That's why I came, Shoshanah. To ensure your safety."

Her eyes widened. For the first time since his arrival, he had called her by her real name. Something intimate tried to wriggle its way into her heart. She resisted it with all her might. What had he said? He wanted her to know that he had not undertaken this violation of her life lightly. In a way, he had come for her sake. He had wanted to keep her safe.

The last of the fight went out of her, and she sank upon her stool. "I am fine."

He shook his head. "I want you to take care. Be watchful. At least until I determine what is going on here."

The look he gave her twisted her insides. There was too much of the past in it. Too much of the man who had once made her feel cherished and safe by his protective overtures.

She had no right to any of it.

He wasn't here as that man. He stood before her as the queen's agent, looking after Esther's concerns. And Sazana was merely one of those concerns. If a bit of his old, protective feelings colored this mission, it hardly signified. She would be a fool to forget that.

17

Jadon

Jealousy is fierce as the grave.
Song of Solomon 8:6

I have searched every potter's station and spoken to every man here. None of them betrayed your trust, not even when I prodded hard." Jadon had waited until nightfall to have this meeting with Shoshanah and Arta. He had barred the doors and closed every shutter as they sat in the lamplight to hear his final report. "Regardless of my best efforts, they remained loyal to you both. A couple of them almost landed a fist in my nose when I pressed them."

He had wanted to plant his own fist in a few ribs when several of the men rose to Shoshanah's defense a little too passionately. The heat of his response had taken him unawares. After all these years, he had assumed she would be married. Have two rosy-cheeked children following in her footsteps. Run a happy household. They would have been a good defense for his heart.

It had come as a shock to find her without a husband. A shock and a relief.

He certainly understood the men's response to her. His own reaction to them, however, left him reeling.

At his report, Arta's rigid back relaxed. "Praise be to God. They are good men. Most of them have worked with me for over a decade. I would hate to think ill of any of them."

Jadon wished he felt the same relief. But he could not shake a niggling doubt in the back of his mind. He sensed that he had missed something. For all his pressing and prodding, some important detail had escaped him.

That nagging suspicion had kept him awake into the small hours for the past two nights. Shoshanah's safety depended on the thoroughness of his investigation. Yet he could think of nothing. No possible loose threads that he had not pulled on already.

"You mean you are finished?" Sazana leaned against the wall, her arms crossed tight in front of her chest. "Now you will leave?"

He could not tell if relief colored her voice or a tinge of disappointment. Perhaps, like his own heart, she felt the confusion of both feelings at once, nipping at her like unruly puppies.

He bowed his head in assent. "Arta, perhaps tomorrow you can make a point of dismissing me. A nice public scene?"

Arta's eyes sparkled. "I will be sure to place my boot on your backside and give a mighty shove in front of everyone."

He had no need of quite so much enthusiasm. Then again, why curtail the man's pleasure? "A sound plan."

"I will make it look real, you need not worry on that score."

He raised a brow. "I applaud your eagerness to serve the queen."

Shoshanah did not crack a smile, barricading herself behind those crossed arms. Even Arta's animated plans did not seem to amuse her. Jadon felt a sudden need to explain his departure.

"The queen still needs me to pursue an important matter. The edict that Haman concocted against the Jews has not gone

135

away. The king could not undo it, for it became law. Instead, thanks to Esther's courage, he has given us the next best thing. But in eight months, an attack will come. And though the Jews can now defend themselves, I must still find a means of weakening that attack as well as strengthening our people's resolve to stand against it."

Arta straightened, his smile vanishing. "What means would accomplish that?"

Jadon shrugged. He did not have Hathach's permission to speak freely of his other mission. "Whatever I can find. Whatever would encourage our people. Some manner of strengthening their hearts as they wait for that fateful day to come upon them. Or else, some way of dissuading the Persians from attacking altogether. Both, if I can."

Arta's usually open expression shuttered. Behind his pursed lips, Jadon could have sworn the man held a secret, all curled up and tight. He leaned forward. "You have something you wish to tell me?"

Arta almost flipped over backward on his stool, he pulled away so fast. "Tell *you*? I think not. What would I have to tell you?"

Shoshanah swiveled her head to study her guardian with a frown. Whatever she was thinking, she kept to herself. Then again, she had a talent for that. He should know.

"Arta, this is the queen's business. I hope you are not hiding anything that concerns Her Majesty."

A thin film of sweat had broken out over Arta's face, shining in the lamplight. "What do I have to do with queens and palaces? Kindly place your nose in someone else's affairs. Mine have nothing to do with you."

Jadon looked down. They were not finished, he and Arta. He would have to get the man alone and work to loosen that tongue. He thought back over their conversation. What had first dragged that shifty expression on to Arta's face?

Ah yes. He had mentioned a means of weakening the attack upon the Jews and strengthening their determination to stand strong.

He rubbed his chin with a tired hand. What did the old potter have up his sleeve? How could *he* help diminish the potency of Haman's edict? Too many sleepless nights were befuddling his mind. He would have to add this question to the ones that already nagged at him.

"Shoshanah." He tried to squelch the heat that rose from his belly and spread through his blood when his gaze landed on her. "Remember what I told you before. You must have a care. You might still be in danger."

Her arms tightened over her chest. "You just told us everyone here is loyal."

"I did. But I may have missed something. I can't shake this feeling that I have overlooked an obscure detail."

To her credit, she did not dismiss his instincts. "We will send for you if something seems out of turn."

He nodded. He would have to be satisfied with that. "You can send for me at home." He handed her the directions he had written out earlier. "I have a small house in Susa now."

Her brow rose as she studied the short scrap of papyrus. He understood her surprise. When they were planning to marry, they had intended to add a couple of rooms to his father's house, a modest villa sitting in the middle of a farm outside Susa. Property within the city proper came at eye-watering prices. The idea of purchasing a home of their own had never even crossed his mind. Those were different days. They had been young and poor. Arta had wanted to sell the house he and Shoshanah occupied to help them, but they had refused. Neither of them wanted to see him displaced.

Now Jadon felt pressed to explain. "My father's house is too far from the palace. This suits me better. It is only a four-room dwelling with barely a courtyard in the back, big enough to have a couple of pots of mint. Those are more often dried-up sticks, since I am rarely home, and when I am, I forget to water them."

What was wrong with him? Why was he running at the mouth with the speed of a cavalry officer charging down the Royal Highway? Shoshanah's brown eyes widened at his list of unnecessary revelations.

He cleared his throat. "If I'm not at home, send a message to Hathach. He'll know how to find me."

One corner of her mouth lifted as though she wanted to suppress a smile. "Arta will manage it."

He felt heat spread under his skin and knew he was blushing like a girl. Turning, he took a step away from her, desperate now to put an end to this painful conversation.

"Wait," she said.

It was humiliating how fast his feet turned back. "Yes?"

She held out a wrapped package. "For the queen. It is the blue ewer she ordered. Would you see that she receives it, please?"

Keeping his mouth shut lest more useless words slipped past his guard, he nodded and took the package, careful to avoid her fingers. He exhaled, reminding himself that he represented Esther, that the queen's business had brought him here and the same business must carry him out that door.

Before walking away one last time, he decided to have another conversation with Arta. He cornered the man near one of the windows. "Arta, if you know anything that can help me, don't keep it to yourself. If you don't trust me, go to Hathach. Or even ask for an audience with the queen. The Jewish people are safer today thanks to Esther's intervention. But they are not entirely out of danger. That edict offers too much temptation. An attack will come, and it could prove a disaster."

Arta played with one of the slats in the window shutter. "I will consider it."

"Then you do have something that can help us."

"Perhaps."

Outside the window, a slight noise brought Jadon's head up. "Stay here," he barked, grabbing a lamp and running out. The spot behind the window looked deserted. He circled around the workshop and found no one. If someone had been listening to their conversation, he could see no sign of them now. Then again, it might have merely been a fox or wild dog, sniffing around for scraps.

He shook his head at Arta. "Nothing out there. But I want you to have a care. If you do know something, it places you in greater danger."

Arta bit his lip and nodded. "I . . . Perhaps I will speak to you tomorrow." He rubbed the back of his neck. "I need time to think on it."

18

Sazana

Night pierces my bones.

Job 30:17 NIV

Arta, what are you hiding from Jadon?" Sazana rounded on her guardian as soon as they arrived home.

He dropped his gaze. "There is something I have never told you."

"What?"

"Your parents entrusted me with something. Perhaps it is finally time to explain it to you."

She sank on her bed. "Tell me."

He bit his lip. "Tomorrow. I will explain all tomorrow."

"Why not now?"

"Mercy, my girl! For years, I have kept this thing to myself. Now I find it clogs in my throat when I try to reveal it. Give

140

me a few hours to compose my thoughts. And to fetch what I need."

"Is it something bad? Did my parents do something wrong?"

"Elihana and Bani? Never!"

The tight band of worry that had squeezed her chest loosened a little. "Then I can wait."

"Bless you, dear girl. Tomorrow. I will reveal all tomorrow." He exhaled. "In a way, it will be a relief."

Sazana rarely had trouble sleeping. Her head met the pillow and the world faded until she opened her eyes in the morning. Even Arta's strange revelation could not keep her up. But some unexpected sound in the deep of the night woke her.

"Arta?" Her throat sounded scratchy from sleep.

"Yes, dear. Sorry to wake you. Go back to sleep."

"It's the middle of the night."

"Clever of you to notice."

She heard a hinge open and close. Odd time for him to go rooting around in his chest. "Don't cause trouble," she croaked and fell asleep to the sound of Arta's chuckle.

The next time she opened her eyes, the bright sunlight filtering through the closed shutters told her she had slept too long. "Arta! Why didn't you wake me?" Her cry met with a silent echo.

She rushed through her ablutions, not surprised to find that Arta had already left for the workshop. He might have allowed her to have a late morning, but once he woke, he hated to loiter.

She jogged to the workshop, annoyed with herself. Her head was foggy from too much sleep. The odd sight of all the workers crowding in the yard brought her to a stop. Why were they lingering outside instead of working at their wheels?

She approached the small crowd. "What goes on here?"

The low hum of conversation hushed abruptly. As if with one accord, every man seemed to find something fascinating in the dusty ground.

She tried to push through them. Arta would know what ailed the potters. But Cambyz snagged her sleeve. "Wait, mistress. Don't go in there."

She stopped. "Why? Why are the men not at their stations?"

Before he could answer, the door opened, and Jadon strode out. What had brought him back to the workshop? She went still as she took in his white face and the grim line of his jaw. "Jadon?"

"Shoshanah! Thank God! I was just coming to look for you. I thought you . . ." He shook his head.

"You thought what? Jadon, what's happened here?"

His voice sounded hoarse. "I am sorry, Shoshanah. It's Arta."

Some thread in her heart snapped. She tried to push past Jadon and rush into the workshop. His arms wrapped around her from behind, unyielding as manacles, holding her back. "Don't go in there."

She struggled against him. His arms tightened, drawing her back into his chest. At the feel of the warmth of him, at once unyielding and welcoming, the fight drained out of her. "Tell me."

"He's gone, Shoshanah. I came very early this morning and found him."

Sazana moaned. It couldn't be. Arta couldn't be dead. "No!" she spoke the single denial as if it could undo the harsh reality of this incomprehensible loss. "No."

"I am so sorry." Jadon's voice had an odd tremble to it.

"You didn't leave him alone in there?" Jewish tradition required that the body never be left unaccompanied.

"Parnaka is with him."

"I have to go inside. I must be at his side."

"Shoshanah, no. He is in no state. You don't want to see him like this."

She frowned. Something was awry. Why did Jadon not want

her to see Arta? Even the men had warned her not to go into the workshop.

She forced the words through dry lips. "See him like what? Did his heart give out?"

Jadon's arms loosened their hold long enough for him to turn her around. The blue irises stood out against the purple half-moons under his eyes. "It wasn't his heart, Shoshanah."

The tears that shock and unbelief had kept at bay were starting to gather, choking her. "What, then?"

"He was murdered."

Sazana felt her body sag. Jadon's hands tightened around her. Gathering her against his chest, he swung her up into his arms. Striding with long steps, he barked an order over his shoulders, telling the men to remain where they were. Near the small stream that passed through the potters' land, he found a wooden bench under the shade of a leafy sycamore and sat down, Sazana still clutched tightly against him.

The fog of shock had lifted enough for her to realize she was sprawled over his lap and chest. She forced her limbs to work, and gathering the tatters of her strength, scrambled to half sit, half collapse next to him.

"What do you mean murdered, Jadon?"

"You don't need that kind of gruesome detail."

She considered the chalky skin pulled tight over his cheekbones, the shimmer of sweat that shone on his brow. Whatever he had seen had shaken him. And this was Jadon. His years as an Immortal made him no stranger to death.

She gulped. "I need to know. Tell me."

"I don't think—"

"Go on, Jadon."

His jaw squared. "It looks like someone snuck up behind him. They used the sharp wire the potters utilize to separate a pot from the wheel."

Sazana covered her mouth with icy fingers. "Lord, help me."

143

He bent his face closer, his eyes warm with concern. "I warned you it would prove too much."

Sazana fought a wave of nausea. "Did he . . . did he suffer?"

Jadon gave a quick shake of his head. "I am certain he did not. It must have happened very quickly. He did not even have a chance to put up a fight."

She nodded. That, at least, was a mercy. A wave of disbelief washed over her. Arta! Her Arta! "Are you sure it's him, Jadon? I mean, how can you tell?"

"There can be no doubt. I am sorry. Beyond the deep cut, he was not disfigured."

She had started to shake and could not stop. Wordlessly, Jadon stripped his cloak and wrapped it around her. "I will take you home."

"No. I have to bide with him."

"Shoshanah—"

"No, Jadon. Don't try to stop me. For twelve years, that man stayed with me, never letting go, no matter how hard or inconvenient. I can remain with him for twelve hours now." She shrank beneath the folds of the cloak. Still warm from Jadon's body, it smelled faintly of the outdoors, of something green and good and living. It smelled of strength and safety. Of everything that she had lost. "Perhaps you can cover him a little. So I can just see his face."

She could sense Jadon battling himself. His chin dipped with reluctance.

Sazana fought through the shock and sorrow that had muddled her thoughts. "How is it that the men obeyed you when you told them not to go inside?"

"They arrived shortly after I did. I had to explain who I really was in order to take charge of the situation." His eyes slid away. "Before we go in, can you answer a question or two?"

"If it helps catch who did this terrible thing."

"It helps."

She gave him a tired nod.

"Can you tell me when Arta came to the workshop? I arrived very early, expecting to find the place empty. Instead, I found Arta's body."

She frowned in thought. "Last night, I heard him. He was noisier than usual. I remember hearing the sound of his chest opening and closing as though he retrieved something. Perhaps he was coming here. That must have been shortly after midnight, since the moon sat high in the southern sky, directly overhead."

"Do you know why he would come here so late?"

Sazana curled into herself. "He did say he wanted to fetch some things."

"What things?"

"He never mentioned."

Jadon withdrew a scrap of papyrus from where he had tucked it into a pocket of his belt. "I found this crumpled in his fist."

Sazana reached for the scrap with hungry hands. No longer than her middle finger with jagged edges, the papyrus was wrinkled but legible. It bore only eight words, with a partial of a ninth.

She squinted, trying to make sense of it, and failed. "Where is the rest?"

"Gone. Presumably his murderer took it. Arta must have closed his fist around the edge just as . . . I don't think his murderer realized that a small corner of the letter remained tucked inside Arta's fist."

Sazana could not swallow the whimper that rose up her throat.

"I am a clod. Forgive me. I shouldn't have revealed so much." Jadon grew even paler.

She buried her hands in the folds of his cloak. "No. I must know." She studied the crumpled papyrus. In the dry Susa weather, the torn edges were already flaking, fluttering to the ground in powdery specks. The words swam before her eyes, not making sense for a moment.

Jadon. You were right. What I have will help Es

"He was writing you a letter when it happened?"

"Seems that way."

"What do you think he wanted to say?"

"Remember yesterday I asked Arta if he had something he wished to tell me? Something to do with the queen's business?"

She gave a reluctant jerk of her chin.

"Before I left, I asked him again, when we were alone. I told him if he had anything that could help the queen, he should not keep it secret. And he said he would consider it. He even said that he would speak to me today after thinking the matter over.

"He begins his letter to me by saying I was right. And now I am asking you to trust me with that information. Tell me, Shoshanah. Do you know what he wished to tell me?"

19

Sazana

The cords of death entangled me;
The torrents of destruction overwhelmed me.
Psalm 18:4 NIV

In a restless rush, Sazana came to her feet. "I do not know anything, Jadon, else I would tell you." She might not trust him as a suitor. But she would entrust her life to him as the queen's agent. More. As a man who would do all in his power to protect her. "When we returned home, I asked him to tell me what he was hiding from you. He told me that there was something he had never told me. A secret. He promised to reveal all today. That is the only thing I know."

"What kind of secret?"

Sazana tightened her fists in frustration. "He never said. And now I will never know."

"Perhaps he feared it might endanger you."

"What could my Arta have known that might prove so vital?

He served as a workshop supervisor. A potter by training. He spent all his time in this place. He did not run around with spies. You are much more likely to know sensitive secrets."

"Hathach told me once that I shouldn't underestimate minor officials, because sometimes they have more useful connections than a dozen senior men. Perhaps the same holds true of Arta. Just because he served in an ordinary capacity does not signify that he could not have possessed important knowledge." He drew close. "In the midst of my conversation with Arta last night, we heard a noise outside the window. I investigated but found no one."

"You think someone overheard you? That's why he was killed?"

"It seems likely."

She took a step backward, tripping on the hem of the too-long cloak. His fingers tangled in the loose fabric and pulled her forward, keeping her from falling. In the process, he drew her closer until they stood chest to chest. Neither moved. Neither breathed. Then, as if guided by some invisible hand, both inhaled, the sound of air dragging into dry throats loud in the still atmosphere.

He put some distance between them with a quick step, the fingers that had tangled the cloak now tangling his hair in a movement she remembered with aching clarity. He always pulled on his hair when he felt distraught.

"Shoshanah, I fear you are not safe. Whoever did this may assume you know what Arta knew."

She sank deeper into the cloak's folds, trying to find a bit of warmth. In spite of the mounting heat of the day, she shivered. Jadon's new revelation did not come as a shock. Some deep pocket of her mind had known it the moment Jadon had revealed Arta had been murdered.

Murdered! Lord above, help her. How could Arta be gone?

"I want to see him."

He did not deny her this time. "Give me a moment." Leaving her with the potters still lingering outside the workshop, he slipped into the building.

The men gathered around her like a city wall, their demeanor exuding silent sympathy. Cambyz fetched a low stool so she could sit. Rashda made a makeshift awning out of wooden posts and a piece of fabric to protect her from the bright sun.

Slowly, the men started to talk to her. They murmured awkward condolences. They asked if she was hungry. They inquired if she wanted a cup of wine, or a kerchief to dry her tears. This last offer she accepted, though the proffered linen, being none too clean, she quietly tucked next to her, unused.

Somehow, having them close helped. A few of them wiped surreptitious fingers under their own eyes, sniffing loudly. They shared in her sorrow, and like a burden too heavy to carry by just one pair of hands, their tears lightened her load.

Finally, Jadon emerged, his face wiped of expression. Sazana came to her feet, determined to see her beloved guardian one final time. To pour the unction of farewell at his feet like a holy offering.

Jadon had closed most of the shutters and lit only one lamp, sinking the workshop into the gray dimness of a predawn sky. She was grateful for this thoughtfulness. She longed to see Arta, but she also wanted to avoid the gruesome details of his final moments.

Her mind was so focused upon Arta that she barely registered the shocking state of the place. Even the shadows could not hide the brutal carelessness with which someone had rummaged through the chambers, leaving a trail of broken and discarded detritus in his path.

All this she ignored as she approached the man who had been her father for twelve years and a friend since birth. Jadon had laid him out on one of the larger tables in the coarse ware section, covering him with a blanket all the way up to the chin. He looked like he was sleeping, eyes closed in repose, one hand resting on his chest over the blanket. She reached for that hand, a part of her in denial of his death clinging to the fantasy that he might sit up any moment and prove them wrong.

No sooner had she held that hand than she dropped it with a dismayed gasp. The unnatural chill in Arta's skin refuted every notion of lingering life. He was gone. Gone to her and the world, leaving behind a mere shell, empty of everything that was Arta. She bent to kiss his forehead, her tears washing his dear face.

The flood of grief choked her. The sight of him, lying dead, resurrected the memory of her parents' deaths. For long, paralyzed moments, she mourned not just Arta, who had been father and mother to her for years, but also her parents, whose loss had shattered her world. Grief became an avalanche that tumbled over her until she suffocated.

Jadon laid a gentle hand on her shoulder. "I sent one of the men to fetch the leader of the synagogue. He will bring women to tend Arta. You probably wish to anoint his body with spice." He hesitated. "Am I presuming too much?"

She swallowed past the block in her throat. "No. You did right."

"I imagine that being a follower of the Lord, he would have wanted a Hebrew burial rather than a Persian service. As a proselyte, that is his right."

She had not thought that far ahead. Of burials and washings and spices. "He would. Thank you."

An hour later, the women arrived, armed with strips of cloth, spices, a linen kerchief for his face, and water for washing. Their wailing loosed Sazana's tears. She bowed her head and prayed Daniel's prophecy over the cold body. "May you awake to everlasting life after your sleep in the dust of the earth, my Arta."

Jadon did not leave her side for an instant as she helped to tend Arta's cold body. His presence brought a strange solace. Like a wall behind her back, she leaned on him when her strength gave way. Jadon had known Arta—loved him, even— all those years ago when Arta had become so much a part of his life. The five years of separation could not wipe away the close attachment of those months. In his own way, Jadon mourned with her.

When they finished preparing the body, they arranged him upon a wooden bier, which would carry him to a new tomb where he would be laid upon a shelf.

Jadon pulled Sazana aside. "I will shut the workshop and set guards over it. We can return to continue our investigation after the burial."

She nodded. "You are coming?"

"I am coming."

A line of men and women, Arta and Sazana's friends and acquaintances from the synagogue, had gathered outside, and they followed behind the bier, the sound of their lamentations loud. Jadon remained nearby, often only one step behind her, like a shadow that never departed.

In the heat of Susa, burials had to take place quickly. The sight of the tomb struck Sazana like a physical blow. Arta's loss still felt like a dream. A nightmare from which she would surely wake.

Now, watching him laid out on the shelf, the smell of myrrh and aloes thick about her, she tripped backward, dizzy at the sight of the white linen shroud that covered his body. A strong arm wrapped about her, holding her up.

Jadon.

She allowed herself the luxury of leaning back against him before stepping away. They watched as four men set an oval stone into a groove at the mouth of the tomb, sealing Arta inside. She stood before that stone, unable to roll it away, unable to undo what awaited within.

"Sazana." Jadon cleared his throat as though struggling with what he had to say. "I must report to Hathach. The queen needs to know what has happened here."

"I understand." She tried to crush the instant sense of loss she felt at his imminent departure.

"I can't leave you here."

"You need not worry on my account." She pointed at the crowd of women that surrounded them. "They will look after me."

"And when they go home? Your house is no safer than the workshop."

Sazana wrapped her arms around her middle. Once again, he was a few steps ahead of her. She did not know any of these women well. Even if they invited her to their own homes, it would be an uncomfortable stay. And perhaps her presence would endanger their households.

As if hearing the echo of her thoughts, he said, "I want you to come with me."

Her eyes rounded. "With *you*?"

He reddened. "To the palace, I mean. Hathach will likely want to question you."

"Question *me*?" She stumbled over the last word and tried to wipe away an image of herself standing before the queen's sharp-eyed steward. The man would expect her to come up with the kind of fast response to which he was no doubt accustomed.

Yet she wanted Jadon to find the monster who had done this thing. She would do what she could to help him, even if it meant facing Hathach and answering his questions.

"You can stay at the palace," Jadon added gently.

"The *palace*?"

If he noticed that she kept repeating him like a sun-addled fool, he chose not to mention it. "It's the safest place we can hide you for now. Hathach will arrange a spot for you."

Sazana bit the corner of her thumb. What option did she have? She could not spend the night with any of the potters she knew best, most of whom were bachelors. The rest, being poor, barely had space for their own families. She would only be an added burden, her Jewish heritage creating too many added complications, especially at mealtimes.

She felt Arta's loss with new force. His passing made her feel young and orphaned again. Arta had become her family after her parents' death. The four walls of their house had provided a shelter. But Arta had been the one who had made it home.

Now it was all gone. Hearth and home and family. In one fell swoop, some cruel, careless hand had robbed her of everything.

20

Jadon

Hide me in the shadow of your wings,
from the wicked who do me violence,
my deadly enemies who surround me.

Psalm 17: 8–9

The afternoon had turned gray with rainless clouds. The grim sky seemed a fitting backdrop to the day's unfolding horror. Jadon's training gave him the discipline to remain focused on the task at hand. But not far beneath that iron control, his soul lay embattled under a gale of emotions. Grief for a man he admired. Concern for Shoshanah. Confusion at this violent turn of events.

He pushed that bubbling cauldron as far down as he could and focused on the problem at hand: how to apprehend the one who had committed this violent crime. And more importantly, how to shield Shoshanah from a similar fate, for there remained little doubt in his mind that she would be next.

They would hunt her down.

He pointed at his stallion. "We'll have to ride to the palace together." Once, neither of them would have given such mundane matters a second thought. Now nothing was mundane between them. In the five years that had passed since she had last ridden a horse with him, their worlds had shifted, making such an intimacy neither casual nor easy.

She toyed with her lip. "We could walk."

"I have tarried too long already, Shoshanah. I cannot lose more time."

His eyes followed the delicate movement in her throat as she swallowed. "Of course." Without another objection, she approached his stallion and waited for his help. He gave her a smile of gratitude as, wordlessly, he cupped his hands for her and bent low.

Unlike his own, her olive-toned skin rarely gave away her secrets by staining with color. It had been the first thing he had noticed about her—that glorious complexion, shining with dewy perspiration while she worked the wheel.

Now, as he felt heat climb up his neck and spill onto his face in a visible show of emotion, he wished he could keep his own secrets as readily. After a short hesitation, she stepped into his looped fingers and allowed him to heave her upon the stallion's back.

Onyx, unused to her scent, pranced restlessly. Jadon placed a hand on Shoshanah's side to keep her steady as he brought the beast under control. With an agile hop, he leapt on the horse and settled himself behind the woman he had hoped never to see again.

His breath hitched as their bodies touched. Every part of him that came into contact with her, from breastbone to hip, burst into life with wild awareness. Her hair smelled of honey and pomegranates and a hint of jasmine, a scent his mind remembered with too much enthusiasm.

Behind her, he screwed his eyes shut and swallowed. The simple ride created a torturous intimacy that he could do without.

Onyx pranced again, objecting to the added weight and the rigid bearing of his new passenger. Jadon exhaled. "You need to relax, Shoshanah. He senses your tension and doesn't like it."

"That makes two of us," she grumbled.

In spite of himself, he smiled. "Three," he said, and set the horse into motion.

Halfway to their destination, she was knocked back against his chest when Onyx leapt to avoid a fallen branch, jostling them. She quit trying to hold herself rigidly away from him after that. With a sigh, she relaxed against him.

It became Jadon's turn to grit his teeth and lean away. The stallion blew an irritated breath through his nostrils and pulled up his head in objection. Jadon grimaced in silent apology. He would have to give Onyx an extra apple to make up for all the discomfort to which he had subjected the poor beast.

At the sight of the palace, Jadon almost thanked God aloud. Dismounting at the door of the stables, he helped Shoshanah down and surrendered the horse to one of the stable hands. Royal guards at the gate subjected them to the usual battery of questions—*Name? Homeland? Profession? Reason for visit?*—before allowing them entry to the palace compound.

Once inside, they found Hathach ensconced behind his simple wooden desk, dictating a letter to a scribe. He looked up and frowned. "Routine or urgent?"

"The latter," Jadon said.

With a nod, Hathach dismissed the scribe, who was well trained enough to close the door on his way out. Hathach crossed his arms and leaned into the edge of the desk. "What is *she* doing here?"

"Arta was murdered, my lord."

Hathach cast a quick glance at Shoshanah and pointed at the chair the scribe had vacated. "Sit." His normally hard-edged voice held a soft timbre as he pronounced the single word. When she obeyed, he poured a cup of watered wine and pushed it in front of her. Politely, she took a small sip before placing the cup on the desk.

"What do you know?" He addressed the question to Jadon, though his gaze returned to settle on Shoshanah.

Jadon explained everything he had discovered, showing the fragment of Arta's letter to Hathach.

"You have two things to uncover, then." Hathach, sharp as ever, had settled on the heart of the matter. "First, who killed the queen's man. And second, what was the secret Arta knew that could help us."

"Right." Jadon placed a hand behind Shoshanah's chair. "She is no longer safe at home. I wondered if you could provide her with lodgings in the meantime."

"Good thought. I will arrange it." He directed his full attention to her. "First, I have a few questions for you."

21

Sazana

They question me on things I know nothing about.
Psalm 35:11 NIV

She had known it would come. Hathach's round of questions, razor-sharp, with the expectation of instant responses. The prospect made her heart crawl up her throat. She gave him a simple nod and hoped he did not think her rude.

"What do you think Arta was hiding?"

She shrugged. It took her a few moments to think through her answer. To her relief, Hathach waited, his body still, giving no sign of frustration. "Jadon asked a similar question, my lord. I have no knowledge of anything, else I would tell you. Only that he said he had a secret."

Hathach's voice softened. "You may have no overt knowledge. But through the years, you might have unknowingly picked up clues. Our job is to help you recognize those clues. What seemed unimportant or irrelevant at the time might give us an insight that helps uncover the truth."

She dipped her chin in understanding.

"Did he ever go to mysterious meetings that he seemed unwilling to discuss?"

"No, lord. He is not a secretive man. I always know—I mean knew—where he went. Or thought I did."

Jadon leaned toward her. "You said Arta may have left in the middle of the night. Was that a habit of his?"

Could Arta have routinely slipped out of the house without her knowing? She bit her lip. "I don't believe so. I would have noticed if he made a practice of leaving the house in the dead of night. Even last night, it struck me as odd." She shook her head. "Arta had a forthright nature. I struggle to believe he led a secret life behind my back."

"Nevertheless, can you make a list of his friends and acquaintances? People he spent time with, even those he may have seen rarely?"

"Outside the workshop, it won't be a long list. We tended to keep to ourselves, especially after . . ." She left the sentence unfinished.

"I see." Jadon's stance had grown wooden.

Hathach looked from him to Sazana. "See what?"

A tide of red spread over Jadon's face. "Shoshanah and I were once betrothed. I believe she means that after the betrothal broke off, she and Arta grew less social."

Hathach tapped a manicured finger against his desk. "The betrothal broke off? Had a will of its own, did it? I have never known betrothals to do that on their own."

On a different day, she might have smiled. The queen's steward wielded sarcasm like a familiar weapon. Normally, the trait would have set her teeth on edge. But given the way he pointed it at Jadon, she found herself appreciating his talent. "Nor I," she said and turned to Jadon, enjoying the squirming expression on his handsome face.

"It did not break off on its own. I broke it off," he admitted through stiff lips.

"Thank you for clarifying," Hathach said mildly. "You did not think to inform me of that detail earlier?"

Jadon's jaw had turned into a knot. "I told you I knew her."

"Not quite the same." Hathach waved a hand. "Carry on."

Jadon pulled an agitated hand through his dark hair. She could tell he was struggling to regain focus. "Did . . . did Arta ever give you the impression that there was something in particular he wanted to keep hidden from you? Some subject he avoided, perhaps?"

They seemed to ask the same questions over and over again. The way he had phrased this question, however, made her hesitate. She *had* felt Arta wanted to keep something from her. "Nothing that could have any bearing on the situation at hand."

"Meaning?"

"Meaning he knew something personal to our family that he did not wish to tell me. It had no relevance to this situation, or to Haman's edict."

Hathach's gaze became a dagger, boring into her. "Let us be the judge of that."

"It's an old matter."

Jadon captured her gaze. "Old might be what we need."

She twisted her hands together. "My grandfather owned a pottery workshop in Babylon. When he died, my mother took over the running of it. One morning, my parents arrived at work to discover we had been burgled. The thieves had turned everything upside down and left behind a terrible mess. Overnight, my parents decided to sell the workshop and move to Susa. They said they no longer felt safe there."

She frowned. "I never understood the haste with which they did everything. The timing for such a sale proved unfavorable.

Instead of waiting to earn a better price, they gave up our family home and my mother's inheritance for a pittance and headed here."

"Arta lived with you at this time?"

"He did. He worked in the workshop. To my parents, he had become a brother. On account of him, they chose to come to Susa. Arta had been born here."

"Your parents died on the way to Susa?"

She nodded. "A cart ran them over. The innkeeper said the cart driver must have had too much beer in his belly to see straight."

"And you never discovered the identity of the driver?"

"We could not. He disappeared after the accident without stopping to give account of himself."

"Your parents lived long enough to say a few words to you before passing, did they not? I remember you mentioned that once."

She winced.

"I beg your pardon, Shoshanah, for making you relive that day." He sounded painfully sincere, as though he regretted the necessity of putting her through such an ordeal.

"They told me they loved me. Then they placed me in Arta's charge."

"What exactly did your parents tell Arta, do you recall?"

"My mother told him to raise me well. To cherish me. It was a promise Arta never broke." Her vision shimmered, obscuring Jadon's face.

"I can attest to that. It was clear that he doted on you."

"My father . . . he told Arta that I was his girl now. Then he gave him some practical instructions about money."

"Can you remember what?"

"Something about using the money from the sale of the workshop to buy a house. That's how we purchased our home here in Susa. Even when Haman turned us practically into slaves, we were able to hold on to our home, since it belonged to us." She leaned forward. "My father did say one thing at the end that I have always remembered. *'Look after them. Keep them secure with your life,'* he told Arta. I suppose he worried for my safety to the very end."

Jadon tilted his head. "Your father said keep *them* safe? Not *her*? *Them*?"

She grew still. The words had been so much a part of that day, a part of farewells and loss and endings that she had never parsed them. The irregularity of her father's phrasing had never struck her as odd. He had been in pain. He had been dying. No one could expect grammatical perfection.

And yet, now that she thought about it, that was precisely the kind of thing one *could* expect from her father. He had been born to a family of scribes, four generations of them ending with him. A man who chose his words with care, who spoke and wrote with the inherent precision that had been bred into his very blood.

"He said *them*. Not *her*," she confirmed.

"Was someone else traveling with you? A servant, perhaps? A retainer?"

"I never saw anyone else except the four of us."

Jadon stared into the distance, his thick brows knotted. This new revelation had added to the mystery rather than help to solve it. "Well, let us return to your original statement, then." His attention resettled on her face. "You said that you felt Arta had been hiding something from you."

"It had to do with the sale of my parents' workshop. Every time I complained about the unreasonable haste of it, Arta got an odd look on his face. Like he didn't want me to know the whole truth.

"That robbery was not the only reason my parents chose to sell their workshop in such a hurry, I am convinced of it. But whatever the true purpose, I cannot see how it is related to Arta's death. Or to the attack the Jews must face in eight months."

Hathach took a sip from the chalice at his elbow. "It seems we have discovered all we can, for now. Please accept my condolences for your loss, Sazana. I will ask the queen's junior handmaiden to find you a chamber and settle you in."

Sazana rose, relieved to have an end to the interview. She pushed her fingers under her sleeves and hiked them to her elbows.

Hathach lifted his head as though surprised to find her still standing in his chamber. "You have a question?"

Jadon dipped his chin at her encouragingly. Such a small gesture, and yet she felt an instant release of the tension that had sat on her chest with the weight of a brick wall. "I . . . I need to gather a few things from home if I am to stay at the palace."

Some silent communication seemed to pass between Jadon and the queen's steward. After a brief nod from Hathach, Jadon said, "I should have thought of that. I will accompany you to your house."

"Oh, you need not—"

"It is done, Shoshanah."

22

Sazana

The murderer rises in the early dawn
    to kill the poor and needy;
    at night he is a thief.

Job 24:14 NLT

She longed to enter the sanctuary of her home. To be surrounded by the familiarity of those walls. It had been the longest day of her life.

But it seemed their enemy had one more blow in store for her.

As the door swung open, Sazana gasped, her mind refusing to make sense of the jolting sight that greeted her. Furniture upside down, bedding tossed about, pieces of broken pottery strewn on the floor, carpets shoved to corners. The gasp turned into a strangled sound of disbelief when she spotted the ruined fragments of the lamps her mother had made.

How much more would they take from her?

As she moved to step farther into the house, a hand wrapped

around her arm, holding her back. "Wait here." With the economical motions of a trained soldier, Jadon swept through the house, inspecting every nook lest the perpetrator was still hiding within.

His mouth had turned into a white, flat line by the time he returned to her side. "I am sorry. They have left behind a sorry mess in every room."

Sazana gritted her teeth. Grief rolled into a tide of anger. "Did they find what they wanted?"

"No way to know. They certainly looked hard enough."

At a knock on the door, they turned in unison to find Sazana's neighbor standing there. Old Alogune and her two sons lived in the house next door, and although the buildings shared no walls, they stood close enough to see into each other's yards.

"Sazana! I am so sorry. I heard about Arta. What a terrible loss. May the Light bless him."

"Thank you."

The old woman indicated the disarray in the room. "And now this. Are you all right?"

Sazana noticed her neighbor did not seem surprised at the sight of the chaos that surrounded them.

Jadon must have noticed the same thing. "Did you perchance hear anything?"

"I did, indeed." She shook her head. "He was not very quiet while he made this mess. What son of a dog would do such a terrible thing? The thieves today have no shame. They destroy what they don't take." She made a clucking noise with her tongue.

Jadon stepped closer. "Did you see anything that might help us apprehend him?"

"Well, I don't know if it will help you catch the rat. But I saw the man."

Sazana whipped her head up. "You saw him?"

The old woman pulled her chin down in an emphatic gesture. "I thought I heard furniture breaking and came to your door, concerned. I could hear someone moving inside. At my knock, they went still. I knocked again and opened the door, which was not barred. That's when a man came barreling toward me.

"He had no good intention, I can tell you. If not for my son, who had followed after me, I am certain he would have done me harm. But after he took one look at my Zissawis, he thought better of his plan and went running off. Zissawis is built like a tree trunk, near as tall as yourself." She motioned to Jadon.

Jadon said, "Can you or your son describe what he looked like?"

"No, I am sorry to say. He had a wool hat pulled low over his forehead. Who wears a wool hat in the middle of summer, I ask you? Whatever was left of his face, he had covered up with a kerchief."

Sazana pursed her lips in frustration. "When did all this happen?"

"This morning, not long after you left. Before I heard about poor Arta."

Jadon hissed an outraged breath. "If you had still been here, Shoshanah, who knows what he might have done."

Sazana felt too weary to think of it. "Thank you, Mistress Alogune. I am grateful you are not hurt. And thank Zissawis for me."

"That answers one question, at least," Jadon said as he barred the door behind Alogune.

"What question?"

"Alogune interrupted the intruder before he finished searching the place. Which means he did not find whatever he came looking for."

Sazana cast a glance at the destruction left behind in every visible corner. "He searched hard enough. I can't imagine what he missed."

"We will figure it out. You are too exhausted now. What you

need is rest. While you grab a few necessities, I will ask this Zissawis to keep watch over the house until I send a detail of guards from the palace. Tomorrow, we will return to set things right. And to have a search of our own."

"But, Jadon, I am unclean. I touched Arta. I will render everything I touch here unclean. I need to wait seven days before I can complete the ritual cleansing."

Jadon waited a beat. "I understand your concern. I touched his body myself. But, Shoshanah, this is not a matter that can wait for seven days. Even if it means you will have to cleanse the whole house afterward. It is crucial that we find what Arta was hiding. It may be the key to solving his murder. Besides, it could prove helpful to our people in their plight."

The moon sat high in the dome of the sky by the time they arrived at the palace. Jadon led her to the entrance of a long building, where a woman with a handsome but oddly severe face and perfect hair waited for Sazana. "I am the queen's junior handmaiden. Lord Hathach has asked that I give you a private chamber. No small task, with the palace bursting at the seams. This way." She gave Jadon an unflinching look. "Not you."

He bowed. "I will contact you in the morning, Shoshanah."

Sazana had no time to respond. The junior handmaiden headed down a limestone passageway, her heels clicking rapidly as Sazana tried her best to keep up. After several sharp twists, she stopped before a narrow opening to swish back a curtain, revealing a square chamber, more closet than room.

"It's the best I could do."

"I thank you, lady. I will be well content here."

The woman's shoulders came down a notch. "I have sent for fresh bedding along with a jug and basin for washing. Do you need anything else?"

"I have all I need. My thanks."

The junior handmaiden turned one revolution in the room

as though to ensure everything satisfied her high standard. "The queen has assigned a palace guard to your door. I will remain until he arrives."

By the time the bedding came, Sazana would have been content to sleep on the bare floor. She fell asleep before everyone had left her closet of a room, drawing the curtain behind them.

Late the next morning, she awoke to find Jadon outside her chamber. "Pardon! I did not realize you were waiting."

He straightened. "I have arrived too early, I think."

She yawned. "Given the hustle and bustle in these corridors, I believe it's more likely that I have emerged too late."

"I hope you were able to sleep well."

"Not many things disturb my slumber."

"So Arta told me."

It surprised her that he would hold on to such a minor detail after so many years. The realization twisted in her belly, a hunger pang yearning for more. More intimacies he had held on to.

"What do you have planned for today?" she hurried to ask, desperate to distract her own wandering thoughts.

"I want to head to your house first. It will take a few days to comb through everything." He gave her a sidelong glance. "Shall we stop at the kitchens first so you can fetch some food?"

"I am fasting for seven days. Eating the bread of mourners." She lifted the narrow bag she carried in her fist. "The women brought me some at the conclusion of the burial."

"They'll probably bring more to your house. It is one comfort they can offer, ensuring you do not have to worry about cooking as you grieve. I remember we received bushels of the stuff when my mother passed away."

She swallowed past a dry throat. "I heard of her death. May you be consoled from heaven."

His face shuttered. "She grew very ill in the end."

He remained quiet as he guided them to the stables, where a

narrow cart hitched to a mule already awaited them. "I thought this would prove more comfortable."

She exhaled in relief. She did not think she could cope with another ride on his horse, Jadon ensconced behind her like a couch cushion. *No. Nothing like a couch cushion.* Couch cushions were comfortable. They were cozy. They did not line one's back like a wall of rock, hot with memories of a past that could never be. "Cart is good." She almost bit her tongue in her hurry to approve of his choice.

When they were sitting side by side on the narrow seat, she asked, "Can we stop at the workshop first? I want to ensure the potters are well."

"The queen has decided to close the workshop for seven days in Arta's honor."

"The poor potters. Most cannot afford to go without work that long."

"Esther thought of that. She will pay them their wage. And before they return, she intends to send a priest to ritually cleanse the place."

Sazana wondered if henceforth every time she entered the workshop, instead of sensing the magic of the wheel and the cool comfort of the clay, she would only see Arta, lying on the table, eyes closed, his skin stone-cold and lifeless.

When they arrived at her house, Jadon took a moment to speak to the guards at the door. "They report a quiet evening. No doubt their very presence warned off any intruders." He opened the door for her.

A good night's sleep had not made the state of her home appear less shocking. She lifted a determined chin and pointed to the living room. "Let's start there. It seems less tossed about. He can't have looked as hard in there."

"A sound plan."

Sazana stopped. "Wait. What are we looking for?"

Jadon took in the jumbled chest, its innards spilled all over the ground, the shattered lamps, the smashed boxes that held Arta's scrolls. "Something small enough to fit into these."

For the next six hours, they worked together, piling broken furniture on one side, folding linens, sweeping aside feathers from ruined pillows, making heaps of the shattered pieces of pottery. The house started to appear less mangled but also sadder, for as they cleaned and swept, the empty places that once held treasures became more evident. But they saw nothing that pointed to any secrets.

After stopping to eat a few pieces of the mourners' bread, softening hard chunks by dipping them into water, they switched their search to her chamber. Righting the overturned chest, they picked up its contents that had been strewn over the floor, until they came upon her mother's pottery tools.

"I remember these," Jadon said, collecting each discarded item with a gentleness that pressed against her chest like a regretful hand. "They seem intact. Somehow they escaped the man's rough treatment."

"Thank the Lord." One by one, she tucked them into their sack.

He retrieved something that had rolled under a cushion. "What did she use this for?"

"That was my father's. One of the reeds he had cut from the shores of the Euphrates River. He intended to make a stylus with it."

"That's right! I have been so focused on the pottery workshop, I forgot that your father was a scribe."

She gave a sad smile. "Fourth generation. It stopped with me. I have no talent for all that. Languages and writing and sums." She made a face.

"You have plenty of talent elsewhere. The world is awash with scribes. But it has few true artists."

His praise wormed its way into some tender place. Not that she lacked admiration. Her pottery had already received much acclaim for someone so young. But coming from Jadon, the

170

words landed in a different spot, as though he alone had access to a deep corner of her soul.

She found a small smile lifting the edges of her mouth as together, they unearthed her father's tools, which had rolled to every corner of the chamber. The collection in her hand made her frown. "I'm still missing a stylus. His favorite."

"Perhaps it's under your blanket. We haven't shaken that out yet."

There was something oddly intimate about going through her bedding with Jadon. It seemed silly to feel self-conscious as together they took hold of her blanket. But he must have felt it too, for his neck turned pink as he held two corners of the wool and gently shook it.

A few things came clattering out of the folds, including the bone-handled stylus for which she had been looking. She swooped down to pick it up, so focused on her father's stylus that she missed the odd expression on Jadon's face.

He untangled an object from the folds of wool, and it finally dawned on her that he seemed utterly absorbed by whatever lay in his palm.

Her breath hitched when she saw it. Slowly, he looked up. His eyes had turned dark, the sea at night rather than a summer sky. Their gazes locked and held. "My rose," he said. "You saved the petals."

She swallowed, searching for the right words as he waited, not moving a single muscle. "I could not part with them." The truth did not leave much room for pride.

He exhaled, a short puff that came out of parted lips as though he had been punched. "I am glad for it."

She squared her shoulders. "It means nothing."

"Don't ruin it."

"I think you did that all by yourself."

He turned away, one hand tangled in his dark hair. "True."

She almost asked him why. Demanded an explanation. But

she was too tired for this. Too worn out by shock and loss and outrage to rummage through the past with him. It was hard enough to rummage through her upside-down home.

Without a word, she took the kerchief of dried petals from his nerveless fingers, folded it neatly, and settled down to repack her chest, which had somehow survived the intruder's violence.

"Wait." Jadon knelt next to her by the chest.

"Jadon, this is not the time to air out everything that happened between us."

"No. I mean before you pack the chest." He pointed at the bottom of it. "It is not as deep as I would have thought. Look at the base." Together, they examined the outer lines of wood and the short, rounded legs supporting a low belly that almost touched the ground. The discrepancy was minor, so subtle that she had missed it, though it had sat in front of her all these years.

"You are right. I never noticed it before, but the inside is not as deep as the outer shell." Something about that odd discrepancy seemed to finger a distant memory. What was niggling at her?

She hit her forehead with the base of her palm. "How could I have forgotten?"

"What is it?"

"After Haman told us we had to work for him without pay, one night, Arta told me that if anything should ever happen to him, he had left some things for me in my chest. I put the words out of my mind. I didn't want to think of Arta being gone. Besides, I rummage through that thing practically every day and never saw a package from Arta. I thought he must have forgotten about it." She pointed at the chest. "But maybe he didn't. Maybe he put something here, only not where it could be easily found." She leaned close to the ground to eye the bottom of the chest. "It can't be very thick, whatever it is."

Jadon examined the planks, careful fingers pressing and pulling. Nothing budged.

"You aren't going to break it, are you?" she asked anxiously.

"You have enough broken furniture. I will not destroy more."

They laid the chest on one side, then another. To their frustration, no amount of pulling and pushing on the various pieces and slats of wood revealed a secret compartment.

23

Jadon

I will give you the treasures of darkness
and the hoards in secret places . . .
Isaiah 45:3

Jadon knelt by the chest, which now lay on its side, and
studied it from every angle. The rectangular box sat on four
short, rounded feet. Closer examination revealed a thin
layer of decorative bone at the very top of each foot. This distinction, nowhere else evident in the chest, roused his curiosity.

He had already tried pressing, pulling, and twisting the
rounded feet, to no avail. How else could he manipulate them?
He pressed the base of his palm against the side of one of them
and tried to slide it one way, then another. It did not budge.

Shoshanah repeated his movements with the opposite ap-
pendage. Nothing moved. Jadon tried the third foot, sliding away
from himself, not surprised that the spherical wood did not shift.
He slid it toward himself this time, expecting the same result.

With an imperceptible squeak, the foot glided forward and, without warning, sprang open with a snap. Jadon startled backward and landed on his posterior with a jarring thump.

For the first time in days, Shoshanah smiled. Looking inside the open sphere, she shook her head. "It's empty."

Jadon held his lamp over the small depression, a compartment the size of a fist, stained a dark brown. Not even a speck of dust remained to hint at what the tiny chamber might have once contained. He turned his attention to the fourth rounded foot. But like the first two, it proved immovable.

Jadon frowned. The secret compartment in the foot still did not explain the thick lining at the bottom of the chest. Following a hunch, he stuck his finger inside the hole and felt around. On the third try, he found what he wanted: a tiny hook that barely protruded from the wood. Painted the same dark hue as the inner chamber, the hook blended so well with its environment that they had missed it.

"Clever."

Shoshanah leaned over. "What is it?"

"There is a hook in here." He gestured at it. "I can't tug it with my fat fingers. See if you can manage. It is to the right, beneath that small nick."

She pressed her index finger inside and soon found the catch he had described. A loud snap sounded from the bottom of the chest. Together, they scrambled to look inside and sat immobile for a moment, staring at the long slat of wood that had popped open, revealing a shallow container about the length of his forearm, and the depth of half his small finger.

Inside, they found a tight scroll of papyrus, tied around the middle with a strip of leather. Jadon reached within and pulled out the treasure they had unearthed.

The agent of the queen wanted nothing more than to rip the leather and pore over the contents. The other part of him, the one still bound to Shoshanah in spite of the shreds of their relationship, handed the bundle over to her, unexamined.

These were not mere documents to her. They likely held deep ties to her family.

With a grateful glance, she accepted his offering. Whoever had placed the scrolls within the hidden compartment of the chest had taken the trouble to arrange them in chronological order. They found the oldest lying on top, a yellowed rectangle of papyrus with fragile edges that turned to dust as it unfurled. Shoshanah held the scroll angled so that Jadon could read the contents at the same time. From the first line, he deduced that this was a personal letter, written in simple Aramaic, but with a scribe's pristine script.

My son, Libni, it began. On the bottom, the signature read, *Your loving father, Mispar*.

Jadon refolded his legs so that he could draw closer. "Do you know who they are, this Libni and Mispar?"

Shoshanah drew a finger down the side of the yellowed papyrus. He noted the slight tremble in the movement. "Libni was my father's father, and Mispar his father before him. They both worked at the palace in Babylon as scribes."

Jadon nodded his thanks before returning his attention to the letter, starting again from the beginning.

My son, Libni,

In all my years working at the palace, none matched the day the great Cyrus freed Babylon's captives. In one fell swoop, by the command of his lips and the seal of his office, he changed the course of our people's history.

At the time, I worked under the senior scribe as one of several men chosen to make a clay copy of the king's pronouncement. This you knew already.

What I have not told you is that I bent the law that day by making an additional copy, this one for our family.

I made it so that in the passing years, we should never forget God's faithfulness. Cyrus's edict is nothing short of the fulfillment of the promise God made to our captive people over generations.

Protect this cylinder, my son. Use it to teach your children and their children that the Lord our God is constant and worthy of trust. Do not allow it out of your keeping, for herein, I hand you a lasting treasure that points to God's perfect plans.

Your loving father,
Mispar

Jadon inhaled sharply, his mind whirling. He made a quick, silent calculation. Cyrus had set the captives of Babylon free sixty-four years earlier. Mispar would indeed have worked in the palace in that time frame, which supported the claim of this letter. His heart picked up its beat.

Shoshanah gave him an inquiring look. "What?"

He pointed at the yellowed piece of papyrus. "I believe what the queen has assigned me to find might be sitting under our very noses. I have looked for this very cylinder for weeks, Shoshanah, and to no avail.

"Until now, I've been blindly searching after a rumor. A whisper that a copy of Cyrus's famous cylinder had been hidden somewhere right here in Susa. By a scribe, perhaps. This is the first real hint that such a copy might truly exist."

And all this time, the secret to its location had been in Shoshanah's possession and she had not known it.

"Why does Esther want it?"

Given the revelation in Mispar's letter, Jadon decided it time to reveal the nature of his assignment from the queen. "Do you know the edict your great-grandfather is referring to in his letter?"

"The famous one, I suppose. The one that ended the captivity of the Judeans in Babylon."

"The famous one, yes. Can you imagine the power of Cyrus's words for the Persians in our lifetime? How this old edict might shed light upon the new one fashioned by Haman? It would dissuade many from attacking our people even though it is lawful for them to do so in a matter of months. Their most admired king moved his might to show the Jews clemency several generations ago."

Shoshanah's mouth gaped. "They would be inspired to do the same, you mean."

"That is the queen's thinking. And the cylinder will strengthen the heart of our own people. It will inspire them to stand and persevere. As your great-grandfather so wisely pointed out, Cyrus's edict is a reminder that the God who fulfilled his will through a Gentile king still fights on our behalf. Still opens impossible doors."

She raised one eyebrow. "I understand your reasoning. Only, why are you searching for such a famous artifact? Surely you will find copies in the palace records."

"We should. But we have failed to locate even a single copy. Not in Susa. The queen has sent messengers to search for them in the other capital cities. In the meantime, I have been chasing a rumor that a scribe had a hidden copy in Susa." He pointed at her letter. "And here we have proof."

She dropped her head in thought. "You think one of these letters might lead us to the copy my great-grandfather made?"

"That is my hope."

Without comment, she set Mispar's letter to one side, careful not to damage the dry papyrus. The second letter was from someone named Eliezer, a senior scribe at the palace in Babylon. This one had been addressed to Bani, a name Jadon recognized immediately as belonging to Shoshanah's father.

Bani, son of Libni, royal scribe,

Your father and I worked alongside each other for many years before his death. May his memory be a blessing.

I write to tell you of a strange discovery I have made. Recently, for personal reasons, I tried to find the famous Cyrus cylinder in the royal archives. I refer to the edict so key to our people's fortunes.

Bani, I could not find it! Not one copy could I lay my hands on. Not in Akkadian or Elamite or Persian. Every copy of that historical document has vanished from Babylon's archives!

When we worked alongside each other, your father once confessed to me that his own father had secretly made a perfect copy of the original clay cylinder. I assume that since his passing, you have become the keeper of this document.

For this reason, I write you not as a senior scribe but as a fellow son of Abraham. I charge you to keep safe Cyrus's words! Keep them well hidden. Someone has either bribed or robbed their way into the royal archives in order to remove all evidence of this precious chronicle. For what purpose, I cannot say. But a day may come when our people will once again have need of Cyrus's words.

Be mindful, Bani. You are guardian to more than a historic moment. You have been entrusted with a divine promise, fulfilled.

If the one behind the disappearance of the Cyrus cylinders at the palace becomes aware of your copy, he will come after it. Be certain to keep it well protected.

Eliezer, Senior Scribe

Jadon looked for a reference to the date and found none. One thing was for certain. It had been written when Shoshanah's father was alive. At least twelve years earlier.

Jadon's brow knotted. "That makes no sense," he whispered under his breath.

"What?"

He waved at the papyrus. "The copies of the Cyrus edict had already started to vanish while your father still lived. That was twelve years ago."

"You think it strange that no one noticed?"

"That part is plausible enough. Thousands of ancient documents lie neglected in the various palaces of the empire, never consulted. Why would anyone notice the disappearance of a sixty-four-year-old cylinder? If no one has need of it, no one goes looking for it. Even Eliezer mentions that he sought it for personal reasons."

"Then what is it that you find strange?"

"All this time, I assumed the disappearance of the cylinder must be connected to Haman's edict. That Haman himself must have arranged for the theft of the copies. I believed he had reached the same conclusion as the queen: Cyrus's words had the power to weaken his ploy, and he wished to eliminate that vulnerability in his plan. But he only set his plan in motion four months ago."

Shoshanah's eyes widened. "That *is* odd! Haman was never fond of the Jews. But a madness overcame him when a Jewish official named Mordecai refused to prostrate himself before him."

"I know the man. I can well imagine the stubborn tilt of his jaw as he stood up to Haman."

"Why would one man's lack of subservience rile Haman to such a degree?"

"Haman grew incensed by Mordecai's refusal to honor him *after* the king conferred a senior rank upon him. Proud of his new position, he could barely believe that some minor official refused to acknowledge his freshly minted superiority."

Shoshanah tapped her lip with a restless finger. "I remember for weeks afterward, Haman breathed fire down our necks at the workshop. He was in a foul temper. He must have started to draft his edict for the destruction of the Hebrews in those days."

"Precisely. His elevation gave him the royal access and influence he needed to set such a plan into motion. Which brings me back to my point. Why, then, would he have wished to steal all copies of Cyrus's declaration twelve years ago?"

Jadon pointed at the letter. "All I know for certain is that your father owned a copy of the very document we desperately need now."

She swallowed hard. He could tell she was battling tears. Everything in him wanted to pull her against him, to hold her until her tears passed. But she saw him as the enemy. The one who had betrayed her.

And to him, she remained forever out of reach. His mother had made any relationship between them impossible. His mother and grandmother between them. He leaned away, tucking his fingers under his arms.

24

Sazana

The LORD himself goes before you and will be with
you; he will never leave you nor forsake you. Do
not be afraid; do not be discouraged.

Deuteronomy 31:8 NIV

Sazana fought the tears that threatened to choke her. "My
father never told me any of this, Jadon."

He gave her a sympathetic look. "Understandable. He
would have considered you too young. You were only eleven
when he died. I doubt you could have understood the importance of it."

She took a sharp breath. "This letter sheds light on their
sudden departure from Babylon. They must have had reason
to believe that the robbery in my mother's workshop did not
take place at the hands of a simple thief. Someone had come
after the cylinder."

"Yet he could not have found it." Jadon looked at her keenly.

"Else your parents would not have bothered to head for Susa. They still had the cylinder when they left Babylon. That's what your father meant when he told Arta to look after *them*. He meant you—and the cylinder."

Her mouth wobbled. "They gave up so much to keep Cyrus's cylinder safe. Their home. Their friends. Their community. My mother's inheritance. All for a proclamation from an old king."

Jadon reached for her hand. She allowed herself this one short touch. This one comfort. For the length of a breath, she closed her eyes and floated in the security of that feathery connection before he removed it.

"Not only the king's words, Shoshanah. *God's* words echoing through them. Isaiah's prophecy fulfilled. Jeremiah's prophecy proven. History bowing before God. Your parents understood that a single promise fulfilled by God carried more worth than fortunes."

She jerked her chin in acquiescence. "My father became the keeper of Cyrus's cylinder. He saw it as a sacred trust."

"And the day he died, Arta took over as guardian of the cylinder. But I think your father must have intended him to be a temporary keeper until you were of an age to take on the responsibility. Your great-grandfather's letter makes this a familial obligation. Why did Arta never tell you about it? You are a grown woman now, and more than capable of understanding its significance."

She drew her knees to her chest as she considered his question. "After my parents' deaths, Arta wanted to protect me from every hurt. I learned to do the same for him. Having both waded through rivers of loss in so short a time, we tended to shield each other from the shadow of every pain. Perhaps overly so. I suppose Arta did not want to burden me. Revealing the cylinder's existence and its significance would have meant passing a weighty responsibility to me. His silence was just another way of shielding me as he had done for twelve years."

"Yet in the end, keeping you in the dark may have placed you in greater danger." Jadon pointed at the remaining scroll. "Perhaps he will finally reveal the secrets we must uncover."

Sazana unfurled the letter. Her sight grew blurred at the first glimpse of Arta's familiar hand. His absence made the world seem less, somehow. Emptied of something truly good.

Outwardly, her body remained as still as a calmed sea. But within, something staggered under the load of the knowledge that she would never see him again, never hear his fingers snapping as he danced his jolly steps in a moment of happiness.

How often would she find herself helplessly tumbling into these dark caverns of grief that came at her like a fanged monster and swallowed her whole?

She let the grief roll over her, roll through her, trying to ride it out like a wild wave. She was an old hand at loss. An experienced sojourner through its endless night sky. In a moment, the shock of it passed, leaving behind a dull ache. Once again, her eyes were able to focus. To read.

The letter began without a proper greeting:

> *Let me begin by congratulating you for discovering this hidden compartment. I told you I had left you something in your chest. I always knew you would get to it one day. It might have been sooner if you showed more interest in spring cleaning once in a while and took everything out of your chest for a proper dusting.*

She laughed, her emotions springing between humor and grief. Even from the grave Arta could cheer her. Her eyes returned to his words.

> *If I am alive, you have no doubt already run me to ground to demand an explanation. But if I am gone, then there is much I need to share with you.*

Shoshanah, remember that I love you as my own. My own sweet girl. I have been proud of you every day of your life. Other fathers are given their children. But I chose you. Remember that. You are my greatest treasure.

A tear slipped down Sazana's cheek and dripped down her chin. She scraped it away with an impatient hand and continued to read.

If you have not done so, read the other letters before returning to mine. They will help you understand. Suffice it to say that next to you, your parents had one other treasure. This, too, they gave to my keeping.

I never told you. Why add another burden upon your shoulders? Since some evil force seemed intent on taking it, I did not want you to live a life of fear, always looking over your shoulder. I thought to carry that burden for the rest of my days. But if I am gone, the responsibility has passed on to you.

I cannot write openly. If this letter should fall into the wrong hands, you will lose your inheritance. Oh, my dear child, I only hope that God will send you his own helpers in my absence.

No doubt, having read this far, you are impatient for me to reveal the location of this treasure. You will find it in another place you once held dear. That is all I can say.

The Lord bless you and keep you, Shoshanah. May he guide your steps and go before you.

> *Your loving guardian,*
> *Arta*

A few sentences were added at the bottom of this final greeting. The ink, darker than that used in the rest of the letter, suggested that these were a later addition to Arta's letter.

Since our lives have changed at the hand of the queen, I will add one final word, for with the new edict, a new danger stalks us. My dear girl, life moves forward though it stands still. I pray one day soon you will find the way to happiness and discover that new doors are opened with old keys. I am only sorry I will not be there to rejoice with you.

Sazana pressed the letter to her heart, for the moment more interested in the hand that had penned it, in the love that poured through every phrase, than in the mystery it had not revealed. She grew aware of Jadon fidgeting next to her.

He had read the words alongside her, but he must be bursting with questions.

She had to appreciate his silence, the patience he offered in order to give her time to settle her emotions. "You want to know where to find the cylinder?"

He leaned close. "He speaks in riddles I cannot comprehend. Do you know what he means?"

"I do not, Jadon. I am sorry."

He sighed. "That would have been too easy, I suppose." He tapped the last paragraph in the letter. "He added this recently. After the queen took over the workshop. Do you know what he means? He mentions a key. Has he given us another clue?"

A muscle spasmed in the corner of her jaw. She was very much afraid that she did know what Arta meant. And it had little to do with Cyrus and his cylinder. This was Arta's eversentimental heart at work.

Life moves forward though it stands still. He had captured, with painful precision, the rhythm of her life for the past five years. Time marched on, moved ahead, while she stood still, changing nothing, frozen in place.

Arta, having sensed her response to Jadon, had concluded that there was hope for them yet. *New doors are opened with old keys.* Jadon was the old key, he meant, who could still open a new door to happiness.

Oh, Arta! She almost groaned aloud. Five years later, he had still not accepted the hopelessness of this particular cause.

Sazana exhaled, grateful that Jadon had missed the embarrassing allusion. "It is a personal word for me. You won't find any reference to the king's edict in that."

It was her turn to grow fidgety as Jadon read through the paragraph once more. "Are you certain?"

"Quite."

"No matter. We will unearth that clue. Together, we will work out the puzzle Arta has set for us."

Sazana's gaze took in the utter destruction of her home, the broken pieces, the irreplaceable bits that held a thousand memories. A wave of exhaustion washed over her. She treasured so many things here. Which one did Arta mean?

With a supple shift of muscles, Jadon came to his feet. "Before we do anything, let's take you to the palace so you can rest. You can't think clearly when you are worn out. It must be near midnight."

She blinked. After all this time, he still seemed to know her every inflection. "But we need to find the cylinder."

"And we will." He hunkered down in front of her. "In my years as an Immortal, I learned that in war, sometimes you must push through bone-weary exhaustion to fight. Go beyond what your body can manage. Some days, winning a victory requires more than you think you have in you to give. Then there are those days when the wise response is to rest. To stop the march forward and set up your tent and find a quiet place for your body and soul.

"Without those snatches of rest, you will not be able to stand the next battle. Trust me, Shoshanah. Now is the time to pause. We will resume our chase in the morning."

Coming to his feet once more, he held out his hand to her.

She studied it for a moment, those outstretched fingers that had once offered so much more than an impersonal support. With a quiet sigh, she reached out and placed her hand in his, allowing him to pull her up.

Five days later, her house looked pristine, if empty. Broken and torn furnishings had been discarded, her belongings packed neatly, and the few pieces of furniture still intact were arranged tastefully. Every possible hiding place had been searched to no avail.

But the futile search had borne one fruit. Sazana had learned to want that cylinder. To treasure it. She had come to understand her parents' profound commitment to its safekeeping.

Only they had kept it so safe that it had gone missing.

Just when her people needed it most, the responsibility for finding the cylinder and keeping it secure had fallen upon her shoulders. And she did not intend to let them down.

Jadon returned from having answered a knock at the door, holding up two sacks full of mourning bread. "Another fresh delivery."

She made a face. "I will be happy to break my fast tomorrow. If I look at another piece of mourning bread, I might turn green."

"We will feed you a proper meal as soon as we have our mikvah baths at sunrise. With the queen's blessing, I have made one final arrangement, if you consent. While we are at the baths, the priests and a few women shall visit your house and the workshop to perform the ritual cleansing. I believe Esther may even have arranged for your chamber at the palace to be purified."

"How thoughtful. I am grateful for it, Jadon." She felt a weight lift from her shoulders. When practical matters were tied so tightly to religious rules, life could grow complicated. It would be good to feel clean again. To be able to participate in the community of her people once more.

Jadon's tone was gentle. "By the time we arrive at the work-shop tomorrow, it will be purified."

She crossed her arms tightly. "I can't imagine Arta finding a safe hiding place for the cylinder there."

"Nor I. But he might have put another clue somewhere for you to find."

25

Sazana

Do not urge me to leave you or to return from following you. For where you go I will go . . .

Ruth 1:16

THE TWELFTH YEAR OF KING XERXES'S RULE
THE THIRTY-FOURTH DAY OF SUMMER

Sazana's morning plans took an unexpected detour. Just before sunrise, while she awaited Jadon's arrival, the queen's junior handmaiden showed up. "The queen requests your presence in her apartment. You will attend her immediately after your special bath."

Sazana froze. "*My* presence?"

"I will return early to ensure you are ready for a royal visit."

Sazana's eyes widened. What did *ready* entail? Her last and only royal visit had taken place when Esther surprised them at the workshop. Sazana had not needed to prepare in any way, for the simple reason that she had not known about it.

She found out the answer after her mikvah bath proclaimed

her free from the pollution of death. Bathed, scrubbed, perfumed, with hair braided, twisted, and tucked, Sazana stood in her linens, grateful for the warm Susa summer as the junior handmaiden tucked a loosening fold of hair back into place.

She frowned at the garment hanging from Sazana's hand. "You can't wear mourning in the palace. And you certainly can't put on that sackcloth in the presence of the queen."

Sazana set aside the scratchy goat hair garment and fetched her two good tunics for the handmaiden's inspection.

After examining each piece, the woman raised a well-plucked brow. "These show a modicum of style. And they appear new."

"I've never worn either." They had been part of her bridal chest, the tunics Arta had purchased in preparation for her life as a married woman. She had never had occasion or desire to wear them. But since they were the nicest clothing she owned, she had impulsively packed them for the palace.

The handmaiden chose the green tunic. Jadon's favorite color. Sazana owned a lot of unworn green clothing.

"This will do." She tapped her feet as Sazana put on the tunic and adjusted its flowing sleeves over her wrists. She would never be able to wear such a robe in the workshop. The fashionable wide sleeves would only tangle in the wheel and be splashed with the muddy waters of her work.

The handmaiden examined her from head to toe as if she were inspecting a sheep before presenting it at the Temple. She pulled down her chin once, the only sign of her satisfaction. "Remember when you come before the queen, no coughing, no fidgeting, no picking, no sneezing."

"No sneezing?"

"Certainly not."

Sazana wondered how one was supposed to control so elemental a bodily function.

"And no sobbing or tears or weeping of any kind. It is very distasteful."

"I was not planning on it."

"Fortunately, the queen's court is not so formal as the king's."

Sazana choked. "Glad I have no business there, then."

"Did I not mention? No choking or gagging."

Throwing a longing glance over her shoulder, Sazana wondered if it was too late to run in the opposite direction. The junior handmaiden had not mentioned running. Before she could give the possibility serious consideration, the handmaiden ushered her past a palace guard and through a wide set of doors into a hexagonal room. Her first glimpse of the exquisite colors in the chamber made Sazana forget the strain of the coming royal audience.

The walls were covered in a clever mix of tiny tiles, glazed in shades of blue, teal, turquoise, and light purple. The overall effect brought to mind a perfect peacock feather, an impression deepened by the priceless carpets that spread over the marble floors.

These very shades had inspired her latest line of glazed pottery. She took a step closer, intending to examine the tiles more carefully in the silvery light of the lampstands. Perhaps she could guess at some of the ingredients that might have produced these exact hues.

The sound of a throat clearing brought her back to earth. She saw first the indignant expression of the junior handmaiden before her gaze took in the woman standing several steps away, her royal gown richly embroidered in gold that matched the crown on her head.

Sazana could have knocked herself on the head. The queen! She had stood here gawping at Esther's tiles and forgotten to bow. She tried to do so now, her movements awkward with embarrassment.

To her surprise, Esther herself took hold of her hand and drew her up. "You see why I was thrilled to see your new design? It fits my chambers perfectly. Even the king remarked upon it when he came to visit yesterday." She indicated a hand toward a silver table, and there, at its center, Sazana's latest ewer, turquoise and slim-necked, had pride of place.

She gave Esther a look of wonder. By choosing her pottery as a centerpiece, Esther had conferred upon it a worth far beyond its natural value.

That the king and queen had both admired her work seemed like the wild imaginings of a dreamy child. How Arta would have enjoyed this moment. He would have snapped his fingers and shaken his shoulders in a dance of jubilation and proclaimed her a genius.

No! No, no, no. But Sazana could do nothing to stop them. The tears gathered in her eyes. She did everything in her power to hold them back. No weeping, the handmaiden had warned. No tears! Yet even the memory of the handmaiden's severe admonitions could not dam the salty drops. Slowly they spilled onto her cheek and rolled down her jaw to dribble over her tunic, turning the light green fabric into the fir trees of a winter forest where they fell.

"I beg your pardon," she said, or tried to say, though the words caught somewhere on her tongue.

"My poor dear," Esther whispered, and to her stupefaction, Sazana found herself enfolded in the queen's embrace, her back patted like a child's. They were not so far apart in age. No more than two or three years, certainly. And yet in that moment, as Sazana's heart cracked, Esther became a mother, offering sweet comfort.

"Come," Esther said, drawing her to a silver-backed couch, seating herself beside Sazana. "You must miss your guardian."

Sazana gulped in a mouthful of air and finally managed to bring the traitorous tears under rule. "Yes, lady."

"I am sorry for his death. I treasure my own guardian, who like yours, raised me as a daughter. I am grown and married. Yet, even now, I cannot imagine losing him. I would feel as rootless as a fallen leaf in the wind."

That was it, exactly. She felt rootless. Part of Sazana kept thinking she was too old for this kind of grief. Mature enough, at twenty-three, to run her own life. And yet the thought of going on without Arta made her feel like a little girl, alone and lost.

"His death came so unexpectedly, you see. To have him there one moment and taken from me the next."

Esther sat back. "We will catch the culprit." Her face, so tender an instant before, turned hard. "We will give your Arta justice."

"He would like that." Sazana wiped her eyes. "Beg your pardon, Majesty."

"Nonsense. I should think you unfeeling indeed if you did not shed a few tears for the good man who raised you."

She offered the queen a tremulous smile. "He would have been proud to discover my work on your table, my queen."

"You are a true artisan, Shoshanah. I am delighted to have you serving in my workshop." The queen dropped her head in thought. "However, I do not wish to burden you with the responsibilities of your work. Rest. Recover from the shock you have experienced while you search for the cylinder."

Sazana straightened. She pressed her lips tight, lest she commit another gaffe by giving voice to her thoughts without the queen's permission.

"Speak, Sazana. I would know your heart."

"My lady." She prayed for the right words. She prayed for *any* words so that she would not leave the queen hanging in expectant silence. But Esther did not seem perturbed by the passing moments until Sazana finally settled on the right reply. "I wish to return to my work, Your Majesty. Without Arta's oversight, no one knows how to run the workshop. The place will crash to a halt if Arta and I are both gone. Besides, sitting at the wheel always calms me."

Esther considered her words. "If I were to agree to your

request, it would be on condition that you have help. Tell me what you need."

Sazana thought quickly. In Arta's absence, there would be a mountain of correspondence and bookkeeping to tend. "Could you give us the loan of one of your scribes for a few hours each day? I know what we need and where the orders should be placed. But it would take me a long time to write such letters and keep track of the payments."

"Done. What of the yard? Can you run that as well as make pottery?"

Sazana was impressed. In her short visit, the queen had learned enough to ask the right questions. "I know the man to place in charge of it. The kiln master can take on the additional responsibility. He's already familiar with the work."

Esther came to her feet, a signal that Sazana should do the same. "I confess I am relieved. Having received the workshop as a gift from the king's hand, I would be loath to tell him that I could not run it successfully, no matter how valid my excuse."

She paced a few steps. "You cannot return there alone. You must know your life remains in danger. I will assign Jadon to you. He is not to leave your side, unless he appoints a trusted guard to take his place."

"Jadon?" Sazana's eyes squeezed shut. There was no ridding herself of the man now. He would dog her steps until they found the king's cylinder. Until they apprehended Arta's murderer.

"Please do not make this task more difficult for him than it needs to be," the queen said, her voice grave. "Keep him apprised of your movements and take no chances."

In other words, for the foreseeable future Jadon would remain by her side. Not for an occasional interrogation or task. But the way the clay of a new pot stuck to the wheel, no distance between them. From sunup until she returned to her small nook in the palace, they would spend almost every waking hour together.

Still, she trusted no man as much as she did Jadon to uncover the murderous hand responsible for Arta's brutal death. She dipped her chin in acknowledgment of the queen's request.

"Another matter to consider," Esther said. "This one more important, even, than the running of the workshop."

Her unusual inheritance: a king's legendary edict. "Finding my great-grandfather's copy of Cyrus's cylinder."

Esther smiled. "Has Jadon helped you understand the significance of it? Much rides on us having Cyrus's words to hand."

"Yes, lady. I understand."

"Then you know why I want you to give this task precedence above all else."

Sazana bowed her head. "I will give Jadon all the help I can." Whatever the cost to her heart, she would pay it.

26

Sazana

Behold, I am doing a new thing;
> now it springs forth, do you not perceive it?
I will make a way in the wilderness
> and rivers in the desert.

Isaiah 43:19

Sazana spent the rest of the morning taking inventory at the workshop. The damage was more extensive than she had realized. She assessed the pottery they had lost, calculating the pieces they would need to replace in order to meet their standing orders. She tallied the loss and winced. It represented a full week of work.

Tomorrow, the men would return. She would need to plan for how they could make up the missing pieces, adding new vessels to their current roster until they caught up.

She steered well clear of the spot where Arta had died. Thankfully, someone had cleaned the area, the strong smell of lye overwhelming the odor of glaze and slurry and clay paste.

Jadon remained near, searching through records, seeking clues, hoping to unearth something Arta's murderer might have overlooked. He had already spent hours going through the small hill of shattered and cracked pottery they had dumped outside after sweeping through the place to ensure that they had missed nothing.

Her head snapped up when the door of the workshop opened. Being there had made her jumpy, the horrible events that had taken Arta's life still too fresh. An audible sigh of relief escaped her when a young servant girl stepped over the threshold.

Jadon reached the girl's side before Sazana moved. After a quiet conversation, the servant handed him a basket and left.

He carried the round hamper to where Sazana had been writing her ledger of tasks. "Look what the queen sent us."

"What is it?"

He stuck his nose into the basket and inhaled. A wide grin bloomed on his face. "Lunch."

"She sent us food?"

"From her own kitchens."

"We can't eat palace food, Jadon. It's not clean."

"Esther would not send us what she herself does not eat." Without waiting for a response, he cobbled together a makeshift table from an overturned box and a broken plank and set two stools on either end.

"Let's see what we have." Drawing aside a clean square of linen, he withdrew a platter. "Fried chickpea cutlets," he said.

"Oh." That sounded like a gift from heaven.

"A salad, fresh cheese, and a hunk of warm bread." He stuck a piece of it under her nose. "Smell that."

Her mouth watered at the aroma wafting from the buttered wheat. Esther's bread had as much in common with the bread of mourning as a loose rock on the side of the road with the jewel on the king's belt.

Jadon poured a deep purple drink from an ewer into two cups. "Water with mulberry syrup."

The fragrance of fried onions, saffron, and mint had her almost salivating like a teething baby. Sitting on the stool Jadon offered her, she bowed her head as he whispered a prayer.

She had to grin when Jadon closed his eyes and groaned after tasting his first bite.

He waved at the food. "Your turn."

She broke off a small piece of the chickpea cutlet and made a morsel with a piece of bread, trying not to feel self-conscious under Jadon's intense scrutiny. A myriad of flavors mixed in perfect harmony and exploded on her tongue. "Oh." She pinched off another piece of the cutlet. Words were wasted on this meal. Her mouth was too busy tasting.

For a while, they ate in companionable silence. Finally, they had swallowed enough food to slow down a little. "Perhaps we can work as we eat," Jadon said. "Have you found anything interesting in the workshop?"

"Broken pottery, only. You?"

"Our man went through Arta's receipts and scrolls with a fine-tooth comb. I have been collecting discarded papyrus from the floor all morning. The queen's scribe will make more sense of the pile when he arrives this afternoon. But from what I could tell, everything pertains to the running of this place. Nothing out of the ordinary. Nothing that would hint at a hiding place." He took a sip from his cup.

She twirled a piece of tarragon in her fingers. Something did not feel right. Both their home and the workshop were vulnerable to the enemy's attack, as they had already discovered. Would Arta have concealed the cylinder in either place?

Then again, perhaps he had found the perfect hiding place within those walls. *You will find it in a place you hold dear.* What could he mean?

That was a question she and Jadon asked again and again as

they searched her home. What were the places that she held dear in her house? Their hunt through every corner she thought of had proven fruitless.

After a lunch replete with good food for the first time in over a week, Sazana knelt by Arta's upturned work chest. Next to it, she found a clay tablet written in her father's hand and decorated with gold leaf, which in spite of its fragility, had by some miracle escaped damage. She snatched it from the ground, where it lay half hidden by a rag.

"What is it?" Jadon hunkered down next to her.

"A promise from the book of Isaiah. My father made it as a gift for Arta on the occasion of his circumcision."

Jadon grimaced. "The considerable price Gentiles have to pay as grown men if they wish to lay hold of the Lord's covenant. My father went through the same before marrying my mother. Not a painless procedure, he tells me. Arta must have loved the Lord indeed."

She cradled the tablet to her. "He did."

"Which verses did your father choose for him?"

Sazana read the passage aloud:

> "Remember not the former things,
> nor consider the things of old."

Jadon added his voice to hers, reciting the words from memory.

> "Behold, I am doing a new thing;
>   now it springs forth, do you not perceive it?
>   I will make a way in the wilderness
>   and rivers in the desert."

His intonation, deep and thoughtful, brought the promise to life. She pondered the words. Could God do a new thing in the midst of this wilderness that her life had become?

Jadon examined the tablet with minute attention before returning it to her. "It seems to contain only Scripture. No hidden messages that I can see." He wrapped the tablet in the folds of a clean rag before handing it to her. "You rarely spoke of your father. When we were . . . I mean, all those years ago."

"When we were betrothed? No, I did not." When she had been younger, when she had been the woman he had known, she would have left her answer at that. But five years was a long time. She had learned a few things through the pain of loss. Asked herself a few hard questions and discovered even harder answers.

"Back then, I still found it hard to speak of my parents. Their loss, though seven years past, felt too raw." She held the tablet in front of her, like a shield. "But that was not the only reason. I did not speak of them because I felt ashamed."

The well-shaped brows furrowed in that familiar way that still tugged at her. "*Ashamed?*"

"When we first arrived in Susa, all I knew was that everyone else had parents. At eleven, it felt to me as though I had done something wrong to deserve such punishment. Something grievously bad for God to allow so severe a loss."

She clutched the Isaiah tablet tighter. "By the time you and I met, it had become a habit. The shame had burrowed inside me. I thought of my mother and father every day. With longing. With love. They had left behind too many sweet memories for me to forget. But I could not speak of them. Not without shame casting its shadow. Their absence reminded me too much that I was different from everyone else. And different made me insufficient somehow."

Jadon had gone still. "I never knew."

"I never told you."

"You have changed, Shoshanah."

"Have I?"

"Once, you would not have admitted so much. You would not have opened up to me."

She sighed and tucked the tablet inside Arta's chest. Even as it settled into the shadows, hidden from view, the words of the prophet reverberated in her mind.

I will make a way in the wilderness
and rivers in the desert.

Were there deserts that even the Lord could not transform? Impossible places where the ancient deserts of life held sway and never let go? Memories of former things that remained vibrant and powerful, refusing to be forgotten? Refusing to heal?

She noticed the way Jadon stared at her, as though waiting for an answer. What had he said? Ah yes. "I would not have opened up because..." She shrugged. "I was afraid I would lose you if I did." Her smile held a world of irony. "If I revealed too much of the broken pieces in my heart."

"I understand that." His gaze dropped.

"Do you?" she asked, surprised. Something about the rigid line of his shoulders, the way his hands kept fisting and opening, turned the words into more than a casual rejoinder.

He looked up. "I do. And I know something about shame, too, Shoshanah."

She would have pressed him for an explanation if he had not walked away to busy himself looking through a pile of discarded papyrus. The conversation had come to an end, apparently. But his words niggled at her.

What could Jadon know about shame? With his perfect family and flawless life, what did he have to hide from?

27

Jadon

For he knows the secrets of the heart.
Psalm 44:21

Any developments with regard to the Cyrus cylinder?"
Esther took up an ornate fan without opening it.

"Not yet, Your Majesty. We have looked everywhere Shoshanah could think of, both in her house and in the workshop."

"Hathach and I have read the copies of the letters you found in her chest." The queen turned to look into the garden. "It is clear no one other than Shoshanah herself can solve this riddle. The answer must be locked somewhere in her mind."

His shoulders grew stiff. "She is doing her best to untangle Arta's words."

"I did not mean to imply she was not. Only that the answer is within our grasp, if only we knew how to get to it." She gave him a sly look. "Hathach tells me you were once betrothed to our talented potter."

"Once." He ignored the spasm in his jaw.

The queen seated herself on the simple chair that served as her throne, taking her time with each movement, allowing silence to hang between them like a threat. What did she want? A confession? A detailed description of events?

Well, she was not receiving it. He ignored the shaft of pain that shot through his head.

"I see." Her smile had a thin edge. "An interesting circumstance. It could work in our favor. Or it could prove a hindrance."

The pain in his head grew sharper. "How so, Your Majesty?"

"Come, come, Jadon. It's not like you to be obtuse. A blind man can see there is unresolved history between the two of you. Every time I mention your past, you look like you have sat on a thornbush."

He made sure his face showed no reaction.

She waved a hand. "With all this tension between you, your very presence could prove detrimental. Her memory may become tangled up more in you than in Arta's letter. Then again, you know enough of her past to ask intimate questions. To direct the conversation in ways a stranger could not. Your presence might trigger just the right memory."

She snapped her fan open and waved it before her face with unnecessary vigor. "I must discern which way matters stand between you. What do you think, Jadon? Are you a help or a hindrance?"

A fair question. "Perhaps you had better ask her, Your Majesty."

"Who said I won't? Right now, I am asking you."

Jadon swallowed past a dry throat. He called to mind the way Shoshanah had been opening up, telling him secrets she had kept hidden even when they were betrothed. Every day, she seemed less guarded with him. Surely that was a sign that a part of her was letting down her defenses in his presence. That level of trust could only help.

And yet . . . what if this whole affair only ended up hurting her again? What if his mere presence drew her too close? Built up expectations that he could not—would not—meet?

He screwed his eyes shut and ignored the pounding in his temple. "Likely, my presence will help jog her memory."

Esther closed her fan, its noise jarring in the quiet chamber. "That is what I thought." She leaned forward. "I do not know what passed between you, or why you chose to undo a betrothal into which you entered freely. But I will give you this warning. Keep my potter safe. From our foes, yes. But also from your own confusion."

She twirled a finger in the direction of his face. "You broke her heart once. Don't do it again while she remains under my protection."

"It is the last thing I wish to do."

"Then see to it that it does not happen."

The problem, Jadon reflected as he bowed, was that he did not know how to comply. How could he protect them both from another heartache? Another round of wrestling the impossible?

His breath still hitched when he thought of her vulnerable confession, acknowledging that she had felt ashamed and afraid. Afraid that he would reject her.

The irony tasted bitter. The rejection, in the end, had come not because of any shortcoming he found in her, but due to his own insurmountable brokenness.

The pain in his head had become blinding, a hammer in his eye socket.

He knew how to fulfill Esther's command. How to protect her heart. He had to be as brave as Shoshanah had been. He had to rip his life open and reveal everything he had kept hidden from her.

Pride had no more room between them. And an old promise he had once made to a dying woman must be put to rest in order to protect the heart of a living one.

The revelation would prove enough to guard her heart from him. His was lost already.

28

Sazana

Behold, like the clay in the potter's hand, so are
you in my hand.

Jeremiah 18:6

The men arrived before sunrise, bringing warmth into the vacant workshop as they occupied their wheels. They did not even seem surprised by the fact that Sazana had taken on Arta's role as overseer. Offering her comfortable smiles, they received their new assignments, assuring her they would do their best to make up for the lost pottery.

No sooner had she finished handing off the new rosters than the door opened to reveal one of the merchants from the market. "I've come to see if you have more of that blue pottery."

He had barely finished speaking when another man walked in. Glowering at the first man, he rounded on Sazana. "What's he paying you? I will offer more."

By noon, she had received sixteen new orders for blue-glazed pots.

Cambyz scratched his head. "You have caused a sensation, Mistress Sazana."

"Both the Royal and Artisans' Markets are abuzz with it." Rashda adjusted his seat at the wheel. "Tomorrow, you will likely receive twice as many orders."

Sazana frowned. She could not handle the increase in orders. Not alone, while trying to also fill Arta's shoes. She pointed at her two apprentices. "You have just been promoted to full potters. I will have to see to hiring wheel boys for you. You'll be too busy to spot each other's wheels if orders continue to pick up at this rate."

The young men sprang up and hollered with joy. She rolled her eyes. "Start with this order of three-legged bowls. When you are finished, I will teach you the basics of blue glaze."

Sazana sent a longing look at her wheel. Her place of comfort. But having spent most of the morning on her chores as overseer, she knew she should now help Jadon search.

He caught her glance. "Go on. The queen wants this place to succeed. Work for a few hours."

She gave him a nod of appreciation and settled on her stool. Tucking her elbow into the anchor of her thigh, she asked God to guide her hands. Signaling Arash to turn the wheel, she wet her hands. The clay felt familiar and malleable, smooth and cool under her touch.

To her surprise, Jadon pulled up a stool next to her and sat quietly, observing her movements. He watched as she shaped the belly of an urn, creating the curves of the lip, her fingers in perfect harmony with the wheel.

Signaling Arash to stop the turn, she dismissed the boy, putting the final touches on the urn before cutting the piece free. Jadon picked up a lump of clay, playing with it in absent-minded grace as he watched.

"Do you still remember?"

He looked up. "Remember what?"

"How to throw a pot." She had taught him, years ago, how to shape the clay on the wheel. She had laughed with him when his first bowl had broken under the uneven pressure of his inexperienced fingers.

Wrapping her hands around his, she had shown him how to raise sturdy walls, her touch a caress as well as a guide.

They had become distracted, forgetting the bowl, finding each other much more fascinating than the half-shaped vessel. Those were the days he had dared to touch her cheek, her hair, her hands. Days he had murmured endearments into her ear and declared how passionately he awaited their wedding day.

He had eventually learned the rudimentary skills for throwing a pot. But not that day. That day, they had found something better to occupy their minds.

A dull tide of color spread over his face, as if he had been accosted by the same memory.

"You still blush like a pretty girl," she said, grinning.

"I know." He pulled his stool closer to the wheel and slammed the lopsided ball of clay with which he had been playing into the center of the wheel. "Let's see."

She set the wheel in motion with a few quick turns as Jadon wet his hands. He cradled the clay, raising the cone. It grew unsteady, and when he tried to press it down too hard, the tip broke off.

Leaning away, he stared at the lump that lay in his palm, no longer usable for anything. Throwing the piece into her discard bucket, he sighed. "There is your answer."

"You were close." She gestured for him to set the wheel in motion again. With quick, familiar movements, she raised and broke down the clay until it grew pliant for shaping. Pushing her stool back, she waved an invitation for him to take over.

For a beat, he did not move, staring at the lump sitting in the center of the wheel. "How odd."

"What is?"

"We both used force against the clay. We both raised it only to knock it down. But the force I used broke it, whereas you only made it pliable and centered so it could be shaped. I weakened the clay, and you strengthened it. I diminished it, and you held it together."

She shrugged, not understanding the intensity of his gaze as he studied the shapeless mound on the wheel. "I am an experienced potter."

The wheel had long since come to a stop. Dust motes danced above it in the fat rays of sunshine that streaked through the window.

"It makes me think of God," he said into the silence.

"The wheel?" She grasped the allusion. "Jeremiah's potter, you mean."

He smiled. "Yes. Jeremiah's potter: 'Behold, like the clay in the potter's hand, so are you in my hand.'

"Except that for years, when I saw God as the potter, I saw someone with *my* hands at the wheel instead of yours. Someone with too much force, who weakens us and breaks us down. Someone who destroys us. But looking at you just now, I was reminded that you can also be knocked down for good."

Something about the way he sat, the hunch in his shoulders, the ashen skin, the thin sheen of sweat that covered his brow, hinted at an inner struggle. Something deeper than an interesting theological conversation about the meaning of the prophet's words. Something personal.

She found herself surprised by this glimpse into his mind. For one thing, he had never been a man to open his heart with ease. For another, she had not known him to speak bitterly about God before, as though he held the Lord to task for some cruelty. She wondered what he had suffered in the past five years that had made him come to see God as a breaker of his people.

She waited for him to expand upon the allusion. To explain

what he meant, but he was unhelpfully silent. Perhaps he could not find a way to the words.

That, at least, she could sympathize with.

His eyes swiveled to her, and for an instant she saw what looked like despair in their depths. "What you said about being ashamed," he said, his voice hoarse. "You had nothing to shame you. You must know that."

Sazana went still. "And yet you walked away."

"Not because you were an orphan. Not because of anything you said or did. There was no lack in you, Shoshanah. I—"

A movement at the door brought the sudden flood of his speech to a stop. The queen had sent one of her messengers. The man wound his way to them with quick steps and extended a thin scroll to Jadon.

His mouth tightened. "Esther requests our presence."

"Ours? Yours and mine?" Sazana had expected Jadon to be the object of the queen's summons. She pulled on the loosened braid of her hair with a nervous movement.

"Last time I checked, that was the meaning of the word *our*."

"Why?"

"Her Majesty does not elaborate. We best leave. She bids us to hasten."

Sazana grabbed the large platter she had packaged for the queen that morning. "At least this time I will go with something besides my tears."

The queen had no patience for royal dawdling today, it seemed. Sazana was still mid-bow, her rounded package held before her like an upended potter's wheel, when Esther began to speak. "We have received news from our final messenger. Not one single copy of the Cyrus cylinder can be found anywhere in the five royal palaces of the kingdom."

She snapped her fan open. "I want to know who has done this thing. I want to know why they have done it." The fan whipped so hard in her hand that Sazana felt its breeze on her own face. "What have you uncovered thus far?"

Jadon bowed. "We know the cylinders in Babylon disappeared over twelve years ago. Presumably, the same can be said for the copies in the other palaces. And yet Haman's edict and the missing cylinders seem connected. The disappearance of one strengthens the other. There is a twelve-year gap between the two events, yes. But that gap is closed by the powerful interest someone is now showing in Shoshanah's copy. Someone who will stop at nothing to destroy this last cylinder."

His brows knotted. "To me, this suggests that, though he is dead, Lord Haman sits at the center of this tangle. He is connected to both events by the strength of his hatred."

Esther closed her fan. "Dig into his background. Perhaps we may find a clue there. If the matter has roots as far back as twelve years ago, then we must search for our answers in the past as much as in the present."

Jadon bowed again and turned to leave. Sazana moved to follow. The queen raised an arm. "Not you, Shoshanah."

Sazana stopped mid-step, eyes wide. The queen pointed at the rounded package clutched at her chest. "Is that for me?"

"Pardon, my queen. I forgot I had it." She held out the platter, expecting the senior handmaiden to take it from her as court etiquette demanded. Instead, Esther herself reached for the gift, unwrapping the cloth in two quick motions.

The queen studied the narrow-lipped platter. The simple turquoise glaze perfectly matched the ewer on her table. She gave a wide smile, famous around the world for its beauty.

"Everything about it is perfection," she said, handing the platter to her handmaiden. "I am told blue-glazed pottery has become quite a sensation in Susa."

With a subtle move of elegant fingers, Esther dismissed everyone from the room, along with Jadon. When they were alone, she sat on the couch and once again invited Sazana to settle next to her.

Perching on the edge, Sazana held her back straight, wondering why she had been honored with a private visit.

Esther placed her fan on her lap. "Have you restored order to your poor home? I understand the intruder made an appalling mess."

"He did, my lady. We have salvaged what we could."

"Tell me." Esther bent close. "How are you? You have gone through much in recent days."

"I am no closer to understanding Arta's message, my lady. I cannot comprehend it. What can he mean? I have looked everywhere in the house and found nothing. The same holds true for the workshop."

Esther laid a gentle hand over Sazana's twisting fingers. "I meant to ask you as a friend rather than a queen. You have suffered a great loss. Are you sleeping at night? Do you feel your world splintering, or can you hold the pieces together?"

Sazana blinked at the queen. Had she just declared she wished to be her friend?

It came as a new sensation, not only that a queen wished to befriend her, but that any woman would. Long years had passed since Sazana had known the companionship of a woman. Because of her slowness of speech, she had never been good at building friendships. And after the betrayal she had felt at the hands of Jadon's mother, she had kept her distance from her own sex. A thread of warmth shot through her.

"I feel like a clay pot sitting in the furnace. Come morning, I am not certain whether I will be riddled with cracks and find I have become useless, or if I will be rendered stronger."

Esther smiled. "How well you put it. I believe I have been through that blaze myself, and more than once. We all face the flames of life, whether we wear a crown or not." She opened and closed her golden fan. "I beg your pardon, Shoshanah. I know

213

that my needs as queen have added to your burdens when you already carry much."

Sazana's mouth hung open. Had Esther apologized to her? A queen asking pardon of a potter? No. A friend asking pardon of a friend. She smiled warmly. "I only wish I could be a better help to you. To our people."

"Sometimes you have to tend to your own heart before you can help anyone else. Let me ask you a strange question. How well do you remember your parents?"

Surprised by the sudden shift in their conversation, Sazana replied, "I was eleven when they died. Old enough to have many cherished memories."

"I lost my parents at seven. My memories of them have become clouded. I've never confessed this to anyone, Shoshanah. But the truth is, I cannot remember their faces anymore."

Sazana felt the current of the queen's guilt flowing beneath her strangled words. "You were only a little girl."

"Perhaps." Esther's smile had a tinge of sorrow. "I remember the way my mother's hair smelled. The sound of her laughter when she tickled me. I remember the timbre of my father's voice. How safe I felt when he held me. That is the sum total of what I recall.

"But do you know what I remember with vivid accuracy? Their deaths. I remember the terror I felt when they were gone. The cavernous loneliness that swallowed me. I remember the nightmares that chased every dream, the wail of mourners at their burial." She gave a short laugh that held no humor. "I remember their deaths more than their lives."

Sazana gave the queen a nod. For all the wealth of her treasured recollections, she knew what the queen meant. The death of her parents held a special power.

"The heart is vulnerable to pain, especially when we are children. Our sweetest memories cannot undo the terrors of childhood loss." She bent her elegant head toward Sazana. "I will tell you a secret. That ancient pain almost tripped me when I most needed to walk in strength. On the day my cousin Mordecai asked me to intercede on behalf of our people with the king, in a corner of my heart, I was still a little girl whose parents had died in spite of her prayers. That is partly why at first, I told him that I could not do what he asked. I could not help our people. I was convinced that, like my unanswered prayers at my parents' sickbed, God would not answer my prayers for the king's favor."

Sazana, who had never heard of the queen's doubts, felt strangely comforted by this revelation. If even the queen had struggled to rise up to the task set before her by God, then perhaps her own struggles were not unusual.

"I wonder, Shoshanah," Esther said, "if you can understand how I felt."

"Oh yes, my lady."

"I believe you can. And I see from the warmth in your eyes that you do not judge me too severely."

"Never, my queen!" Time ticked by as she tried to assemble her thoughts into phrases that made sense. "Knowing your past, I am now amazed that you were willing to go before the king unsummoned. Surely the little girl whose parents had died, whose worst nightmares had become reality, must have believed you would meet your end as well by coming to the king."

Esther's eyes widened. "How well you capture my feelings. I myself had no awareness of them at the time. I knew only that I held no hope of finding grace in the king's presence. I almost missed God's call on my life because of this festering wound from my childhood. I thought my fate lay in the king's hand, or in my own ability. I forgot about the might of God's provision.

"I tell you this because I want you to show yourself a little mercy, Shoshanah. If you cannot understand Arta's message, it may have to do with the pain of his murder. Or the way his death connects and weaves into the loss of your parents." She took hold of Sazana's hand. "Perhaps a little orphan girl is trying to solve a puzzle that belongs to a woman."

Sazana gave the queen a doubtful look. "You were able to rise above it, my lady."

"I had help. A whole city fasted and prayed for me. Shoshanah, I am finally learning that I am not an orphan. I pray you will learn the same lesson." From the filigreed table next to the couch, she retrieved a scroll. "I had one of my scribes make this for you."

Sazana studied the roll of papyrus with its colorful silk tie, her jaw agape. Hesitantly, she took the queen's offering and, undoing the ribbons, unfurled the papyrus.

With silver ink, the scribe had copied one verse from the prophet Isaiah.

> Yet you, LORD, are our Father.
> We are the clay, you are the potter;
> we are all the work of your hand.

"How beautiful. I don't know how to thank you, my lady."

"No need for thanks." Esther smiled. "As a potter, you must be familiar with this verse."

"I have heard it a time or two, lady."

"Yes. But I want you to set your gaze upon the first line. How can you be an orphan when you have a Father in God? As a potter, you might appreciate the allusion and understand the rest of the verse better than most. But as an orphan girl, you have to learn all about the first claim. Seek your Father, that he may heal you."

Sazana rose when Esther came to her feet. "Come and have supper with me tomorrow night. I do enjoy your company. The palace, full as it is with princesses and aristocratic women, does not always offer a queen many friends."

Taking her leave, Sazana wondered if she had dreamed the

last hour. Had a queen opened her own heart, revealed her own wounds and her own mistakes, in order to comfort her? Had she offered true friendship, laying at her feet the mercy of one who understood her shortcomings and yet offered no judgment?

For the first time since Arta's death, Sazana felt a quiet calm beneath the mountain of grief. She pressed the queen's gift to her chest and smiled.

29

Jadon

> After these things King Ahasuerus promoted Haman the Agagite, the son of Hammedatha, and advanced him and set his throne above all the officials who were with him.
>
> Esther 3:1

Jadon entered the royal treasury, thanks to the special permission Esther had managed to arrange for him, and headed directly for a humble group of rooms hidden at the very back of the otherwise lavish building. Here, scribes worked with diligent concentration, keeping track of payments, receipts, and gifts. Persians loved their records. If a payment was involved, the department of the treasury could provide every manner of detail about it.

Which was why Jadon had decided to search for Haman's background here.

Two hours later, he had a hill of papyrus scrolls and thumb-sized clay tablets piled in front of him. His eyes were not going to thank him. On a receipt for a payment of wine, he found his first clue.

To Lord Haman, of Agazi. He made note of the town, a small place near Ecbatana.

Another note came from a birthday gift to the king from Haman, son of Hammedatha. Jadon wrote down the name of his father next to the town.

But it was a fifty-year-old tablet that captured his interest the most. A merchant named Hammedatha had sold a dozen carpets to the palace. Next to his name, there was a single word. *Amalekite.*

An hour later, Jadon had collected a handful of interesting details. To connect these seemingly incongruent dots, however, he would need some help. And he knew just where to seek it.

Like the trenches of an oft-traversed road, deep lines ran down Gadatas's cheeks. The long grooves that radiated from his eyes attested to a merry disposition that erupted into laughter with easy regularity.

Jadon remembered when Gadatas had been immensely popular at court. Now that age had limited his activity and influence, few sought his company. Palace courtiers mistook his age for feebleness. Jadon knew better. Gadatas had accumulated more information than the ancient library of Babylon, and he had a gossipy woman's love of sharing it.

It had taken Jadon a four-hour hard ride to arrive at his country estate, and he considered the man worthy of every bone-rattling step. He knew if anyone had the kind of intelligence he needed, it would be Gadatas.

"And what brings you to an old man's door so late in the evening?" Gadatas offered his good-natured smile.

Jadon leaned into the comfortable pillow at his back. "I have come to pick your mind."

"According to some, you have already missed that caravan. It departed years ago."

Jadon grinned. "I know better."

Gadatas grinned back. "I am gratified to hear it. It places you in a rather narrow category of men."

"What category is that?"

"The one worth my time." He rubbed veiny hands together. "Let's see if I can help."

"I have come to ask about Lord Haman."

"He is dead."

"That much I know."

Setting out two rare glass beakers, Gadatas poured wine from the ewer Jadon had brought as a gift. "It makes him boring, no?"

"Perhaps not. Some men continue to wield influence from beyond the grave."

"Those are the ones I especially resent. They are like an old man's hair. Gone where you want it and abundantly present where you don't. Well, what is it you want to know about that pimple, Haman? Never did like him."

Jadon's grin widened. "A man of good taste, as always. Tell me what you know about his family. They hail from Agazi, I understand."

Gadatas screwed up his eyes thoughtfully. "His mother's people came from one of the seven noble families. Not a major branch, mind. They had sunk into the backwaters, content with life in the provinces. Respectable enough, but rarely at the palace. They wielded little influence."

"Tell me of his father, Hammedatha."

"What a name! That will break your jaw if you say it too fast. Now, he had an interesting background. How did it go? Let me think." He held up a crooked finger. "He arrived at Agazi as a traveling merchant. Here is the interesting part of the story. Hammedatha chose to settle there because he said the name of the place reminded him of his own people."

Jadon leaned closer. "Who were his people?"

"He was originally from some small watering hole one rarely hears about. The name escapes me. After a few years in Agazi, he had done well enough for himself to marry Haman's mother. No one had heard of him before then."

He sipped from his beaker and smacked his lips. "This is fine grape. I am honored Hathach sent me the good stuff." He pointed at Jadon's untouched cup. "Are you going to drink that?"

"I thank you, no."

"I hoped you would say that." He picked up the priceless glass, emptying half in one gulp. "Too Gentile for your Hebrew laws, am I?"

Jadon shrugged, unsurprised by Gadatas's knowledge. "Can you tell me any more about Haman's father?"

"No, dear boy. That's why it's an interesting story. The man remains an enigma. It's as if his life started when he arrived in Agazi. Haman might have been an Agazite, or as he called himself in their dialect, an Agagite. But only his mother's line traced themselves to the place. As for his father, no one really knows."

Jadon froze. "What did you say?"

"Quite a lot, actually. Which part interests you?"

"What do the people of Agazi call themselves?"

"Agagite. A silly name, don't you agree? It sounds rather like someone retching on sour milk."

Jadon did not smile. His mind had become too occupied. He had heard that name before. Vaguely, he called to mind a boyhood lesson. But it had not been at the palace school.

For once, he wished he had paid more attention to the rabbi when he had expounded on the history of ancient Israel. What had he said about that name? Why did the name *Agagite* pluck some thread in his memories?

30

Sazana

Blessed be the LORD!
　For he has heard the voice of my pleas for mercy.
The LORD is my strength and my shield;
　in him my heart trusts, and I am helped;
　my heart exults . . .

Psalm 28:6–7

After her audience with Esther, Sazana decided to return to the workshop since there would be more than two hours of daylight left by the time she arrived. She needed to inspect the day's work and determine if they needed fresh supplies. Tasks Arta usually managed.

Her heart clenched at the thought. Ordinary, everyday moments like this, when she would have taken Arta's presence for granted, now grew into a constant reminder of his absence. Of the cavernous hole he left behind.

In many ways, he had prepared her well, teaching her how to

run the workshop and look after their personal finances. He had by no means raised a helpless woman, dependent upon others. Yet, being capable and being alone were very different things.

Exiting the queen's apartments, she found Jadon nowhere in sight. Instead, a palace guard waited for her at the threshold. "Master Jadon assigned me to your care, mistress," the young man said. "I am to accompany you wherever you go."

"I hope I am not taking you away from more important duties." She suspected she was little more than a nuisance to the young man with the soldierly bearing. But she felt relieved by his presence, appreciating that in pursuing his own line of investigation, Jadon had not left her to her own devices.

"It is my pleasure to serve," the soldier said politely. Palace guards were well trained in more than combat duties, it seemed.

"I hope you like a good march. The queen's pottery workshop lies almost an hour's walk east of the palace."

The guard smiled. "It will be a pleasant diversion. I come from the country, myself. Long walks pose no threat to these legs."

He proved an amiable soul, keeping her entertained with stories from his childhood growing up on a farm. At the workshop, he seemed content to wait at her elbow as she calculated the fresh materials they would need to purchase. The queen's scribe saw to writing the necessary letters, so Sazana found herself free to return to the pottery wheel after a couple of hours.

She set to doing the work of her heart: the shaping of a vessel. She smiled at the wheel boy, whose countenance had brightened when she sat across from him. "Missed me, Arash?"

"It's like the sun goes out when you're gone, mistress."

"Aren't you the poet?"

The tips of his ears turned red. She gave him an encouraging nod. Over recent weeks, it had become obvious that Arash had formed a boyish attachment to her, which he would outgrow soon enough. In the meantime, she did her best to handle his youthful heart with care as well as appropriate distance.

He wriggled on his stool. "Sorry about Master Arta. I miss him."

"Thank you. I miss him too."

An anguished look passed over his face. "Why did they do that to him?"

"We are trying to discover that. Those who are responsible will be brought to justice. It won't replace Arta. But it will help."

They sank into companionable silence as she shaped a bowl. She had finished her third piece when she realized the place had emptied of everyone save her, the wheel boy, and the guard. Someone had thoughtfully lit the lamps on their way out, so she had enough light to work by even though the sun had set.

"It must be later than I thought." She stretched. "I have kept you too late," she told Arash. "There are still two more pieces I want to finish. But I won't need the wheel for that. You run along to your house. Your mother will worry if you don't arrive soon."

"You sure you don't want me to stay?"

"It's all right. I'll leave in an hour or two. See you in the morning."

She spent a quiet hour shaping handles for the new pieces. The handles, whorled and complicated, stuck above the rim of the bowl, which prevented them from being stacked. This made them more expensive, for they required more room for storage.

As she worked, she thought about Esther's advice that she show herself mercy. That she resist living life as an orphan. Sazana had a feeling that her mother would have agreed. The woman who had made a habit of anchoring her life to God would want to know him as a Father.

Sazana smiled as she wiped her table clean of clay dust. A strange sound outside the window brought her head up. "What was that?"

The palace guard strode toward the door. "Stay here, mistress, while I investigate."

A chill went through her, making the hair on the back of her neck stand. Something similar had happened on Jadon's final day as he had conversed with Arta. Like the palace guard, he had gone running into the night, chasing the sound to no avail.

A few hours later, Arta had been murdered.

She hugged herself, running trembling fingers up her chilled arms. Outside, she heard a shout and the sound of running feet. Rushing to the window, she opened one shutter. In spite of the bright moon, she could see nothing.

In the workshop, all remained still. Nothing moved. Nothing whispered, warning her of danger. And yet an odd sensation, like a hand running over her scalp, caused her to turn her head, eyes wide.

In the periphery of her vision, she saw a large form, hands reaching out toward her.

A small whimper escaped her. Before she could scream or take a step, the hands looped over her head. The experienced potter, familiar with the paraphernalia of her trade, knew instantly what those fingers held. What they intended.

The sharp edge of the wire cutter slipped against the skin of her neck and pulled violently.

One thing alone saved her. Because she had turned and seen his approaching form, she had time for one small response, one minor reaction. She slipped her right palm, fingers pressed against her left shoulder, under the wire.

Her throat began to close as the wire pulled tight, trapping her hand, palm out. Her own ligaments and bones pressed hard into her flesh, gagging her. But it also saved her from the brutal edge of the iron wire. She bunched her free hand against it, trying to loosen its merciless hold, to no avail.

The man panted in her ear as he hefted the wooden edges of the wire cutter closer together. She felt her palm split, the cut a fire in her skin, burning hotter as it deepened. She struggled hard, her body heaving backward as she choked, barely managing to inhale.

One short breath. One tiny gulp of air.

Blood dribbled down her tunic. Her strength dwindled. Death drew near. So near. She felt its breath, more cloying even than that of her assailant's as he tightened the iron noose on her neck.

Dying was lonely business. No one could enter that inscrutable arena with her, not even the man who delivered death, his body so close she could hear the thunder of his heart against her back. The pain, the suffering, the slow ending, all this she had to bear alone.

And then the realization came to her. In this moment, as her eyes grew dim and the world started to fade, she was not alone. She was not alone at all.

The Father was with her. The Father of her people. The one...

As through the depths of a pool, she heard a shout in the distance and the sound of running feet. The wire tourniquet around her throat loosened. The arms that had held her in the embrace of death fell away, and she collapsed to the ground. Consciousness came and left, like the light of stars on a cloudy night.

"Mistress!" someone cried as hands loosened the knot of wire at the nape of her neck. A groan. "Please don't die! He'll kill me for certain if you die."

She recognized that voice. It belonged to the palace guard. She tried to reassure him that she still lived, but she found that she could not form the words.

Some things, it seemed, never changed.

A weak cough escaped, mewling and painful. The world pitched as muscular arms lifted her. She closed her eyes and let the darkness claim her.

A confusion of sights and sounds greeted her when she next opened her eyes. The train of a lavender gown, a pair of hands pulling through dark curls, the scent of a woman's perfume mingling with something medicinal.

"Is she going to be all right?" She knew that voice, now stifled with some anguished edge, as though he could barely bring himself to ask the question.

She lost the response to the clouds that obscured her mind.

"Will you have to stitch that hand?" a woman asked. *The queen*, she thought. *The queen is here with me.*

"Yes." The voice, calm and assured, belonged to a stranger.

"Will she be able to work the wheel again?"

Another lost answer. Her throat ached. But the gash in her hand pulsating with pain drew her focus most. She tried to sit up.

A pair of hands held her down, at once velvet soft and firm. "Hold still, dear heart. Hold still."

"Jadon?" Her voice emerged a croak.

"I'm here. Be calm."

Her arm and wrist were held down and instinctively she tried to wriggle loose. Not so long ago, someone in the workshop had imprisoned her in an iron grasp and the panic of those moments came to her now, turning her feeble struggle into a mighty heave as she blindly sought freedom.

"Easy now." Jadon's face came into view, the blue eyes looking almost black against his chalk-white skin. "You're safe."

His presence, the quiet timbre of his voice, and the faint familiar scent of evergreens acted like a calming elixir upon her stretched nerves, and she relaxed.

"The physician has to suture that cut in your hand." He drew a tangle of hair away from her eyes. "He won't be able to do it right if you keep wriggling. Will you hold still for him?"

"I'll try," she whispered.

"Brave girl. I'm here with you. Hold my hand with your un-injured fingers. Squeeze if it hurts."

She squeezed.

He gave her a small grin. "He hasn't started yet."

She swallowed. "Practicing."

"Practice to your heart's content."

Sazana was starting to feel more alert. "Did you call me *dear heart*?" Had she imagined the endearment, the tenderness with which he had uttered it, her frightened mind concocting its own comfort? For some reason, it became very important to know the answer.

"He certainly did. I heard him." An elegant face came into view, long earrings dangling against a perfect cheek.

"Majesty!"

"I find when sutures are involved, it's best to remain on familiar terms. You may call me Esther." She turned to Jadon. "Not you. Your hand is not being sewn up."

"Might be worth a stitch or two," Jadon said dryly.

"I would be happy to oblige." The stranger's voice, warm and deep, had a pleasant quality. The physician, she assumed. "If you are interested, you better stand in line. I am currently busy."

A dark-eyed man bent his face into view. "I'm Adin, one of the royal physicians. How do you feel?"

She thought about it. "Alive?"

He chuckled. "In my profession, we call that a good answer. You have significant damage to your hand, though I suspect from the marks on your neck that it saved your life. Now we must repair the damage."

"Sutures?"

He dipped his chin. "Nice, tiny ones. That bruise on your neck should heal on its own, though I suspect it feels uncomfortable now."

Recalling the queen's earlier question from the fog of her mind, she asked, "Will I be able to continue my work? My pottery?"

"I am going to do my very best."

The room sank into a kind of pall. The ramifications of the

physician's answer, which left room for an ominous doubt, became a wall against which all of them crashed, though none so hard as Sazana.

Her throat, swollen and scratchy, felt like it might close. And somewhere in the distance, another door with it. The wheel! Her life had been stripped bare of everything that held value or offered comfort.

She was drowning, drowning under the pressure of this grief, this unendurable, final loss.

At first, she missed the tug on her good hand. Then it came again, gentle and insistent. "He did not say *no*." Jadon's fingers caressed her hair, feather soft. "He said he would do his best to ensure you could. Don't you dare give up hope before he even begins. I have seen Adin's work on the soldiers around here, and he has mended far worse cuts than this."

"True," the physician agreed. "It will take a few weeks of careful tending, and a longer period of further remedies after that. But you have a chance. The torn cords and ligaments in your hand may be restored, with God's help." He patted her shoulder. "Now, I really must begin. And I am sorry. This will hurt. I think it unwise to give you a draft that might help the pain. Your throat is too swollen. I do not wish to risk choking you."

Sazana nodded her understanding. She thought it unlikely that she could swallow anything just then.

Under his breath, Adin whispered a prayer. She caught the Hebrew words "Blessed art thou, O Lord . . ."

"You are a son of Abraham!" she said in surprise after he had finished.

"At your service. Me and my needle." He held up a long metal thorn with a pierced eye at one end, threaded with fine mesh.

At the first sharp poke into her flesh, Sazana hissed a breath and another and another, holding still, clinging to Jadon. The room held a tense silence, undergirded by the constant movement of the needle, held in calm, capable, but inexorable fingers.

Sazana's first prayer started as a desperate plea, a stuttering, tearful entreaty. Then Jadon began to pray softly next to her, and the queen joined in, and something shifted. The press of the needle going in and out remained an agony. Yet in spite of her shrinking flesh, her heart started to settle into something other than the claim of that pain.

She began to realize that beyond the pain lay hope. Lay, as the queen whispered, healing.

Adin knew his craft well. He sutured the deep cut more quickly than Sazana had expected, though to her, every moment had lasted an age. Applying a salve that stung unbearably at first before numbing the fiery misery of her wound, he soaked a fat wad of wool in liniment and curled her fingers around it.

"Bandaging your fingers in this position will place less stress upon the cords you have cut." He bound the hand in a large swathe of dressings before fashioning a sling. "This will keep your fingers from moving. That is important. I have sewn several tears in your ligaments. Any sudden movements and you could cut through a ligament completely. We want to avoid that."

She released a shaky breath. "My thanks, Master Physician. Your salve has calmed the pain."

"That, and the fact there is no more needle poking your flesh." The queen came to her feet. "I will send my handmaidens to set up a proper bed for you. A bedroll is no place to recuperate from a murder attempt."

"Thank you, my lady, for biding with me."

"Esther," she reminded.

"Esther." Few were the queens in all history who would trouble themselves to sit beside a low retainer at such a time. Fewer still who would count her as friend. She considered how protected the queen was in her day-to-day life from unpleasant scenes. From coughs and sneezes and blown noses, let alone bleeding wounds. "I know it must have been unpleasant."

Esther patted her arm. "More so for you than for me, I should think."

Sazana thought of one final question. "How long before I can work with my hand again?"

Adin paused. "The cords in the hand take time to heal. Eight weeks, if all progresses well. Sometimes longer."

"*Eight weeks?*" She gaped at him. Who would look after the workshop while she recuperated? Who would fulfill her orders?

Esther pressed her shoulder reassuringly. "Do not forget your Father. He will provide."

31

Jadon

The Lord will cause your enemies who rise against
you to be defeated before you. They shall come out
against you one way and flee before you seven ways.

Deuteronomy 28:7

Jadon bowed as Esther made her way out of the small chamber, her face rigid and white. She looked as strained as he felt. The acrid bite of nausea still clawed up his throat.

When he had arrived at the palace in the small hours of the morning, Hathach's assistant had merely informed him that Shoshanah had been attacked and gravely wounded. He could not even assure Jadon that she had survived.

The shock of that dreadful possibility—the possibility that she was dead—had almost brought him to his knees. He had cut the ties of their relationship five years earlier. But the knowledge that she lived somewhere in the world had always shored up the foundation of his life.

Having her so close again had resurrected old feelings, strengthened them in ways he had not expected. He needed her to be alive. To be safe. Else his world would topple from its axis.

He had run all the way to her chamber, legs shaking, heart pounding like the march of a battalion of foot soldiers. Outside her door, he ran into the palace guard he had assigned to her, looking so wan and miserable that Jadon's string of angry rebukes had dried up.

"Is she dead?" How the words had made their way out of his lips sounding so calm, he had no idea.

"I thought so, at first. But she lives, Master Jadon." He pointed a thumb to the drawn curtain. "She's in there now, being tended by the queen's handmaidens."

Not a good time to burst in, though every part of him longed to barge into that room in order to reassure himself that she would recover. He ground his teeth. "What happened?"

The guard, though young, knew his business enough to give a well-organized report.

"You mean the sound you heard outside could not have been made by the man who tried to murder her?"

"No, master. I could hear him running ahead of me. Mistress Sazana's attacker slipped in while I still chased him, though he seemed to disappear like smoke."

"There are at least two men, then."

"Seems so."

"Why were you there so late?"

"She wanted to finish some pieces."

Jadon scrubbed a hand over his jaw. How had they known just when to attack her? How had they known she would be there later than usual, with only one man to guard her? Were these people seers? At every junction, they seemed three steps ahead of him.

When the queen's women exited, Jadon knocked on the threshold and entered. For a moment, he had eyes only for

Shoshanah, lying on a bedroll, sheets pulled up to her chest. She seemed unconscious, though the steady rhythm of her chest rising and falling beneath the linens reassured him that she lived.

In spite of the palace guard's detailed report, the sight of the livid bruise across her throat chilled him to the bone. His gaze found the bloody rag wrapped around her hand, and he pressed his fingers to his mouth. She had come so close to dying.

A slight movement in the shadowy corner of the room caught his attention. Jumpy from the news of the attack, he had his dagger drawn and his knees locked, ready to spring at anyone who dared to violate the safety of this room.

"Put that away." She stepped into the light, her scalloped skirts dancing around her feet. "You will find no enemy here."

"My queen!" Jadon paled, dropping into a low bow. Pulling a dagger on royalty could earn the offender's head a rather uncomfortable resting place atop tall gallows. "Beg your pardon. I feared—"

She waved a hand. "I know what you feared." Sighing, she knelt by the pallet. "I have sent for my own physician. He will arrive soon." She motioned for him to join her on the other side of the bed.

He dropped to his knees. "How is she?"

"She has opened her eyes a few times, only to lose consciousness. I don't know if it is the shock or the injury that keeps her insensible."

The queen straightened a wrinkle in Shoshanah's blanket. "I am the one who sent her to the workshop. The one who insisted she find that cylinder."

Jadon gave her a sharp glance. Did that explain her presence here? Guilt? "You are not to blame for what that murderer has tried to do."

She exhaled. "We each bear our own manner of responsibility."

He opened his mouth to argue, but she forestalled him with

a hand. "The point is, they are harming my people. I want it stopped, Jadon."

"Yes, lady."

"We will tend Shoshanah's wounds. Then we will put an end to this hunt. I am done being the prey to some invisible foe. Agreed?"

"With all my heart."

The physician had arrived then, and Jadon's attention had turned from the vagaries of his work to Shoshanah as she stirred awake. He had wanted to fall on his head a few times, knowing how she suffered body and soul from the wound that might rob her of her gift.

Now, with only Jadon and the physician left in the chamber, Jadon's gaze remained glued to Shoshanah's sleeping form.

The physician put away his bandages and the other paraphernalia of his business, sealing his medicine chest. "The greatest danger now is the putrefaction of that wound. I will return twice daily for the first week to examine it and to apply a special salve. For the present, we must ensure that she keeps the hand immobile."

Jadon looked at her face, its alluring color leached out by pain and shock. "She won't like that."

Adin winced. "I fear very little of what I do is likable. Hopefully, she will like the results." He sighed. "Those rest in God's hands more than mine."

Though he knew the queen had sent two guards to stand at Shoshanah's door, he could not bring himself to leave her side yet. The small chamber, more closet than room, lacked a window. He had no way of knowing the time, though his tired body told him that it must be well past sunrise.

Not long after the physician's departure, the curtain swished open silently, admitting Esther's promised handmaidens, followed by a couple of burly servants who dragged an iron bed frame behind them.

"Watch it," Jadon barked as one of them tried to maneuver the bed in. "I'll have to move her out first. In this tight space, you are liable to trample her, and she is injured enough already."

Tenderly, he lifted her against his chest, bedroll and all, careful to tuck her hand over her chest. In the hallway, he hunkered down with his back against the wall, cradling her against him, ready to take off anyone's head who dared approach too close. The handmaidens made quick work of the bed, their feather mattresses and pillows and silk coverlets creating a sleeping couch fit for a royal occupant.

Shoshanah never stirred when they settled her inside her plush nest. At least she would recuperate in comfort.

Esther's junior handmaiden pointed her chin at Jadon. "I will sit watch. You can leave."

"I prefer to remain."

"That was not a suggestion. The queen orders it. She suspected you might prove stubborn. She said to remember your duty, which is not as nursemaid. Go and catch whoever did this. You can visit later."

Jadon felt his face heat. Never had he needed a reminder to do his duty. Esther had the right of it. He could not afford to give in to personal feelings. Giving Shoshanah's good hand one last gentle squeeze, he slipped out.

32

Sazana

Why is my pain unceasing,
my wound incurable,
refusing to be healed?
Jeremiah 15:18

THE TWELFTH YEAR OF KING XERXES'S RULE
THE THIRTY-SEVENTH DAY OF SUMMER

A soft cloud cradled her. Sazana opened her eyes, feeling the confines of an unfamiliar bed. The mattress supporting her back, stuffed with feathers, made her feel as though she floated in the air.

"Finally!" A female voice pronounced the word with crisp satisfaction. "You took your time waking."

Turning her head one slow degree, Sazana found the junior handmaiden occupying a narrow stool on the other side of the bed. The iron contraption had taken up so much room in her nook that apart from two stools on either side of her, no other furniture could fit.

The handmaiden rose and walked around the bed to the other stool, where someone had placed a jug and clay cup. "Thirsty?"

Sazana found that her throat had turned into an arid desert. "Yes." She tried to reach her good hand for the cup, but the handmaiden slapped it away.

"The physician stopped to have a look at you again. He said you ought to be able to drink a bit of water if I spoon it into your mouth."

Sazana grimaced. No one had spoon-fed her since her days as a babe. By its very nature, the task could not be pleasant to either party, though if the handmaiden resented the duty, she took care to conceal it. Carefully, she poured spoon after spoon of water into Sazana's mouth.

As soon as she coughed, the handmaiden stopped. "Enough for now."

Far from sated, Sazana gave a longing look at the cup.

"I will give you more when your throat has had a chance to recover."

"Thank you, mistress." The light of the lamp caught the woman's face as she turned, and Sazana noted the dark circles under her eyes. "Have you been here long?" Her voice sounded scratchy, matching the way her throat felt. "You must be weary."

The handmaiden shrugged. But the severe expression on her face softened a small degree. "It is nothing."

"To me, it is something. I do not have many people who would go sleepless in order to nurse me."

An odd expression flickered through the dark eyes. "Well, now you do." She ran a hand over her hair, which in spite of her sickbed vigil, had not dared to budge from its elaborate tucks and braids.

"It's a marvel that you can keep your hair so beautifully tidy.

Mine would be a mess." She touched a tangled hank lying on her shoulder with her good hand. "*Is* a mess."

"That is certainly true. It's the silky nature of your hair. I can tame it for you. Do not worry on that score."

Sazana's brow rose. What had she gotten herself into? "Perhaps before I worry about the state of my hair, I should tend to more urgent matters."

"What could be more urgent than the state of your appearance?"

Sazana gulped. "Well. Certain things come to mind." She pushed herself up on an elbow. "Certain . . . functions?"

The junior handmaiden actually cracked a smile. "I can help with that also."

She proved quite adept at helping with that, as it turned out, her matter-of-fact attitude and expert handling of the daily concerns of life lending dignity to a situation that could have reduced Sazana to stuttering embarrassment.

"Is it day or night?" Sazana asked once she was garbed in a fresh tunic, her braided hair lying neatly over one shoulder.

"You slept through the day and night. The sun has already risen."

Sazana gasped. "I have never slept so long my whole life."

"You have been through much."

A knock sounded at the threshold, and the curtain lifted to reveal the physician, bulky chest cradled in his arms. "How fares my patient on this summer day?"

"Quite well, thanks to the efforts of the junior handmaiden."

Adin smiled. "She makes a capable nurse, indeed." He poured some sweetened wine down Sazana's throat with a long-handled spoon and watched her swallow. "Good. I will ask the queen's kitchen to prepare some soft food for your lunch."

"Your name is Adin?"

"Adin ben Zerah, at your service." His deep voice held the edge of an exotic accent.

"From Egypt?"

"I grew up on the Elephantine."

That explained his broad shoulders and hard-muscled physique, as well as his Hebrew lineage. A great many of the men on the island of Elephantine were Jews who served in its massive garrison as soldiers. If he grew up there, likely he spent his youth receiving basic military training.

She watched as he unwrapped her hand. The sutures sat like a row of tiny black ravens over the dark brown of clotted blood. "How does it progress?"

"Very well. I see no sign of putrefaction in the wound. That is the most important element in your recovery." After applying salve, Adin once again shaped her hand around a wad of liniment-soaked wool before binding her hand with thick bandages. "Keep improving at this rate and you shall soon outgrow the need for my services."

She tried to make her voice sound casual. "You think my hand will be as good as new?"

He shrugged. "Nothing is impossible with God."

Her heart caved. "You mean it would require a miracle for me to have my hand perfectly restored?"

"Perhaps. Though I will try for *almost*-perfect restoration."

He smiled, but she could not join him. The difference between perfect and almost perfect may have sounded small. But to a potter who created fine ware, even a slight loss of supple movement in one hand might mean the loss of the quality that made her work unique.

Sazana pulled her knees close to her chest once the physician slipped out of her room. The junior handmaiden resettled the blanket over her. Outside, she heard his murmured conversation with someone and assumed he must be greeting the guards. But a moment later, someone rapped on the threshold, and at her invitation, pulled aside the curtains.

"Jadon!" In a sudden rush, she remembered his presence by

her side after her injury, and the sweet way he had held on to her hand as the surgeon applied his needle.

He gave her a formal bow. Standing at the foot of the bed, he studied her. "How did you sleep?"

"Dead to the world. I have not lost that talent, at least."

His eyes narrowed. "You have not lost any talent. The physician tells me he is satisfied with your progress."

She did not argue. "It is good of you to visit me."

"Your voice still sounds hoarse." He turned to address the junior handmaiden. "You have been here overlong, mistress. Why not take your rest? I will remain with Sazana." When the handmaiden looked as though she might argue, Jadon raised a hand. "Her Majesty is sending your replacement soon."

After a slight hesitation, the handmaiden nodded and turned to Sazana. "Behave, or I will hear about it," she said. "Do not even attempt to rise from bed."

Sazana gave a wan smile. "Thank you for your care, mistress."

Jadon lowered himself to the stool that the handmaiden had vacated. "I have news."

She noticed, then, that in spite of the pallor of his skin, his eyes sparked with a barely contained energy. "After our audience with Esther two days ago, I went directly to the king's royal treasury for a little research. I discovered that Haman comes from a small town called Agazi. But it is only his mother's family that hails from there. His father, one Hammedatha, was an Amalekite."

She blinked. "What?"

"Interesting, no? It gets better. I followed my research with a visit to a man called Gadatas. If an ancient library were to marry the town gossip, the child of their union would be Gadatas. He knows everything when it comes to palace life and its courtiers."

She found herself smiling. "He sounds entertaining."

"Let's say I have never been bored in his company. Last night, Gadatas told me something interesting about the lineage of Haman's father."

Judging by the suppressed glee in Jadon's narrow smile, the discovery held some importance.

"According to Gadatas, Haman's father had once claimed that he settled in Agazi because the name reminded him of his people. I could not understand who he meant until Gadatas mentioned that the Agazites refer to themselves in their dialect as *Agagite*."

She frowned. "How do I know that name?"

"Ha! That is exactly what I thought. Except I also remembered that I had heard it in some lesson at the synagogue. I rode as fast as I could back to Susa to resume the thread of my investigation. I am afraid by then the hour had grown quite late." He wriggled uncomfortably on his stool. "Quite. But I needed the help of the ruler of the synagogue."

"You did not! You dragged Master Sheber out of bed in the middle of the night to ask him a lesson in Hebrew history? Knowing him, he treated you to a few heated glowers."

Jadon grinned. "If I had not hidden behind Esther's skirts, so to speak, I do believe he might have thumped me."

"Attempted to, you mean."

"I would have had to let him, considering I could not explain the reason for my sudden interest in the chronicles of our people."

She shifted, trying to find a more comfortable position. Casually, he reached out to resettle the pillows behind her.

"Better?" he asked.

If forgetting to breathe was an improvement. "Thank you." She cleared her throat. "What did you find out?"

"An instructive lesson. One that stretches as far back as King Saul."

"Gracious! How did you go from Haman to Saul? That must have been hundreds of years ago."

"Over sixteen generations." Jadon nodded. "Here is the connection I discovered. God charged Saul to destroy the Amalekites because of their sins against Israel."

"Wait! Did you not say that Haman's father was an Amalekite?"

"You begin to grasp the connection. King Saul defeated the land of Amalek." He held up a finger. "But contrary to God's command, he pounced on the spoils, destroying whatever was worthless and keeping the best of the sheep, oxen, and other valuables."

"How does all this concern us now?"

"Because not only had the king saved the fat cattle, he had also spared the king of the Amalekites, a man whose sword had made a widow of many a Hebrew woman."

Sazana sat up. "That's how I know the name! The Amalekite king was called Agag! Oh, I see! Haman's father said the name *Agagite* reminded him of home. You think Haman's father belonged to the king's lineage?"

"It fits."

"Wait, Jadon. That cannot be right. Saul may not have killed the king, but the prophet Samuel put Agag to the sword."

"So he did. But Master Sheber told me there is no proof that every one of Agag's sons were killed at that time. Saul, having spared one man, may have spared more. Or one of the sons might have been traveling at the time of the battle. Or might have managed to hide. We will never know for certain.

"What we do know is that Haman's father claimed that *his* people were also named Agagite. Which explains one thing: If a descendant of Agag had survived, he would have reason to bear a deep hatred for Israel and her God. A hatred malevolent enough to be passed from generation to generation."

He sighed heavily. "After hearing Master Sheber's history lesson, I rode back to the palace, arriving here in the small hours of the morning. I planned to give a brief report to Hathach before heading home. But what did I find? You . . ." He waved his hand toward her. "Half dead and unconscious."

"Is that when you called me *dear heart*?" She drew out the words in an exaggerated imitation.

"Might have been." Pink tinged his skin. "Heat of the moment. The salient point not being what I said. But—" He waved his hand at her again. "This whole business of you almost dying. I am highly opposed to it. Highly. Please do not repeat that performance."

For all the teasing in his manner, she sensed the weight of his concern for her. She supposed even a broken betrothal and the distance of years could not completely erase all that had once passed between them. "I will consider your suggestion."

33

Sazana

Yet you, LORD, are our Father.
We are the clay, you are the potter;
we are all the work of your hand.

Isaiah 64:8 NIV

She looked away, trying to pluck the threads of his narrative from the distraction of their personal lives. "Let us return to your story. An old line descending from a king, held together by the common bond of hatred for Israel."

Jadon nodded. "Their hate festered, and each generation fostered more hate in their sons and their sons after them."

How their people must have rejoiced when Assyria took captive the northern kingdom of Israel! How they must have danced in the streets when Babylon destroyed the southern kingdom of Judah. Sweet revenge for an ancient wound when stone-faced soldiers demolished the Temple of the Lord.

Until Cyrus.

The Persian king brought freedom in his wake, pronouncing the edict that allowed all Jews to return to their homeland. To begin rebuilding the very kingdom that had crushed Agag.

"You think Haman's father is behind the theft of Cyrus's cylinders?"

Jadon leaned forward. "The old king's proclamation would have been a stench in his nostrils. The undoing of Israel's enslavement. Haman's father could not reverse Cyrus's old command. But he understood the value of an edict that proved the faithfulness of the Lord. Cyrus, though a Gentile, demonstrated God's power at work through the ages. With the mark of his royal seal, he fulfilled the promises of God and proved the Lord's love for his people. He vindicated them.

"Haman's father, a man influenced by generations of hate, would have longed to destroy those words, along with the testimony they carried for future ages."

She considered his words in painful silence until they formed a question that could no longer be denied. "Jadon, do you think he was responsible for my parents' deaths? Could Hammedatha have arranged for them to be run over by that cart because they had a copy of the cylinder?"

Jadon gave her a steady look. "There is no way to know for certain. But I think, given what we have uncovered about Haman and his father, there is a good chance that your parents' deaths were no accident."

"But the man has been dead many years! Arta and I were still new at the workshop when Haman closed the place down for a week in honor of his father's passing. That was eleven years ago. He cannot be behind these recent attacks. He cannot be the one responsible for Arta's murder."

"Haman has ten sons. He will have passed that generational hatred to them. Like his father before him, one of them has turned to murder, knowing that the Cyrus cylinder could once again foil their plans to destroy the Jewish people."

"One son." She swallowed. "Or perhaps all ten, colluding together?"

Jadon's expression hardened. "The Ionians have a legend they call the hydra, a monster with nine heads. When you cut one off, two grow in its place. The descendants of Agag have become such a monster. The queen cut one head off. Now we have ten more to contend with."

"Have you told her?"

"Both her and Hathach. As we have no proof, the queen cannot raise a hand against Haman's sons. We only have conjecture, none of it solid enough to convince the king. He cannot go around putting his courtiers to death without proof."

Sazana plucked at the sheets. A ten-headed hydra, he had called their enemy. A shiver went through her. "What do you plan to do next?"

He grew quiet. She gave him a suspicious glance. "What is it?"

"This attack on you proves one thing. Someone in the workshop is spying for the enemy. Someone who knew that you planned to work late last night. The guard told me he had ensured that no one followed you from here. During the day, he made several excursions around the perimeter of the workshop and found nothing suspicious. Your attackers came later. They came knowing they would find you alone and vulnerable."

"But I thought you had already ruled out all the potters as potential spies."

"I could never shake the nagging feeling that I had missed something. I must start from the beginning and unearth what I failed to uncover last time."

She dropped her head. The men had become dear to her over the years. She knew each one, knew the names of their wives and children, knew whose mother had aching joints and whose brother faced debt. The knowledge that even one had turned against her—had caused Arta's death—lodged in her belly like a stone.

A soft knock at the threshold revealed a young woman bearing a tray. "I'm Sisy. The queen's cook sent me with puree of almonds." She set a steaming bowl on the stool next to the water jug. Her shy smile revealed a missing tooth near the front.

Sazana returned her smile. "My thanks. It smells delicious."

Sisy's genial face turned pink as she looked at Jadon before slipping out. Sazana could not blame her. He had the same effect on her insides, if not on her complexion.

Jadon gestured at the bowl. "Would you like me to help? I can manage to feed you without scalding you if you sit very still and avoid blinking."

Just then, the curtain swished open, revealing one of the queen's handmaidens. "No need. I am here now."

The handmaiden whispered something to Jadon. He rose quickly. "Hathach needs me. I will return to visit as soon as I can. Don't get into trouble while I am gone."

Sazana shrugged. "I would have to get out of trouble first."

He looked as if he could not decide whether to smile or frown, and his face settled somewhere in between, brow puckered, one corner of his lip tipped up. A fist squeezed her heart as she watched him leave. Over the past few days, they had spent so much time together, shared such depths of emotions, that her defenses had slipped. Every small inflection, every gesture had come to mean more than it should.

He cared for her, she could see that. Not enough to wish to marry her. But the thought of her dying had unsettled him. Shaken him enough to call her *dear heart*. His old endearment.

She would have to be careful. So careful. Or the gash in her palm would be nothing to the wound reopening in her heart.

Something told her that it was already too late.

She thanked the handmaiden, who held the bowl of almond puree for her as Sazana fed herself one-handed. At least she did not have to suffer through the indignity of being fed like a babe again.

Afterward, exhaustion and Adin's pain physic overcame the last of her strength, and she slept again, her dreams disturbed by muddled images she could not remember upon waking. Still, when she opened her eyes to lamplight, she felt better.

The junior handmaiden had returned to her bedside, looking refreshed. She had come armed with the paraphernalia of her trade. "Would you like me to arrange your hair?"

Sazana tried to hide her horrified reaction, knowing the woman meant the offer as a kindness. "Perhaps when I feel better?"

"I suppose you have a good excuse." She sniffed. "But it doesn't do to grow slovenly."

Sazana had an idea that their ideas of *slovenly* might differ a great deal.

To her surprise, the queen arrived with her usual unassuming entry. Sazana attempted to rise and offer a bow.

Esther held up her long-fingered hand. "I forbid it. Remain in bed, else you will have me to deal with."

"Your Majesty, how gracious of you to visit me again."

Esther settled on the stool the junior handmaiden had vacated, dismissing the woman with a wave. When the two were alone, she studied Sazana. "Other than the bandages encircling your hand, no one would believe you almost died two days ago." She leaned forward. "How do you feel?"

"Better, my lady."

"I am relieved to hear it." An awkward pause followed.

Esther took a breath and held it. "My husband, the king," she said, "sends his men into danger with painful regularity. Sometimes they return home injured or maimed. Sometimes they do not return at all. It is a burden that comes with his crown, a duty he must fulfill. Perhaps he bears it so well because he was born to it. Bred for it." She lifted an elegant, bejeweled hand toward Sazana. "I find I have no stomach for it."

Sazana's eyes widened. Did Esther feel guilty because she had almost died? "Your Majesty, you did not send me into battle. If I was in the workshop, it is because I do not wish to be elsewhere. If I search for the cylinder, it is because it is my heritage. Serving you is an honor. But you bear no responsibility for what happened to me. Or to Arta."

Esther's eyes shimmered before she looked away. She tugged her chin down once. When next she looked up, she had managed to put away the wavering emotions. "Did Jadon apprise you of his findings?"

"About Agag? He did."

"Jadon is a clever man."

"I can't disagree."

"Foolish to have let you go. But clever."

Sazana felt a smile tug at her lips. "I can't disagree with that either."

"What happened between you? Not that you have to answer. A fine line separates a good queen from an interfering woman."

It took Sazana a few moments to form her response. "His mother disapproved the match."

"His *mother*?" Esther's voice dripped with disbelief. "You mean to tell me that my bold, intrepid agent broke a betrothal because his *ima* objected? I don't believe it."

"Neither did I, for a long time." Sazana shrugged. "And yet I have the broken contract to prove it."

The queen sniffed. "We shall return to this discussion at a more opportune time. First, tell me how you are, truly." She pointed at Sazana's hand. "That is no simple gash. Not for you, Shoshanah. It must weigh on your heart. It must feel like your very future is struggling to survive under those bandages."

Sazana's breath caught. She had not expected the queen to understand the underlying deprivation caused by her wound. Save for a miracle, she would be stripped of something core to her very being. As always, words would not come when she most wanted them. The queen waited, her doe eyes kind.

"Forgive my slowness, Majesty." Sazana fisted her good hand under her breast. "I sometimes lack the ability to express my thoughts as I ought."

"Rubbish! You express them well enough. Most people's minds are like a shallow puddle. It does not take long to draw things out of it. You are a deep pool, my dear. Deep pools need a little more time."

"Then I wish I were a shallow pool."

"What nonsense!" Esther drew herself up. "Never belittle your creation," she said in a queen's voice. "You are fearfully and wonderfully made. God, in his design of every part of you, created an awe-inspiring and wonderful being. If you change one part, reject one thing, who knows but that you would ruin the whole?

"If God intended your mind to be a deep pool even though he knew the cost of it would be a slower speech, then trust the wisdom of his decision. I, for one, bless his choice for you. Be sure and do the same, my dear. Else you reject God's own intention. His very creation. Only a fool would do that, and you are no fool, Shoshanah."

She exhaled. "Besides, your words are worth the wait."

Sazana had never thought of her slow speech as God's design. God's good intention rather than a defect of her mind.

Had she done what the queen accused? Had she rejected God's wondrous creation by hating this part of herself? She chewed her lip.

She had always thought of herself as a tolerably good person. She did her best to keep the commandments. When she could, she helped the widows and orphans. She tried to love God. Yet in the short time the queen had known her, she had fingered two serious shortcomings in her, not in a condemning manner that disparaged Sazana. But with caring, with understanding, with grace. And with truth.

Sazana would never have noticed her own tendency to live

as an orphan. To forget God's fatherhood, relying instead on her own ability. Or fearing her own weakness.

And now the queen had helped her see how her attitude toward her speech was a rejection of God's own design. Until Esther pointed out these flaws in her thinking, she had not considered them a sin.

Now? It came to her that she needed to repent. She had diminished God and enlarged her own role by forgetting his fatherhood. His provision. His protection. And she had belittled his creation when she had belittled herself.

"My lady," she told Esther who waited in patient silence. "I have sinned."

Esther nodded. "Haven't we all?"

For four days, Sazana found herself imprisoned by her injuries, confined to her closet of a chamber when she desperately wished to be of use. She wanted to help the queen make a success of the workshop, to finish the pieces she had started, and to complete the orders that required her attention. She wanted to help her people by searching for the cylinder.

Instead, God had allowed her to become imprisoned within these four walls, availing nothing for anyone.

At first, the empty hours chafed, leaving too much opportunity for fretting. From her childhood, she had learned to find comfort in her work. Now even that comfort had been snatched away. Lacking her usual occupation and the familiar consolation it brought, she struggled to find peace.

Her eye fell on the queen's gift nestled at the foot of her bed, atop her narrow travel chest. She unfurled the treasured papyrus and studied the silver verses from the prophet Isaiah.

> Yet you, LORD, are our Father.
> We are the clay, you are the potter;
> we are all the work of your hand.

She had known these words before. Appreciated their sentiment, even. But now, in the maddening confinement of illness, they took on a deeper meaning. The longer she considered them, the more her soul understood Esther's intention in giving these verses to her. What the queen had wanted to teach her through them.

Lying in this bed of iron was the orphan child. The orphan who stared at the gash in her hand, anxious for her future. The orphan who wondered when the next disaster would arise to crush her.

But the orphan was wrong.

She had a Father. God had not left her to her own devices. He did not expect her to resolve her own problems, heal her own wounds, determine her own solutions.

She studied the rest of the prophet's words. Esther had the right of it. Sazana understood the role of clay to a potter better than most.

How often she had walked by a row of jars she had recently shaped on the wheel and touched them with joy, with gladness for their very existence. How often she had celebrated when they emerged from the kiln just as she had intended.

Did God not care for her more than a potter for her clay?

For four days, Sazana sank into those verses like a pot being dipped into glaze, absorbing its truths, its promises, its strength, until the little orphan girl was, if not healed, then certainly soothed.

God, in his mercy, had pulled her out of the urgency of the world to remind her of an even more urgent truth.

On the fifth day, she felt like a pot seasoned on the drying rack. Ready to face the fire that her life had become.

The day before, the physician had replaced her sling with a sturdier one to keep her hand steady when she walked about. "Does this mean I may return to work?" she asked Adin as he checked on her stitches.

He raised a thick brow. "What do you mean by 'work'?"

"I know I can't throw a pot. But the workshop needs oversight. Orders must be placed. Supplies replenished. Our men need supervision. I have been missing too long."

The physician put away the jar of salve he used daily on her wound and closed his medicine chest. "As long as you keep your hand immobile, I see no reason for you to remain stuck in this chamber."

"Bless you!"

He laughed. "Feeling a little desperate to end your confinement?"

"Except for the amount, you have diagnosed the condition perfectly."

Adjusting her tunic, she slipped her feet into her shoes, ensuring that the thick sling kept her hand steady. She left her hair loose, unable to manage a braid. There was only so much she could do with one hand. When she slipped the curtain open, she came face-to-face with one of the king's Immortals instead of a regular palace guard.

"Mistress." He slapped his spear to his chest.

When the soldier did not budge from her path, she shifted her weight from foot to foot, finally pointing to the hallway.

He did not budge. "If you leave, I follow."

"I see." She tried to look around him. "What happened to the palace guard?"

He bent to pick up his shield from where it rested against the wall. "The guards are not bad. But the Immortals are better."

Her eyes narrowed. "Did Jadon arrange this?"

He grinned. "Who else?" He held up a finger. "Lest you mean to argue, you should know the queen approved his recommendation. Which is to say, before we leave the palace, we stop at Lord Hathach's chambers to report your movements."

She tried to cross her arms before remembering her bandaged

hand, and left one arm dangling at her side and the other resting in its sling across her chest like a lopsided chicken. "Anything else?"

"Please don't faint on my watch. I am not fond of contending with fainting women."

"You are a friend of Jadon's, aren't you?"

He bowed with perfect grace, managing not to poke himself in the eye with his long spear. "I have that dubious distinction. Mazares, at your service."

"Well, Mazares, I have no intention of fainting today. I plan to spend the day at the queen's pottery workshop. And I'm not riding your horse."

"It's fortunate for me, then, that they teach us how to walk reasonably well in the army."

34

Jadon

Even my close friend in whom I trusted,
who ate my bread, has lifted his heel against me.

Psalm 41:9

THE TWELFTH YEAR OF KING XERXES'S RULE
THE FORTY-SECOND DAY OF SUMMER

When Jadon arrived at the workshop, he found Shoshanah deep in conversation with the queen's scribe. "We are running short on quartz," she said, consulting her list.

At the scribe's blank expression, she explained, "I use it as temper in my clay."

"Temper. Right."

Jadon could tell she was trying to corral her smile. "It's something you add to the clay to improve its quality. Make it stronger, less likely to break."

The scribe nodded. "Very good. Where should I send the request?"

"You can copy Arta's last order." She handed him a scroll with her good hand. "A new batch should last us to the end of the year. Also, the kiln master told me that he is running low on seaweed."

The scribe scrunched his nose. "You use seaweed in your clay?"

"In the clay, no. In the kiln's fire. The salt and minerals from the sea improve the colors of the glaze."

She seemed animated as she explained to the scribe the basic business of running the queen's workshop. Her skin had lost the pallor of sickness. Jadon found himself exhaling with relief.

Spotting Jadon, Mazares slapped him across the back. "Knew it wouldn't take you long to get here." He subtly nodded toward Shoshanah. "Figured I would be too much competition, eh?"

Jadon sighed, refusing to take his friend's bait. "Thank you for stepping in to help during your leisure hours."

"I nosed around to see if I could find anything useful." He shrugged. "Just a bunch of potters. Nothing suspicious."

"That's my problem. Something smells rotten, and I can't find the source."

"You will." Mazares yawned, displaying his magnificent teeth as well as a broad tongue. "I'm off to bed. The rest of the boys are lined up to help when you need us."

Jadon smiled with gratitude. "Thank them for me."

When Shoshanah finished her conversation with the scribe, he wound his way toward her. "Glad you have recovered enough to return to work."

She had left her hair loose, and it hung down her back, reaching all the way to her hip. As she turned to face him, a silky curtain of hair fell over the side of her face and shoulder. His breath hitched at the picture she made, the olive skin perfect over the rounded cheekbones, the full lips, the strong line of her shoulders. He itched to tuck the hair behind her ear and shoved his hand into his belt to keep temptation at bay.

257

She must have noticed him staring. "I couldn't braid it with one hand."

He almost offered to help. He was quite adroit at braiding, thanks to years of caring for his horse. It took more effort than he liked to admit to curb his tongue. "How are things here?"

"The kiln master has done a fine job of running the yard. The quality of the clay we produce has remained consistently high. In the workshop, the men have managed the best they can in my absence. But I need to create a new work roster for the week. Cambyz and Rashda have made good progress throwing the pots in the fine ware section. They are waiting to start a new batch of the blue glaze. I wish I could make it myself." She worried her lip. "With my guidance, I trust they will manage."

"The place needs an overseer as well as a potter. With Arta gone, the workshop depends on you, whether you can ply the wheel or not."

She threw a longing glance at Arta's corner, where he used to sit at the close of the day to study his scrolls, and occasionally, if time allowed, to throw a pot on his old, wobbly wheel. His empty stool had a forlorn air, a long crack running through the middle of the aging wood.

"I miss him," she said. "I can never replace him. He taught me the business of running the place. But he had the head for administration. I am only a potter." She sighed. "Or I was."

He frowned. "You're still a potter, Shoshanah."

Her smile held an edge of irony. "A one-handed potter?"

"For now."

"Perhaps." She shrugged. "I am learning to anchor my soul to God better than I used to do before all this happened."

His chest filled with something warm and tender. She had always known how to surprise him. "That will serve you even better than pottery."

"True."

Over her head, he saw the wheel boy hunkered against the

258

wall, his gaze following Shoshanah. A film of tears made his eyes shimmer. The boy seemed to be drowning in despair. Jadon pointed his chin. "Perhaps you can find something for Arash to do while you are recuperating."

Shoshanah turned, taking in the boy's stooping figure. "I forgot about him. Poor thing. He must be afraid he will lose his job without me working the wheel." She strode away, squatting before Arash and speaking softly. She motioned to the coarse ware section.

The boy bowed his head in agreement and rose to plod behind Shoshanah as she wove through the potters. The dark shadow on his face did not lift, not even when Shoshanah smiled at him. His gaze slid away from hers, avoiding her eyes.

If Jadon didn't know better, he would have thought the boy felt guilty. What fathomable reason would the child have for that?

Time slowed. The noise of the workshop faded around him. Blood pounded in his ear.

Guilt!

The pieces started to fall into place. The rotten stench he could not pinpoint, the crack in the workshop he had missed.

The boy's youth had clouded his judgment. That, and the fact that he clearly carried a torch for Shoshanah. He would never hurt her, of that Jadon was certain. Not intentionally.

He strode toward them, his steps long and urgent. Spotting his purposeful gait toward them, Shoshanah hesitated.

Jadon skewered the boy with an unblinking glare. "Arash, please join Mistress Sazana and me in the fine ware section."

The child paled, stepping backward. His eyes widened, and he looked around wildly. For a moment, he seemed to consider making a run for it.

Preparing for a mad dash, Jadon bent his knees and tilted his body forward. "I only want to talk to you. Running won't solve anything."

Shoshanah gave Jadon a confused glance before placing her good hand on the boy's shoulder. "It's all right, Arash. Come with me. No one means you harm."

At her touch, the fight went out of the boy. His head drooped, and he followed them to the fine ware section. His legs folded beneath him as he collapsed on his stool.

Jadon dismissed Cambyz and Rashda, sending them on a break. He drew the curtain that separated the two sections, enclosing them in a bubble of privacy.

He knew he had to strike the right tone. Too harsh, and the boy would shut down. Too gentle, and he would wriggle out of their grasp. He had to find the perfect balance.

In the back of his mind, he was aware that Shoshanah's silence indicated the kind of deep trust he had not earned from her. She had not questioned his actions, but stood near Arash, her hand on his shoulder, her face concerned.

Questions must be clamoring around her clever mind. He appreciated the fact that she chose not to voice a single one. Instead, she gave him room to maneuver as he needed.

Jadon dragged Shoshanah's pottery stool over to where the boy sat, his back hunched, his skin damp with sweat. Sitting across from him, he began. "Arash, who did you tell?"

The boy cringed.

Jadon waited a beat, and when Arash remained mute, he pressed. "You told someone what Master Arta said that last night. It was you I chased. You were listening outside this window here. And you heard what Master Arta and I talked about. You heard him say he would consider helping me."

The boy curled into himself and remained silent. Jadon needed a different tack. "How did you do it? How did you evade me? I ran out of here fast. There are not many grown men who can outpace me, yet you managed to disappear. How?"

The ghost of a smile touched the boy's lips at this compliment. "I did not outrun you."

Jadon did not betray his satisfaction at this oblique admission of the boy's presence that night. "No?"

"I worked in the yard for a whole year. You learn good hiding places in a place like that. I ran a short distance before diving under a pile of wood near the kilns."

At this tacit admission of guilt, Shoshanah pressed her hand against her mouth.

Jadon continued, hoping to break the boy's defensive walls. "Clever. I never saw you."

A shrug. "Didn't want you to."

"Who did you tell? Lord Haman's son?"

"Don't know him."

"Tell me the truth and I will do my best to protect you. I am sure you did not intend to harm Master Arta or Mistress Sazana."

At the mention of Sazana's name, he dropped his head, the tips of his ears turning fire red. He played with a clean kerchief tucked into his belt.

Shoshanah followed the movement, her eyes narrowing. She crouched next to him. "You aren't trying to protect yourself, are you, Arash? You are worried about someone else. Someone you care for very much. Someone like your mother?"

A tortured sound escaped his lips. "Please! I don't have no one else. You've been an orphan, mistress. You know how bad it is. Don't take her from me."

She pressed her hand over his in a calming gesture. "The queen has a tender heart for orphans, Arash. Like you and me, she lost her father as a child. Her mother too. For your sake, she will do what she can to shield your mother. But you must tell us everything."

Jadon sent Shoshanah an admiring glance. She had deciphered the boy's silent anguish. Though he had taken note of it, he had not been as quick to understand its source. To realize the boy wanted to protect his mother more than himself.

261

Shoshanah had an agile mind to which she did not give enough credit. The twists and turns of that mind, gentle and unique, able to draw conclusions that most, including him, missed, was one of the beautiful things about her.

He forced himself to focus on the present task. Time to find the answers they needed.

He steeled himself to the pain he was about to cause. "Arash, you must know that whoever has done these things is an evil man. If your mother knows him, she is not safe. He will not wish to leave any witnesses behind. Best you tell us all you know so that we can protect her."

35

Sazana

For you equipped me with strength for the battle . . .
Psalm 18:39

Sazana's heart could not catch up with the unfolding drama. Of all the people in the workshop, Arash had been the last person she had suspected. Half of her wanted to scream at him, to protest his betrayal. The other half bowed under the weight of pity.

"It started simple," he said. "After Lord Haman died, my mother would ask me questions every day. *Tell me what happened at work. What did Mistress Sazana say? Where did Master Arta go?* At first, I thought she was just curious. You know. Because the queen owns the place now and everything.

"Then she started asking for more. Like making me go back in the evenings and listen at the window. I told her it wasn't right. But she said I was too young to understand."

He sniffed and wiped his nose on the kerchief his mother laundered every day. "The night Master Arta died . . . That day,

I had come back home to tell my mother what I'd heard him say to you, Master Jadon. That he might know something to help the queen. That's when I seen him."

"Who?" she and Jadon asked together.

"That Nabonassar who used to work here. He came to our house. I saw my mother speak to him. When Master Arta got murdered later that night, that's when I knew. He done it. He done it, and it was my fault for opening my big mouth."

Nabonassar! Haman's spy. Sazana had assumed that with his master dead, he had packed his bags and set off for greener pastures. Instead, he had remained close. Who did he serve now? One of Haman's sons? All of them?

Her mouth tasted like the old clay she dumped into the leftover bucket. "They were spying on us from the time Haman died."

"It's the reason Hathach sent me here to begin with. He worried they might seek a way to ruin the workshop. To make the queen seem incompetent before the king. Even to harm you in order to diminish the workshop's income. Hathach was right. They couldn't stand for the place to succeed without their father." Jadon rubbed the back of his neck. "But over time, the information they collected added up to something more interesting. Something even you and I didn't know."

A picture began to emerge as Sazana deliberated over what their enemies had discovered. Haman had already known that she and Arta had arrived from Babylon twelve years earlier. She had even told him that her father had been a scribe.

But the pieces must have started to fall into place when he discovered her Jewish heritage.

Haman had known that another copy of the cylinder existed somewhere because his father's men had failed to retrieve it from her mother's workshop. Even after her parents' deaths, Hammedatha had not recovered their cylinder, and his son had known it. Like the queen, Haman might have heard whispers of its presence in Susa.

If she had told Haman her true name when she had first started working here, he would have made the connection. But because she had kept her heritage secret, he had remained in the dark for twelve years.

The recent revelation of her Hebrew lineage had opened the first door to the discovery of her connection to the cylinder. Haman would have taken notice: A Jewish child from Babylon who had arrived in Susa twelve years earlier. A girl with a talent for the wheel. Eventually, that single fact might have triggered a memory in Haman. The memory of another female Jewish potter. Another rare talent.

When Arta practically admitted to the queen's agent that he had a means of helping her and the Jewish people, Haman's sons must have come to the right conclusion.

She and Arta had brought the cylinder from Babylon after her parents had been killed.

"From the beginning, they were a step ahead of us," she said.

"We were operating blind. Arta kept his secret too well, while Haman's brood knew everything." His jaw knotted. "They knew they could not delay any longer, not when Arta practically agreed to help the queen. He had to be eliminated. I wish he had trusted me that night."

"Or me, for that matter. He promised to tell me his secret the next day. But he never had the chance."

From the frown on his face, Arash had lost the trail of their conversation. He had gathered enough, however, to realize that his reports had somehow led to Arta's demise.

"My fault. 'Cause I told them what I heard that night." A sob escaped him. "After Master Arta died, I told my mother I wouldn't do it anymore. I wouldn't tell her anything else. But a few days later, that Nabonassar came back. And he beat her. She had nothing to report 'cause I refused to say nothing. So he beat her bad."

Sazana winced. Poor boy. The anger she had felt at his betrayal shrank to a small ember. "I am sorry, Arash."

"It's me who is sorry, mistress. I shouldn't have said nothing to her. But I swear to you, I didn't know what he would do."

Jadon's tone had grown soft. "To protect your mother, you told her that Mistress Sazana was staying late at the workshop that night, didn't you?"

"I'm so ashamed, mistress! My mother begged and begged me. Black and blue she was from her last beating. I didn't dare refuse her. I thought for certain he would kill her."

Jadon pressed again. "After you told her, you decided to come back here."

He hung his head. "I thought perhaps I could help if he tried to do her harm like he done to Master Arta. But that guard chased me, and I had to hide from him. I did no good by coming and caused more harm, on top. Instead of chasing after me, the guard could have stayed to defend the mistress."

"He could have. Then again, Nabonassar might have hurt him too. Who knows. Perhaps chasing after you saved the guard's life." Jadon came to his feet. "We need to go and collect your mother. We'll take you both to the palace for now."

The boy's eyes grew round as the king's newly minted coins. "To put us to death, you mean?"

"No. The queen will determine your punishment. But no one is dying today. Of that, you may be certain."

Sazana felt an odd relief. Since Arta's death, she had started to feel like a hunted animal. Like every corner hid a monster bent on harming her. Not knowing who wanted her dead or how they managed to always remain a step ahead. Not comprehending how they always showed up at the precise moment that would inflict the most damage.

Jadon's insight into Arash's involvement had changed things. By convincing the boy to confess, they had discovered the identity of Arta's murderer. More, they now knew how he had managed to collect his information.

"I don't feel like a hunted animal anymore," she murmured.

Jadon's mouth flattened. "Because you're not. The tables are turned. Now we become the hunters. We have severed their source of information. They don't know it yet. But they have just become deaf and blind."

His smile had little in common with the man of her youth. It had a razor's edge, with no hint of pity to soften it. "I will find Nabonassar. And he will answer for what he has done."

Esther listened to Jadon's report. "Excellent work, Jadon."

A trail of pink stained his skin. He pressed a fist to his heart. "I live to serve, lady." He pointed his chin at Sazana. "I ought to mention that Shoshanah guessed the boy wanted to shield his mother. Knowing his motive helped me crack through his defenses."

"I always suspected you two would work well together. Tell me, what do you plan next?"

Jadon's brows lowered. "Finding Nabonassar won't be easy. He used to bunk at the workshop when Haman was alive. That's a dead end. He also owns a cottage outside Susa that's occupied by distant relatives. I have sent a couple of men to nose around, though I doubt he will be staying there. I suspect he's too slippery to make it that easy for us. I aim to interrogate the boy's mother. If she knows anything that could help us, I will draw it out of her."

The queen sat on the edge of one of Hathach's narrow chairs. "We need Nabonassar. Not only is he a murderer and must be punished for killing a valuable man, but he can lead us to his master."

"Or masters. For all we know, all ten may be involved."

"Knowing Haman as we do now, I do not doubt it." She adjusted her scalloped skirts. "We still need to find that cylinder. Given how desperate they are to lay their hands on it, I am certain they have not given up looking, and neither can we."

Sazana bit her lip. It always came down to that. Her inability to understand Arta's message.

But no. That was not true. She did not have to solve this puzzle alone. She was not an orphan. God would help her. He had brought her this far. He would take her the rest of the way. For the sake of his people, he would guide her through the wilderness of her confusion.

36

Jadon

… and my eye has looked in triumph on my
enemies.

Psalm 54:7

Jadon had already spent a whole hour with Arash's mother,
having little to show for his time. She seemed to know
nothing useful about Nabonassar. The man had crawled
into some hole they could not uncover.

If they could not find Nabonassar, that meant that Nabonassar must find them.

He exhaled. This had been his least-favorite option. Too
many variables that could go wrong.

"How did you know when he would come to visit you?" he
asked.

"I never did, master. He came and went as he pleased, like
an ill wind."

"When do you next expect him?"

"I couldn't say. He came for news when he wanted."

"Then we will have news waiting for him. I need you to return to your house. The boy too. And he must resume his work at the pottery workshop." He lowered his eyebrows. "It's temporary, you understand? When we catch him, you return to the palace and await the queen's pleasure."

She gave an anxious shake of her head. "He'll hurt me, master. Please don't send me back."

"He will not have a chance. We'll be there with you."

"Even if I survive him, the queen will have me killed." She beat her breast. "Ay! What's a poor mother to do? My son will be left with nobody to look after him."

"Stop your sniveling," Jadon said, out of patience. "The queen has no plan to execute you. Likely, she will put you to work at the palace laundry until you learn to make do with honest gain rather than set such a poor example for your son."

Everyone at the workshop seemed to sense the unease that filled the air. The men had grown more quiet than usual, the sound of their conversations muted. Arash swept the floor with a long-handled broom, picking up pieces of dried clay and dirt.

Though Jadon felt fairly certain that the boy would not repeat his offense, he and Shoshanah made sure not to mention anything important in his hearing.

They needed to give the impression that this was a day like any other. Arash had arrived as usual to tend to his work. If Nabonassar had the boy and his mother under surveillance, he would not detect any unusual activity. Knowing that this might be an option from the beginning, Jadon had ensured the secrecy of their transport to the palace.

He had their house and the workshop surrounded by his men. He did not intend to take any chances. A tightly woven net awaited Nabonassar. All he had to do was show his face and they would have him.

Sazana sat in a corner, guiding Cambyz as he mixed glaze. Once in a while, she looked up at Jadon, brows knotting. He tried to give her a reassuring smile.

She did not return it.

His heart squeezed. Too many things remained clouded between them. Too many unexplained matters stretched between them like a military rampart separating two armies.

He had been about to delve into the past when they had been interrupted by the queen's man. They had no future together, he knew that, although God had seen fit to throw them into each other's paths with generous regularity.

He had convinced himself that his lack of proper explanation for his abandonment of her made little difference. He had, after all, assured her that none of it was her doing. Having now spent time with her, he realized the depth of his error. His silence had gored her like an ox's horn. Into that open wound, she had poured all manner of untruths. He had been half gored himself at the time, watching the pieces of his life fall at his feet. His decisions had not always been perfectly executed. He had to make up for that.

He blew out an exasperated breath. Thanks to her injury and the paucity of time, he had not had a single moment to explain himself. He could not mend the betrothal. But he could at least wash away the lies she had told herself.

He had wounded her twice. First by walking away, and then by not telling her why. His promise to his dying mother had been made under duress. Surely God would forgive him for breaking it. For it was the only way he could show Shoshanah that none of the fault lay with her.

As soon as they caught Nabonassar in their trap, he would set the past to rights. Perhaps God could heal the wounds Jadon had dealt her. He squeezed his eyes shut. His own would never heal.

He pulled Arash aside as he was about to leave. "You know what to do, yes?"

The boy nodded, face wan.

"You will be safe. I have eyes on you and your mother."

Arash's lower lip quivered. "I'll do right."

"Good boy. We count on you."

Shoshanah watched him leave. "Will he be all right?"

"He is more surrounded today than the king of Persia on his way to war. No harm will come to him, I promise."

"You think you'll catch Nabonassar?"

Jadon shrugged. "If not today, then soon. He is bound to come sniffing again. They have been his best source of information. He has no reason to give up on them."

Nabonassar did not show. Nor did he come on the second or third day. Everyone kept up the charade, Arash and his mother living at home, shadowed by Jadon's men, Shoshanah working at the workshop. When the sixth day came and went with no sign of the man, Jadon began to despair he would ever show. In spite of Jadon's best efforts, Nabonassar must have grown suspicious of the boy and his mother.

He started to review other options, other traps he could set, though he had no liking for any of them. They all involved endangering Shoshanah, and he refused to consider that.

By the end of the week, the mood at the workshop had grown strained to breaking point. Although the men had no knowledge of the trap Jadon had set, nor of the part Arash had played in Arta's death, they picked up on Shoshanah's quiet tension. His own body felt so wound tight that when he climbed into his bed at the end of the night, his neck and jaw ached.

Arash suffered the most. He grew paler by the day, jumping at every sound. They could not continue like this. The boy would unintentionally give them away.

That night, after he had dropped Shoshanah off at the palace, he returned to Arash's home to join his men. Another fruitless watch, he reckoned.

The sun had already set, giving way to a bright moon, when the man came skulking like a wild dog. His great paw wrapped around the boy's arm, pulling him up until he stood on tiptoes. Whatever foul threat he intended to deliver, he did not have the chance to complete it.

"Nabonassar, I presume." Jadon crept soundlessly from behind, pressing the tip of his dagger into the man's jugular. "I have been eager to meet you."

His quarry, knowing himself betrayed, hissed in anger and twisted his hold on Arash's arm. The boy yelped.

Jadon shoved the knife tip hard enough to cause damage, but not to kill. "Do that again, and I will have a very enjoyable night. You have no idea how I hope you will try."

Nabonassar dropped his hand. Jadon's men made short work of trussing him up. He resisted enough to earn himself a few fat bruises before being thrown into a dirty cart.

Catching him turned out to be the easy part. Getting the man to talk proved a bigger challenge.

He passed a long and fruitless night trying to convince Nabonassar to reveal the names of his masters. Jadon would give the villain one thing. He knew how to keep his mouth shut.

He fell into bed just as the sun rose over the horizon, exhausted but convinced that in a matter of days they would find the proof they needed to cut the hydra's head off for good.

37

Sazana

. . . a time to keep silence, and a time to speak.
Ecclesiastes 3:7

Nabonassar's arrest meant they had come one step closer to conquering their enemies. Sazana hoped that soon they would enjoy greater safety—the queen, the workshop, and every Jewish man or woman who might one day suffer from the consequences of Hammedatha's generational hatred.

But they had come no closer to unearthing the location of Cyrus's cylinder. Only one person could find that irreplaceable document: Sazana herself. And she was confounded.

Having spent five full days searching through her home without anything to show for it, she had not bothered to return there except for a quick trip to fetch more personal necessities. She had already looked through every corner she could think of to no avail. But finding the workshop likewise devoid of a single helpful hint, she decided to begin her search afresh.

The morning after Nabonassar's arrest, once again she found Mazares at her door, yawning like a cat curled up in the sunshine.

"We have to go to my house," she said without preamble.

His jaw snapped shut mid-yawn. "And a good morning to you. This house of yours, are we going there so you can prepare a magnificent breakfast?"

"You must have fallen asleep on your feet, because it is clear you are dreaming."

He grinned. "Can't blame a man for trying."

"If you don't mind, bestir yourself and follow."

He trailed a step behind. "First, we report to Hathach."

"Fine. We report. We report. Pick up your Immortal feet and tell me what happened last night as we walk. Jadon sent me a message to let me know he had captured Nabonassar. I don't know what took place after that. Did Nabonassar divulge any useful information?"

"Not yet. Last I heard, we left him to pickle in his misery for a while. Perchance it will loosen his tongue."

"I see." She pursed her lips. Her question, she had hoped, would encourage Mazares to mention Jadon. But the man proved infuriatingly unhelpful.

She could ask a direct question. Then again, she could only imagine the teasing to which he would subject her if she did. She gnawed her lip.

She had heard nothing more from Jadon after his brief update on Nabonassar's arrest the previous night. Managing to run Hathach to ground, she had insisted on a few details. The eunuch had assured her that Arash and his mother were safe and residing within the safety of palace walls. But his parsimonious account had left out any mention of Jadon.

"You seem preoccupied," Mazares said. "Anything on your mind?" He gave her an innocent look.

"No," she snapped.

"That's too bad. I felt sure you might want to ask me about Jadon."

Her hardest glare failed to put a dent in his smile. Or to loosen his tongue. She lasted halfway up the hill before she gave in. "How is Jadon?"

"Aren't you relieved to spit it out? His pretty name must have stuck in your throat like a burr." To her annoyance, his grin widened. "Jadon, as far as I know, lies snoring in his cozy bed. You do know he snores? Not a bargain, that one."

She rolled her eyes. "But he is well? Uninjured?"

"Of course. He stayed up half the night trying to get Nabonassar to talk. Man wouldn't break. Near sunup, Jadon decided to go home and catch a few hours of sleep. He will return to the palace soon enough, and Hathach will send him to find you. He will be standing at your door before noon, I wager."

Sazana's shoulders lowered from around her ears. Jadon was unharmed. She had needed to hear those words. Somehow, in her diminishing world, his safety had come to take on mountainous proportions.

When they arrived at her house, Mazares called a familiar greeting to the two men who stood guard. In spite of their presence, the Immortal insisted on searching the house himself before he would allow her to step inside. She was beginning to comprehend where Jadon had formed some of his habits.

"Are you certain there is no breakfast to be had in the place?" Mazares pinned hopeful eyes on her.

"I gave away all the food when I moved to the palace."

"That's sad." He heaved a tragic sigh. "What brings you here, then?"

"I am searching for something."

Mazares looked through one window, followed by the next. His actions seemed casual, but she realized that beneath the cheerful exterior and the teasing manner, he was all soldier.

Every look, every step revealed a military man focused on his business.

"You think they will send someone else? Now that Nabonassar is caught? You expect my house to be ransacked again?"

He shrugged. "Nabonassar is only a tool. A good one. But a tool, nonetheless. Tools can be replaced." He flashed his ready smile. "If they manage by some miracle to get past those two out there, they'll have me to contend with."

"True. Then again, you must be weak from hunger, having skipped your morning meal."

He cracked a knuckle. "Starved or not, I am twice any man who tries to walk through that door."

Jadon chose that inopportune moment to step across the threshold.

"As I said." Mazares looked pleased as a fox.

Sazana burst out laughing. Jadon looked between the two, taking in the smug expression on Mazares's face and Sazana's sniggering convulsions. "I don't want to know," he said.

"Nothing new, in any case. Another proof of my superiority."

"Another dream in your head, you mean." Jadon placed a canvas bag on the dining room table. "My thanks for taking another shift, Mazares. I will take over now."

"Just in time, too, before the poor man faints from hunger," Sazana said. "And we all know how much Mazares loves fainting."

"Other people's fainting," the Immortal retorted, looking cagey.

"Oh, Mazares has no problem with fainting. In fact, I would call him an expert in the field." Jadon fetched a short stack of dishes and set them on the table. "He once swooned for two whole hours without fluttering an eyelash."

"I did not swoon! I passed out, thanks to a Greek arrow sticking out of my thigh. Anyone would do the same."

Sazana laughed again, enjoying the good-natured harassment.

Enjoying the friendship it implied between the two men. And most of all, enjoying the sight of Jadon, hale and hearty, safe from Haman's posthumous darts.

Jadon withdrew an oval loaf of stone-baked bread from the canvas bag and set it upon a plate, followed by a square of white cheese.

"You brought food!" Mazares reached for the bread.

Jadon slapped the back of his hand. "Manners!" From his bag, he withdrew a package, covered in thin cloth and wrapped with twine. "I asked one of the queen's cooks to prepare this for you. You can eat it as you walk."

Mazares sniffed at the package and peeked inside. "Sour cherry jam and cream! My favorite."

"Can't risk you swooning in public. Gives a bad name to the Immortals."

Mazares lifted his breakfast triumphantly. "Say what you like. I forgive you."

After the Immortal left, Jadon set out the rest of the food he had fetched from the queen's kitchens. "I heard you left without eating."

She gaped at him. "There are no secrets in that gilded palace."

"You begin to understand court life." He placed a broad pat of butter next to the cheese and followed them with two small clay pots. She lifted their lids and found honey in one and sour cherry jam in the other.

"Quite the feast."

"A more delightful aspect of the palace. One eats well."

She set aside the empty amphora of wheat she had been searching and joined him at the table. Jadon prayed over their meal, blessing the Lord for bringing forth bread from the earth. Breaking off a ceremonial piece, he dipped it into salt before eating.

"No news?" she asked when he finished.

"Nabonassar remains silent, but it will not last. He will crack soon enough. Until then, we wait. And you?"

She shook her head. "I thought I better search the house again. Perhaps it will jog my memory and help me understand Arta's hint."

"I am glad you are here." He looked at his hands.

The mood, light and laughter-filled with Mazares there, shifted, becoming heavy and layered, like a cloud-covered day that refused to rain.

"I have wanted to speak to you for some days. But the world has interfered." Jadon pointed at her sling.

She took a bite of her bread, training her gaze on him. A bright flush ran from his neck to his cheeks. Lowering his head, he refused to meet her eyes.

"What eats at you?" she asked, her tone gentle.

He gave her a surprised glance before lowering his head again. "You always had a knack for reading me."

And yet he left her confused. She wondered if Nabonassar had said something. Revealed some bad news Jadon preferred not to share. Perhaps something had gone awry with Arash.

But the line of his rigid shoulders and that grinding jaw hinted at something more personal.

He picked up a piece of bread and placed it back on the plate. "I want to explain. About what happened between us."

Her heart stuttered. She had waited years for him to account for his actions. Years of wanting to hear from his own lips what she had already deduced from his actions. That he had walked away to please his mother. That she had never mattered enough to warrant a fight.

And yet she realized with sudden insight that a part of her did not want to hear the words. Did not want the finality of such an explanation. Did not want to be proven right.

A part of her wanted to stop him now. To demand that he keep his mouth sealed tight.

She bit her lip, tasting blood. Best to finish with the past once and for all.

Perhaps that was why God, in his wisdom, had allowed Jadon back into her life. The only way to be truly free of him was to expose the nub of the putrefaction that lay between them. Clean away the poison. Perhaps then she could move on with life.

"Tell me," she said, trying to brace herself against the agonizing truth.

38

Jadon

For God alone, O my soul, wait in silence,
for my hope is from him.

Psalm 62:5

Jadon came to his feet, his movements restless. "I thought, at the time, that if you knew the full truth, you would insist on remaining with me. On sacrificing yourself at the burning pyre my life had become."

Sazana shook her head in confusion. "Of what do you speak?"

His lips had turned white. "I speak of my mother, and my grandmother before her."

"Your grandmother? I never even met the woman. She died long before we were betrothed." Surely he could not blame her for displeasing another woman in his family.

He held up a hand. "I know. I know."

She inhaled. "What of her?"

"There was a reason I rarely spoke of her to you. As a boy,

I adored her. I remember her being a sweet, doting presence throughout my childhood. She baked treats for me and laughed at my antics. I could do no wrong in her eyes."

"She sounds lovely."

His smile held a bitter edge she did not understand. "Lovely, yes. The grandmother everyone wants to have. Then, something changed when I turned twelve. By then, the palace school took up most of my time. But when I came home to visit, I noticed a difference in her.

"They were small things at first. She grew wan and suffered from colic. She seemed tired all the time. We became concerned as her symptoms worsened. She suffered with frequent headaches and grew alarmingly thin. Physicians dosed her with their remedies. None helped."

"How painful for you and your family, Jadon. I am sorry."

He waved away her response as though she did not understand. "I have more to tell. This is the part you need to hear. My grandmother's symptoms took an odd turn. She started to grow irritable. A woman who had been gentle all her life would snap at us for little reason. We assumed the illness made her short-tempered and did our best to soothe her.

"The spasms began not long after. Tremors she could not control. She grew terse. Without reason, she would become angry and scream at us. She accused us of absurd things." He shook his head. "Some days, it was unbearable to watch."

At the age of twelve, he must have found his grandmother's incomprehensible transformation confusing. "How awful," she said, her voice warm with sympathy.

"You do not understand. She grew mad, Shoshanah. In the end, she suffered from terrible delusions, going from silent exhaustion to sudden outbursts no one could calm. I will not bore you with more of the terrible details. My parents carried the brunt of it. I had my training to attend."

Sazana leaned toward him. "I am so sorry, Jadon."

"So am I." He pulled a hand through his hair. "We mourned her, though we were relieved that her suffering had come to an end. No one should live through that.

"You can imagine my horror when almost two decades later I started noticing similar symptoms in my mother. The ashen color. The colic. The unremitting fatigue. The headaches.

"At first, my father and I tried to discount it. We called it a passing malady. But then the irritability came. The outbursts of anger, so unlike my sweet mother."

Sazana pressed a hand to her lips.

"That night . . ." Jadon seemed unable to go on.

She decided to put an end to his palpable suffering. "Don't speak of it. Not when it brings you such torment."

"No. It's long past time. You must understand why I made the decision I made. That night, that final night we were together, when my mother screamed at you, remember?"

As though she could ever forget. She jerked down her chin.

"Her outburst, her unreasonable suspicions, her belief that you wanted to take me away from her, her desire to hurt you . . . none of that was my mother. The disease had a hold of her, you see."

"Jadon, I am so sorry." She could think of no other words. *Sorry* seemed such an anemic response to so great a tragedy.

She did not think it the right moment to express her confusion. What had any of this to do with the end of their betrothal? She could see that his mother's fate weighed heavy upon Jadon. Weighed beyond loss and grief.

It covered him like graveclothes.

He waved a hand. "I knew that night what the end would be like for her. I remembered it too well from my grandmother's final months. But I also realized something else. Something that ended any chance of happiness between you and me."

She stilled. "What can you mean?"

His eyes had turned the sea-gray of tempestuous waters. "It's in my blood, you see. This madness. Through my mother's line."

Sazana gasped. She pressed a fist against her lips.

"My father believes that it does not affect the men. My mother has two older brothers, neither of whom have been afflicted." He slumped against the wall. "How to know? Perhaps the madness skips sometimes. But even if my father has the right of it, I could have a daughter. I could father girls.

"Shoshanah, I could not do that to you. I could not subject you to such pain. It would mean watching your child grow into womanhood, into maturity, and then bit by bit, be consumed by madness."

He shook his head. "You deserve better. You deserve to have healthy children and a husband who will not start frothing at the mouth and try to choke you to death. That, Shoshanah, is why we can never be married."

Sazana tried to absorb this leap in his reasoning. The fear of the disease that had chewed away the sanity in his mother and grandmother. What he had witnessed in the end, two dear lives twisted by more ugliness than any human should see, had left an indelible mark. A scar that shaped his view of himself and his future.

She had not had time to think through this revelation. But already she knew that she would reach a different conclusion from Jadon.

There was always hope.

She frowned. "Jadon, you made a decision that changed my life without even consulting me. I had a right to know."

"Why?" he barked.

"Because I might not agree."

He shook his hand at her. "That is why I could not tell you. I could not allow you to waste your life on me. You are too willing to sacrifice yourself. I could not let you ruin your chance at happiness by shackling yourself to such as me."

He sank onto a stool. "My mother, in one of her states of confusion, made me promise to never tell anyone of her affliction. She felt convinced everyone would hate her. I made the promise. She begged it of me, and I could not refuse. I gave my word.

"I could not tell you the truth for that reason." He shook his head. "Listen to me, how noble I make myself sound. Me, a keeper of promises. That is laughable, as we both know." He gulped in a deep breath. "In truth, I could not let you know how rotten I was. How broken. How unworthy."

His head dropped into hands that shook. "At the time, I was certain of one thing: That by walking away, I gave you a chance at a better life. A good future." He lifted his eyes to her. "I never thought I would find you unmarried five years later. No children, no joyful home, no warm hearth welcoming a growing family. That is *my* due, not yours! Never yours, Shoshanah. You must move on."

Outside, she could hear the chatter of sparrows, the murmur of leaves as they danced in the summer breeze, the hum of some bird she did not recognize. Life went on, sunny and cheerful.

Inside, the world had come to a halt, as though every word ever created by human mind had shriveled and died. Neither of them spoke for long moments. She did not know how much time passed. An hour or a day.

Her mind had become a violent gale where nothing could remain still. Her thoughts spun so fast she could not make sense of them, now turning to one phrase, now to another that had nothing to do with the first. The chaos within refused to be ordered.

Emotions dashed about with abandon. One moment she felt euphoria that made her dizzy. *Does this mean he loves me?* The next sinking into a pit so deep no light could penetrate. *There can be no future for us. He will not allow it.*

Whatever he felt or thought, he kept to himself. Having emptied himself of the confession he had carried for five years, he now seemed vacant, his gaze bleak as he stared at nothing.

Finally, he rose. "I must return to Nabonassar. I will bring you back to the palace."

Outside, she discovered that he had driven a cart to her house, allowing them a tiny hedge of space as they sat next to each other on the wooden seat. Perversely, she wished he had ridden on his stallion, forcing him to hold her.

The silent drive proved a torment. It was the way Jadon held himself apart, every muscle rigid as an iron bar, every breath of air that separated them a declaration.

We can never be married. We can never be married. We can never be married.

It felt like the day he broke their betrothal all over again. Incandescent hope for a moment, followed by immutable despair.

She had scarcely had time to return to her chamber when the junior handmaiden arrived. "The queen wants to see you."

She could not remember walking to the queen's chamber. She had blinked, and there she stood in Esther's hexagonal reception room. Had she bowed? Had she forgotten?

Whatever Esther saw in her face made her take a sharp breath. She sprang to her side, wrapping her spangled arm around her. "Come. Come and sit. You are pale as a dish of yogurt." She settled her on the teal sofa, covered her in the folds of a soft blanket, and shoved a gold cup bearing a warm liquid into her hand. "Drink."

Sazana obeyed.

"Now tell me. What ails you?"

"Jadon's mother."

"I thought the woman had died."

"Poor Rachel. Even in death she ruins my life."

39

Jadon

The enemy came to an end in everlasting ruins.
Psalm 9:6

As a soldier, Jadon had learned long ago to tuck personal concerns into a tidy box and bury them where they could not interfere with his work. He strode into the small dungeon attached to the soldiers' barracks, his face impassive, the earlier flood of emotions that had threatened to drown him in Shoshanah's presence now concealed so deep that even he could not reach them.

After that wrenching encounter, Jadon thought his day could not grow any worse. He found he was wrong.

As he strode into the outer chamber leading to Nabonassar's cell, he noticed a palace guard delivering a cup of water to the prisoner. His eyes widened in alarm when the guard stepped too close to the prisoner.

Jadon cried out a warning. The soldier looked over his

shoulder, not comprehending the danger in which he had placed himself.

The prisoner, his form slumped, appearing semiconscious, came to sudden life, throwing the chains that bound his wrists together around the soldier's throat. Jadon leapt inside the tiny cell, but no man could travel that fast.

Nabonassar had already done his worst. The guard's knife in hand, he dropped the unconscious man roughly to the stone floor.

Jadon stopped just out of his reach. "Well played, but useless. Where do you plan to go, chained as you are to the wall?"

Nabonassar waved his fingers at Jadon, motioning him to step forward.

Jadon crossed his arms.

"Too scared, pretty boy?"

No point in answering.

"Don't worry. It is not you I mean to harm, though it would be a pleasure to take you with me." He turned the point of the dagger to his neck.

Jadon's eyes widened. He took half a step forward. What he needed was a good distraction. "Put down the knife, Nabonassar. You'll get a lot more with a loose tongue than with that sharp blade."

"I will get death either way."

"Perhaps not. The queen might exercise leniency."

"That Jew?" He spat on the ground.

"You are an Agagite?"

A flash of surprise passed over Nabonassar's handsome features. Good. Jadon needed to keep the man off-kilter. He took another half step forward.

Nabonassar lowered the knife a finger's breadth. "What do you know of us?"

"I know your master was an Agagite. Or should I say masters now? I assume you belong to the same lineage?"

The face, swollen and bruised with patches of purple and green from the struggle he had put up before being loaded into the cart, still managed to emanate pride. "We are the descendants of an Amalekite king. Your murderous prophet put an end to a noble man. But Samuel failed to wipe out his royal line. We are still here. A tribe whose strength and determination you cannot match. We have survived the ages to get our revenge."

"I see that."

"I'm sorry I won't be there in person seven months from now to watch the Jews wiped from the earth. The world will sigh in relief the day it is cleansed from your kind."

"Give me the names of your masters and I promise that you will live to witness the events of that day." Another half step. "Of course, I doubt it will unfold as you wish."

"The law has passed. It is done. My master will make certain that our revenge is complete."

Jadon frowned, unsettled by the man's confidence. What made Nabonassar, chained as he was and powerless to save himself, so sure of their success? And what *master* did he mean with Haman dead? Had one of the sons taken lead? "That law has lost its claw, or did you not hear? The king gave the Hebrews permission to defend themselves. Tell me the name of the man you serve now. Or should I say men?"

Nabonassar flashed an ugly smile. "I will tell you *your* name. You are called Doomed."

The knife pressed for home. Jadon had mere seconds to get to him. He leapt over the distance that separated them, arriving just in time to shackle his fingers around Nabonassar's wrist, preventing it from pressing farther. Blood dribbled down the man's neck, but it remained a rivulet, not the flood that would kill him.

In spite of his hours of captivity, Nabonassar remained strong. Perhaps it was the long years of hatred that gave him an edge.

Jadon twisted the struggling hand, pulling the blade one

breath and then another away from its target. Another moment, and he would disarm the man. Keep him alive to feed them the information they desperately needed.

From the corner of his eye, he saw the palace guard stir on the floor. The young man rose on unsteady knees and turned toward them, a second dagger in hand.

"No!" Jadon shouted.

He twisted to kick the man out of harm's way while at the same time striving to keep Nabonassar's dagger from pressing into his bleeding jugular. The world slowed. His foot landed on the guard's chest, pushing him back. *Safe*, he thought.

But at the last moment, Nabonassar grabbed the guard's wavering wrist, still clutching its dagger, and shoved the hand, dagger and all, with every bit of his waning might into his own belly. The dagger buried itself inside the muscular wall of his stomach, leaving only the plain hilt of a palace-issued weapon.

"Beat you," Nabonassar said. His eyes rolled back, and he joined his royal ancestor in the sleep of death.

40

Sazana

You will not fear the terror of night,
  nor the arrow that flies by day,
nor the pestilence that stalks in the darkness,
  nor the plague that destroys at midday.

Psalm 91:5–6 NIV

Esther tapped her gilded fan against her lips. "The question is, what do you want?"

Sazana slumped against the sofa's plush back. "Begging your pardon, Your Majesty. But it seems to me that what I want hardly matters. Jadon has made up his mind. My desire does not come into it."

"Jadon is guided by his fears. They have chased him for years, haunted his nights, and pursued his every thought. I imagine every time he has suffered a headache, he has wondered if the disease is upon him. You have a clearer head. Are you of the same opinion as Jadon? Do you think it best to forget him? To begin your life afresh, elsewhere? I ask again. What do you want?"

"What do I want?" Sazana threw up her hands. "I want Jadon! But he will not budge. This bleak future to which he ascribes takes no account of God at all. It's as if the disease determines our destiny, not the Lord.

"Think, my lady, of all the ways Jadon could be wrong. As his father believes, the disease may not pass through the male line. Or God may not even bless us with children. Or if he does, they may all be sons. And if we have a daughter, who is to say that the Lord will not find a cure?

"The patterns of the past do not always determine our future. Because Jadon's mother and grandmother died this way, does it mean God cannot spare any daughters he gives us?" Sazana's wild discourse finally ran itself to ground.

Esther smiled. "That, my dear, is the longest speech I have heard out of your mouth. And I applaud every word. Now, go and give it to Jadon. He is the one you need to convince, not I."

Sazana's face crumpled. "He will not listen. He has committed himself to this course and refuses to veer from it."

"Then it appears Jadon is not the only one who has forgotten there is a God. You give Jadon all the power, and the Lord none."

The queen's admonition had an odd effect on Sazana. Instead of thinking herself diminished, she felt herself lifted up, like a tiny wooden boat that refuses to drown in the swells of the ocean. Something sweet settled within.

Hope.

A smile broke through her spasm of despair. Solomon was right. Many waters could not quench love. Nor could they quench hope, it seemed. Not if she chose to remember she was not an orphan.

"You have the right of it, lady."

"This is a lesson I ought to know well." Esther came to her feet. "Look at me, a simple Jewish woman who has become the beloved consort of the king of Persia. My example should teach you one thing: If God intends for two people to come together, he will open the door. And if he does not, then best you give up on this dream not for Jadon's sake, but for your own."

In the morning, Sazana once again found Mazares guarding her door. The warm greeting on her lips died at the sight of the man's knotted jaw and grim mouth. "What has happened?"

"Nabonassar is dead."

After the great pain he had caused, she held no affection for the man. Yet the news of his death came as a shock. "How?"

"He killed himself." The Immortal's lips barely moved as he said the words.

"Before he gave us the name of his masters," she guessed.

"As you say."

"Does Jadon know?"

"He was there."

She took a sharp breath. "Is he all right?"

"He sustained no injuries."

The pulse bashing against her eardrums quieted a little. No wonder Mazares looked so grim. "Jadon blames himself?"

"As any Immortal would."

"What happened?"

"The Immortals had been pulled on double duty for the king. None of us was available to help guard Nabonassar. Jadon had to rely on the palace guard. Only one man was there when he arrived. The second has disappeared."

"Dead?"

Mazares shook his head. "Bribed, more likely. Never showed up for his shift. The guard who remained lacks experience. He came too close to the prisoner, and Nabonassar divested him of his dagger. Jadon did what he could."

"If Jadon could not stop him, then no one could," she said firmly.

Mazares cracked a faint smile. "Well said."

"Can you take me to him?"

"He is with Hathach."

The sound of hurried steps had Mazares shoving her behind him, only to find Jadon rushing toward them. "You heard what happened?" he asked, not bothering with a greeting.

"Mazares just told me. I am sorry, Jadon."

Jadon's hand tightened around the hilt of his dagger. "Nabonassar displayed an odd confidence in the success of Haman's plans. In spite of the man's death, in spite of the king's new edict, he did not seem shaken.

"I do not like it. There is more to their plans than we know. I suspect with Nabonassar dead, they will come harder after you, Shoshanah. Now the cylinder is the only other thing that seems to threaten them. They are afraid of the power it holds. And you are the only remaining connection to it."

"If only I knew where to find it."

"For the present, the important thing is to ensure your safety."

Mazares frowned at Jadon. "If I have to give up a month of sleep, I will. No one is going to harm your Shoshanah. And I know our friends all feel the same."

Jadon did not correct his friend's assumption that Sazana belonged to him. "My thanks, Mazares."

She straightened. "Wait! This means they're scared of me. Your hydra is scared of what I can do. That's why they want me dead."

Jadon arched a brow. "One way to look at it."

If her enemy feared her so much, it was past time that she realized the power she had in God. She was starting to truly understand what her mother had meant when she told Sazana to anchor her heart to God.

"They may want the cylinder," she said, "but not half so much as I do. Let us return to my house. I want to read those scrolls again."

"Good plan," Jadon agreed. "The sooner we find the cylinder, the safer you will be."

She narrowed her eyes. "The sooner we find the cylinder, the weaker they will become."

At the house, Jadon and Mazares helped her empty the chest so that she could retrieve the scrolls from the secret compartment. First, she established the timeline of the cylinder from the year her great-grandfather had made it.

"For sixty-four years, the cylinder remained in my family's keeping. From the day Mispar carved those words into the clay of the Euphrates River, it never left our possession," she said. "My family considered it a treasure for all Judah. A religious artifact as much as a historical relic. Which means that all those years, they would have kept it close by."

Jadon gave her a sharp glance. "In their house, you mean?"

"I believe so. The house I grew up in had belonged to my father's father, Libni. Likely, he had already created a hiding place for it. Some inconspicuous hole in the ground, a generation before my father came along."

Jadon leaned forward. "Then they had to leave Babylon to keep the cylinder safe."

She gave a slow nod. "And they would certainly have had it with them when they left. With them when they traveled."

She tried to grasp hold of the fleeting idea that seemed just beyond reach. "I always assumed that Arta would have hidden it again, once we arrived in Susa. He was the only one who could have. But what if . . ."

She unfurled the letters, quickly finding Arta's missive. She searched through the now-familiar lines and found the ones she wanted.

No doubt, having read this far, you are impatient for me to reveal the location of this treasure. You will find it in another place you hold dear. That is all I can say.

Her gaze sought and found the sentences he had added later to his original letter.

Since our lives have changed at the hand of the queen, I will add one final word, for I sense the shadow of a new danger stalking us. My dear girl, life moves forward while it stands still. I pray one day soon you will find the way to happiness and discover that new doors are opened with old keys. I am only sorry I will not be there to rejoice with you.

She had thought the words pertained to her and Jadon. And they had. But . . .

"I was wrong! I was so wrong."

"Wrong about what?"

"This later entry in the letter. I felt sure Arta meant you and me. My life coming to a standstill after you broke our betrothal." Jadon winced. "I thought he meant to encourage me, hoping I would give you another chance. You are the old key that opens a new door to happiness. You see?"

Jadon shoved a hand into his hair.

"Don't give yourself a sour belly. We can speak of that later. My point is that while Arta, clever man that he was, meant exactly that, he also meant another thing entirely."

Jadon snapped to his feet. "You know where it is! You have cracked his reference."

"I have." She bit the corner of her thumb. "At least, I think I have."

She pointed to the second part of Arta's message. "Look at what Arta writes. *Moves forward while it stands still.* That's a reference to a parked cart! A cart is made to move forward but stands still when parked."

She unfurled the top part of the papyrus. "In the first section, he says the treasure is in another place I hold dear. When my parents left Babylon, we traveled in an old cart that had belonged to my grandfather. It was so long ago that I had forgotten it. I rode in it all the way from Babylon. It smelled like my mother's perfume. My father let me carve my name into it. And after my parents' deaths, I refused to leave it for the inn at night."

Jadon's eyes bored into her. "Where do you keep it? I have

never seen you or Arta ride in any cart other than the one belonging to the workshop. Not even five years ago."

"That's because we never used one. With only the two of us, we had little use for it. Arta must have boarded it in a stable somewhere. I have not seen it since our first year in Susa. But I know Arta did not sell it because he would have consulted me about such a thing, especially since he would have considered that cart part of my inheritance."

"Boarding it does not sound very secure. Why would a man as careful as Arta have left the cylinder on a cart parked in a public stable where anyone might steal it?"

"I don't know. But it's the only thing that makes sense."

Jadon headed for the door. "Arta's receipts!"

Mazares followed, grumbling. "I suppose this means I have to skip lunch again."

41

Sazana

Not one word of all the good promises that
the LORD had made to the house of Israel had
failed; all came to pass.

Joshua 21:45

They spent the next two hours sorting through a hundred
documents in the workshop. Even the queen's scribe, who
happened to be present at the time, joined in the search.
For all their diligence, they found nothing useful.

No trace of anything that hinted at the location of the cart.
Not a single record of payment to a stable or farm where Arta
could have conceivably stashed it.

Mazares threw down a record for the purchase of wood shavings. "Perhaps he has the cart hidden in another potter's yard.
All these documents belong to pottery-related materials."

Jadon straightened slowly, dropping the papyrus scroll he
had been perusing back onto the pile that had gathered in front

of him. "That is unlikely. He would want to keep the cart in a protected place, and a pottery yard is too exposed. But you do have a point. Arta would think like a potter. He would hide the record in a place that would make sense to a potter."

He turned to Sazana. "Where would *you* hide a scrap of papyrus if you didn't want anyone to find it?"

Sazana barely had to consider her answer. "Somewhere in my wheel."

"Did Arta have a wheel?"

"As a matter of fact, he did." She leapt to her feet. "He rarely had time to use it as an overseer, but he refused to let us move it. Once in a while, he would make a vessel to keep in practice."

She led them to the corner of the fine ware section where Arta's old stone wheel sat collecting dust. "I don't know what he saw in this thing. It has wobbled for years."

"How could he make anything on a wobbly wheel?"

"He couldn't." A smile tugged at the corner of her mouth. "He had to stick something under the base so it would turn properly."

Jadon dropped to his knees and examined the base of the pedestal. Using the tip of his dagger, he coaxed a square wad from under the heavy stone. They stared at the squashed square resting in the palm of his hand. Arta had folded several sheets of papyrus into a neat pad.

When Jadon carefully untucked the folds, they found eleven small sheets of papyrus, each bearing record of payment for one year, to a stable.

For the length of a heartbeat, no one moved. Then Sazana jumped in the air and cheered. "That's Isaac's place!"

"I know it," Jadon said. "It sits just outside the Artisans' Market. Many of the merchants keep their carts and mules there during the day."

Sazana had scrambled out the door before Jadon could refold the papyrus.

Isaac studied the receipt. His eyes welled with unexpected tears when he looked up. "He said one day you would come to fetch it. I was to give it to no one but you. I have tucked it in the back where it's secure."

Jadon gave the man a curious look. "You know what's inside?"

"He never told me." Isaac waved a hand in the air. "He only said that I was to keep it safe. I promised him that I would protect it with my life."

Mazares whistled. "I didn't think the rent he paid was that high."

"Ha!" Isaac faced Sazana. "Ever known that guardian of yours to pay a high price for anything?"

She grinned. "Not Arta."

"Why, then?" Jadon stood rock-still, his gaze unflinching. "Why did he trust you with the cart and its contents?"

Isaac held his gaze. "He saved my son's life, years ago. My only son. Dan was going through a rough patch. Youth, you know, can be a swine to live with. Arta came upon him at just the right moment. Saved my boy. Dan is happy now. Married and a father of three. But I will never forget the debt I owe Arta. I told him then that he could have anything. Silver. Horses. Anything. He only asked that I hide his cart. Keep it safe from thieves. Protect it from everyone, save for this young woman." He pointed his thumb at Sazana. "Arta even insisted on paying me, though I would have kept it for free." He shrugged. "No one has come near that cart except for me, when I clean and oil it, and Arta himself. Whatever he put there, you will find there still."

He led them to the rear of the building. Sazana looked at the wall in confusion. It looked like there was nowhere else to go. But Isaac pulled on a wooden slat, and the wall slid to one side, revealing a small room behind it. He grabbed a torch from the wall and handing it to Jadon, walked away.

Though she had not seen it for over a decade, Sazana recognized the cart instantly. Isaac must have looked after the cart well over the years, for the wood showed no signs of warping or peeling or decay. It seemed smaller than she remembered, empty and forlorn in the dim light of the stable. She ran a hand over the side, her gaze seeking and finding her name carved next to her grandfather's. Her pulse raced.

If she had truly cracked Arta's clues, then soon she would hold Cyrus's cylinder in her hands. Her heart pounded.

Jadon slid the secret stable door into place, creating a private oasis. Light flared into the room when he ignited another torch that sat against the wall.

Mazares, already inspecting the back of the cart, tapped the shaft of his spear against the high side. "Might be faster if we break the thing down plank by plank."

Jadon walked around the cart, examining the boards with careful hands. "We could damage the cylinder. It's over sixty years old and likely delicate."

Sazana sighed with relief, glad to be spared the destruction of yet another possession. "Arta wrote that an old key would open a new door."

"*New* meaning the planks that created the hiding place were newer than the rest of your grandfather's cart. Presumably, your father installed a hiding place before leaving Babylon."

"Everything looks aged to me," Mazares grumbled.

Jadon held up a hand. "Patience." He circled the cart a second and third time before climbing inside. Crouching, he studied the different sections closely. "Clever."

"What?"

"They used the same type of wood to create their compartment. But they were in a hurry and left behind a few clues."

She stepped on a spoke in the wheel and tried to pull herself inside with one hand, wavering. Jadon sprang over to wrap an arm about her waist. "Careful."

She allowed herself to lean into him, forgetting, for a

heartbeat, about the cylinder and the queen and the whole blessed world.

Jadon turned the bright red of an autumn apple as they stood at the edge of the cart, chest to chest, lost in each other until he came to himself with a loud cough and stepped away.

She smiled.

Still smiling, she asked, "What clues did you find?"

"Ah." He pulled on the tip of his ear before crouching again. "Here, see? The rest of the cart has been put together by an able craftsman. He used dovetail joints everywhere, perfectly fitting the pieces. But in this section"—he pointed to a slat that ran across the back of the cart—"they used no joints that I can see. And look. Though the wood seems distressed, there are fewer cracks. Your parents did what they could to make the wood appear aged. But under careful scrutiny, you can see the difference."

"You think they hid the cylinder somewhere behind this section?"

"Let's see."

But no amount of manipulation shifted the slat. Stubbornly, it refused to budge.

"We may have to hammer it loose after all," Mazares said. "Or at the very least, press the edge of a dagger between the joints and try to pry it off."

Jadon sat back. "Too risky. We need that cylinder undamaged."

He moved the torch, shifting the shadows in the cart. Sazana knelt to examine an oval mark at the bottom edge of the slat. "I had not noticed this before. What is it?"

Mazares held the second torch closer, and Jadon and Sazana bent their heads low to see it better.

"It looks like the impression from a stamp of some kind," Jadon said. "Perhaps the seal of the carpenter?"

Sazana gasped. "An old key!" She straightened and reached for the seal hanging from the chain at her neck. Drawing it loose, she fit her mother's seal into the oval. It did not fit. She hissed in frustration.

"Turn it upside down."

Following Jadon's suggestion, she felt the seal fall into place perfectly. The slat of wood yawned open, revealing its dark interior. Within its shadowy depths sat something wrapped in folds of wool.

"Ah!" Three deep breaths expelled from three awestruck pairs of lungs in perfect unison.

"Jadon, you do it. I don't want to drop it." She lifted her sling.

He picked up the woolen bundle with the care of one of the Hebrew midwives delivering a male babe in Pharaoh's Egypt. With slow, deliberate movements, Jadon untucked one wrap at a time. Inside sat a small, clay cylinder. The three of them stared in silence.

Cyrus's historic declaration. The words that had saved lives and could do so again.

In all, it was an unimpressive object, the length of her forearm, thicker in the middle, tapered at the ends, and a dark ecru in color. Dense writing covered every available surface in parallel lines. Sazana could not read a blessed word. It had been recorded in Akkadian cuneiform.

"What does it say?"

Jadon studied the tiny writing. "It begins: 'I am Cyrus, king of all the universe, the great king, the powerful king,' so on and so forth." He turned the cylinder half a revolution. "Here, he goes on to say that having conquered Babylon, he will . . . now? . . . No, he will at once allow the peoples whom Nebuchadnezzar and Nabonidus captured and made into slaves to go free. Cyrus declares that he will let them return to their countries." Jadon turned the cylinder again. "And here, he says that he will restore to them the religious articles and ceremonial vessels that the Babylonians confiscated from them."

"That's it?" Mazares scratched his head. "All the fuss, murder, bribery, and bloody attacks for this bit of clay?"

Jadon cradled the cylinder to his chest. "It means more than you know. To those of us who are of Jewish heritage, it is a divine promise fulfilled.

"And for those of us who have Persian blood, it is a reminder that Cyrus allowed the people of different nations to live in freedom. To worship their gods in peace. To enjoy liberty. This small cylinder demonstrates the clemency of a good king toward all the peoples that occupy his lands, regardless of their background. It is the very antithesis of Haman's edict.

"I pray every Persian who hears these words will think twice before attacking the Jews in seven months. By law, a man may have the right to murder and pillage on that day." He pointed at the cylinder. "But by Cyrus's own standard, he will not wish to. Not when the meaning of the cylinder is made clear to him."

Mazares whistled. "Maybe it's worth a missed meal or two."

"It should make you even more proud to be a son of Persia, my friend."

Sazana caressed the knobbly surface of the clay. She had finally found her inheritance. The treasure her family had kept safe for sixty-four years.

But it no longer belonged to her. "We should deliver it to the queen at once."

Esther, having heard from Hathach what they had in their possession, left some formal palace function to meet them in a plain chamber at the back of her apartments. She stood in the center of the rectangular room, looking like a bright jewel, her ruched purple skirts dancing gently at her feet. "You have it?" she said, her hands clutching her fan.

Jadon bowed formally at the waist and held out the treasure that Sazana's family had guarded for over half a century. "May it serve you faithfully, Your Majesty."

Esther passed her fan to her handmaiden, who stood next to her, and stretched her hands to receive the unassuming cylinder. Her fingers, Sazana saw, trembled. "I will look after it with my life."

She turned her head. "Hathach!"

"My lady?"

"We begin at once. Send out the first invitations for tomorrow night. And send me two or three trusted scribes to make copies in this room. We need to have it translated into Persian and recorded on papyrus as well as clay. But I do not want to let it out of my sight for even a moment."

"At once." With a bow of his head, Hathach exited the room.

Esther placed the cylinder upon a silver table. "To begin with, we will show the contents of Cyrus's cylinder to the most powerful women of the court—wives, daughters, and sisters of important men who can carry the message where it will make the greatest impact. Each shall receive a copy as a gift, recorded with gold ink upon papyrus. We will ensure that word of Cyrus's edict spreads throughout the land. Let it serve as a reminder of what Persia and the Persians stand for."

She rested her hand upon the cylinder. "My husband's second edict laid the foundation of our defense. Now we make certain of our victory by weakening the attack."

She turned to face Sazana. "My deepest thanks to you, my friend." As if she found the words somehow insufficient, she folded Sazana in an impromptu embrace. "I know the price you and your family have paid to keep Cyrus's words safe. Know my gratitude goes with you always, Shoshanah."

Sazana blinked hard. "We owe it all to our God, my lady. The Father who gave the promise and saw to its fulfillment has also kept this testimony secure."

42

Sazana

> . . . he uproots my hope like a tree.
> Job 19:10 NIV

Sazana woke bleary-eyed to the sound of quiet voices speaking outside her room. Having discharged what felt like her most important duty, she had experienced a sudden wave of weariness, which had sent her to an early bed the night before.

Yawning, she slipped into her tunic and opened the curtain, only to take a hasty step back.

Jadon, Sisy the serving girl, the physician, and the junior handmaiden turned in unison to face her.

She gulped. "Are you holding a banquet out here and you forgot to invite me?"

The physician lifted his chest. "We all happened to arrive at the same time."

Sisy held out a tray bearing various bowls and plates. "You

were asleep. We were trying to decide whether to wake you or leave you in peace."

"Wake you, obviously." The junior handmaiden sniffed. "Who sleeps past sunrise?"

Jadon leaned against the wall. "I was just on guard duty."

Sazana blinked. "I thought the discovery of the cylinder would bring an end to my need for a guard. Why would they harm me now? No sense in closing the barn door after the horse has run off."

"Hathach and I have discussed it. Once the content of the cylinder becomes common knowledge, you will certainly be safer. That won't happen for another week, at least. In the meantime, we will make certain they can't reach you again."

Sisy shifted the tray, which looked heavy. "The queen commanded that we serve you a nourishing breakfast."

"How kind. Well, you had better all come in."

"I have come to arrange your hair," the junior handmaiden announced, setting her large basket at the foot of the bed.

Sazana threw her an alarmed glance. "What's the occasion?"

"The queen wishes you to attend her feast tonight. Tell the ladies the story of the part your family played in saving Cyrus's cylinder."

Sazana sank onto the edge of the iron bed. "She wants me to do what?"

Jadon bit his lip.

"You better not be smiling right now," she snapped.

"Wouldn't dream of it."

She tried to keep her voice from trembling. "Speak at the queen's formal banquet? I would rather make a pot on the wheel one-handed."

"Speaking of one-handed." The physician placed his bulky chest next to Sazana on the bed. "I have first rights to the patient. It has been two weeks since her injury, and today she will have the sutures removed from her hand." He gazed at the steaming dishes on the tray. "You can eat before I begin my work."

Having her hair arranged by the junior handmaiden may well prove more torturous than having her stitches removed. In either case, eating seemed like the best choice.

She examined the contents of the tray, which held a bowl of jiggly almond cream, quince blossom paste, fig jam, fresh cream, warm bread, cherry juice, and a steaming egg dish with apples, raisins, and dates. "It smells delicious. And there's enough here to feed the Persian cavalry." She cut a piece of bread and passed it to the physician. "You all better help me."

Jadon accepted the portion of fluffy eggs she placed on a plate for him. "Poor Mazares. He will be aghast to discover that finally there is food to be had and he missed it."

Sazana dolloped cream and fig jam on bread before rolling it up and setting it aside. "You can take that to him later."

The handmaiden passed Sazana an empty plate. "Never you mind about everyone else. You eat," she ordered.

"Only if you join us, mistress." Sazana pressed the almond cream bowl into the woman's hands. "I remember from when you nursed me that you are partial to almonds."

The handmaiden's lips parted. For once, she seemed lost for words. Hadn't anyone ever tended to her needs the way she did for others? Probably not, given her reaction. Most people would be too intimidated to try.

Sisy gave a longing glance at the tray. "It sure does look good." The junior handmaiden recovered her wits enough to direct a glare at the poor girl. Rolling her sleeves, Sisy sidled toward the door. "But I have to return to the kitchen. Those assistant cooks have left me a mountain of dishes to clean."

Sazana handed her the rolled bread she had set aside for Mazares. "Eat this on the way there. I will make Mazares another." Sisy took the offering with a wide grin and slipped through the curtains like a mouse slinking to its hole, too fast for the junior handmaiden to reprimand.

For a few moments, silence reigned in the small room as

everyone enjoyed the excellent fare from the queen's kitchens. When the food had disappeared from bowls and plates, the handmaiden gathered the tray. "I will return after the physician has tended to your hand."

Sazana exhaled. Reprieve. "I would rather have twice as many stitches removed than go to the queen's feast and speak in front of everyone."

Jadon leaned against the threshold. "You can practice with us. It will take your mind off the discomfort."

She cleared her throat. "Have you ever had sutures removed?"

"A few."

"Does it hurt?"

"Depends who sewed you up. Adin's are delicate as spider webs. It will be over before you know it."

The physician grinned. "It also helps that I have kept the threads supple by applying a special ointment daily. We have kept the wound clean, and it has closed nicely. I have every confidence no screaming shall issue forth from this chamber today."

Sazana sputtered. "I will try to be comforted."

"Remember, though we are removing the stitches, the ligaments are not yet healed. That takes time. You will need to be patient for another six weeks. I will splint the hand, and you must continue to rest it."

A tangle of obstinate thoughts attacked at once. Every terrifying question she had set aside while chasing after the cylinder decided to bang at the door of her heart at once, like a line of bailiffs demanding their due.

What if in six weeks, in spite of all of Adin's efforts, she did not regain the dexterity of her fingers? What if she had lost full flexibility? What if she had lost her pottery?

Jadon, reading something in her expression, straightened from his spot at the threshold, and not waiting for an invitation, sat beside her. "Want to hold my hand again?"

"Are you going to call me *dear heart* if I do?"

Something about his earlier confession had loosened her tongue. Though he had never claimed to still love her, she had sensed it. And the knowledge made her bold.

Because she certainly loved him.

He coughed. "Will it help?"

She had come to the end of her words, it seemed. Shrugging, she held out her bandaged hand, palm up, for the physician. "Do your worst."

"Thank you. But I intend to do my best."

He untied the bandage and washed the wound with a mix of wine and some stringent compound she could not name. "Clean as a princess's laundry," he declared when he examined the cut across her palm. "No hint of putrefaction."

From his chest, he withdrew a pair of long-nosed tweezers and began pulling on the end of the first black knot. She felt the pull, and a sharp pain that made her wince. But the physician had the right of it. She would not be screaming today.

Fifteen tucks and pulls later, and her hand was free of sutures. A thin red line ran across her palm. Her hand felt stiff as the physician created a splint and applied a fresh bandage, this one smaller and less awkward, thankfully.

Jadon slapped her lightly on the shoulder. "If you saw the manner of wounds the Immortals recover from, only to send their arrows and throw their spears and wield their swords as straight as ever after recovery, you would have hope. It means hard work. That's all."

She looked at the physician. He gave her a slight nod. "I have seen it. Not every time and not every wound. But is it possible? Indeed. For now, rest that hand."

By the time the setting sun had turned the sky into a blazing dome, Sazana, bathed and perfumed, had her long, straight hair arranged into a long braid twisted at the nape of her neck, little wisps curling against her cheeks. A twisted circlet of stiff gold ribbons crowned her head. Her face bore the faintest trace of cosmetics that made her eyes appear huge and her lips as red as sweet cherries. She barely recognized herself in the polished bronze mirror the junior handmaiden held up for her inspection.

Sazana reached for her green tunic, only to have the handmaiden rap her lightly with two fingers on the back of the hand. "Not that one. You are going to a royal feast. We must dress you accordingly."

"Pardon. You will find the green to be as *accordingly* as you will find in my chest. I own nothing more *accordingly* than that."

The handmaiden's mouth tipped up. "You do now. The queen has sent you—" she bent her head close, as though whispering state secrets—"a gift."

Sazana's mouth opened without issuing a sound.

The garment the handmaiden spread before her was worthy of being described a royal gift, a special impartation, usually from the hand of the king, saved only for those retainers and courtiers who pleased him best. That the queen had chosen to send her such valuable finery showed a sign of her public favor.

Sazana fingered the silky fabric, dyed scarlet and decorated with a gold border at the edge of the sleeves and the hem. "Angels in heaven have nothing more beautiful."

"Let's put it on you and see how you look."

Median in design, the dress had a long, pleated skirt, and a short cape on top that danced around her arms like wide sleeves. A thin gold belt tied in the front, matching a chain of gold that hung at her breast. "Is the queen loaning me her jewelry?" she asked with a squeak.

"Are you not listening? Gift, I said." The junior handmaiden adjusted the fall of the skirt and sleeves and gave a nod of satisfaction. Holding up a pair of soft leather shoes with heels as high as her little finger, she commanded Sazana to put them on. The rigid leather soles had been decorated with red appliqués.

"Who decorates the bottom of a shoe?" Sazana asked.

"Don't be so uncivilized. Top or bottom, a lady must look her best from every angle."

"I'm not a lady. I'm a potter." Sazana pulled on the leather shoes, hoping to manage the unfamiliar heels.

The handmaiden stood back and studied the results of her four-hour handiwork. "She'll not be ashamed of you tonight."

"Not until I open my mouth."

Still, it might have been worth the excruciating hours of preparation, not to mention the terrifying notion of having to speak before a crowd of pampered, aristocratic women, to see the expression on Jadon's face when she stepped out of her room.

His eyes rounded. A tide of red matching the scarlet of her skirts rose up his neck and spread to his cheeks. His lips parted, but no words emerged. For once, he appeared like her, mute as a brick. With a grin, she realized she did not mind it at all.

He had dressed as a soldier tonight, high boots and fawn-colored trousers that clung to his calves. As though the short tunic had cut off his breathing, he tried to loosen his collar and swallowed.

She had hoped for some pretty compliment but decided that his tongue-tied response spoke more volubly. Entertained by the sidelong looks he continued to cast her way as they walked to Esther's apartments, she forgot to be petrified. At least until he bowed formally and handed her inside the queen's chamber.

One of Esther's handmaidens took charge of her as soon as she entered and never left her side. Esther's formal reception room was overflowing with fashionable women this night. Sazana gave up counting at forty-two.

"That one is the king's sister-in-law," the handmaiden whispered, pointing discreetly to a woman dressed in purple. "And the one standing next to her is His Majesty's cousin."

In all, there were thirteen princesses milling about, wafting expensive scents. Being a royal in that room was like being an egg in a chicken coop. Nothing remarkable.

Little seemed required of Sazana as the women ate and gossiped. After a time, her shoulders dropped from around her ears, and she enjoyed the food the queen sent her from her own special dishes.

At the end of the meal, Esther came to her feet and began to tell the tale of Cyrus's conquest of Babylon, a story familiar but dear to all Persians. But Esther's telling focused more on the beloved king's mercy than it did the political and military genius of his campaign. Slowly, she wound her tale to the disappearance of the cylinders.

By now, not a sound could be heard in the hexagonal chamber. The outrage of it had the women sitting up rigid. The outrage of anyone daring to rob the palace of its precious records.

Thus it was Esther herself who told most of the story, pointing at Sazana upon occasion and only asking her to fill in a few words here or there to add authenticity to the account. This, Sazana found, she could do without much effort, for the queen set up each scene with such expertise that Sazana merely had to slip into the telling a few of her own experiences.

Esther said nothing that would undermine her husband. Neither by word nor expression did she censure her husband's decision with regard to Haman's edict. What she did was to raise up a king already beloved. To shine the light upon his actions. And to make it very clear that the Cyrus who had once saved the Jews from slavery and oppression would surely do so again, had he lived in this age.

A long silence fell over the room when they finished their account. Then, as if orchestrated by a master musician, the sound of deafening applause filled the room.

Afterward, not a single woman remained on the side of Haman's edict. He had become the enemy. The edict an injustice that could not be tolerated. Every woman there proclaimed herself committed to Esther's cause, not because they felt close to her personally, but because they wanted to honor Cyrus's memory.

Esther meant this as only the first of many gatherings. The first step in changing the mind of a nation, removing from it the poisonous dart of Haman's savage hatred.

After the formal presentation, many sought Sazana, admiring both her pottery, which the queen had displayed with great prominence, and her courage in saving the history of their nation by keeping the Cyrus cylinder safe. Sazana felt she had done little to deserve their praise. It had been her parents and Arta who had knowingly sacrificed so much to preserve Cyrus's words.

Once again, Jadon accompanied her to her chamber. At her door, he dropped his head. "May I come in? I will not disturb you long."

Her heart, which had finally calmed after the queen's feast, picked up its tempo again. With a small nod, she waved him through the curtain.

Detaching a small sack from his belt, he held it out to her. "I want to give you something. I have always felt this rightfully belongs to you. You kept nothing of mine after I broke our betrothal, though it all should have been yours." He pulled a hand through his hair. "Now that you know the real reason for my mother's actions that night, you must realize she meant nothing by what she said. The illness drove her."

He undid the sack and pulled out a solitary object.

Sazana pressed a hand against her chest. "Your grandmother's cup."

"Had things been different, this would have come to you upon my mother's death. I want you to have it. Let it be a reminder that what we had was real. I don't want you to ever feel that my mother meant her words, or that I took what she said to heart. Let this be a sign of your worth."

He pressed the silver goblet into her hand, wrapping her fingers around the smooth stem before turning and walking away.

Sazana stared at the cup, for years an object of despair and resentment in her memories.

It still remained a barbed thorn, as far as she was concerned. She knew what Jadon meant by it. He wanted her to understand that any tie between them was truly severed. Severed forever.

This last silvery memory meant only a debt paid. A chapter closed. He thought by giving it to her, he could set her free to begin a new life. Walk through the new door to happiness to which Arta had alluded in his letter. Only not with him.

43

Jadon

You will forget your misery;
you will remember it as waters that have
passed away.

Job 11:16

THE TWELFTH YEAR OF KING XERXES'S RULE
THE FIFTIETH DAY OF SUMMER

Sazana sat at her wheel, her injured hand resting in its sling. The sun had set, emptying the workshop of all the potters. She remained alone with him, staring at the empty, still stone.

"I feel the stiffness in my hand, under the bandage and Adin's clever ointments. What if nothing changes, Jadon?" She did not look up. "What if, despite all the effort and the pain, my hand stays half frozen?"

Jadon was sitting across from her on the wheel boy's stool. He bent forward, capturing her gaze. "Then you will learn to live with it. But first, you try everything. Everything. What you do on the wheel, it is a gift from God, Shoshanah. If he wants to take it away, then so be it. He will give you other things in its place. I only say that you ought not to give up easily.

"Sometimes the pain in the pursuit becomes part of the gifting. Part of the way God's call is formed. This injury may not be an end, but God forming something deeper in you."

She narrowed her eyes. "Did *you* pursue everything? With us? Because to me, that also felt like a gift from God."

The unexpected twist in the conversation made him flinch. He rose. "Shoshanah."

"I deserve an answer, Jadon."

He pressed the heel of his hand into his eye socket, trying to squeeze the pain away. "Yes, I tried everything. I told you. No one had a cure for my mother or grandmother."

She came to her feet. Her hair had come undone again from its braid, and it lay in a silky curtain down her back, beckoning him like an invitation.

"Well, I say you didn't. You placed all your trust in that terrible disease. You trusted it to come for you. You trusted it to come for your children. You trusted it to destroy all of you."

"When a man is falling down the side of a mountain, he can trust his skull will cave in by the time he arrives at the bottom." He tasted the bitterness of his words on his tongue.

"That is not the same. There is not near so much certainty in your situation as you have made yourself believe." She took a step toward him. "You have convinced yourself that your mother's illness will one day pass to you. Even your own father does not believe it. Name another man in your mother's family who suffers from the malady. Likely, you will be spared."

Another step, and now she stood too close. A reach of his arm, a tug of his fingers, and she would be in his arms. "I am not willing to take that chance," he said hoarsely. "I will not subject you to what my father endured."

317

"That is for me to decide." Her voice, iron-hard, brought him up short. "You have wronged me, Jadon." He gaped at her, for a moment unable to comprehend her meaning.

She pressed in, her tongue unusually fluent and bold. "You wronged me by taking the decision from me. It was not for you to make that choice. Not alone. You should have given me the right to have a say in my own destiny."

Sazana

She resisted the urge to thump his arm in frustration. He stood, his back rigid with righteous indignation, as though her words made no sense. She tried to explain herself, but the phrases tangled in her mind, and she could not form them. She pressed a fist to her mouth.

The heat in his eyes cooled. Gently, he tugged on her wrist, pulling her fist away. "I can wait for the words to come."

At once his assurance calmed the rising tide of confusion. Her thoughts settled, and she found she knew what to say. "Jadon, you have left so much out of this decision. Most importantly, you have left God out of your calculations. Is God incapable of imparting heaven's healing? Does your future not rest in his holy hand? You are living as though this disease is the God of heaven and earth and you are subject to it alone."

He had turned pale. "It is not true. I have only accepted what he has deemed to be the right path for me."

"You don't know God's intention for your future, Jadon. Not with any certainty. Is there a possibility that you will suffer this terrible outcome? I acknowledge there is. But look at my hand. Not long ago, I was whole, with no notion that in moments my life would diminish. None of us can count on a perfect future."

"But some of us can count more assuredly on an imperfect one."

"If there was no God at all in the world, then yes. If he had no mercy in him. If his steadfast kindness did not undergird our very being. In that case, you could count on your miserable future."

He took a few steps away, putting more distance between them.

Without hesitating, she closed the gap, like a lioness in pursuit of her prey. "Esther told me that I was living as an orphan. Living as though my future depended only on my own strength. My own solutions. I tell you, Jadon, though you grew up with the love of both your parents, you are more orphan than I! You have forgotten God is your Father."

He blinked.

"I," she said with some force, "remember it well. Leastways, when it comes to us. You think I want to marry you because I desire to sacrifice my life at the altar of your disease. I do not! I want to marry you because I believe God can protect you from this disease. And if he does not, then he will give us the strength to go through it. But not before we have had years of joy together.

"What did you just tell me? That what I do on the wheel is a gift from God? But what we feel between us is no less a gift from heaven. As you so wisely pointed out, if in time, God chooses to take this blessing away by allowing the sickness to eat your mind, then so be it. He will sustain us through even that heartache."

His skin had turned the white of ship sails. He tried to swallow again and again.

Her voice softened. "If I ought not give up too easily on what is only clay and wheel, how much more ought you not to give up on us? On love? On me?"

Time to be brave. Time to be bold. Time to take her destiny in hand. She pressed herself against his chest, and with her good hand, tangled her fingers in his hair, pulling down his head until their lips met.

For a fraction, he remained unyielding. Then his skin turned hot, and his hand crept up her waist, and with a groan, he pressed her against him, careful of her splint. The kiss turned wild in a moment, carrying with it the yearning of years and the desperate hunger of long-suffered denial.

Against her lips, he whispered her name, his voice husky. Pulling her closer, his fingers seemed intent on removing every last breath of distance between them. The years had changed them, and their kiss reflected the change. They were no longer shy and youthful. They had matured, body and soul, and they kissed with the melting wonder that their years afforded.

He stopped to take in a shaking breath. "You don't know what you are taking on."

"But I know *who* I am taking on, and more importantly, with whose help."

"Shoshanah, I never stopped loving you."

"Nor I you."

"I knew that."

She did thump his shoulder then.

"Truly, you are not sacrificing yourself? You are willing to take this chance?"

For answer, she kissed him again. Finally, feeling dizzy and dreamy, she took a half step away. "Does this mean I am betrothed again?"

As he pulled his fingers through his hair, she saw that they shook. "It seems that way. It seems God wants me to trust him. Trust him with this illness. Trust him with your future as well as my own." He drew in a deep breath.

She hugged him, laying her cheek on his shoulder. "All will be well. What did you tell me? 'Sometimes the pain in the pursuit becomes part of the gifting.' Perhaps this separation was merely God forming something deeper in us."

"I am wiser than I realized," he said. He cradled her, his arms tender now rather than passionate. "I love you beyond words. I am sorry for all the pain I have caused you."

Those simple words started the healing, closing the wounds of his rejection, of his sudden abandonment. They had not disappeared yet, whispering that he might change his mind. That he might leave her again. But the whispers were weak, and growing weaker with every proof of his love.

She caught sight of the splint that hid her scar, a red marker of her brokenness. As she rested in Jadon's arms, his heart beating its steady rhythm into her ear, she felt her soul rest. God could heal even this, and if not, he would give her what she needed to find joy in a life without the wheel. Without the fame and praise of her profession.

He would make the fulfillment of his will for her life more than enough.

"The queen's scribe reports that your blue pottery has become the new rage in Susa, if the orders are any indication." Jadon leaned against the wall of her chamber, where they were waiting for Adin's nightly visit. "How are you keeping up?"

She smiled. She had smiled a lot in the past three days with Jadon by her side. "Cambyz and Rashda are managing, though we cannot yet accept orders for more complicated designs. The simpler pots keep selling, though. It's the glaze people seem to want."

Jadon pulled his sleeve down. "My only concern is with Haman's sons. They cannot be pleased with this increased success under the queen's rule."

She shrugged. "Good."

He pulled gently on a hank of hair before tugging it behind her ear. "I mean you are not entirely safe yet. Esther wants the workshop guarded. And you shadowed, still."

"Will you be my guard?"

"When I can. Today, the king gave Esther permission to officially use a small detachment of his Immortals. That means my friends no longer have to work overtime to help me."

While grateful for this additional protection, Sazana longed to have life restored to normal. To move back home and walk down the street without always looking over her shoulder and jumping at every unexpected sound.

She jumped at the sound of a knock and grinned weakly at Jadon.

The physician conducted his routine examination of the cut and added new ointment to the bandage. "I am satisfied with your progress." He tied the fresh dressing around the wound, before reaching for the ewer of water on the stool to rinse his hand. Catching sight of Jadon's ornate chalice, which she had set next to the water, he grew still.

"May I?" He gestured to the cup.

Sazana nodded.

Lifting up the chalice, he held it carefully to the light of the wall sconce. "Beautiful."

"It belonged to Jadon's mother, and her mother before that. It was a gift from the wife of a wealthy man who owned mines."

"Silver mines?"

"How did you guess?"

"As a young physician, for some months I served near a silver mine in Laurion, a little south of Athens. That's where I saw this combination of metals used together."

The physician lowered his dark brows. "I hope you will not be offended by what I am about to suggest. Set this chalice on a shelf and enjoy its elaborate carvings. But never drink from it."

Sazana, who still could not bring herself even to touch the object, gave him a curious look. "May I ask why?"

He picked up the cup and turned it to show the smooth insides. "If I am not mistaken, the inner cup is made of cast lead, while the outside carving has been fashioned from silver.

Those of us physicians who tended silver miners quickly came to see a group of symptoms that the men suffered, sometimes leading to their early demise. I will tell you, even cows and horses could not be pastured too near the mines, else they, too, would succumb to terrible colic and die.

"My colleagues and I have different theories as to the cause of these symptoms. There are a number of byproducts that form in the mining of silver. Some believe the sickness results from the noxious gases produced during silver mining. Others blame mercury and its volatile nature.

"While neither of those elements will do much for your health, I align with those who blame a third cause: lead. I have since avoided drinking or eating anything from lead vessels." He pointed at the lining of the chalice. "Like this."

With an awkward motion lacking his usual grace, Jadon snapped to his feet. "What are the symptoms?"

"You need not worry if you have sipped from this cup a few times. I doubt it will harm you."

"Please. The symptoms."

The physician frowned. "It depends how bad a case you have. Sometimes it's merely a loss of appetite along with stomach cramps and headaches. Fatigue and weight loss are also common."

Sazana gasped.

"In bad cases, I have witnessed nervous spasms and uncontrollable tremors as well as irritability and unnatural excitement. One man who had worked long in the mine began to suffer delusions, and toward the end, frothed at the mouth."

Jadon pressed a hand against the wall as though he needed help to stay upright. Having an inkling of his thoughts, Sazana maneuvered her way to him in the tight space and wrapped an arm about his waist.

The physician rose as if to join her. "Are you unwell, Jadon? You've gone very pale."

Jadon flung up his palm. "I am well." He licked dry lips. "Tell me, can all this happen even if you don't work in the mines? If you merely drink from a cup such as this?"

"I told you already, you needn't worry if you took a few drinks from it."

"Not a few drinks, only. But years of them. Decades of hot wine and cold water? Of mulled grape and warm honey drinks?"

Adin rubbed his chin. "From that lead cup? To my mind, it would be possible—indeed, probable—though I have no proof. As I said, different physicians postulate various theories. Why? Do you know someone who suffers these symptoms?"

Jadon slipped to the floor, pulling his knees into his chest. "I did."

"Your mother?" the physician guessed.

"And grandmother."

"Both suffered the symptoms I described?"

"Yes," Sazana whispered. "Poor women."

The physician's words were only just beginning to come together in her mind. The disease that Jadon had feared all these years! The one that had cast its shadow over their lives with such darkness did not travel through his bloodlines at all. "Oh, Jadon! It was that cursed cup all along."

His body shuddered against her. The blue eyes were drowning, his thick, short lashes sticking together in sharp spikes. She drew him against her and felt him shake uncontrollably. From the corner of her eye she saw the physician slip out, giving them the privacy they needed.

In time, a hint of color returned to Jadon's complexion and the racking shivers of his body calmed. "When I think of their needless suffering . . ." he whispered.

"I know, my love."

A beat of silence. Then, "You know what this means?"

"That I have been right this whole time?"

He huffed a laugh. "You have been right, yes. And perhaps

almost as important, I do not bear that cursed disease in my veins."

"Thanks be to our God! You are free of it."

He kissed her, lips trembling against hers, his skin feverish. "The Lord be praised," he mumbled. He lifted his head. "Shoshanah, do you realize if the physician had told us about the cup only three days ago, the outcome would have been the same? I would have married you.

"But because he did not, I stopped leaning into my own strength, my own understanding, and I laid my life down. I finally chose to trust God with my whole heart."

44

Jadon

Two are better than one . . .
Ecclesiastes 4:9

The Twelfth Year of King Xerxes's Rule
The Fourth Day of Autumn

They married forty days later. After a five-year wait, neither of them had patience for a long betrothal. With Shoshanah's help, Jadon and his father arranged a modest celebration in deference to the fact that she was still in mourning for Arta.

"Are you sure you don't want to wait?" Having taught himself to give her up entirely, Jadon now found himself oddly resentful of every additional hour he had to spend apart from her. But he would delay their wedding if it made her happy.

She kissed him on the cheek. "I think my dear Arta would not have wanted us to wait. 'Delay?' he would say in his raspy voice. 'Not on my account.' He would have shaken his shoulders and danced a few merry steps and told me that he had been right all along. Remember his note to me? Our love was the old key that opened the new door to our happiness. He never gave up on us."

Jadon had found himself missing the man who still managed to reach from the grave to bless them.

Forty days, though short, had felt an age to Jadon. His father, Lord Arsaces, hosted the wedding at his villa outside Susa, filling the place with music and dancing. In accordance with his Persian heritage, he served enough food during the festivities that even Mazares patted his belly and declared himself fuller than a stuffed grape leaf.

Lord Arsaces had not stopped grinning for days, though he had shed tears of joy when Jadon told him of his intention to marry Shoshanah. "Five years ago, I told the boy not to break his oath to you." He had taken hold of Shoshanah's hand and not let go for a good hour. "Said it would all work out. But he had to have his own way."

Shoshanah had treated him to her sun-bright smile. "He is hardheaded, your son."

His father took hold of Jadon's hand and joined it to Shoshanah's. "But softhearted."

"Which is much more important when you are a bride-to-be," she said.

On their wedding day, she arrived in her finery and veil, without bandages on her hand for the first time since sustaining her injury. As they sat before the small gathering of friends and family, his beloved whispered so only he could hear, "You are blushing like a bridesmaid."

He pressed his lips to her ear. "In a few hours we shall see who will blush."

At his words, heat rose up in her cheeks, and for once, her complexion betrayed her. At the sight of that beautiful and rare pinkish hue, he threw his head back and laughed, longing to make her blush all night long.

Jadon basked in his new role as husband, though he still played the queen's agent by sticking close to his bride, lest Haman's sons chose to work some fresh mischief in the workshop. He could barely wrap his mind around the joy. After five years of living half a life, of giving up any hope of personal happiness, it seemed as if every moment had become a miracle.

He watched as his bride tried to create a cone from the lump of clay lying at the center of her wheel. Her right hand would not cooperate. Within moments, the tip broke.

She had been at it for seven days without sign of improvement. He pressed her shoulder, trying to pour strength into her.

"Try again."

She blew out a frustrated breath. But after a beat, she picked up a new lump of clay. This time, she managed to raise the cone twice before it broke.

"You're improving."

Without a word, she threw another lump of clay onto the wheel and tried again. "My brave girl." He kissed her forehead.

The incandescent joy of their marriage could not erase the injury to her hand and her increasing anxiety that she might never regain her ability to work the wheel.

Nor could it blot out the looming shadow of the coming attack from Jadon's mind. The queen's bravery had earned them the second edict, which meant the Jewish people could defend themselves. That knowledge alone would restrict the number of attackers, for the Hebrews were no longer easy prey.

Esther had also used the Cyrus cylinder to ensure that many Persians, especially those unafraid of a fight, had lost their desire to come against the Jews, no matter how tempting the law. But Jadon had not forgotten Nabonassar's final words, nor the odd confidence in the man's eyes as he faced death.

It came as no surprise when Hathach summoned him, and he arrived to find Esther already ensconced in the eunuch's rooms. What threw him was the presence of his own wife.

"Shoshanah?"

She shrugged. "Her Majesty sent for me."

Jadon sent a curious glance at the queen. His stomach dropped at the marble expression on her face. "We must make ready for the battle that comes," she said.

He had no quarrel with that. What he wanted to know was why his bride needed to be here. He bowed, keeping his disquiet to himself. "My queen."

"I have new information." Esther pointed to a small clay tablet on Hathach's desk. "We have found something that might help us."

Jadon studied the tablet and wondered what light this ordinary-looking document shed upon their situation.

Esther tapped the clay with a henna-red nail. "When the king condemned Haman to death, he presented me with some of his property, including the pottery workshop and Haman's villa in Susa. The day he transferred the house to me, he ordered Haman's family to vacate the property, giving them until sundown to comply.

"I always knew that with so little warning, they could not have had time to strip the place bare of everything. For some months, my women have searched, hoping to find something useful there for our purposes. We have failed to uncover anything that might openly incriminate Haman's sons before the king. But this morning, we discovered this deed." She pointed to the clay tablet. "It is to a farm two hours' ride north of Susa. I am betting you will find Haman's sons and their followers holed up there."

"I will dispatch a couple of men to surveil the place at once."

"Good. But we need more than that."

Jadon understood. Keeping an eye on the brothers would be

merely like keeping a poisonous snake in one's sight. The viper could still strike. It could still kill, pumping its venom before there was a chance to run. "You have a plan, I take it?"

The queen lowered her chin. "You will not like it."

He edged closer to his wife.

Hathach crossed his arms. "It all comes down to the workshop, Jadon. Though most of the potters are Persian, it is owned by a Jew. Queen or not, she remains subject to Haman's edict. One can make a strong case that on the appointed day, Haman's sons will be allowed to attack it, if they wish."

He should have seen this coming from thirty parasangs away. Jadon ground his teeth. "No."

Shoshanah threw him a shocked look. He grabbed her hand. "Your Majesty, it is my honor to serve you. But my wife is a potter. Not bait."

Hathach bristled, his eyes throwing fiery darts. The very fact that he could speak to the queen so boldly demonstrated that he served an uncommon woman. Another monarch would have his head on a spike by now.

Esther smiled sadly. "Shall we ask her?"

He squeezed his eyes shut. She did not need to separate his head from his neck. She had no need for his opinion at all, and she knew it.

"Absolutely not." Jadon whipped around and walked away in a straight line before returning. "I forbid it."

Esther had wisely dispatched them from her presence so that they could sort out her request in the privacy of their home. The queen had known that his wife's persuasion would accomplish her royal intentions more quickly than anything she herself might say.

"It is a good plan. If we do not draw them out, we may have to contend with them for years to come, a shadow hanging over our heads. I do not want that."

"Neither do I, Shoshanah. But there has to be another way. How many times have I almost lost you? Don't ask me to do it again."

She looked at him appealingly. "In truth, I have no particular desire to risk my neck one more time. Then again, I want this threat gone. For myself and you, yes. But also for our people.

"Jadon, you know better than I that we must destroy this hydra. Cut off its head once and for all. The queen's plan gives us the best chance of doing so. Haman's sons will come for the workshop. They will not be able to resist when they discover we will be conducting business as usual on the appointed day. They will have expected us to close our doors in fear and lock everything tight against them."

"Because that is the sane response." He threw her a stormy glance. "They will not only come for the workshop. They will come for you."

Gently, she kissed him. "I trust you to protect me. You will think of a way."

"I thought Esther was your friend."

"She is, Jadon. But she is also a queen who must protect more than those she loves best. It is what makes her worthy of our obedience."

45

Sazana

I will rejoice and be glad in your steadfast love,
because you have seen my affliction;
you have known the distress of my soul,
and you have not delivered me into the hand
of the enemy.

Psalm 31:7–8

THE THIRTEENTH YEAR OF KING XERXES'S RULE
THIRTEEN DAYS BEFORE THE FIRST DAY OF SPRING

As Sazana sat in her familiar spot in front of the open window, she ruminated on how the first months of her marriage had taught her a deeper love than she ever thought possible. They had given her time to carve out a home with her husband. They had deepened her faith and thereby increased her peace, in spite of the approaching war.

They had turned the livid scar in her palm to a faded pink. Her ligaments had regained some of their strength so that she could shape vessels on the wheel once more. But she knew she would never be the artisan that Susa had once celebrated.

She had learned to make do in spite of the weakness in her hand. She had incorporated the resulting imperfections into the design, using unusual glazes and metallic finishes to cover some of the inevitable marring. Her pottery no longer bore that perfection that had once been the hallmark of her work. But it held a different kind of beauty. Her pieces were more unique than ever and, perhaps because of it, still as much in demand as before her injury.

She had had an inward battle on her hands, adjusting to this loss, for loss it was. Part of her—the part that had known itself as a superior potter, had named itself by that ability—was lost. Gone forever. She had shed tears over that loss. A piece of her very self had been cut away.

But time had shown her that God had made her so much more than the Sazana who could create perfection upon the wheel. She was a wife. A teacher. An overseer. A friend. And yes, still a potter. She placed a hand upon her belly. Soon to be a mother, by the grace of God. She smiled. But none of these things made her truly who she was.

Above all, she was a daughter to a Father who was worthy of her every sacrifice.

Jadon appeared at her side, his steps silent as a cat's, interrupting her musings. "Be ready. A single rider approaches."

"A spy?"

"Looks that way."

Mazares, dressed as a potter, leaned his weapons of war against a wall, out of view from the window, and subtly shifted his muscled torso to stand in front of her. With a gentle shove, she pushed him aside. "We want them to see me, Mazares."

Jadon scowled, but after a beat, nodded at the Immortal. "We have him in our sights. If he reaches for an arrow, I'll drop him." He bent to give Sazana's hand a kiss before slipping out silently.

She felt his absence immediately, like a hole where there should be ground. Setting the wheel in motion, she turned it once, twice, three times, until it gained enough speed to begin work. Though she had replaced Arash with a quiet youth, she had ordered the wheel boy to remain home today. This was no place for him. Without his help, throwing the clay would be more complicated. But she only intended to look like she was making a pot. She doubted her trembling fingers could actually achieve anything useful today.

The place had grown eerily quiet, and at a signal from Mazares, the hum of quiet conversation and turning wheels filled the place. They wanted everything to look as it customarily would.

She stared at the clay, her mind not on her work.

The spy, whoever he was, must know his business. She never heard nor saw him. Until Jadon returned to her side some time later, she had no idea that he had sniffed around the workshop and left already.

"I just received word they are all coming this way," Jadon said grimly.

"All?"

"All."

She dropped her chin. It had arrived, her battle. Around Susa—indeed, around 127 provinces in the land of Persia— other Jews were facing their own battles today. "How many men altogether?"

"Forty." He bent down for a lingering kiss, in spite of the audience. There were hoots and cackles from the eighteen potters, who were not potters at all, but his Immortal friends, dressed as workshop laborers over their fine armor, their weapons hidden in easy reach.

She felt her face heat and knew he had managed, again, to make her complexion betray her. He never tired of reducing her to a blush.

"Stick to plan." His voice had turned hoarse.

She appreciated the strain she heard in the short command. She was feeling her own share of strain, knowing he would face mortal danger today, more even than she, given that he had surrounded her with some of the best fighters in the world.

"Don't do anything rash," she said.

He flashed a smile, kissed her again, and vanished outside.

Unlike their single spy, their cavalry made no effort to hush the sound of their arrival. Even the deaf could not have missed their approach, forty sets of hooves beating the ground like a wild stampede. Sazana's throat turned dry.

She coned the clay in front of her and flattened it again and again until the clay became overworked beyond use, and still she went on. Her elbow sat anchored against her thigh, and she prayed softly as she anchored her heart to the Father. *God, let our plan succeed.*

The door flung open. Men rushed in, screaming, swords drawn, daggers naked and sharp like hungry wolf fangs. They had expected easy prey. Helpless potters befuddled by terror. Instead, they found a lethal enemy, cool as the boulders of the Zagros Mountains.

Still, there were only eighteen of them to their forty. Their spy had already searched the yard and found no guards posted outside. They came in at once, leaving their backs unprotected, as Jadon had hoped.

Jadon's second cohort rose then. They had concealed themselves in all the useful hiding places Arash had shown them, covering their gear and armor with a coat of dry clay to blend in with the earth.

When they hurtled in, their roar like the rushing waters, Haman's sons and their men knew themselves trapped between two mighty pincers. They fought with wild desperation, but they must have known their cause hopeless.

Sazana was grateful that they had removed all the pottery and delicate paraphernalia of her trade out of the workshop, else everything would have shattered to pieces within the first moments.

Mazares never left her side, his sword in one hand, shield held high before her. How he managed it, she could not say. But every once in a while, he threw a dagger or a spear, and a man would fall.

Needless, needless violence, spurred on by generations of ruinous hatred.

"Watch it!" Mazares cried, tucking her behind him, and she saw the man sprinting toward her, somehow swerving out of the reach of every knife and spear that headed his way. Just behind him came Jadon, eyes blazing blue fire, his sword bloodied from an earlier encounter.

Familiar with the layout of the workshop, Jadon cut left, then right again, arriving in front of Sazana before the man could reach her. He stood loose-jointed and graceful, wiggling four fingers at the Agagite in invitation.

"Tell me your name that I may know whose blood I spill. I am Jadon, son of Arsaces."

The man raised a dark brow. "I have no quarrel with you, Persian. I come for the Jew." He spat the word as he pointed at Sazana.

Jadon gave him a cold smile. "That is my wife. Tell me your name before I send you to your forefather Agag."

The man raised a brow, seeming surprised at the mention of his people. "I am Parshandatha." He raised his sword.

"Haman's oldest." Jadon bowed his head. "It is my pleasure."

Sazana had to close her eyes then. She could not bear to watch her husband prancing a mere breath away from a naked sword. Had this been her idea? This tangle? This trap? No wonder Jadon had opposed it so vehemently. Now she wished she had listened.

Lord, Lord, Lord, she chanted under her breath, that mighty name her only strength and prayer.

A hand thumped her back. "It's all right. He lives. Look." Mazares lifted his sword to point at Jadon, who knelt by Parshandatha's prone body.

She dropped to her knees next to him. "You are bleeding!"

He touched his forehead. "Flesh wound." Turning, he gave her a quick look. "I thought we agreed you would not move from Mazares's side."

"This doesn't count. I am by *your* side." She pointed at the pale man. "Is he dead?"

"He breathes, though not for long." He shook the man roughly. "Parshandatha, look around and see your defeat. Your men have surrendered."

Haman's son opened bleary eyes. "If you think we are finished today, you don't know us. The best of us remains free. We are not done, your kind and us."

Sazana gave Jadon a wild-eyed look. No! After all this, were they still to be tormented by more threats, more menace, more death?

"The best of you? Your little sister, you mean?" Jadon taunted. "Your father is dead, his head upon his own gallows. Your nine brothers are yonder, lying dead in the workshop you failed to take. And you will soon join them, your line blotted out and your hatred with it. Speak no great boasts, Parshandatha. Your delicate womenfolk cannot accomplish what you failed to do."

Parshandatha smiled through swollen lips. Perhaps it was the gravity of his wounds that addled his mind. Perhaps his pride could not bear Jadon's taunt. Whatever the cause, he spoke, and though his words were few, he said too much. "You will find my uncle not so delicate as all that."

Jadon bowed his head. "My thanks for the tip."

In Jadon's quiet response, Sazana found what all the victory in the day's battle had not given her. Reassurance.

337

From the Secret Scrolls of Esther

And Esther said, "If it please the king, let the Jews who are in Susa be allowed tomorrow also to do according to this day's edict. And let the ten sons of Haman be hanged on the gallows."

Esther 9:13

Thirty-Two Years Later
The Twenty-Fifth Year of King Artaxerxes's Rule

Over the decades, some have criticized me for being too bloodthirsty. Those who do not know the full story of that day accuse me of a hard heart. My one wish, after all, was not for peace, or forgiveness, but to extend the edicts by one more day in Susa, thereby opening the door to more bloodshed.

As if that were not enough, I asked the king to hang the bodies of Haman's ten sons on the gallows. A gory display. Vindictive, some say. But I had my reasons.

Those bodies were my invitation to the last of my enemies. A goad he could not refuse for all his sly preparations.

By the end of the first day, my husband told me that

five hundred men had been killed in the citadel of Susa alone when the Hebrews defended themselves and overcame those who wanted their land and riches.

"What then have they done in the rest of the king's provinces!" he said.

In his eyes, I read both admiration and wariness. As king, he certainly understood the need to send your enemy a decisive message, and he admired our ability to do so. But he also did not want the Persians to look weak. Any Persian defeat, even one as just as the one suffered that day, left a bad taste in his mouth. Worse, it set a nasty example in a vast empire that ruled by balancing mercy with a healthy dose of fear. Our victory could lead to numerous uprisings.

Still, he wanted to shield the wife he loved. And he felt he owed it to me, having placed my whole race in danger of genocide when he accepted Haman's words at face value.

He flinched when I made my request to extend the edict by one day in Susa. In Susa, only. But he granted my wish.

Over the years, I have reflected upon that request. Spent sleepless nights wondering about it.

I could think of no other strategy that would dry up the vein of savage hatred that had coursed through the ages with such bitterness. But do not think that I never regretted the cost.

I saved my people, a task God himself placed me in the Persian palace to accomplish. But my hands, once innocent, are stained with blood. I know it.

More blood for that second day.

I wonder, often, if I could have thought of a better solution. A more forgiving one. A more peaceful resolution. I have never found one. But I still wonder.

46

Jadon

May the LORD give strength to his people!
May the LORD bless his people with peace!
Psalm 29:11

THIRTY-TWO YEARS EARLIER
THE THIRTEENTH YEAR OF KING XERXES'S RULE
THIRTEEN DAYS BEFORE THE FIRST DAY OF SPRING

You know, I'm a lot prettier if you visit me at a decent
hour of the day." Gadatas pressed a hand over the thin
strands of hair that stood at odd angles over his pate.
"What time do you call this?"

"Forgive me, Lord Gadatas." Jadon placed the large amphora
of wine in front of the man. "Compliments of Hathach. He
said to tell you that you will find it better even than the last."

The old man sniffed. "Well. When you are my age, you can
always sleep. Interesting company is more difficult to find. Have
a seat." Jadon made to sit on the ornate chair facing the man's

desk. But his host pointed at a plain, wooden stool farther away. "You do rather smell of horseflesh and battle. My nose still works in spite of all the wrinkles that surround it."

"Beg your pardon." Jadon covered the bloodstain on his tunic with the edge of his cloak. "There was no time for proper ablutions. It is an urgent matter."

The old man rubbed his hands together. "More lessons in genealogy?"

"I fear so." He leaned forward. "Did Haman have a brother?"

Gadatas poured himself a small thimble of the queen's wine. "A brother, you say." He slapped his thigh. "Why, of course! A man by the name of Parshandatha."

Jadon's shoulders slumped in a combination of disappointment and weariness. It had taken him a four-hour ride to arrive at this place, after an exhausting day of fighting, while anxiously trying to keep Shoshanah safe. He had hoped for at least a morsel of information.

"Haman's oldest *son* held that name. I met him just this morning. It proved a short acquaintance."

"Did it? Poor fellow." Gadatas took another sip of his wine. "Haman named the boy after his brother. Parshandatha. Another jawbreaker of a name, do you not agree?"

Jadon straightened. "You mean Haman also had a brother by that name?"

"His younger brother. I met him only once. He seemed strangely reluctant to show his face in the palace. Haman had inherited all the charm in the family, it seems, and left none for the younger sibling."

"What did you think of him? Beside the fact that he lacked charm?"

"He struck me as a surly fellow. Big as a tower, that one. I prepared to write him off as all muscle and no mind for clever schemes. Then I managed to draw him out, and I had to admit myself wrong. Much cleverer than Haman, it turns out."

"Is he a man who can be manipulated into action?"

"At first he seemed cool as a block of ice. But that day, the king had shown clemency by pardoning a dozen men in honor of his birthday. Parshandatha, when he heard this, came close to treason by calling the king soft. He is sly as a king's vizier. But I think you can push him over the edge if you find the right goad. There is a hot head under all that ice."

Jadon's heart picked up speed. "As ever, you prove useful, my lord."

Gadatas twirled a finger in his direction. "Better watch your step. Parshandatha's sting is deadly. If he has set himself against you, don't leave him wounded. Cut off his head while you can, or make ready to fall victim to him later."

By the time Jadon arrived at the palace, the world still lay in pitch-darkness. He was not surprised to find Hathach's offices filled with activity under the burning light of dozens of lamps. At the center, a sleepy Master Sheber sat, blinking with confusion. At least this time Jadon had not been the one to wake him.

In an act of defiant confidence, months ago, the Jews of Susa had already planned to hold a celebration, scheduled to take place the day after the edict. Their confidence had proven justified. They had overcome their enemies. God had sustained them through a day of hard fighting.

Now the people intended to gather in the synagogue that very afternoon for a joyous feast, giving God thanks for answering their prayers. The queen had sent Jadon to discover whether they should cancel the feast or keep it.

Jadon waited in a corner for Esther to arrive. Exhausted to the marrow of his bones, he took a soldier's nap, the kind he had learned at the palace school—sitting up and surrounded by noise and light.

He awoke instantly at a soft kick to his ankle. "Master Hathach."

"The queen comes." Hathach gave him a towel damp with warm water and scented with some pleasant perfume.

Jadon made quick work of wiping his face and hands. Accepting a clean cloak from the eunuch's hand, he exchanged his own filthy garment with the proffered linen, doing his best to cover the stains of his garb with its folds.

He doubted that the towel's perfume would manage to cover the full stench of him. Nothing he could do about that. He doubted the queen would complain.

She arrived pale, purple half-moons under her eyes testament that her own night had been no more restful than his, though at least she had not spent it on the back of a horse. He offered her a tired bow as Hathach sent everyone from the chamber and sealed the door shut.

"Anything useful?" she said.

Jadon told them what he had learned from Gadatas. "I recommend we go forward with the planned celebrations. The sight of his ten nephews on the gallows will spur him to action. Though wisdom might whisper caution, I suspect he will not be able to resist the temptation that feast offers—all the Jews of Susa gathered in one place, helpless before his sword."

Esther nodded. "Poor Master Sheber. He will have a hard day and night ahead."

Jadon rose. "I will help him."

"So you shall. But not before you rest for a few hours, or you will prove useless to me later. Go home, Jadon. This part of things Hathach and I can handle. Return in time to see to your part."

Though Jadon knew that he would face his deadliest enemy in a few hours, he felt a deep peace as he lay in his wife's arms. Sleep came for him quickly. But even as he sank into its blessed depths, he thought he felt Shoshanah place his hand on her belly.

Jadon watched the people arrive at the synagogue in small groups, carrying covered platters of food and large amphoras of wine. The women had modestly covered their hair, holding on to their bowls and dishes with a tight grip that hinted at the pride with which they had cooked the food within. The men clapped one another on the back.

If under closer examination their faces appeared too pale and their smiles strained, no one paid any attention. They had, after all, fought for their survival not a few hours earlier.

From inside, the strains of harp and flute drifted out, joyful songs to commemorate their victory. It was a celebration like no other his people had ever known.

The queen had asked her kitchen to deliver additional food, roasted vegetables and thick soups of legumes and herbs, and the smell of costly spices made the bellies of passersby grumble. They waved at their neighbors, no doubt wishing they could attend the gathering and taste the food that was making their mouths water. No one invited them.

Mordecai stood next to Master Sheber at the door, welcoming the members with a blessing. Jadon hoped they were the only ones who could see the platters shaking in trembling hands, causing the daggers and knives hidden beneath the lids to rattle noisily. And the only ones to note the shadow of beards already growing back on the recently shaven cheeks of some "women."

Still, the people came, and the synagogue filled with the sound of celebration. Hard to miss all that joyous laughter and the stamping of dancing feet. Anyone hearing that clamor would assume that the wine must be flowing freely indeed.

The people inside the synagogue could not see the thirty men who prowled toward the door, dressed in black tunics, their faces hidden behind dark scarves. But Jadon could. He waited until the right moment, until half had slithered inside, like the front end of a hissing snake, before he led his Immortals against their flank.

Half in and half out, Parshandatha's men were once again caught off guard on both fronts. For within the synagogue they did not find themselves facing inebriated merchants and laborers along with their fat wives, unable to run faster than an injured turtle. Instead, they came face-to-face with dead-sober Jewish men who had prepared for battle for eleven months. And though few of them were truly warriors, there were three for every one of Parshandatha's men. Enough to overcome.

Outside, the Amalekite warriors fared no better. Expecting to sneak in and slaughter a helpless enemy, instead they fought Jadon's lethal Immortals.

Jadon recognized Parshandatha immediately. A head taller than most of the men there, and half a head taller than Jadon, he slashed his sword with a mesmerizing fluidity that no one seemed able to withstand.

He could not watch his friends fall under the man's blade. They had come to lend a hand of support to his cause, not to die. Jadon flung himself before Parshandatha.

He grinned. "Your fight is with me, I believe, Agagite."

Parshandatha turned. Taking Jadon's measure, he grinned back. "To you I owe all this trouble, I believe?"

"Some, in any case."

Their conversation did not progress beyond that. It became all thrust and block, counter and guard, stabbing blades and bleeding wounds.

Until the end came. Jadon saw it and could not defend himself. Parshandatha had pulled out a dagger with his other hand, and as Jadon deflected a sword thrust, the dagger came straight for his gut.

At the last moment, the tip of another sword pressed itself

between them, and rapping hard on Parshandatha's wrist, loosened his hold on the dagger. Mazares stepped next to Jadon.

Parshandatha screamed in frustration. It was the last sound he ever made. He toppled like a great tree with shallow roots, and with him came down centuries of Agagite hatred.

Jadon watched the river of scarlet drain from the massive chest, feeling nothing save for cold relief and a forlorn sorrow for the waste of it all. Here lay an extraordinary man, strong, capable, and gifted. A man who could have lived to bring peace and prosperity to his people and had instead ruined their lives on the altar of empty vengeance. Jadon wiped his eyes with the back of a bloody hand, unable to stop the hot tears.

Then he thought of his friend Mazares who had risked his own life to save him. Of his queen who had been willing to die to save her people. Of his precious wife who had sat so bravely before that open window, willing to play bait in order to end this violence. For all the ugliness of these savage days, there were a thousand moments of beauty, of courage well spent, of love freely offered, of hope and sacrifice and virtue. He thought of all the good that had managed to survive through the ugliness and smiled through his tears.

47

Sazana

The blessing of the LORD makes rich,
and he adds no sorrow with it.

Proverbs 10:22

TEN MONTHS LATER

Jadon whirled about the room, his daughter clutched in his arms. Sazana tried to suppress a laugh and failed when the baby spat up a large glob on his shoulder.

"Aaah!" Jadon stopped. "Unfair, my lady," he said to the babe.

The child grinned at him, a feat she had only learned a day earlier.

Jadon almost fell over his head with elation. "Did you see? Did you see that? She smiled at me. For the second time today, I will have you know."

Sazana took the babe back into her arms, wiping her rosebud mouth with the bit of soft cloth she had learned to always carry close at hand. "I saw. I saw. Very impressive. Our child is a prodigy." She handed him the cloth. "You might wish to wipe that off." She pointed at the bit of white spit that was sinking fast into his shoulder.

"If only she had taken after her mother when it came to sleep," he said, wiping hard at the spot.

"Or her father."

"Mine is a learned talent. According to my father, as a babe, I kept the whole house up with my wailing."

Sazana grimaced. "When did you become a good sleeper?"

"Around the age of eleven or twelve. I'm a quick student."

Sazana held out her daughter so she could look into the blue eyes. "Don't even think about waiting that long. You will learn faster. We will begin today."

The three of them headed for the bedroom, where a wicker basket served as the child's bed. "Now, you behave yourself, or your father will take it into his head to teach you to dance again. Which will make you spit upon his shoulder even more of that lovely milk your ima fed you. Do you agree?"

The child made an indeterminate coo.

"I will take that as a yes."

She laid the baby in the basket. For a moment, all was still.

"Quick," Jadon whispered. "Let's lie down. Perhaps she will let us sleep."

Sazana tiptoed to the bed and found her husband already there. She sighed with relief as she stretched out next to him. He pulled her into his arms. "Have I told you how brilliant you are?"

"For . . . ?"

"For finding such a good husband."

She grinned. "Not half so brilliant as you are for finally marrying me."

The blue eyes, so much like their daughter's, sparkled. "I knew I could get you to admit I was the more brilliant one."

She laughed, and he caught the sound in his kiss. "Sometimes," he said, "I can't quite believe how blessed I am."

"Nor I."

"I think it is because we have learned to appreciate what we have rather than worry about what we don't. Learned to see God in the threads of our lives."

Sazana nodded. God had taught her she could be happy with a hand that was less than perfect, happy in spite of so much loss, happy with their small home and their lack of sleep and Jadon's dangerous work.

All of it, every single thread, came to her through a God who was a Father to her people and to her. She leaned in and kissed her husband, deeper this time, full of a melting love. They had just wriggled closer when a wail made them freeze.

The baby's cry grew louder and more insistent, reverberating around the walls of their chamber.

Yes, happy even with the wailing of their babe.

From the Secret Scrolls of Esther

And I will give you a new heart, and a new spirit I will put within you. And I will remove the heart of stone from your flesh and give you a heart of flesh.

Ezekiel 36:26

Thirty-Three Years Later
The Twenty-Fifth Year of King Artaxerxes's Rule

Let me tell you a secret: The feast of Purim sometimes makes me weep. Though it is a day of celebration, a day Mordecai set apart for remembering that God turned our sorrow into gladness, there are moments when I remember the cost.

You, my dear Nehemiah, have fought enough battles to know that every victory has its own sharp edge. It leaves its own bruises.

We celebrate Purim now as a holiday, a time of feasting and joy, days for sending gifts of food to one another and presents to the poor. To God goes the glory, for he accomplished what I alone could not. He overcame an enemy who was greater than we were.

I celebrate that. How could I not? In the end, a generation of my people were spared the genocide of Haman. That is a great thing, no?

And as if that were not enough, God mended my marriage. For my husband returned to my arms, unwilling to give me up. That, too, is a cause for celebration, if to no one else, then for my own little heart.

But that story I have already written about and shall not bore you with more on that score.

I have now told you the story of Purim, the day we defended ourselves against our enemy throughout Persia and vanquished the great evil that rose up to swallow us. And the second day, in Susa, when I set the bodies of our enemies hanging upon ten gallows as tall as the heavens. I had never thought of myself as that kind of queen. That kind of woman.

Bloody and hard.

You who spent your own money to buy back our enslaved people from our harsh enemies also lifted your hand in warfare. One hand to build a wall, the other to hold a sword. You will understand what it means to foster mercy in your heart and yet choose to be merciless.

It is the fate of broken humanity, I suppose. We cannot always find peaceful measures to resolve our enmities. Perhaps it requires a move of God himself to give us that manner of peace. Perhaps he will have to give us a new heart and put a new spirit within us, as he once promised the prophet. How I wish I could live to see that day!

I am no longer a queen. It has been many years since I wore a golden crown.

This, I have found, is a relief.

May you find relief at the end of your own work, dear Nehemiah.

Author's Note

The clock is ticking, and I am edging past the deadline for this final touch to *The Royal Artisan*. So I will be brief. Which can be a challenge for a novelist.

First of all, yes! There really is a Cyrus cylinder. Years ago, I saw it in the British Museum and became enchanted. It is one of those rare moments when archaeology and history and biblical narrative and prophecy all collide in one small package.

Since so many people remain unaware of the existence of this extraordinary relic, I decided to give it its own storyline here. Of course, that part is made up. As far as I know, the Cyrus cylinder never went missing from Persian palaces, and it never played a role in the salvation of the Hebrew population during Esther's time. To be fair, it had already discharged its purpose in that regard sixty-four years earlier.

Our knowledge of Persian pottery from this period remains limited because few pieces have survived. The color of the palace bricks in Susa as described here is historically accurate since some of them actually survive. Try visiting the Metropolitan Museum of Art for a glimpse. But no blue pottery from this period is in existence, though later Persian potters had a love for the color. That thread in the story is fictional.

Images of potters from this period or earlier sometimes show potters squatting, though I found two images of potters sitting on stools. I loved Sazana too much not to offer her that bit of comfort.

Several ancient seals bearing women's names have been unearthed, one of which bears the name of Elihana bat Gael. While some scholars cast doubts on its authenticity, others believe it to be genuine. As a novelist, I thought it was too good not to use. Of course, I made my Elihana a potter and changed her father's name, because I don't want to be sued by her family for slander. (That's just a joke, folks. It's late, and I am growing slightly eccentric.)

One final note: The QUEEN ESTHER'S COURT series will tell Esther's story three times, focusing on a slightly different vantage point with each telling. But the true heroines of these books are Esther's fictional friends. I hope these novels will take readers deeper into Esther's fascinating world.

At the same time, no version of any of my stories can compare with the original biblical narrative. These stories in no way replace the transformative power that the reader will encounter in the Scriptures. For the original account of Esther's life, please refer to the book by the same name in your Bible.

For updates and to sign up for my monthly newsletters, please visit my website at TessaAfshar.com. I love hearing from my readers.

Discussion Questions

1. What were some of the challenges Esther faced when she first arrived at the Persian court?
2. Arta has been a father to Sazana for twelve years. Name some of the qualities that you like in him as a father figure.
3. Both Sazana and Esther adopt names that are not their own in order to survive. What would you imagine are some of the complications they faced in doing so?
4. In what ways does Jadon realize that Sazana has changed since she was first betrothed to him? What are some events in your life over the past few years that have changed you?
5. Why is it so important to Esther that they find the Cyrus cylinder? In what way did this old royal edict demonstrate the faithfulness of God to the Jewish people in Esther's day?
6. In spite of the fact that Jadon has broken off their betrothal, he demonstrates that he is far from indifferent toward Sazana. What are some of the ways we can see that he still cares for her?

7. Why did Sazana's pottery mean so much to her? What was the lesson she learned when she could no longer produce the same quality work as before?

8. How does Jadon finally learn to trust God with his whole heart? Are there areas of your life where you need to do that?

9. What was your favorite scene or lines in the book and why?

10. What was your favorite Scripture used in the book or as an epigraph? Share why.

Acknowledgments

Thank you for picking up this book and spending your precious time romping around ancient Persia with me. I am more grateful than I can express to readers like you, without whom these books would not be possible.

A special word of gratitude to Dr. Rhonda Wells, whose medical knowledge, both ancient and current, proved an exceptional resource. I can't imagine writing those scenes without her gracious insight and guidance!

My profound thanks to Carole Wolaver of PotteryLady.com, who willingly read a whole novel written by a total stranger and spent precious time helping me get my descriptions of pottery right. Or at least almost right.

So thankful for dear Janet von Wodtke, my treasured beta reader who jumped into the gap with willing alacrity and blessed me with her encouragement.

What a privilege to work with the marvelous Bethany House fiction team. My deepest gratitude to Andy McGuire for taking a chance on these stories and on me. Rochelle Gloege and Jennifer Veilleux, thank you so much for your guidance, which helped elevate *The Royal Artisan* to a whole new level. Kate Jameson, thank you for helping to further refine the story.

I owe a debt to the amazing Bethany and Baker publishing team, whose genius ideas and hard work ensures this book is accessible to readers: Raela Schoenherr; Karen Steele; Lindsay Schubert; Rachael Betz; the sales team. Jennifer Parker, I appreciate the beautiful cover design with just the perfect blue urn! Also, Design Team, I LOVE that awesome map. Thank you.

Always thankful for my spectacular agent, Wendy Lawton, who found the right home for this series, and the right home for all my books.

Utmost love and honor for my husband who accompanies me on research trips, helps me plot ideas, gives me the strength to overcome the discouraging days, and champions me through life's highs and lows. Thank you hardly seems enough.

And above all, praise to God who opens impossible doors and calls us to impossible things.

Coming Soon:

THE PALACE SPY

Don't miss the thrilling conclusion of the QUEEN ESTHER'S COURT series.

Homeless after the sudden death of her father, Danna is traveling in search of work when a runaway horse takes off with its royal rider. Danna, who has grown up around horses all her life, brings the wild mare under control, only to discover that its occupant is Esther, the queen of Persia. When they realize this is no simple accident, Esther secretly employs Danna to find out who is behind the attempt on her life. But Danna cannot accomplish her mission alone.

Allon tends his expansive apple orchards, determined to spend the rest of his days as a simple farmer. But when Esther summons him for one final task, he cannot refuse the queen he once served. Having paid a steep price for being the king's spy, his new assignment resurrects the ghosts of his haunted past.

As if her new role as the queen's spy is not confusing enough, Danna finds that teaming up with the enigmatic Allon can tie even the steadiest of hearts into knots. Now the two of them must race against time to save Esther's life and establish her in the safety of a new identity.

This gripping finale to the QUEEN ESTHER'S COURT series unveils a glimpse into Esther's life beyond the iconic biblical tale.

AVAILABLE FALL 2026.

Tessa Afshar's biblical fiction has been on *Publishers Weekly*, CBA, and ECPA bestseller lists and has been translated into twelve languages. Tessa's books have received the Christy, INSPY, and ECPA Christian Book of the Year Awards, and are Carol, Christy, and ECPA Christian Book Award finalists. Born in the Middle East, Tessa spent her teen years in England and later moved to the United States. Her conversion to Christianity in her twenties changed the course of her life. Tessa is a devoted wife, a mediocre gardener, and an enthusiastic cook of biblical recipes. Learn more at TessaAfshar.com.

Sign Up for Tessa's Newsletter

Keep up to date with Tessa's latest news on book releases and events by signing up for her email list at the link below.

TessaAfshar.com

FOLLOW TESSA ON SOCIAL MEDIA

Tessa Afshar   @TessaAfshar

Be the first to hear about new books from Bethany House!

Stay up to date with our authors and books by signing up for our newsletters at

BethanyHouse.com/SignUp

FOLLOW US ON SOCIAL MEDIA

   @BethanyHouseFiction